Praise for the Zoe Chambers Mystery Series

"I loved *Bridges Burned*. The action starts off with a bang and never lets up. Zoe's on the case, and she's a heroine you'll root for through the mystery's twists and turns—strong and bold, but vulnerable and relatable. I adore her, and you will, too."

— Lisa Scottoline,
New York Times Bestselling Author of *Betrayed*

"New York has McBain, Boston has Parker, now Vance Township, PA ("pop. 5000. Please Drive Carefully.") has Annette Dashofy, and her rural world is just as vivid and compelling as their city noir."

— John Lawton,
Author of the Inspector Troy Series

"I've been awestruck by Annette Dashofy's storytelling for years. Look out world, you're going to love Zoe Chambers."

— Donnell Ann Bell,
Bestselling Author of *Deadly Recall*

"An easy, intriguing read, partially because the townfolks' lives are so scandalously intertwined, but also because author Dashofy has taken pains to create a palette of unforgettable characters."

— *Mystery Scene Magazine*

"Dashofy has done it again. *Bridges Burned* opens with a home erupting in flames. The explosion inflames simmering animosities and ignites a smoldering love that has been held in check too long. A thoroughly engaging read that will take you away."

— Deborah Coonts,
Author of *Lucky Catch*

"Dashofy takes small town politics and long simmering feuds, adds colorful characters, and brings it to a boil in a welcome new series."

— Hallie Ephron,
r of *There Was an Old Woman*

"A vivid country setting, characters so real you'd know them if they walked through your door, and a long-buried secret that bursts from its grave to wreak havoc in a small community—*Lost Legacy* has it all."

— Sandra Parshall,
Author of the Agatha Award-Winning Rachel Goddard Mysteries

"A big-time talent spins a wonderful small-town mystery! Annette Dashofy skillfully weaves secrets from the past into a surprising, engaging, and entertaining page turner."

— Hank Phillippi Ryan,
Mary Higgins Clark, Agatha and Anthony Award-Winning Author

"Discerning mystery readers will appreciate Dashofy's expert details and gripping storytelling. Zoe Chambers is an authentic character who will entertain us for a long time."

— Nancy Martin,
Author of the Blackbird Sister Mysteries

"A terrific first mystery, with just the right blend of action, emotion and edge. I couldn't put it down. The characters are well drawn and believable...It's all great news for readers.

— Mary Jane Maffini,
Author of *The Dead Don't Get Out Much*

"Intriguing, with as many twists and turns as the Pennsylvania countryside it's set in."

— CJ Lyons,
New York Times Bestselling Author of *Last Light*

"Dashofy has created a charmer of a protagonist in Zoe Chambers. She's smart, she's sexy, she's vulnerably romantic, and she's one hell of a paramedic on the job."

— Kathleen George,
Edgar-Nominated Author of the Richard Christie Series

CRY
WOLF

**Books in the Zoe Chambers Mystery Series
by Annette Dashofy**

CRY WOLF

A ZOE CHAMBERS MYSTERY

ANNETTE DASHOFY

HENERY PRESS

Copyright

CRY WOLF
A Zoe Chambers Mystery
Part of the Henery Press Mystery Collection

First Edition | September 2018

Henery Press
www.henerypress.com

Trade Paperback ISBN-13: 978-1-63511-392-1
Digital epub ISBN-13: 978-1-63511-393-8
Kindle ISBN-13: 978-1-63511-394-5
Hardcover ISBN-13: 978-1-63511-395-2

Printed in the United States of America

To Ray

ACKNOWLEDGMENTS

As always, the creation of this novel has been a team effort. The seed of the idea came from a conversation with Edith Maxwell at a writing retreat led by Ramona Long. Thanks to both of you and to all of Ramona's morning sprinters, without whom I'd never get enough pages written to meet my deadlines.

I had a lot of technical help on this one. Thanks to Stephanie Szymowski for helping me with the details of Franklin Marshall's illness, to Chris Herndon for eagerly answering my coroner questions, and to Kevin Burns and Terry Dawley for keeping my cops real. Any inaccuracies in any of these areas are my fault alone.

On the subject of cops, thanks to Lee Lofland and his amazing staff at the Writers Police Academy. So much of this book was fleshed out through my experiences there.

I want to thank Phyllis Walden and her family for allowing me to use their restaurant in this story. Walden's is real and if you're ever in southwestern Pennsylvania, you should stop in. Tell them I sent you!

When it comes to actually getting words on the page and having them be the best I can make them, my support team is invaluable. My critique group (Jeff Boarts, Tamara Girardi, and Mary "Liz Milliron" Sutton) pushes me to work harder and create a stronger tale. My beta reader, Edie Peterson, cuts me no slack. And my eagle-eyed proofreaders, Wanda Anglin and Anne Slates, find everything else I've missed. Thanks to all of you. And dear readers, if you still find typos, accept my apologies. It's not for lack of effort to eliminate them.

Thank you to the crew at Henery Press—Art Molinares, Kendel Lynn, and Christina Rogers in the front office; my editors Maria Edwards and Sarah Billman; and the creator of my cover art, Stephanie Savage.

I would not be published without my friends at Pennwriters and Sisters in Crime, including National, the Guppies, and my Pittsburgh Chapter. You are the foundation of my street team. The rest of my team resides on Facebook at Zoe Chambers Mysteries and Friends. Look us up and join. We have way too much fun. Thanks to each and every one of you.

And to the Mysterious Magnificent Six (you know who you are), thanks for the friendship and support.

Finally, I couldn't do any of this without the love and support of the man behind the curtain, my husband Ray. Thanks for always being here for me. I love you to the moon and back.

ONE

Zoe Chambers glanced at the dashboard clock of Monongahela County EMS's Medic Two. Six thirty on a Sunday evening and they'd had back-to-back-to-back calls since before noon.

Her partner, Earl Kolter, rode shotgun, slouched in the passenger seat, arms crossed, and his cap tipped forward over his face. "I'm gonna punch the next person who tries to tell me there's nothing to this full moon thing."

Zoe maneuvered the ambulance around a series of Pennsylvania potholes blossoming along the edge of Route 15, the main road between Brunswick and their station in the borough of Phillipsburg. "You don't need to resort to violence. Just drag them along on a full-moon weekend."

And it had been a classic. On duty since eight a.m. Saturday, all three teams on their crew had rotated through a plethora of "interesting" runs. So far, Zoe and Earl had responded to such diverse emergencies as a man who fell off a ladder while taking down Christmas lights even though it was now mid-April, a three-vehicle traffic collision caused by a woman plucking her eyebrows while driving, and—Zoe's personal favorite—the elderly woman with chest pains, who they discovered had some body piercings one wouldn't expect on a person of that age. Earl had gladly turned over the job of removing them to Zoe before patching the patient in to the cardiac monitor.

He squirmed in the passenger seat and sat up, repositioning his ball cap. "I'm starved. I wonder if anyone back at the station had time to cook supper."

"I doubt it."

"Maybe we should stop for takeout."

Zoe let off the gas as they approached the sweeping turn leading into the village of Dillard. "You think we're actually gonna have time to eat before our next call?"

"We've been on what? Six calls already today? There can't be any more sick or stupid people left in this corner of the county. I have a feeling the rest of the evening is going to be quiet."

As if mocking him, their radio burst to life. "Medic Two, this is Control. Respond to 125 Silver Maple Drive, Phillipsburg. Report of a man cut by a machete. Be advised, police have been notified and are en route."

Earl grabbed the aluminum clipboard and the mic. "Control, this is Medic Two. Ten-four," he replied to the EOC—Emergency Operations Center—dispatcher. He shot a look at Zoe. "Did he say 'machete'?"

Zoe tamped down a burst of adrenaline and flipped on the lights and siren. "Yes, he did. It's all your fault. 'The rest of the evening is gonna be quiet,'" she mimicked. "You jinxed us."

The address the EOC had given was for Phillipsburg, but Silver Maple Drive was located about five miles outside of the borough in one of the housing plans popping up where farmers sold their property to developers. A hundred acres of upscale homes sandwiched between a row of 1950s vintage houses on one side and a pristine horse operation on the other. One-twenty-five was the first address on the right once they turned off the main route. Its backyard bordered the horse farm, and Vance Township Police Department's SUV sat in the driveway, emergency lights flashing red and blue.

Earl unclipped his seatbelt. "Isn't that Pete's vehicle?"

"Yep."

"But it's Sunday."

Zoe pulled the ambulance in behind the SUV and shifted to park. "They're still short an officer, so everyone's working extra shifts."

Earl bailed out and yanked open the side patient compartment door to grab their jump kit. Not sure what to expect, Zoe followed raised voices to the heart of the action in the backyard.

Flexible vinyl fencing separated the immaculately groomed lawn from the pasture. An orange riding mower towing some sort of sweeper/bagger contraption sat idle next to the fence. Beside the small tractor, a man cradled his arm, wrapped in a white towel with a blotch of red seeping through. He shrieked at another man, who stood next to a mound of fresh, fragrant grass clippings—and a large knife—on the pasture side of the fence. Vance Township's Chief of Police, Pete Adams, had positioned himself between them like a referee.

The man standing over the clippings pointed a finger at the guy with the towel. "I've asked you, pleaded with you, how many times? Don't dump your damned clippings in my pasture."

"You nearly cut my arm off, you cretin."

"I barely scratched you. And I told you to stop. You don't listen to reason."

"You think coming after me with a machete is a reasonable response?"

Zoe stopped short of the melee, meeting Pete's gaze. She knew him well enough to recognize he'd reached the limit of his patience with the pair, but he gave her a quick nod. With Earl on her heels, she approached the man with the bloody arm and introduced herself and her partner. She motioned to a nearby lawn chair. "Would you like to sit down?"

"No, I would not. My legs are fine."

Okay. "Can you tell us your name?"

"Of course, I can. My arm's been severed, not my throat."

She glanced at Earl. Yep. Full moon.

Her partner touched his pen to the run report on the clipboard. "What is your name, sir?"

"Kristopher O'Keefe." The man watched Zoe finger the wrist of his uninjured arm, checking his pulse. "*Professor* Kristopher O'Keefe. With a 'K,' not a 'C-H.'"

Professor Kristopher-with-a-K's pulse was strong and steady. Not what she'd expect from someone suffering severe blood loss. His cheeks were ruddy and his skin was as cool and dry as the air that spring evening. No signs of shock. While Earl finished gathering their patient's pertinent information, Zoe checked his BP and respiration, both slightly elevated.

She and Earl exchanged a look. He tipped his head toward the ambulance. "Air splint?"

"And extra bandages."

He handed her the clipboard and jogged away.

"Hey, Doc?" Machete Man called.

Zoe realized he was speaking to her.

"Is he gonna be okay?"

Before Zoe could give a non-committal response, Professor K moaned dramatically. "No, I'm not okay, you buffoon. What kind of maniac are you, anyway? Chief, I hope you're going to make sure he never sees the light of day again. The man's a menace."

"How many times do I have to tell you? Just stop dumping your grass clippings where my horses can get them."

Zoe looked up at Machete Man, suddenly aware of what was really going on. She turned to her patient. "Don't you know fresh grass clippings can founder or even kill a horse?"

Machete Man's eyes lit up, having recognized a kindred spirit. "Thank you."

Professor K blew a raspberry. "Don't be ridiculous. They eat grass all the time. I just like to lure them over here so my grandkids can pet them."

Zoe made a point of looking around for the nonexistent children.

His head bobbled a little in acknowledgement of their absence. "I also enjoy seeing the horses up close. Magnificent animals."

She sputtered, wanting to point out how fragile those magnificent animals could be. How the fresh clippings would ferment inside them. How they'd eat themselves into permanent lameness or even death. But she suspected Machete Man had already explained the facts of horse digestion with Professor K ad nauseam.

"Let's see how bad this is." Zoe unwrapped the towel. Had the patient appeared to still be bleeding, she'd have left the makeshift bandage in place. But most of the blood was already dry. Combined with his strong vital signs, she figured it was safe to start a fresh—and sterile—bandage.

Earl jogged up with an armload of supplies as she lifted the towel away from the wound. Gaping? Yes. And in need of stitches. Probably a tetanus shot. But not as bad as she'd first feared.

Professor K, however, threw his head back and groaned. "Oh, dear lord, I'll never have proper function of my arm again. And my dominant arm at that."

Earl rolled his eyes and unsealed a bottle of sterile saline.

She took the bottle and held it over the gash. "This might sting a bit." Too bad it wasn't alcohol.

From the patient's yelp, it very well could have been.

While Zoe tore into a stack of gauze squares and secured them in place with a roll of Kling wrap, she noticed Pete ordering Machete Man to climb over the fence. She glanced up long enough to watch Pete cuff Machete Man's hands behind his back. As much as she enjoyed watching Pete at work, this time she didn't agree with him.

Zoe secured the rolled gauze with some tape and caught Earl's attention. "Can you finish up?"

He unfolded the clear plastic air splint. "Sure."

She excused herself from the professor and strode toward Pete and his prisoner. "You're arresting him?"

Pete appeared surprised by the question. "Yes."

"He was defending his property."

Pete studied her for a long moment before replying. "With a machete."

Zoe pointed at the weapon lying next to the mound of grass clippings. "That?"

Pete's expression continued to darken. She knew he was letting her get away with way more than anyone else who would dare challenge his authority. "Yes. That."

"That's a corn knife. It's a farm tool."

If Machete Man hadn't been cuffed, he might have hugged her.

Pete continued to glare. "It's still a lethal weapon."

Zoe stepped to the fence and started to reach through the vinyl rails.

"Don't touch it." Pete grabbed a handful of her jacket. "It's evidence. As soon as I secure my prisoner, I'll bag it." Still gripping her coat, he pulled her closer and whispered in her ear. "What the hell are you doing? You know better."

She did. But from across the pasture, a small herd of horses had spotted the activity, or caught wind of the clippings, and ambled their way. Zoe had been a horsewoman longer than she'd been a paramedic. And much longer than she'd been Pete Adam's girlfriend. "Okay. I won't touch your evidence."

He hesitated a moment and then released her. "Good."

"At least not the knife." She grabbed the post, placed one foot on the highest band of fencing she could reach, and vaulted the fence into the pasture.

"What are you—?"

She scooped up an armload of the fresh grass and flung it over the fence into Professor K's yard.

"What the bloody hell are you doing?" The professor waved his uninjured arm at Pete. "Aren't you going to stop her?"

Pete, however, kept quiet. Zoe caught a hint of an amused smile. Apparently, he had no plans to bag and tag the clippings as evidence.

Professor K sputtered, glaring at Pete. "You cops are useless. Every one of you."

By the time Earl had inflated the air splint around an unhappy Professor K's arm, Zoe had transferred the entire mound into the yard.

Pete and Machete Man kicked it far enough from the fence that the inquisitive horses couldn't reach the delicious and toxic treat. Zoe climbed back over and brushed off her uniform. She looked at Pete, who'd wiped the smile from his lips, although it still gleamed in his eyes. "Okay?"

He shrugged. "Okay."

"Thank you," Machete Man whispered.

She nodded and headed toward her partner and their patient. "You ready?"

"Yep," Earl said. He turned to the professor. "Let's go."

"Wait." Professor K continued to hug his arm, now encased in a clear balloon. "That's it? Aren't you going to give me an IV? I've lost a lot of blood you know. I probably need a transfusion."

Zoe and Earl exchanged a look.

Full moon.

The next morning, Pete stepped out of his township-issued Ford Explorer in the parking lot of Golden Oaks Assisted Living and waited for Zoe to compete with a small red car for one of the spaces. The small car had better options than Zoe in her multi-colored gas-guzzling dinosaur three-quarter-ton pickup truck. Pete had dropped off some paperwork at the county courthouse and learned the machete-wielder had already been arraigned and released on bail. Zoe had a meeting with her boss at the Coroner's Office at twelve thirty, so she'd agreed to come into town early and accompany Pete to visit his father.

After securing a parking spot, she approached Pete, the morning sun creating a halo of her honey-colored curls. That sexy-as-hell swagger of hers never failed to put him in a sweat. Lately, their work shifts had them saying hi and bye in the doorway—proverbial ships passing in the night—and he missed the hell out of her.

She slipped into his arms for a quick, safe-for-public-eyes kiss. "Good morning."

"Good morning, yourself." He resisted her half-hearted attempt to step away. "How was the rest of your shift?"

She sighed and made a face. "Earl and I finally hit our bunks around three. At least I'm off duty all this week. You don't have that luxury."

"No, I don't." This time, he released her from his embrace. He took her hand and they headed toward the nursing home's front door.

"How's Seth?"

His errant full-time night-shift officer. "Still not ready to come back to work."

Seth Metzger saved Zoe's life last winter but had taken a life in the process. His first. And in spite of having been cleared in the investigation by the Pennsylvania State Police and having completed the mandatory psych eval, he still wasn't handling it well. Pete wasn't sure how much longer he could keep juggling schedules and working double shifts to cover for the young officer.

Zoe leaned against Pete's arm. "That's too bad."

Pete recognized the guilt in her voice. "It's not your fault."

Her expression told him she didn't buy it. "I'll give him a call later this morning."

Arriving at the massive entrance doors put an end to the discussion.

Whoever had designed Golden Oaks' interior had gone to great lengths to make it look homey. Polished wood. Floral draperies. Antiques—or reproductions. But he still thought of the place as a nursing home. At first, he'd hated that his father lived here. Harry, however, seemed remarkably content. Confused much of the time, but at least he was safe.

Pete and Zoe headed toward the staircase to the second floor. She greeted several of the residents by name. He loved how she managed to make friends with these older folks. He especially loved how she never minded that his father, more often than not, had no clue who she was.

At the base of the stairs, a table held a bouquet and a framed portrait of a sweet, wrinkled face. Next to the photo, a card printed with "In Memory of..."

"Aw," Zoe said. "I always enjoyed talking to her."

The downside of making friends with folks at Golden Oaks. Pete squeezed Zoe's hand.

A gruff, masculine voice grew louder as they climbed to the second floor, emanating from what Pete had come to know was the activities room at the top of the stairs. At first, he thought someone was being combative, but a burst of laughter punctuated the shouts. They paused at the doorway and peered in.

Harry Adams spotted them and shuffled in their direction. "Son, I'm so glad to see you."

Pete patted his father on the back. "Hey, Pop. Do you remember Zoe?"

"Of course, I do."

Pete doubted it.

Harry drew her into a hug. "Good morning, Sunshine. Have you and my boy got married yet?"

Okay, maybe he did.

She laughed. "Not yet."

Harry jabbed Pete in the gut with one gnarled finger. "You best get on that, Son. This girl isn't gonna wait forever, you know."

Across the room, the gravel-voiced man held court with a half dozen or so women and two of the male caregivers, regaling his audience with what sounded like war stories. Something about the guy struck Pete as familiar. "Who's that?"

"Not now." Harry clutched Pete's arm and leaned closer. "I need to talk to you."

"Sure, Pop. What about?"

Harry glanced around furtively. "Not here. In private." His voice dropped to a whisper. "I think a woman's been murdered."

TWO

Zoe stayed inside the activities room while Pete and Harry stepped into the hallway. She could see Harry pleading his case, while Pete listened, his expression stoic. They went through this every time someone at Golden Oaks passed away. Even on his best days, Harry didn't seem to grasp that he was in a senior living facility or that people here died of old age or various natural illnesses. She and Pete had investigated the place. There was nothing suspicious about any of the deaths.

She turned her attention to the speaker and his audience and spotted Barbara Naiman, the lovely older woman who had become Harry's "lady friend." Wearing a pale pink sweater and her ever-present strand of pearls, she sat tall and proud in one of the home's faux-vintage chairs, her upswept platinum hair sprayed to perfection. Zoe crossed to her and rested a hand on her shoulder. "Good morning, Barbara."

"Well, hello." Barbara started to rise, but Zoe motioned for her to stay seated and pulled a vacant chair closer.

"I don't recognize that man. Is he new?"

"Yes. He moved in a couple days ago, I believe. His name's John...something." Barbara leaned toward Zoe and lowered her voice. "He's quite the rogue. Speaks his mind, shall we say, whether anyone else agrees or not."

John cleared his throat, and Zoe noticed he was giving her and Barbara the stink eye. Having gotten his message across, he turned his attention back to the entire group. "So, we just let these two assholes keep beating the shit out of each other. Wear themselves down a bit, you see. When they started slowing down some, my partner and I stepped in. But damned if he didn't grab the little guy and leave the big fat one for me." He held up two fists in a boxing pose. "Bubba took a swing with his big ol' paw." John mimed the action. "Knocked me flat."

"Then what'd you do?" one of the male aides asked.

"I pulled my baton." John mimicked swinging a baseball bat.

"And I busted his kneecap. It really is true what they say. The bigger they are, the harder they fall."

One aide chuckled. The other didn't appear amused.

One of the women in a wheelchair gasped and touched her frail fingers to her mouth. "How awful."

John turned to her with the same look he'd given Zoe and Barbara. "What's the matter, you old biddy? You live your life in a damned convent? The world's not all sunshine and rainbows, you know."

The woman immediately started to whimper, and the unamused aide dropped to his knees in front of her.

"Oh, dear," Barbara said to Zoe with a sigh. "See what I mean? He just says whatever he wants and doesn't take anyone else's feelings into account."

Another elderly gentleman stomped to the sobbing woman's side and put an arm around her frail shoulders. He glared at John. "Now look what you've done. You know what you are?"

John puffed his chest. "I'm sure you're gonna tell me."

"You're a bully. An old bully. That's what you are."

John started toward the other man. "And you want to know what I think about you?" He might have appeared menacing if he hadn't stumbled and nearly fallen.

The aide who'd enjoyed John's colorful tale caught his arm and tried to shush him. The one who'd been kneeling at the sobbing woman's side climbed to his feet. Zoe thought he was going to help steady John, but instead, he moved in close and jabbed a finger into the older man's chest. He spoke too softly for her to make out his words, but his menacing posture hinted they were less than pleasant.

"What's going on?" Pete asked from behind Zoe.

She turned to discover he and Harry were back. "The new guy isn't very good at making friends."

Harry waved a dismissive hand. "Oh, that's just the way he is. And Gladys there bursts into tears if you look at her cross-eyed."

The second aide caught the angry one's arm and whispered at him. The only part Zoe could hear was "Get some air and cool off."

The unhappy aide glared at John and then his coworker before wheeling and storming out.

Harry acted like the confrontation was an everyday occurrence. "Come on, son. I want you to meet the new guy. He used to be a cop, just like you."

Which explained the partner and baton comments. Zoe excused herself from Barbara and tagged along when Harry guided Pete toward the kneecap buster, who was shaking off the remaining aide.

"Let go of me. It's not my fault if that old biddy's feelings got hurt."

Pete stepped in front of the man, arms crossed. "Do we have a problem here?"

The sight of an over-six-foot tall man in uniform shut John up. He took in Pete's boots, uniform, and duty belt. His gaze paused on Pete's name pin. A smile spread across his thin lips as he lifted his eyes to Pete's. "Well, I'll be damned."

Harry elbowed in next to Pete. "John, this is my son, Pete Adams. He's a police officer too."

"He knows who I am, Pop."

Startled, Zoe looked up at Pete to find him smiling broadly.

"John Kinney, you old son of a bitch." He reached a hand toward the older man. "How the hell are you?"

Kinney's gait reminded Pete how bad the injury from the accident had been, but the retired cop refused Pete's attempt to steady him. "I'm fine." He suggested he and Pete catch up someplace more comfortable, so with Harry and Zoe tagging along, they claimed a table at the currently deserted area dubbed the "Bistro" at the entrance to the dining room. On the far side of the staircase, someone was tinkling the ivories on the piano with a handful of residents and family gathered around.

Kinney barked at a passing aide. "Bring us some coffee."

"You haven't changed a bit." Pete waved off the young woman who appeared eager to satisfy the demand. "Still giving orders."

"They get paid to take care of us." Kinney leaned back in the chair and crossed his arms over his barrel chest. "I figure they should earn their money." He cast an appreciative gaze toward Zoe. "And who is this? Please tell me she's your sister."

"Still flirting with every woman you meet too. Hands off, John. She's spoken for."

"By you?"

"You bet."

"Damn."

Pete chuckled at the flush of red in her cheeks. "Zoe Chambers, meet Sergeant John Kinney, Pittsburgh Bureau of Police. And my first FTO."

She shot him a puzzled scowl. "FTO?"

"Field Training Officer." Kinney reached across the small table to shake her hand. "Pleased to make your acquaintance."

The fact he held her hand longer than a typical brief introductory handshake wasn't lost on Pete. "Enough already with the charm, Kinney. How'd you find your way from Pittsburgh out here to Monongahela County?"

Kinney leaned back again. "My wild youth started catching up with me."

Pete understood. Referring to the accident as his "wild youth" meant he didn't want to discuss it in front of Zoe and Harry.

"My sister started getting after me, insisting it wasn't safe for me to live alone like I've been." Kinney shrugged. "Just because I fell once or twice, they thought I was gonna hurt myself. My sister and her husband moved out this way last fall." He gestured toward the patch on Pete's shoulder. "Your jurisdiction, by the way. Got a place in Vance Township. She thought it would be nice to have us close together." He made a face at the word "nice."

"So, they moved you here." Just like Pete's sister Nadine had done with Harry.

"I moved my own damned self," Kinney said indignantly. "I'm not helpless. And I kinda like this place." He glared at Pete. "Except when people stop the hired help from bringing me coffee."

Zoe pushed back from the table. "I can get us some."

Kinney reached out and caught her hand. "Nonsense. Sit down. I don't really give a damn about coffee. I just like to see the staff earn their wages." He broke out a more yellowed version of the lady-killer smile Pete remembered. "Besides, I don't want *you* going *anywhere*."

She blushed. "I bet you have some stories to tell about when Pete was a rookie."

"Lordy, do I. Has he ever told you about the time..."

Pete listened to the piano music wafting from the sitting area instead of the embellished details of Kinney's narrative. He took poetic license, mostly to play up his heroics. But the truth was there, every detail exactly as Pete recalled. The man hadn't lost a beat mentally.

Unlike Harry, who gazed blankly around the room. Lost again.

Physically was another matter. Besides the falls Kinney had mentioned and the other after effects of that long-ago accident, he looked...old. Pete did the math. Kinney had to be seventy or so. Back in his days as Pete's FTO, he'd been in his mid-to-late forties. About the same age Pete was now. Dammit. How the hell had that happened?

He studied Kinney and Harry. One with his mental faculties firmly in place. The other, not so much. Pete thought of his father's claims of murder...murders, plural...around here. Kinney would be the perfect insider to "investigate" Harry's claims and put them at rest. And hopefully put Harry's mind at ease.

"You mean that really happened?" Zoe asked as she and Pete strolled through the parking lot toward their vehicles. She hadn't known whether to believe John Kinney or not.

Pete grinned. "It really happened. Maybe not exactly the way he said, but beneath his embellishments, yeah."

Zoe stopped at the back bumper of her Chevy pickup and turned to face him, stuffing her hands in her jacket pockets. "I overheard you asking him to look into Harry's claims. Were you serious, or just giving your old boss busy work?"

"No one needs to give Kinney 'busy work.' If there's any truth to Pop's claims, Kinney will root it out. And if he can reassure Pop, I'll owe the old reprobate a case of Iron City." Pete placed his hands on her shoulders and gazed at her with blue eyes the shade of Arctic ice. "With him on the inside and you and Franklin Marshall in the Coroner's Office watching over things, I feel confident any discrepancies won't be overlooked."

"You have my word." She slipped her right hand from her pocket and raised it, as if taking an oath. "Golden Oaks will be the most scrutinized senior living facility in the state."

"I have no doubt." Pete glanced at his watch. "I better get back to the station." He tipped her face upward with a crooked finger beneath her chin and pressed a lingering kiss to her lips.

They'd been "dating"—sort of—for almost a year, living together—sort of—since last November, and the touch of his skin on hers, the taste of his mouth, still sent an electric sizzle through every nerve in her body.

Pete turned to walk away. "Let me know what the big meeting's all about," he called over his shoulder.

*   *   *

At half past noon, Zoe found County Coroner Franklin Marshall seated at the Colonial-style desk in his funeral home.

He looked over the rim of his glasses at her and pointed at a chair across the desk from him. "Have a seat."

As she complied, she noticed he appeared even paler than usual. "Are you okay? You look tired."

Franklin dismissed the question with the wave of a hand. "I wanted to speak to you and the other deputy coroners in private to let you know what's going on."

"Is this about the election?"

He lifted his head in surprise. "You've already heard?"

Zoe shrugged. "I've seen the campaign signs." A lot of them actually.

"For the first time since I took over the office, I have someone running against me. Dr. Charles Davis is challenging me for the position."

"Is he a viable threat?"

Franklin huffed. "He has money, and he has the backing of two of the three county commissioners. How much of this do you already know?"

"Not a lot. I'd heard there was someone else on the ticket and he's running on promises of big changes, but don't they all?"

"Yes, but Davis isn't a politician. He's a forensic pathologist who's worked on some of the biggest cases around the country." Franklin picked up a pencil and started doodling on the notepad in front of him. "And his platform of change? He's promising that once he gets into office, he'll work with county government to do away with the coroner system and replace it with a Medical Examiner one like they have over in Allegheny County. Goodness knows, he has the credentials to run it."

Zoe pondered the implications.

Before she had a chance to ask the big question, Franklin answered it. "If I lose my job, you and the other deputy coroners will lose yours too."

The news wouldn't have mattered so much a year ago. Back then, she'd had doubts about her second career. Now, however, she was beginning to embrace the job. "I thought having an ME's office was too expensive for a county like ours." She decided to keep the rest of her thought to herself. If Davis won, but the coroner system remained intact, perhaps the deputy coroners would keep their jobs. She winced. Poor Franklin would be out of a gig, and here she was, worrying about surviving the sinking ship without him.

The tired smile crossed his face again. "Even if Davis fails at pushing through the change to a Medical Examiner system, he'll bring in his own staff."

So much for being subtle. "I guess I should get out there and campaign for you then."

Franklin's laugh was as tired as his smile. "I hate politics. I hate begging for votes. Maybe I'm just a dinosaur who's outlived his place in the world."

Zoe'd never known him to be defeatist before. And once again, she noticed the pallor of his skin. "Are you sure you're okay?"

"I'm fine. And yes, if you'd be willing to help with the campaign, I'd appreciate it."

Zoe disliked politics too, but Franklin was a good guy, a good boss, and a good coroner. "I'll do everything I can."

His phone rang. "Excuse me," he told Zoe and reached for it.

She stood. "I'll let you get back to work."

Zoe had made it halfway down the funeral home's hallway when she heard Franklin call her name. She turned to see him at his office door, motioning for her to come back. Curious, she retraced her steps.

Franklin was still on the phone, making notes on a legal pad. "Uh-huh...Yes. Certainly...I'll send someone right over." He hung up, ripped the top sheet from the pad, and held it out to her. "You have a case."

"What is it?" She took the offered page.

"City police phoned it in. Deceased elderly male. It's probably nothing more than an accident, but the police want a coroner on the scene."

She skimmed the few details Franklin had scribbled. No name had been given, but she froze when she saw the location.

Zoe's heart threatened to explode out of her chest as she wheeled her old truck into Golden Oaks parking lot for the second time that day.

Dear God, what if it's Harry.

A City of Brunswick Police Department cruiser sat at the front door along with a plain black sedan.

She informed the receptionist she was with the coroner's office and was directed upstairs. The room number wasn't Harry's.

Zoe's panic edged down a notch.

She took the stairs two at a time. Made a left instead of a right to Harry's room. A uniformed officer stood cross-armed in the hallway speaking with County Detective Wayne Baronick. Two women, one in a wheelchair and one on a walker, watched the pair from a distance, a blend of curiosity and dread on their lined faces.

Wayne looked up at Zoe's approach, his expression lacking its trademark smile. He'd seen the body. He would know if it was Harry. She tried to read his face for some clue.

"What are you doing here?" he asked.

Under different circumstances, she'd have slugged him. Not hard, but a good thump on the arm. "Franklin sent me." She swallowed. "Is it...?"

Wayne's brow creased in confusion for a moment before he realized and his eyes widened. "Oh. You think...No, it's not Pete's father."

For a moment, she thought her knees were about to fail. Wayne must have thought the same thing. He reached to steady her, but she recovered. Was she a horrible person feeling relief that someone else had died? Anyone but Harry.

Or Barbara. Or—

She'd come to know and like so many of the residents. Maybe Franklin losing the election and her losing her position in the coroner's office wasn't the worst thing that could happen.

Wayne squeezed her arm. "You okay?"

"Yeah. Where's the body?"

He thumbed at the room. "Inside."

A man in a flannel shirt and khaki pants sprawled prone next to the twin-sized bed. His head was turned away. A floor lamp lay on the floor, its base near the deceased's feet, the cord looped loosely around his ankles.

Wayne pointed. "Looks like he got tangled up in that and fell."

Zoe dug in her purse and withdrew a small camera Franklin had given her. She snapped pictures of the body, the cord, and the lamp. She also captured photos of the bed, rumpled as if someone had climbed out and "made" it by doing nothing more than throwing the spread over the un-straightened sheets and blankets. "Did you get your pictures?" she asked Wayne.

He patted his pocket. "Yep. You ready for me to turn him?"

"Yeah."

Wayne waved the uniformed officer in. Zoe's paramedic mentality kicked in and she moved to the victim's feet. While the men handled the deceased's upper body, she grasped his legs as they log-rolled him. The cops stood and stepped back, giving Zoe her first glimpse of the victim's face.

She felt she'd been sucker punched. "Crap."

"You know him?" Wayne said.

"Yeah. His name's John Kinney."

THREE

Tuesday morning, Zoe stood in the county morgue's autopsy suite wearing a surgical gown, waterproof apron, and gloves. As she gazed at the remains of Pete's Field Training Officer, a lump as heavy as lead sat in her stomach.

She'd returned to Golden Oaks with Pete last evening to check on Harry, only to find him having one of his "bad" nights. Anxious and uncooperative, he'd recognized Pete, but not Zoe. Harry was concerned about going home, not about murders.

Franklin and Doc Abercrombie, the forensic pathologist the county employed to handle autopsies, looked over the notes and scanned the x-rays and the photos taken of the deceased. She didn't need to see them again. She remembered the man who only yesterday morning had been regaling her with stories of Pete as a young rookie. The same man whose body she'd processed a few hours later.

From her jeans pocket beneath the protective gear, her phone sang out its generic tune. Franklin, Doc, and the young assistant turned to look at her.

"Sorry." She dug through the layers to extract the device. The number wasn't familiar or local. She muted it and retreated into the morgue's office to drop the phone into her purse.

The door to the entrance swung open and Wayne Baronick breezed in. "Good morning." He glanced around. "I thought Pete might be here."

"He couldn't get away." They'd talked about it. Pete had given her the "too busy" excuse. Vance Township was a small department. Even when fully staffed, Pete worked the daylight shift solo. Still, he usually managed to attend autopsies. "And he's taking Kinney's death pretty hard. I don't think he wanted to see the man like this."

Wayne gazed through the window, toward the body on the metal slab. "When a brother in blue dies, even a retired one, we all feel the loss."

"Is that why you're investigating? Because he was a cop? Or do you suspect foul play?"

"From what I found out yesterday, nothing appears suspicious. The staff at the facility all report he was notoriously unsteady on his feet and refused to use a cane or a walker."

Zoe could attest to that much having seen Kinney yesterday.

"He was found on the floor of his room." Wayne shook his head. "Looked like he got his feet tangled up in an electrical cord and fell, striking his head on the corner of his nightstand."

The elderly lived in places like Golden Oaks to be safe and supervised. Apparently for John Kinney the move had failed on both counts.

"I'll bet there'll be a lawsuit if the facility is deemed negligent," Wayne added. He motioned to the door to the autopsy suite, and she led the way.

Franklin tucked the paperwork under his arm as he and Doc moved to the stainless steel table. Doc glanced at Zoe and the detective, his gaze settling on her. "Are you ready?"

"Just tell me what to do."

Doc nodded toward Franklin and Wayne. "Keep them company. You've earned your autopsy survival badge."

Had there been such a thing, she'd wear it with pride. She'd lost count of how many times she bolted from the morgue to the woman's room across the hall. The smells still curdled her stomach, but she'd learned to grit her teeth and bulldoze through it.

The young assistant began the dirty work while Doc kept watch.

Franklin handed the envelope with the x-rays to Zoe. "You might want to take a look at those."

She removed the films and held them up to the light. "Wow." Both of Kinney's legs contained metal plates and pins. "That's some impressive hardware."

The detective tipped his head to view them too and whistled. "I'll say."

"Pete mentioned he'd been in an accident."

The assistant cranked up the bone saw and set the whining blade to Kinney's skull. The stench of burning flesh and bone filled the air.

Wayne nudged Franklin with an elbow. "How goes the campaign?"

Franklin grunted. "Wonderful." His tone said otherwise.

Zoe took a long look at him. The stress of the upcoming election was evident on his thin face. The harsh lighting couldn't take all the blame for the dark shadows under his eyes. "Are you okay?" she asked.

Franklin's glare was as dark as those shadows. "Wonderful," he repeated.

Okay. He did not want to talk about the election. Or his health.

Wayne must have gotten the hint as well. He moved closer to her. "How's Metzger doing?"

The detective had been there that snowy night when Seth had saved her life. "About the same, I guess. I need to stop at his place and visit him."

"Any idea when he's coming back to work?"

"Not that I know of."

"Pete still working double shifts?"

Zoe looked up at Wayne. He wasn't usually this concerned about the Vance Township Police Department. "Yeah. Why?"

He shook his head, suddenly riveted to the autopsy. "No reason."

In spite of a mountain of paperwork—on which he couldn't focus—Pete climbed behind the wheel of the township SUV. Maybe patrolling would distract him from the thought of his FTO on a slab in autopsy. John Kinney was one of those men who seemed too tough to die.

Especially from a fall in a nursing home.

Without thinking, Pete pulled into a driveway less than a block from the station. He stared up at Seth's house. Maybe his subconscious wanted to quell his grief over the old cop by rescuing the promising career of a young one.

Pete barely recognized the man who answered the door. Seth's longish hair hadn't seen scissors or even a comb in much too long and his face hid behind a thick growth of beard. His t-shirt and sweatpants looked dingy and rumpled.

Seth stepped aside, allowing Pete to enter. "You checking up on me, Chief?"

Dirty dishes overflowed the sink. A pizza box and several Chinese takeout boxes toppled from the full trash can. The place reeked of spoiled food and sour milk. "Looks like you need it."

"My housekeeper quit."

It was a lame attempt at humor. Pete narrowed his eyes at the young man. "I know taking a life is tough. If you weren't affected by it, you wouldn't be the kind of man I want working for me. But you need to realize you did the only thing you could do."

Seth didn't appear convinced. "If I'd waited another second—"

"Zoe would likely be dead." Pete put a hand on Seth's shoulder and squeezed. "Frankly, I'm grateful you reacted how and when you did."

Seth ducked away from Pete's grasp.

The last time he'd been here, he'd left a business card for a shrink on the kitchen table. He crossed the room to see if the card was still there among the stack of papers. "Did you call the therapist I recommended?"

"Not yet." Seth scurried to the table to intercept Pete. He reached to gather the papers, but not before Pete identified a résumé on the top of the pile.

Pete placed a hand on the papers, pinning them to the table. "Seth? Is there something you want to tell me?"

The young man's face lost its color. He opened his mouth, but words didn't come.

Pete knew all too well what Seth was going through. "I realize you did the mandatory psych thing, but you need to talk to someone else. Burying all that shit won't make it go away."

Seth kept his head lowered. "Did you go for additional therapy after you shot that kid?"

"You bet I did." A memory flashed through Pete's mind. One he hadn't thought about in years. A conversation much like this one, but with him on the receiving end of it—and John Kinney on the giving side. Except Kinney hadn't let him wallow for months. "You're a damned good cop, Son. I'd hate to see you give up a career you love."

Seth lifted his face to look at Pete. "I don't know that I love it anymore."

"That's one of the reasons you need to talk to someone. Deal with what happened and then figure out where you go from here."

Pete's cell phone rang. He ignored it, his gaze pinning Seth in place in the same way his hand pinned the résumé and what appeared to be job applications to the table.

But Seth averted his eyes. "You should answer that."

Pete willed the kid to look at him. And failed. The phone kept ringing.

Reluctantly, Pete released the papers, which Seth scooped up and carried into another room. Caller ID revealed Zoe's name and photo. He swiped the answer button. "Hey."

"Where are you?" Her voice sounded strained.

Pete looked around at the filthy apartment. "On patrol. What's wrong?"

"I'm at your station with the autopsy report," she said. "You're gonna want to see this."

"On my way." He hung up. Seth was still in the other room, his back to Pete. "Make the phone call to the therapist. If you don't, I'll make it for you."

As Zoe hung up, she noticed the tiny icon indicating she had a voicemail. That ignored call.

"I'm gonna wait in his office," she told Nancy.

The secretary waved her back. "You know where it is."

Zoe dropped the large envelope with the autopsy report on Pete's desk and, once seated in the visitor's chair, she touched the icon on her phone.

"My name is Jason Cox and I'm trying to reach the Zoe Chambers whose father was Gary Chambers of Monongahela County, Pennsylvania. I've been doing some research of my DNA and ancestry and I think we may be related. Please call me at your earliest convenience."

The phone number he left had an area code she didn't recognize.

The voice echoed in her ears. Gary Chambers. Her dad. May be related. An uncle? No. Zoe remembered stories about how her father's only brother had died when they were kids. She replayed the message, this time jotting down the phone number on a piece of note paper from Pete's desk.

The bells on the station's front door jingled, disrupting her thoughts about calling the guy back. A moment later, Pete strode into his office, bending to plant a kiss on the top of her head. "What's going on?"

For a moment she wondered how he knew about the cryptic message. Then she realized he meant the report. She pointed at the envelope. "Take a look."

Pete slid around his desk and into his chair before putting on his reading glasses and picking up the envelope. Steeling himself, he pulled out the report and photos.

Zoe stood and moved behind him, leaning over his shoulder to read along. "We originally assumed Kinney had gotten his feet tangled up in his lamp's electrical cord and fell striking his head on the corner of the bedside stand." Zoe tapped the report with one finger. "But see here? The shape and size of the contusion wasn't consistent with what we'd expect to find from striking a sharp corner."

Pete flipped from the printed summary to the photo and back. "What do Marshall and Doc think caused it?"

Zoe lightly backhanded Pete's shoulder. "And me. I'm in on this investigation."

"Pardon me. What do the three of you think caused the contusion?"

She perched a hip on the desk beside him and held up her fist. "We think someone decked him."

Pete half turned in his seat to look up at her. "Someone punched him hard enough to kill him?"

"Not exactly." She gestured to the report. "The blow probably stunned him. Maybe even knocked him down, as unsteady as he was. But cause of death was suffocation." She reached down and flipped a page. "White cotton fibers were found in his mouth, nose, and trachea."

"The kind of fibers you'd find—"

"In a pillowcase."

Pete leaned back in his chair. "Someone knocked Kinney down with a punch and then finished off the job by smothering him with a pillow."

"Looks that way. Not very original."

"But effective. And definitely homicide." He rubbed the stubble on his upper lip. "Does Baronick know about all this?"

"Yeah. He headed over to Golden Oaks right after the autopsy to collect Kinney's linens."

"Good."

"I thought you'd want to take over the investigation yourself."

Of course he did. His father was in that place. "Not my jurisdiction."

"Jurisdiction?" She arched an eyebrow at him. "This is Harry's home we're talking about. That makes it your jurisdiction, township boundaries be damned."

She knew him all too well. Under different circumstances, he'd have been on the road to Brunswick this very minute. Hell, he'd have been at the autopsy. But Seth wasn't available to fill in. Both Kevin and

Nate, his two remaining full-timers, had already accumulated more overtime than the department's budget could bear. And his part-time officers were tied up with gigs at other departments. "Baronick's a good cop."

She choked a laugh. "I'm surprised to hear you admit that."

"I wouldn't admit it to *him*. And if you tell him I said that, I'll deny it."

Zoe crossed her arms. "You're gonna be on the phone with Wayne the minute I walk out of this office."

"Probably."

Her expression shifted to one Pete couldn't read, and she picked her phone up from his desk, studying it.

"Expecting a call?"

She walked around to the visitor's chair but didn't sit. "I already got one. Or a strange message anyway."

Pete's shoulder muscles tightened. "What kind of strange message?"

Zoe handed the phone to him. "Listen for yourself."

He played back the recording she'd keyed up. Then played it a second time. He'd heard of these DNA and ancestry search things. "You've never registered with one of those websites, have you?"

"No."

"How'd this Jason Cox track you down?"

"I have no idea."

"You haven't called him back yet?"

"I just picked up the message while I was waiting for you to get here."

Pete studied her. "Are you going to?"

Zoe appeared surprised by the question. "Yeah." She shifted her weight, reminding Pete of a kid digging a guilty toe in the sand. "I mean, why not? The only real family I have left—that I know of—is my mother, and you know how well we get along."

He knew. They didn't. At all.

"And there's Patsy..." Her recently discovered second cousin. "Maybe I have another cousin out there somewhere on my dad's side of the family."

Pete scribbled the name Jason Cox on his notepad. "Do me a favor?"

"Anything."

"If he says anything about meeting face-to-face, let me check him out first."

She grinned. "You're being a little overprotective, don't you think?"

"You bet."

Zoe's cell phone rang out an old rock tune by The Who. "That's Franklin," she said as she dug it from her pocket.

Pete rose and moved to the coffee pot to fill his empty mug. He picked up a clean one and held it up to her. Her face had grown tense and she shook her head. If Zoe Chambers turned down caffeine, something was definitely wrong.

Her lips moved, but Franklin Marshall apparently wasn't giving her a chance to speak. After several false starts, she said, "Have the doctors given you any idea?"

Pete carried his coffee back to his chair.

Zoe gave a few uh-huhs and okays. She looked at Pete, her eyes troubled. "I'll head there now. You just concentrate on taking care of yourself."

Pete waited until she finished the call. "What's going on?"

She set her phone on the desk and stared into space for a moment before looking at him. "Franklin's in the ER. He collapsed sometime after I left. They don't know what's wrong yet, but they're running tests and plan to admit him." She swallowed. "He's temporarily put me in charge of the Coroner's Office."

FOUR

The drive back to Brunswick was a blur. Zoe's mind churned out and revised a plan of action for the job that had been dropped in her lap. While she was worried about Franklin, she had to admit the prospect of taking the lead on a homicide case—and being able to see it through—excited her.

The idea of being in total charge of the department—even for a few days—terrified her.

At least the timing was good. After the long shift she'd been on last weekend, her EMS crew didn't pull another shift until next week. She had six days to devote to filling in for Franklin. And he had the same six days to get over whatever bug he'd picked up.

Wayne Baronick leaned against his unmarked sedan in the Golden Oaks parking lot, scanning his phone. He looked up when she approached. "Franklin called and told me you were on your way."

"Did he give you any idea of what's wrong with him?"

"Nope. Just that he was in the hospital and you were filling in. On this case, at least." The detective gave her one of his devilish smiles. "Looks like we'll be spending a lot of time together."

Zoe ignored the innuendo. Wayne made a game of hitting on her, suggesting if she ever got sick of Pete, he'd be happy to fill the void. But they both knew it would never happen and, in spite of a rocky first meeting, she counted Wayne as a friend. "Did you collect the bedding from Kinney's room?"

The smile faded. "Unfortunately, no. Housekeeping had already stripped the linens and sent them to the laundry."

"From a crime scene?"

"I spoke with the woman in charge and she was appalled. But they didn't realize it was a 'crime scene' until I told her, and management has harangued the staff about cleanliness so much that housekeeping was trying to be conscientious."

Zoe wondered if getting a vacant room turned around quickly for a new paying resident might have something to do with the conscientiousness. "Did you talk to the person who cleaned the room?"

"Yep, and I don't believe she was trying to destroy evidence. Besides, she didn't do anything else except remove the bedding. I've sealed the room until our crime scene techs can go over it."

"So, we're stuck for now?"

"Not completely." He thumbed toward his car. "I have the footage from the security cams in my backseat. Hours of it."

"From Kinney's room?"

"They don't have cameras in the residents' rooms. Privacy issues. But the hallways and entrances are monitored. We should be able to see who came and went during the time of the homicide." He grinned and winked at her. "Feel like watching some movies? I'll bring the popcorn."

Zoe looked toward the window on the building. "I promised Pete I'd check on Harry." She wondered if he knew he'd finally been right about someone being murdered.

A black box truck with the county seal printed on the door and Monongahela County Crime Scene Unit painted in gold on the sides turned into the lot and stopped in a no-parking zone.

"There's my team." Wayne pushed away from his car. "You go make sure Adams Senior is all right. I'll get the techs started and then head back to headquarters. That's where I'll be if you want to help view the security footage."

Zoe left Wayne consulting with the CSU team and headed inside. She found Harry seated alone in the Bistro, a half-full chocolate milkshake in front of him. "That looks good," she said, expecting to have to introduce herself to him all over again.

He squinted up at her and smiled. "Hello, Sunshine."

"Mind if I join you?"

He gestured toward one of the empty chairs. "Of course I don't mind. Is Pete with you?"

She camouflaged her surprise. "Not this time. He's at work."

"That boy works too damned hard. When you get married, make sure he takes time for you. Being a workaholic is what ruined his first marriage. Well, that and the fact he married a bitch."

Zoe choked. Regaining her composure, she said, "I never really got to know Pete's ex-wife."

"Just as well. You're nothing like her." Harry brushed away the subject with a wave of his hand. "And here I am, criticizing my boy when I'm being anything but gentlemanly. Would you care for a milkshake, my dear?"

"No, thank you."

"You sure? They're really good. Better than most of what they call food here."

"I'm sure." Zoe leaned forward on the table. Harry was sharper than she'd seen him in months and these windows of opportunity were not only rare but could close at any moment. "I suppose you heard about John Kinney's death."

"John Kinney?"

"The new guy. Used to be Pete's Field Training Officer in Pittsburgh."

"Oh, sure. I know who you mean now. He died?"

She nodded. "Yesterday."

Harry scowled at his drink, as if his memory was mixed up with the ice cream. "Yesterday? Yeah. I do seem to recall something about that."

Zoe wasn't sure she believed him. Harry had become proficient at covering his memory lapses. "We're pretty sure it was murder."

Harry snapped out of his bewilderment, his ice-blue eyes—so much like Pete's—locking with hers. "I knew it," he exclaimed, a note of triumph in his voice. "I've been telling Pete that people have been getting killed around this place."

"Now, I don't think there's been anything nefarious about any of the others, but in this case...maybe."

"You all think I've been crying wolf. But I'm telling you. Weird shit goes on around here."

"Why do you say that?"

"Because they wheel someone out of this hotel once a week or so."

Zoe wanted to point out it wasn't a hotel but had seen Pete get into this same argument with his father. "Have you seen any suspicious activity?"

"People getting wheeled out in body bags isn't suspicious enough for you?"

Maybe she should have accepted the offer of a milkshake. Preferably with something stronger added. "I mean anything that might help us catch who did it."

"Oh." His eyes widened. "*Oh*. Like people sneaking around, being where they ought not be."

"Exactly."

Harry leaned back in his chair and rubbed his upper lip thoughtfully. "There was a stranger in here the other day. Was it yesterday? No. Maybe the day before. Oh, hell, I don't remember. But he was looking around a lot. You know. Casing the joint." He smiled, apparently pleased with himself for using crime slang.

Looking around. Casing the joint. Probably being given the same tour Pete, Nadine, and she had been on when they were considering Golden Oaks for Harry. "Was this guy alone?"

The question puzzled Harry. "Alone?"

"Was he with that woman that runs the place?"

"Oh." He pondered a moment. "No. Wait. Maybe."

Zoe sighed. The security cams should give them a more reliable report of any strange comings and goings. "Okay. You let me or Pete know if you see him again. Or anything else out of place."

Harry blew a raspberry. "Pete thinks I'm off my rocker. And sometimes I think so too." He tapped his head. "But I'm not a total goner yet."

Zoe dug a scrap of paper from her purse and jotted down her name and number, sliding it across the table, careful to keep it out of the condensation puddle pooling around the milkshake glass. "You call me. I promise I won't think you're off your rocker."

Harry picked up the paper and studied it. "Zoe." He nodded and then smiled. "We'll be a regular crime fighting duo around here."

She left him tucking the paper into his trousers pocket and imagined the person doing his laundry finding it and tossing it away. Not that it mattered. Harry likely wouldn't remember the conversation by the time he finished his drink.

Nevertheless, Zoe stopped at the business office to ask about any tours they may have given in the last day or two. The director had gone for the day, so Zoe left a message with the concierge, who promised to have her call as soon as possible.

The exchange reminded Zoe of the voicemail on her phone. She listened to it again on her way to the parking lot. Once behind the wheel of her Chevy pickup, she keyed in the number he'd left.

A masculine voice answered.

"I'm trying to reach Jason Cox," she said.

"Speaking."

"This is Zoe Chambers. I'm returning your call."

"Zoe, thank you so much for getting back to me." The words tumbled through the ether in an excited rush. "I was afraid you wouldn't bother."

"You mentioned my dad, but his only sibling died when he was a child, so I'm not sure how we could be related."

The line fell silent for a moment before the voice said, "Oh. I see. You thought we might be cousins."

"Well...yeah."

"I'm sorry. No." Another pause. "Zoe, Gary Chambers was my father too. You're my sister."

Pete's morning had segued into the afternoon without more than a fleeting moment to ponder Kinney's homicide, Harry's proximity to a murder, or Zoe's new DNA match. Something must be in the light drizzle, driving all the locals to file complaints against each other. The culmination of the string of calls came from Kristopher O'Keefe, who demanded Pete come to the scene of the machete incident immediately.

O'Keefe, donning a raincoat and carrying an umbrella, stood in front of his garage door as Pete stepped out and tugged his ball cap onto his head. "What can I do for you...?" He pondered the title. "Is it *Doctor* O'Keefe?"

The man's chest puffed. "*Professor* O'Keefe."

"I assumed you had a PhD." Pete watched the man's mouth narrow into a thin line. "My college professors always preferred to be called 'Doctor.'"

"It's *Professor* O'Keefe," he repeated, biting off each syllable.

Pete shrugged. "What can I do for you, Professor?"

He huffed. "Did you know that homicidal maniac neighbor of mine is out of prison?"

"I understand he was released on bail, yes."

"Bail? The man is a menace to society. And my life is in danger. My word, what's to keep him from coming over here and finishing the job he started two days ago?"

"Has he contacted you since his release? Made threats?"

"He's too smart for that. He'd plan a covert attack, I'm quite sure."

Pete winced at the headache boiling behind his eyes. "Apparently the judge determined that Mr. Anderson wasn't a threat to society or to you."

"What exactly is there to keep him from evading justice by fleeing the county?"

Farmers with family and livestock weren't usually considered a flight risk, but Pete didn't think O'Keefe could grasp the concept. "Look at it this way, Professor. If he runs off, he won't be around to cause you more harm."

O'Keefe crossed his arms. "Now you're just being insolent, Chief Adams."

"What exactly do you want me to do?"

"Put him back behind bars."

"That's not how it works."

"You mean you can't do anything until he kills me?"

"I can't arrest the man until he breaks the law or misses his court date."

The swish of rubber on wet pavement behind Pete drew his attention. A dark blue Toyota Camry pulled into the driveway and edged to one side, leaving room for Pete to back out. A woman with short well-groomed hair climbed out and clung to the open car door as if she might otherwise collapse. She glanced from O'Keefe to Pete. "Oh, dear God. Now what's wrong?"

"Nothing, dear." O'Keefe shifted his weight like a kid being called in front of the school principal. "I'm simply trying to prevent further trouble by asking the police to take that nefarious heathen back into custody."

"You mean Boyd Anderson?" The woman heaved a sigh that sounded equal parts exhaustion and exasperation. "If you would just quit..." She clamped her mouth shut and shook her head. "I'm so sorry my husband dragged you out here."

Pete noticed O'Keefe with his umbrella had made no move toward his wife whose formerly pristine hairdo now glistened from the drizzle. "No need to apologize, ma'am."

O'Keefe puffed his chest. "I should say not. Chief Adams is only doing his job." The Professor glared at him. "Or he will be if he arrests that machete-wielding madman."

Mrs. O'Keefe slung a purse over her shoulder and slammed the Camry's door. "He's already arrested the man. Boyd's out on bail. They can't keep him jailed just because you're scared of him."

"I am not."

Pete rubbed his upper lip to hide his smile. He liked this woman in spite of her bad taste in spouses.

She trudged toward the house, pausing to look at her husband and then at Pete. Her brow creased. "Chief Adams," she said as if testing his name on her tongue. "I feel like we've met."

Pete had to admit he'd had the same sense of recognition, but studying her, he was fairly certain he'd remember. "I don't believe so, ma'am." He caught a glimpse of bloodshot eyes.

She approached him and extended a hand. "Elaine O'Keefe. What's your first name?"

Her grip was firm, confident. And her eyes were definitely red. "Pete, ma'am."

She repeated his name while clearly trying to pull a memory from the recesses of her mind. Then she shook her head. "I still feel like I know you from somewhere. Anyway, I'm sorry my husband called you back out here for nothing." Shooting a look at the professor, she turned away.

"Excuse me, Mrs. O'Keefe." Pete took the umbrella from her husband and handed it to her. "Take this."

She seemed surprised, but a smile crossed her lips. "Thank you, Chief Adams." And she walked away.

Zoe inhaled slowly. Sister? "I'm sorry. I don't understand."

A nervous but melodious laugh filtered through the line. "I'm the one who should apologize. I just kinda sprung that on you, didn't I? You see, I'm adopted, and I recently tracked down my biological mother. She and your—our—father had an affair and she became pregnant with me. Before he married your mother, I mean."

The idea of a tryst was far from foreign to Zoe. She'd been a wild child herself. But her father? "I don't believe it. If Dad had gotten a girl pregnant, he'd have done the right thing."

"You mean get married? According to her, he wanted to, but her parents wouldn't let them. They packed up my mom and moved her to Philadelphia. When I was born, she put me up for adoption."

Zoe listened, a million half-formed questions flooding her brain.

From the other end of the line, another laugh, this one more relaxed. "Information overload, right?"

She managed a short laugh of her own. "You could say that."

"Look. I still live near Philadelphia, but I'm in Pittsburgh on a business trip. I was hoping we could get together. How about having dinner with me this evening?"

"This evening?" Zoe remembered Pete's demand to be informed before any face-to-face meeting. "Um. I can't. I'm working on a homicide case, and I—"

"Homicide case? I thought you were a paramedic."

"I am. But I'm also a deputy coroner."

"Really? Cool."

"Anyhow, tonight isn't good." Which was true. Besides her promise to Pete, she wanted to see those security recordings.

"Oh." His disappointment was tangible. "I'm leaving for home in the morning."

Zoe echoed his deflated "Oh." Did she dare bypass Pete? Forego viewing the footage from Golden Oaks? The case Franklin had entrusted her with? No. "I'm sorry. Maybe the next time you're in town? We can email in the meantime."

"Yeah. I guess." He sighed. "You know, the hell with it. I can reschedule the meetings I have waiting for me at home and stick around another day. How about coffee tomorrow? Or lunch?"

"That would be great."

They arranged to meet at a small restaurant in Phillipsburg for lunch and said their goodbyes. Zoe sat in her truck and stared at the phone. A brother. She had an older sibling she'd never known about. After thirty-six years as an only child, the revelation left her torn. Memories of her dad played on a loop across the movie screen of her mind—the memories of an eight-year-old. Distorted. Jumbled. But she could still picture him. Tall, blond, broad shouldered. And a smile that put everyone at ease.

He'd had a child before her and never let on.

Did her mother know about it?

Zoe thumbed to her phone's contact page and froze. Calling Kimberly was never a fun experience. Extracting information about her first husband was akin to torturing covert details from a war-hardened spy.

No. Zoe would meet Jason Cox first. Then she'd call her mother. Or not.

FIVE

True to his promise, Wayne met Zoe at the county police headquarters with a large bag of fresh popcorn in hand.

She pointed at it. "You must really love popcorn."

"Don't you?" He grinned. "This might end up being dinner."

Not the day she'd planned when the invitation to watch security footage had first come up.

Zoe followed Wayne into a small, dark room filled with electronic equipment, control panels, a couple of computer keyboards, and numerous monitors. He pulled up one of three chairs on rollers and signaled for her to grab another. Plopping the bag of popcorn on the control console, he crossed an ankle over his knee and balanced a keyboard on his lap. "Here we go."

Grainy black and white footage flickered onto one of the screens. Overhead views of people coming and going, passing through the hallways.

Popcorn for dinner? They might still be here for breakfast if they had to go through all of this.

Wayne tapped some keys and the image switched to a different camera. And another and another. "There." He leaned forward and pointed at the screen. "That's the door to Kinney's room. I think this angle will give us the best view of anyone who entered and exited around the time of his death." Wayne played with the keyboard and mouse, rewinding and fast-forwarding the footage. "According to the report, an aide found his body shortly after noon on Monday when he didn't show up in the dining room for lunch. What time were you and Pete there?"

"Between nine and about a quarter 'til ten."

"Okay." Wayne pecked the keys, sending the figures on the screen racing backwards. "We know Kinney was alive when you left, so that's where we'll begin."

Even with the speed set at fast-forward, Zoe expected to be there a while, waiting to see someone enter or leave Kinney's room. Apparently, Wayne did too. He reached for the bag of popcorn.

A blurred figure disappeared into Kinney's room. "Wait," Zoe said. "There."

Wayne clicked the mouse, freezing the picture. "What? I missed it." He reversed the footage, still faster than normal.

The person in the image sped backwards into the hall. "There," Zoe said again.

"I saw it." He stopped the film and advanced it at normal speed.

This time the figure hobbled into the frame and turned into the room. "It's John Kinney."

"Yep." Wayne touched the corner of the screen where the time and date were printed. "9:56."

Wayne let the footage roll at normal speed for a few minutes. Kinney remained inside and no one else entered the frame. The detective reached for the keyboard, but before he could click to fast-forward, someone wearing a ball cap appeared on the monitor. As Zoe watched, the figure stopped at Kinney's doorway, paused, and entered the room.

She glanced at Wayne. "Did you see that?"

The detective's face revealed no sign of his trademark smile. "Yeah." He uncrossed his legs and leaned toward the screen. "Timestamp, 10:02."

Exactly eight minutes later, the person stepped into the hallway and headed toward and under the camera, out of the frame. The bill of a Pittsburgh Pirates ball cap shielded his face from view.

The skin on Zoe's neck prickled. "Do you think—?"

Wayne lifted a hand to silence her. "Too soon to tell."

But almost a half hour later, after fast-forwarding to the point where the aide entered at 12:10 and immediately rushed back out, they determined no one else had come or gone from the victim's room.

Wayne reset the footage to 10:10 where the man in the ball cap stepped back out into hall after apparently committing murder. Freezing the frame, the detective stared at the image. "Yeah," he said. "I'd be willing to bet that's our killer."

Zoe studied the monitor, willing the man on the screen to lift his face. "Who is he?"

"Now's when the real fun begins. We get to watch the rest of the security footage to track his movements and try to catch a glimpse of his face." Wayne leaned back in his chair. "Better have some popcorn."

*   *   *

The day's light drizzle had let up, and the sun, low in the western sky, split the clouds and sparkled off the damp spring-green grass. Zoe slid down from the cab of her pickup in Pete's driveway, next to his township vehicle. She stepped through the kitchen door—no one but strangers ever used the front one—into an invisible cloud of garlic, onion, and tomato.

Pete turned from the stove. "Glad you could finally make it."

She inhaled deeply, her mouth watering. "You made spaghetti?"

He held up a wooden spoon coated in sauce. "Sort of. I hope doctored-up jar sauce is good enough."

One of Zoe's orange tabbies trotted over to greet her as she collapsed into the chair next to the door. "I'm so hungry, even canned ravioli sounds good." She despised canned ravioli.

Pete made a disappointed face. "Well, I suppose I can toss this and see if I have anything like that on the shelf..."

"Don't you dare." She unlaced her boots and tugged them off, setting each next to the chair. The cat meowed, and Zoe picked her up. "Hi, Jade."

The tabby squirmed in protest, wriggling free, preferring to rub on Zoe's legs.

Pete stirred the pot and set a lid on it before crossing the kitchen to stand in front of her. "How'd it go?"

She called him a couple hours ago to let him know she'd be late but hadn't gone into any details. "We think we found the killer on the security footage."

"Oh?"

Zoe stood and slung her jacket and purse on the hall tree. "Male, wearing a ball cap."

"That's not a lot to go on."

"I know." She sighed and stepped into Pete's arms, burying her face against his chest and breathing in his freshly showered scent. Even better than the aroma of pasta sauce.

"Could you identify him?"

"Nope. He kept his head down. We couldn't find a single frame with his face visible. There's a lot of footage to go through yet, but from what we could piece together, he wandered around a while. Then he went into John's room, came out eight minutes later, and exited the building. Never once looked up. He even tipped his head away from some of the cameras that might've caught a profile."

Zoe could hear the rumble in Pete's chest. "He was street-smart enough to keep his face shielded."

"Or the killer was aware of the cameras' locations. Wayne and I figure he's spent enough time there to know his way around and know about their security."

"That's a good probability."

She eased out of Pete's embrace. "Anyway, Wayne said he'd have some of his men go through the rest of the footage from yesterday and from the days leading up to the homicide. But without a face to match, all the guy has to do is change clothes and wear a different hat, or no hat at all. There isn't much of a chance we'll ID him."

Pete gazed over her head, his expression stoic.

Zoe made a guess at his thoughts. "You're worried about Harry."

Pete's jaw twitched. "Hell yes, I'm worried about Harry. I had qualms about Nadine's insistence on moving him there last winter. He seemed to settle in well though, so I dropped it. But now..."

She filled in the blank. Now a murderer had shattered the illusion of security. "Have you spoken with your sister?"

"I called and left a message."

"You know she'll insist on moving him."

"It'll be the first thing we've agreed on in a decade."

"I checked on him today."

"Oh? How was he?"

"Good. Better than most days. He knew who I was. And he said he saw a stranger wandering around the place the morning of the murder."

Pete's eyebrows shot up. "Really? He was sure it was that morning?"

"Kinda. Sorta. Maybe."

Pete nodded. "That's what I figured. Besides, *everyone* is a stranger to Pop."

"My point is you need to quit worrying so much. Your dad is fine." Zoe fingered Pete's arm, sliding her hand down to clasp his. "And we're gonna catch this guy before he can do any more harm."

The corner of Pete's mouth tipped into a hint of a grin. "We?"

"Yeah. Me and—"

He groaned. "Do not say 'Wayne.' I'm getting a little tired of you being so buddy-buddy with that guy. Especially talking about him when I'm holding you in my arms."

She knew Pete was teasing, but she stood on her toes to give him a quick kiss. "You have nothing to be concerned about."

"Yeah? Prove it." His arms encircled her waist drawing her to him and the kiss he returned threatened to divert the conversation into the bedroom.

When his hands slid lower, she ducked out of his grasp. "Later, I promise. But I need some of that spaghetti because I'm too weak from starvation right now."

He aimed a finger at her in a mock threat. "I'm holding you to that promise." Turning, he headed back to the stove. "By the way, did you ever call that guy claiming to be related to you?"

Crap. She'd been so focused on the case, she hadn't mentioned her lunch plans to Pete when they'd spoken earlier. "Uh, yeah."

"And?" He lifted the lid to peer into the pot.

"He's my brother."

The lid clattered to the stovetop, splattering pasta sauce. Pete ignored the mess, facing her. "Your brother?"

"Half-brother." She explained about her father's premarital affair and the resulting child.

Pete fell silent for a few moments before asking, "Did he mention how he found you?"

"He tracked down his birth mother who told him who his father was. From there it wouldn't be hard."

"No." Pete's voice was pensive. "It wouldn't." He returned to the pot and the mess he'd made, grabbing a dishrag to wipe the counter. Over his shoulder he asked, "Have you talked to *your* mother about this?"

Zoe cringed. "Not yet. I thought I'd meet him first."

"You're meeting him? When?"

"Tomorrow for lunch." She braced for the impending storm surge. Hurricane Pete.

He wheeled, dishrag in hand. "When exactly were you going to mention this?"

"I just did."

"You have no idea this guy's for real."

"I know that. We're meeting at Walden's. There'll be people around. And once I see him, I'll know if he's really my brother."

"How? Do you have some built-in lie detector I don't know about?"

Pete's surly tone grated on her. "Yeah. The same one you do," she snapped. "You call it your gut. I call it intuition."

He flung the dishrag into the sink. "Dammit, Zoe—"

"I know what my dad looked like. If this guy is his son, there'll be a resemblance. I mean if he has dark hair and eyes, he's probably not my brother." Unless Cox's biological mother had dark hair and eyes, but Zoe would deal with that possibility when and if the situation called for it. "And it's lunch in the middle of Phillipsburg, not a clandestine encounter in a dark alley somewhere."

Pete crossed his arms. "I'll meet you there. What time?"

Zoe stuttered. "No."

His eyebrows shot up. "No?"

"No," she repeated firmly. "If Jason Cox is my brother, I want to hear what he has to say. Having a cop, especially one looking like..." She gestured at Pete's cross-armed power stance. "...*you*...sitting across the table from him, isn't going to be conducive to relaxed conversation."

"It'll encourage honesty. What time?"

Zoe bit back a frustrated scream. "No. I mean it, Pete. I don't want you there."

Her words stung. She could see it in his face. "Look, I just want to get a feel for the guy, one-on-one, this first time." She cocked her head and gave him her best flirtatious grin. "Then I'll set up another lunch for the three of us, at which point you can do your best to scare the crap out of him."

The muscle twitching in Pete's jaw told her he wasn't backing down.

"Besides, how long does it take you to run a background check? I'm not meeting him until noon. You do that thing that you do..." She mimed typing on a computer, "...and if you find out Jason Cox is on some terrorist watch list, I'll bring you along and you can arrest him."

The muscle in Pete's jaw stopped jumping, but he didn't relax his stance.

Zoe sashayed over and placed a finger at the center of his chest. "I know you want to protect me. But I need to handle this my way." She traced a path down to his belt. From the hint of a groan on his breath, she knew she'd won.

"You don't play fair."

She raised onto her toes, bringing her lips near his ear and whispered, "Not when I'm starving. You're about to burn the spaghetti sauce."

SIX

There wasn't enough coffee in all of Monongahela County to clear Pete's mental cobwebs Wednesday morning. He sat at his desk, a cup cradled in one hand, his head in the other.

Zoe had a brother. Half brother. A connection to the father she'd lost when she was a child. Blood kin, but a stranger nonetheless.

Do that thing you do, she'd said. A background check before noon.

Right.

He dug out the note he'd written to himself last night. Jason Cox. Who the hell was this guy and where had he come from? After another sip of coffee, he pulled up his police database and typed in the name. For Zoe's sake, he hoped he drew a blank.

Instead, a list of at least two dozen Jason Coxes greeted him. Great.

He was Zoe's older brother. How much older? Pete typed in a DOB date range, eliminating anyone younger than she was. That narrowed the number of possibilities to seven.

A half hour later, Pete had eliminated three of them. One had died in a car crash. Another had been killed during a robbery down in Orlando, Florida. The third was still incarcerated.

Four names. Of those, two weren't racial matches. One of the final pair was bone-thin and had all the tell-tale features of a hard-core drug user. The other looked like he carried the skinny guy's weight on top of his own plus maybe half another man. Pete noted the last known addresses of both. Just in case.

Changing tactics and databases, Pete tried the social media route and again typed in Cox's name.

A common one there too, as it turned out. Zoe had mentioned he was from Philadelphia. That narrowed down the search, and this time, Pete found a possible match.

He studied the face in the photograph. Wavy blond hair and blue eyes. Just like Zoe's. Except a fair percentage of the world's population boasted the same coloring. He squinted, trying to determine if there were other similarities. Features. Bone structure. The shape of his nose. His chin.

Pete shook his head. He wasn't an anthropologist. Maybe the guy looked like Zoe. Maybe he didn't.

Clicking a few of the links associated with Cox brought up a work history in computers and data communications, storage, retrieval, and other terms Pete didn't understand. What he did understand was the guy's employer was one of the big-name banks based in Philly.

And this Jason Cox was not in his police database.

Odds were good this was the man Zoe was meeting for lunch instead of the other two. But he didn't crumple his note yet.

He closed out both programs on his computer and stared at the township seal on the screensaver. Maybe he'd drop in at Walden's for lunch in spite of Zoe's protests. After all, he had to eat somewhere.

Pleased with his plan to meet this new member of Zoe's family, Pete turned his attention to his own sibling. He still hadn't been able to reach Nadine.

A man in the same building as Harry had been killed. Knocked senseless and then smothered. John Kinney was no easy mark. At one time, it would have taken three men to restrain him and even then they'd have had a fight on their hands. But the old guy Pete had seen on Monday? How much brute force would it take? Still, if the attacker had managed to overpower Kinney, what chance did Harry have against a similar assault?

Who was this killer? Most likely someone who knew Golden Oaks well enough to be aware of the camera locations. Another resident? A staff member? Or a frequent visitor?

The bells on the station's front door jingled followed by a familiar masculine voice exchanging pleasantries with Pete's secretary. A moment later, Baronick appeared in his doorway, a large Starbucks cup in each hand.

"That better be for me," Pete growled.

"My. Aren't we in a cheery mood this morning." Baronick entered, thumped a cup down in front of Pete, and flopped into the visitor's chair. "Don't suppose it has anything to do with me spending all yesterday afternoon with Zoe, does it?" The detective winked.

"You didn't come here just to bring me coffee. What's up?"

"I assume Zoe told you about the man on the security footage."

"You IDed him?"

"Unfortunately, no."

Dammit.

"I emailed you a photo of the guy. The best angle we could get, and it still sucks."

Pete clicked the computer icon for his email and waited for it to load. "Suspects?"

The detective's chuckle held no humor. "John Kinney had more enemies at that place than he had friends." Baronick read from the notes he kept on the phone. "Most of the residents I spoke with referred to him as rude, abrasive, and condescending."

"That was Kinney, all right." Pete opened the email Baronick had sent and pulled up the grainy black-and-white photo. A man in a Pirates ball cap—the same kind of cap owned by more than half of the region's population—wearing a light jacket. A hint of jaw. Clean shaven. The rest of his face was hidden by the hat's bill. "You have to be kidding."

"I told you it sucked." Baronick took a long drag from his coffee. "There was one guy in particular who didn't seem at all upset that Kinney had been killed. Called him 'an old bully' and said—and I quote—'good riddance.'" Baronick scrolled through his notes. "Name's Robert Welsh."

"The man Kinney was arguing with the other day?" Pete mused out loud.

"There was mention of a recent disagreement. Something about Kinney making a lady cry?"

"That's him." Pete pictured the old man comforting the weeping woman and compared the memory to the photo on his computer. He pointed at it. "*That* is *not* him."

"Agreed. Welsh is in great shape for an older guy, but his gait's all wrong. The man in the security footage moved like a younger guy." Baronick set his cup on the desk. "For what it's worth, one of the few residents who liked Kinney is your dad."

Pete chuffed a laugh. "Pop appreciates law enforcement. Good natured or not. So much for residents. What about staff? I witnessed one male employee get hot under the collar during that same incident with the crying woman."

Baronick thumbed his phone's screen. "That would be Daryl Oliverio. His grandmother happens to be Gladys Oliverio—"

"The woman Kinney made cry."

"You guessed it."

"Still, seems like a pretty thin motive for murder."

Baronick angled his phone toward Pete. "Not if you have a history of anger management issues and have been reprimanded for getting confrontational with residents in the past."

Pete took the phone and read. "Daryl Oliverio was charged with simple assault two years ago, but the charges were dropped when he agreed to take anger management classes."

"Which he did and passed with flying colors." Baronick took his phone back. "But word has it he's very close to his grandmother, and, as the Golden Oaks director told us, he's 'extremely protective' of her."

"That's one way of putting it. Could he be the man in your video?"

"Physically, he's a good match in size and build. The problem is he was on duty and had on the standard green polo shirts all the staff wears."

"But he left right after that incident." Pete told Baronick about the aide who broke up the confrontation between Kinney and Oliverio. "The other guy told him to get some air. Oliverio stormed out, and I didn't see him after that."

Baronick mulled over the new information. "Interesting. I'll head over there as soon as I get back to Brunswick and show the photo around. See if anyone, especially Oliverio, reacts."

"Keep me posted."

The detective shifted in his seat. "On a different subject, what's the status of Seth Metzger?"

The change in direction startled Pete. "He's still on a leave of absence."

"Are you planning to hire someone to replace him?"

Pete bristled at the word replace. "You looking for extra work?"

"Me? No. But I have someone in mind. Young. Eager. Good cop. Been working over in Marsdale for a couple of years."

Marsdale was a good twenty-five miles south of Vance Township, on the other side of Brunswick. "He looking to move?"

"She. And for a full-time position, yeah."

"Girlfriend of yours?"

Baronick's expression turned sour. "No." He shifted again. "My sister."

"You have a sister?"

"Yes, I have a sister. And I'd rather she not know we talked."

Pete studied the detective. He'd never seen Baronick quite like this. Uncomfortable. Asking for a favor. "She's part-time now?"

"Yeah. And two male officers with less experience have been bumped ahead of her for the full-time shifts."

Pete drummed his pen on the desk as he thought. Seth was a good officer. Pete wasn't ready to give up on him yet, but he pictured that stack of résumés on the kid's table. "I don't know what Metzger's plans are. If he wants his job back, it'll be waiting for him. However, if your sister is willing to fill in for now, settle for part-time if that's the only thing available, tell her to send me her résumé. Your say-so isn't enough for me to promote her over another one of my part-timers for a permanent full-time position, but if she's the most qualified, she'll get it."

Baronick nodded. "Fair enough."

Pete rocked back in his chair. "Speaking of sisters, Kinney mentioned having one who lived here in Vance Township, but he didn't mention her name."

"I have it here somewhere." The detective thumbed through his phone.

"Good. I'd like to pay a condolence call before the funeral service."

"One of my men already spoke with her. Ah. Here it is." Baronick fiddled with his screen. "Her name's Elaine O'Keefe."

Zoe sat at a table in Walden's, the small family-run café on Phillipsburg's Main Street. The tin ceilings and walls had survived from the building's earlier life as the Phillipsburg Pharmacy. She had vague memories of her father bringing her here when she was small. He'd fill a prescription or buy some aspirin and allow her to pick out a comic book. *Casper the Friendly Ghost.* She smiled. Friendly ghosts, indeed, roamed this place.

She repositioned her chair so she could watch both the front door and the rear, which opened into a potholed public parking lot. Locals used either entrance, although she expected Jason Cox—her brother— would use the one facing Main Street.

Her brother.

She had a brother. Not an easy concept to grasp. She wished she had one of her old faded photographs of her dad. Their dad. But her scrapbook and boxes of old pictures had perished in the house fire that claimed everything she owned except for her horse and her cats. And her memories.

The front door opened, bells on it jingling much like the bells at the police station. She looked up eagerly. But two men in mechanics' uniforms entered and moved to the other side of the dining room, leaving her alone. She checked her watch. Five minutes before noon.

A thump and scrape from the other direction spun her around to find a man in a pale blue button-down shirt and khakis standing inside the rear entrance. His eyes settled on her, and he smiled. "You have to be Zoe."

"And you have to be Jason." She was on her feet without realizing it.

He closed the distance between them in three long strides and threw his arms around her.

Zoe'd had no idea how she would react. Would they feel like awkward strangers? A sibling blind date? Or would they instantly be comfortable together? What she hadn't counted on was the rush of tears, the choking sob, and the sudden sense of being whole for the first time in...forever.

He took her by the shoulders and drew her an arm's distance away from him. "Are you okay?"

She laughed, realizing her face was wet. "I'm fine."

"You look exactly like I pictured you. I searched online but couldn't find you."

Zoe gestured to the table and they sat. "I'm probably the only person left who doesn't do all that social media stuff. I don't have time." She blew out a breath to regroup. Studied the man across from her. Tall. Wavy blond hair. Blue eyes just a shade different than those that looked back at her from her mirror. And a wide smile with teeth as white as Wayne Baronick's.

"I guess you don't. Paramedic and coroner. You're a busy gal."

"Deputy coroner," she corrected. "Plus, I have a horse. And a farm that needs a lot of work."

"I love working with my hands. If I was gonna be in town longer, I'd help you out."

A waitress arrived with flatware wrapped in paper napkins for each of them. "Can I get you something to drink?"

In unison, they said, "Coffee."

Zoe laughed.

The waitress looked at her then at Jason. "You two look alike."

"We should." Zoe's cheeks ached from the strain of smiling. "He's my brother."

* * *

Pete hadn't been able to shake the feeling that he should know Professor O'Keefe's wife in spite of his certainty that they'd never met. Now he knew. She had the same bone structure as John Kinney. Softer, but the family resemblance was there. Her eyes matched her brother's as well, but she'd worn smudged makeup. Pete recalled they'd been red too, no doubt from tears shed in grief.

He pressed the button next to the O'Keefes' front door and listened to the muffled chimes from inside. Braced for another encounter with the professor, Pete was grateful when the wife opened the door.

"Chief Adams." She sounded pleasant—polite, but tired. "Oh dear. What has Kristopher done now?"

Pete removed his VTPD ball cap. "Nothing. I'm here to see you. May I come in?"

Her face registered surprise. "By all means." She stepped aside.

The entryway ceiling soared two-stories high, a brass chandelier lighting it and the staircase. She directed him into a living room to the right boasting spotless white modern furniture on a white carpet. Track lighting illuminated a series of framed photographs of various subjects, including several of the neighbor's horses. "Your home's lovely." Pete didn't mention it wasn't to his taste. He preferred the appearance of history in a house. Other than the photos, this stark showcase for some interior designer sorely lacked personality. He probably had items in the back of his refrigerator that were older than this place.

"Thank you." She curled a leg under her as she claimed one end of a sectional and tipped her head at the pictures. "I see you've noticed my husband's work."

"He took those? They're good."

She shrugged. "He teaches photography."

Pete thought of his earlier exchange with the man. "He's a professor of—"

She rolled her eyes. "He likes the sound of being called 'Professor.' But he's simply an instructor." A weary smile crossed her lips. "Please don't tell him I said that."

"Your secret is safe with me."

"Thank you. Now, what did you want to see me about?"

Pete remained standing, his hat in his hand. "I wanted to express my condolences in the passing of your brother. He was a good man."

The surprised look returned. "You knew...?" Then realization lit her eyes. "Pete Adams. Now I remember where I've seen you. John had an old photo of the two of you in uniform back at his house." She smiled. "You were much younger then."

"I just learned this morning that you were his sister."

"Please sit down. It's hard on my neck looking up like this."

Pete obliged, glad the weather had cleared and both his boots and his uniform trousers were clean and dry. "I understand visitation is tomorrow in Pittsburgh?"

"Yes." She heaved a weary sigh. "All day. And all day on Friday with the service on Saturday. Will you be there?"

"Absolutely." Kinney may have been retired, but Pete felt certain officers from departments all over Pennsylvania and surrounding states would be represented at the funeral.

"Good." She lowered her eyes and nodded. When she again met his gaze, her expression had turned troubled. "John's death wasn't from natural causes. Nor was it accidental." Statement, not question.

"Yes, I know."

"That's why you're really here, isn't it? To ask if I have any idea who might have wanted John dead?"

Pete studied his hat. "I wanted to pay my respects, first and foremost. However, if you have any information that could help the investigation..."

"I spoke with a detective from Monongahela County yesterday. I can only tell you what I told him. John made his fair share of enemies in his life. It comes with the job, don't you think?"

"I suppose so."

"But he never forgot a face." She smiled sheepishly. "Unlike me. Anyhow if there was anyone at Golden Oaks with whom he had a past relationship, good or bad, he'd have known right off, and he'd have told me."

"What about new enemies. I understand he rubbed a few people there the wrong way."

Elaine laughed. "John rarely rubbed people the right way. He was always blunt, even as a child. But with age he became...brutally honest. If you wanted to have your ego stroked, don't look to my brother."

"Did he and your husband get along?"

She gave Pete a wry look. "Speaking of egos, you mean?"

"I guess I'm not very subtle either."

"That's probably why John liked you. Birds of a feather and all that." Her eyes grew thoughtful. "No, John and Kristopher didn't get along. In fact, they haven't spoken in years. I honestly believe one of the reasons Kristopher wanted to move here was because of the distance it placed between us and John."

"Whose idea was it for your brother to move to Golden Oaks?"

"Mine," she said defiantly. "My husband may have liked to keep us separated, but I did not. When John started having more mobility issues, he asked me to help find a place where he could live without worry of falling and not being found for hours or days. When I took him to see Golden Oaks, we agreed it was the perfect solution."

"What was your husband's reaction to the decision?"

Elaine raised a perfectly groomed eyebrow at him. "You've met my husband. What do you think?"

Pete had a pretty good idea. "I'd rather hear it from you."

"Kristopher was livid. He has a very clear picture of how he wants his life to be. When anyone or anything interferes with that vision, he throws a temper tantrum to rival most two-year-olds."

"Does your husband ever get violent?"

The question appeared to startle her. "Violent?" She laughed. "Kristopher? You're asking if I think Kristopher is capable of killing my brother?"

Pete didn't bother to respond.

"No. Kristopher doesn't get violent. Not in the way you mean. He's more into passive aggressive behavior. Always the victim." She shifted her gaze to the large window looking out at the horse pasture. "To be honest, if the situation were reversed, I wouldn't have been at all surprised if John had killed Kristopher. And I think my husband was well aware of that possibility."

SEVEN

By the time their meals arrived, Zoe and Jason had exhausted the small-talk topics. He lived in Abington, north of Philadelphia, and worked in IT for a big banking conglomerate in the city. She told him about her years with Monongahela EMS and her love of farm life and horses.

They fell into a few minutes of silence as they dived into the food. Zoe had selected a BLT with fries but thought her brother's loaded cheeseburger looked pretty good too.

He must have caught her drooling over his choice and held it toward her. "Want a bite?"

"No, I'm good. Thanks." She smiled to herself while she chewed. Lunch with family. More specifically, a pleasant lunch with family. When was the last time that had happened? Other than with Patsy, whom she still thought of as a friend more than a cousin.

Jason studied his burger as if it held the secrets of the universe. "Tell me about our father. What was he like?"

Zoe swallowed, wiped her mouth with the paper napkin, and let a flood of memories wash over her, all viewed through the filter of an eight-year-old. "He was tall, handsome. I can close my eyes and still see his smile. Sometimes I can still hear his laugh."

"But what was he *like*? Did he enjoy sports? Did he fish or hunt? What kind of music did he listen to?"

The questions left her at a loss for a moment. She hadn't thought about her father—really thought about him—in a long time. "He loved horses. I guess that's where I get it from." She remembered seeing him on horseback. Except...no. She remembered a photo of him on horseback. A photo she no longer owned thanks to the fire.

"What else?"

Zoe dug deep, searching for details. "I remember he liked country music." A mental flash of her dad and her mother two-stepping around their kitchen brought a smile. "And he was a good dancer."

Jason chuckled. "I guess I didn't inherit that particular gene. I'm an awful dancer."

Zoe laughed.

"Do you have any pictures I could look at?"

Her laughter faded. "I lost them all when my house burned down."

"Oh. I'm sorry." He chewed a moment. "What about your mother? Certainly she has some she could have copied for you."

Zoe had long wanted to ask Kimberly about that but was afraid her mother would refuse. Or worse, would tell her she'd destroyed all links to her past, including any evidence of her late husband's existence. "My mother and I aren't on the greatest of speaking terms."

Jason added ketchup to his fries. "I thought you said she gave you a farm."

"Yeah, well. It's something of a handyman's special. The house is unlivable right now. I've been spending every penny I make to fix up the barn for the horses."

"So, not much of a gift, huh?"

"Right. But I can't complain too much. I needed to move my horse out of the other place. I don't know where I'd have gone otherwise."

"What other place? What happened?"

"I was managing a boarding operation owned by an older couple. Mr. and Mrs. Kroll. They owned the house that burned too. Anyhow, they decided to sell the property. The new owner wanted all the horses out of there immediately." Zoe snorted. "And, wouldn't you know it, he hasn't done a thing to the place yet. It's sitting empty. Huge barn. Acres and acres of pasture. Indoor arena."

"And you could've still been using it?"

She shrugged. "Maybe." Her phone rang. A glance at the screen showed a number she didn't recognize. She tapped the ignore option, turned down the volume, and seized the momentary interruption to steer the conversation in a different direction. "I want to know about you. Are you married?"

He choked. "No."

"Dating?"

"Well, yeah. I date. But no one in particular at the moment." He grinned. "Do you have a friend you could hook me up with?"

"I could probably arrange something."

He laughed, and Zoe could almost hear her father's laughter echoing through the decades. "I'll keep that in mind," Jason said.

"What about you? Anyone special in your life?"

Thoughts of Pete warmed her cheeks.

"You're blushing. I take that as a yes."

"I'm...yeah."

Jason sipped his coffee. "I want a name. It's a big brother's duty to make sure his baby sister is being treated well."

Baby sister? This was going to take some getting used to. "His name's Pete Adams and he's the chief of police in Vance Township."

"A cop?" Jason whistled. "And you're a coroner. I guess you must work together a lot."

"*Deputy* coroner. I've only officially worked a couple of cases. But yeah, we work together some."

"Is it serious? Between you two, I mean."

Serious? She pondered the word. "Yeah."

Jason finished the last of his burger and wiped his mouth. "You don't sound convinced."

Zoe toyed with her fries. How much of her personal relationship with Pete did she want to divulge to a relative stranger, even if he was her brother?

Jason leaned back, draping an arm over the back of his chair. "If you don't want to tell me, that's okay."

"No, it's not that. It's...complicated."

He studied her. "How complicated can it be? Do you love him?"

"Yeah. I do."

"Does he love you?"

She pictured the way Pete's eyes softened when he looked at her. "Yeah."

"Does he treat you well?"

"Absolutely."

Jason threw up both hands. "There you have it. Not complicated at all."

Zoe laughed. "I suppose you're right." She picked up one of the fries. "We've both screwed up relationships in the past. He's divorced. And I'm..." She didn't want to confess she had the worst taste in men in the history of the world, so she let the sentence die. "He's overly protective. And I'm a little independent."

"Just a little, huh?" A grin played on Jason's lips, but the rest of his face had grown serious. "Let me guess. He has concerns about me."

She opened her mouth to deny it, but the lie wouldn't voice itself. She closed her mouth, dropped the fry, and pushed her plate away.

"I don't blame him."

Her surprise must have registered in her eyes.

"Hey, if I had a girl, and a stranger showed up out of the blue claiming to be a long-lost relative, you bet your sweet ass I'd be concerned. Hell, I'm surprised he isn't sitting right here giving me the third degree."

Zoe covered her mouth, concealing her smile. "If it was up to him, he would've been. I told him I didn't want him to come."

"Why?"

"I was afraid he'd intimidate you."

Jason threw back his head and laughed that familiar laugh again. Then he came forward, resting his arms on the table. "I don't scare that easily. Next time I'm in town, you bring him along."

She stuttered. "Next time?"

Jason lifted a hand to their waitress and mouthed "check" at her. "I have to head home first thing tomorrow."

"Tomorrow? No. I—" What? Wanted to get to know him better? Wanted to hold onto the feeling of having a brother?

Wanted to hold onto the feeling of having a piece of her father back.

Jason dug his wallet from his hip pocket. "I have to get back to my job. But I'll come visit. Maybe in a couple of weeks. That'll give your cop friend time to run a complete background check on me." He grinned. "Just please tell him I will pay those parking tickets. I promise."

She laughed in spite of herself.

The waitress arrived with their check, and Jason handed over a twenty and a five. "Keep the change."

Zoe protested. "No fair. I should pay."

"Uh-uh. I'm the big brother. I get the check."

"So, it's going to be like that, huh? Playing the big brother card every time you want to get your way?"

He flashed a smile that slammed her with an image of her father. "Yep. It's my job to look out for my sister. And I have a lot of catching up to do."

Zoe lowered her face to conceal the dampness in her eyes. "Yeah," she said. "We both do."

Pete left Elaine O'Keefe and responded to a call from a local mom who asked him to have a come-to-Jesus talk with her rebellious teen son. No sooner had Pete left the kid reconsidering his life choices than a report came in about a vandalized vending machine outside a mechanic's garage in Dillard. By the time his radio fell quiet, he realized he'd missed Zoe's lunch date.

Annoyed, he strode into his station to find Nancy on the phone. The look on her face when she glanced up stopped him from continuing down the hallway.

"What's going on?" he asked.

She signaled him to wait with a raised finger. "I understand. I really do," she said into the phone. "Hang on a sec. The chief just walked in. I'm going to let you talk to him."

Pete reached a hand to take the receiver, but she held up the finger again.

"Okay. You're sure?" she said to the caller. After a long pause, she nodded. "All right then. I'll tell him. You take care of yourself."

"What was that about?" Pete asked after she'd set the receiver back in its cradle.

Nancy pivoted her chair to face him. "That was Seth." She picked up a pen from her desk and clicked it. "He said to tell you he's decided to tender his resignation from the force."

Pete swore. "I was afraid this was coming. You should've let me talk to him."

"I tried. He didn't want to."

Because he feared Pete might talk him out of his decision. "I'll go over to his place after I finish my paperwork."

"Good."

He collected his messages—a half dozen slips of pink paper with requests for his attention to a few non-emergency situations around the township—and retreated to his office. For the umpteenth time that day, he checked his phone. Nothing from Nadine. Nothing from Zoe. No missed calls. No text messages. She could have at least let him know how lunch went. If he called her, she'd harangue him for checking up on her.

Dammit, he *was* checking up on her. He hit the little green phone icon next to her name and listened to the ringback tones play for several seconds before directing him to Zoe's voicemail. "Call me," he said and hung up, cursing his lack of eloquence.

Pete jiggled the mouse to wake up his computer. The monitor opened to his email. At the top, a message from Abigail Baronick with the subject line: *Résumé.*

That was fast. He clicked on it and scanned the young woman's law enforcement credentials. Impressive. A degree in Criminal Law from Pitt. Graduated from the Pittsburgh Police Academy near the top of her class. Excellent marksmanship scores. She'd taken a job with Marsdale right after graduation and had accumulated a number of commendations. She also had a number of continuing education credits listed. Baronick's sister was dedicated to her craft. At least on paper.

Pete picked up the phone and punched in the number she had listed. Unlike the other women in his life, this one answered.

"This is Abby Baronick." Her voice sounded strong. Confident.

Pete identified himself. "I received your résumé. When can you come in for an interview?"

A momentary pause. "I'm on second shift right now, so mornings would work."

"How about nine a.m. tomorrow?"

"I'll be there."

After hanging up, Pete scanned the rest of his inbox, deleting most, making a couple of notes on others, but nothing else required his immediate attention.

The bells on the front door alerted him that someone had entered the station. The fast *clip, clip, clip* of footsteps in the hall warned him the newcomer was wearing high heels and was headed his way.

His sister stormed into his office. "What on heaven's green earth is going on?"

"Hey, Nadine."

"Don't 'hey, Nadine' me. I just got home from a peaceful vacation to the news of a murder at Golden Oaks. Why didn't you tell me?"

"I've been trying to reach you."

"'*Call me,*'" she mimicked. "That's not much of message."

"You didn't call me back though, did you?"

"You didn't tell me it was important. My God. A man is murdered just feet from our father and you don't even mention it? Just 'Call me.'"

"You're right." Arguing had never been an effective tool where Nadine was concerned. "So, what are we gonna do about Pop?"

"We? Me. I'm going to have to move him back into my house since you cops can't manage to keep old folks safe around here."

Nadine was being ridiculous now. Not that Pete would say as much. He knew better. Let her rant.

"I don't suppose you have any idea who did it, do you?"

"The homicide is under investigation."

She clenched her fists so hard her arms trembled, and if her face got any redder, steam would start shooting from her ears like one of those cartoon characters they watched when they were kids. "Do not feed me the company line. This is our father we're talking about."

"When you're done venting, we'll do just that. Talk."

Nadine glared at him. For a moment he expected her to punch him. But the crimson in her cheeks faded to pink, and her hands and shoulders relaxed. "All right." She closed her eyes and took a few breaths. "So, you agree we need to move Dad back in with me."

Pete studied his sister with her perfectly colored and styled hair, her crisp jeans, and high-heeled shoes. He remembered the haggard version from last winter when she'd first come to him about placing Harry into assisted living. That Nadine had graying hair and dark circles under her eyes. "No."

Her eyebrows shot up. "No?"

"No." Pete couldn't believe what he was about to say. "We'll move him in with me."

"What will Zoe say about that?"

"She adores Harry. Besides, it'll just be temporary. Look, you were right to move him into Golden Oaks. He may not always know where he is, but he likes it there. He has people his own age to talk to. I don't believe John Kinney's death is an indication of ongoing criminal activity. Once the killer is captured, Pop can go back, and he'll be safe."

"Who's going to take care of him while you're on duty?"

"Zoe doesn't go back to work until Monday. I'm sure she'll be happy to hang out with him."

Nadine caught her lower lip between her teeth, thinking. After a few moments, she lifted her chin. "Okay. When can we pick him up?"

"This evening." He had eight hours off before he had to cover the midnight shift.

She glanced at her watch. "Okay. I'm going to head into Brunswick now to see him. I'll stick around until you get there."

Pete waited until he heard the bells before picking up his phone and trying Zoe's number again. And again, got her voicemail. *Dammit.* "Call me."

EIGHT

As Zoe sat in the parking lot behind Walden's, she remembered she'd silenced her phone. Three missed calls. The first—the one she'd ignored when having lunch with Jason—was from Connie Smith, the director at Golden Oaks. The other two were from Pete.

She listened to Connie's message. After identifying herself, the director said, "I'm returning your call about setting up a meeting. I'll be in my office until five this afternoon. Feel free to call me back or stop in."

Zoe decided she'd prefer to meet Connie face-to-face. She phoned Wayne.

"Thanks," he said after she told him about the message. "I'm heading there now. I'll let you know how it goes."

She bristled. "I want to be there too."

"There's no reason for you to make the trip to town."

Zoe ticked off the list to him, starting with Harry and including the facts that she'd been the one who contacted Connie in the first place, and her position as acting coroner.

"I'm the cop," Wayne said with that placating tone she knew infuriated Pete. "You've done your part. The coroner's duties don't extend to this portion of the investigation."

The hell they didn't. She cranked the ignition and the old pickup roared to life. "I'll be there in twenty minutes." More like thirty or thirty-five, but she didn't think he'd agree to wait that long.

"You don't need to make the trip." He sounded like he was biting off each word. "I've got this."

"I'm on my way. Wait for me." Before he could argue, she jabbed the red button.

She thought of Pete's two call-me messages and imagined the conversation they'd have. That discussion would have to wait until later. She texted him, *Lunch went fine. Talk to you soon,* and shoved the phone in her purse before reversing the big Chevy three-quarter ton out of the parking spot.

Zoe made the trip to Golden Oaks in just over thirty minutes. As she pulled into the facility's driveway, she spotted a grouping of political signs, most of them touting Dr. Charles Davis for County Coroner.

She really needed to start campaigning for Franklin.

She found Wayne inside the atrium, studying the memorial set up for Kinney. A vase of daffodils, a photo of him that appeared to have been taken only days ago, and a framed copy of his obituary from the paper sat on a round table.

Wayne looked anything but pleased to see her. "I told you—"

She cut him off with a wave. "Is there anything new on the case?"

Wayne made an irritated growl deep in his throat. "Not yet. The lab's still working on fibers. The few viable fingerprints the crime scene unit lifted belonged to Kinney and two of the staff. Female. Both have been cleared."

Before Zoe could ask about the security cam footage, a thin, rosy-cheeked woman wearing an ill-fitting business suit and a pair of glasses on a decorative chain around her neck approached. Unlike the other times Zoe had seen Golden Oaks' director, the woman's face bore lines of tension across her forehead and around her eyes. She forced a smile and extended her hand. "Sorry to keep you waiting. I'm Connie Smith. You're Zoe, right?"

"Yes. Thanks for meeting with us." Zoe introduced Wayne.

"Detective?" Connie cast a puzzled look at Zoe. "I thought you wanted to talk to me about touring the facility."

Wayne opened his mouth to reply, but Zoe beat him to it. "We're investigating John Kinney's homicide."

"Oh." The pink drained from Connie's cheeks. She motioned to a door next to the Bistro. "Let's go in here." She ushered them into a bright and cheery conference room and offered water or coffee, which they refused. Once they were seated, Connie looked at Zoe. "I believe I've seen you around here before, haven't I?"

"One of your residents, Harry Adams, is a friend of mine."

"Oh, yes. You were with the family the day I showed them around the first time."

The woman had a good memory for faces. Maybe she'd be able to identify their mystery baseball cap guy.

Wayne thumbed his phone before handing it to Connie. "I have a picture I'd like you to look at. See if he looks familiar."

She put her glasses on and studied the photo. "It's not a very good angle."

"We know. It's the best one we have. The man was aware of your security cameras and intentionally avoided showing his face."

Connie looked up at Wayne, her eyes wide. "You think this is the man who killed Mr. Kinney?"

"Yes, ma'am."

"Oh, dear." She enlarged the photo on the screen. After several long moments, she shook her head. "No. I'm sorry. Like I said, it's not a good picture. That could be my own son and I wouldn't be able to recognize him."

"Can you think of anyone who might have wanted Mr. Kinney dead?" Zoe asked.

Wayne nodded toward his phone. "Especially if they happen to match the build of the man in the photo."

Connie handed the phone back. "I hate to think someone here had anything to do with it."

"I realize that," Wayne said.

"And I'd hate to cast suspicion on an innocent person." She removed a logoed pen from a container on the table and rolled it between her fingers.

"We'll be discreet." He smiled at Connie. That well-practiced comforting smile Zoe had seen him use a number of times. Including on her.

Connie set the pen down. "I truly want to help, but I can't think of anyone here who's capable of such brutality."

Wayne slung one arm over the back of his chair, striking a laid-back pose. "What can you tell me about Robert Welsh?"

Connie appeared startled by the question. "Everyone loves Robert. He's polite to the staff. Helpful to the other residents. He and Gladys Oliverio have a not-so-secret romance going on. It's very sweet."

"You mentioned Gladys Oliverio," Wayne said. "What do you know about her grandson?"

"Daryl? He works here."

"Are you aware of his history of anger management issues?"

"He underwent therapy for it."

"I'm not sure the therapy worked," Zoe said softly.

Connie swung to face her and appeared ready to protest.

"I've seen his temper." Zoe leaned forward, resting her forearms on the table. "As a matter of fact, I saw it directed at Mr. Kinney the morning he was killed."

The director's shoulders sagged. "Oh, dear."

Zoe looked at Wayne. "There was another aide there at the time." She turned to Connie. "Shouldn't he have reported it?"

"Yes. He should have."

"Do you have a name on this other aide?"

"I'll have to check the work schedule." The director's jaw tensed. "I'll speak with him and have him contact you."

"What about Daryl Oliverio?" Wayne asked. "Is he working today?"

"No. He'll be back on duty tomorrow morning."

"Can you think of anyone else who may have had a disagreement with Mr. Kinney? Or anyone he knew from before he moved here?"

"No, I'm sorry. His previous address was in Pittsburgh. Other than his sister who visited regularly, I don't believe he knew anyone else."

"I know you're busy, so we won't keep you any longer." Wayne rose and held out his business card. "Make sure the aide who witnessed Oliverio's disagreement with Kinney contacts me. If you think of anything else..."

Connie stood and accepted the card and a handshake. "Likewise, if you have any other questions, please don't hesitate to call me."

The director bustled out ahead of them. Alone in the conference room, Zoe caught Wayne's arm. "What are you going to do next?"

"I'm going to have another chat with Robert Welsh for starters. And if this other employee doesn't call me, I'm going to track his ass down."

"Do you think Daryl Oliverio is our Baseball Cap Man?"

"Maybe." Wayne shrugged. "I know I want to talk to the man. *And* I want a closer look at those security videos."

Although everything at Golden Oaks appeared to be status quo when Pete walked through the doors, a palpable nervous energy vibrated the air. The residents seemed fine, however the usually friendly staff wore strained smiles on their faces like masks hiding their concern.

He'd texted Nadine from the parking lot, and she'd responded that she was with their father in his room. As Pete headed for the elevator, the door to what he knew was a conference room opened.

Baronick and Zoe stepped out.

She spotted him, and a smile lit her face as she approached. "What are you doing here?" But the smile immediately faded. "Is Harry all right?"

He wanted to tell her she would know had she returned his calls instead of simply texting him back. "Nadine's worried about him. I've decided to move him in with us until the person responsible for Kinney's homicide is arrested."

Zoe's mouth formed a silent "oh."

Pete turned to Baronick. "Any progress?"

"Nothing worth mentioning." He gestured toward Zoe. "She can tell you about the meeting we just had." He turned to her and added, "I'm gonna track down Robert Welsh. I'll let you know if I find out anything."

"Thanks. And thanks for letting me sit in on the meeting."

Baronick grunted. "As if you gave me a choice."

Pete watched the detective go and turned to Zoe. He had enough questions for her to fill a good-sized notebook, but they would have to wait. "I could use your help."

"With Harry? Are you taking him home tonight?"

"That's the plan. Nadine's upstairs with him now."

"Okay. Let's go."

Pete trailed Zoe up the stairs and fell into step beside her at the top. Trying to sound nonchalant, he asked, "How'd your lunch go?"

Her pace slowed, and he caught a glimpse of a smitten grin. "Good. Really good."

"You think he's on the up-and-up?"

She stopped. The look she gave him made him wonder if he'd sprouted a second head. "Yes, he's on the up-and-up."

"How can you be sure?"

"I just am." Her expression softened, and she continued down the hall. "I can't explain it, but it was like we'd known each other all our lives. Like...I dunno...like he's always been a part of me." She glanced at him. "He wants to meet you."

"Good," Pete said. Because he sure as hell wanted to meet Jason Cox too.

NINE

They found Nadine and Harry in his room. One glance at his sister told Pete it was not a pleasant visit.

"Look, Dad," she said, her voice tight. "Pete and Zoe are here."

Harry had been gazing out his window, his back to them. When he turned, his jaw was set. "Their being here doesn't change anything."

Pete made no effort to cover his sarcasm. "Nice to see you too, Pop."

Harry shook his finger at Pete. "I'm not taking any bullshit from you either."

Nadine rose from her chair and looked at Pete. "Can I talk to you for a minute? Please." she whispered.

"Sure."

She looked at Zoe. "Could you keep an eye on Dad?"

"No problem."

Pete watched Zoe round the bed to speak softly to his father. Harry's expression relaxed. The old coot even smiled.

Out in the hall, Nadine pressed both hands to her head as if attempting to keep her brain from exploding. "He's being a stubborn old jackass."

"And this is new?" Pete gave his sister a teasing grin hoping to lighten the tension.

She lowered her hands and glared at him.

"Okay, tell me what I missed."

"I told him he's was going to go to your house to visit for a while. He refuses. Hell, he actually stomped his foot." She shook her head in frustration. "Dealing with him is like dealing with a six-year-old child."

"Did he say why he doesn't want to come to my house?"

"He just kept saying 'no, no, no.' Over and over."

Pete checked his watch. It was after five. "We should have known better than to do this in the evening. He's always more cooperative early in the day."

Her look said *duh*. "I've been telling you that for ages. But you're always too busy to deal with him during the daytime hours."

Reminding her of his work shift would have been redundant. "Let's do the best we can. Maybe Zoe can keep him calm."

Nadine huffed a laugh. "Zoe. The Dad Whisperer."

Back in the room, Zoe and Harry sat on the edge of the bed, hand in hand. True to form, she seemed to have defused his temper. At least until Pete approached. Then the stubborn set returned to Harry's jaw.

"Hey, Pop." Pete offered his father a big grin. Fake. But big. "Zoe and I want you to stay with us for a few days. You know. A vacation."

"Vacation, my ass. You're just trying to get me out of here."

"Well. Yeah. We thought you'd like a change of scenery."

"The scenery here is fine."

Pete crossed his arms, baffled by the reaction. He'd thought Harry would leap at an opportunity to blow this joint.

Harry held Pete's gaze for a moment before turning to Nadine. "Take Zoe here out and get her a milkshake. They're free, you know." His gaze came back to Pete. "I want to talk to your brother. Man to man."

That didn't sound good. Pete responded to his sister's unspoken question with a slight nod.

Once the women had left the room, Pete narrowed his eyes at his father. "Okay, Pop. What's up?"

Harry stood and moved closer. Keeping his voice low, he said, "You and I both know there's weird shit going on around here."

"All the more reason to get out for a few days."

Aggravated, Harry shook his head. "No, no, no. You don't understand. I need to stay here. I can do more good if I *stay here*." His expression and his tone grew more intense. "Barbara has nowhere else to go. I can't protect her if I'm away on vacation."

His father's clarity shocked Pete into silence.

Harry leaned in even closer. "I can help you with the investigation from here too." He tapped one temple. "I see things. Hear things. No one pays any attention to me because they think I've lost my marbles."

"What have you heard?"

The befuddled look returned. "Oh. I don't know. Nothing yet. But if I do, I can tell you about it."

Pete sighed.

Harry looked around the room before his gaze settled again on Pete. The confusion was gone, replaced by stubborn determination.

"Besides, I've done all the moving I intend to do."

The moment they stepped into the hallway, Zoe and Nadine agreed neither wanted a milkshake. Instead, they leaned against the wall outside Harry's room and eavesdropped.

Nadine's eyes glistened. "I really can't stand this." Her voice, low enough that only Zoe could hear it, was as damp as her eyes.

Zoe wondered what her dad would have been like in old age. On one hand, she'd been spared watching time and illness ravage his mind and body. On the other, she'd give just about anything to have him in her life, no matter what shape he'd be in.

Not that she'd say anything to Nadine—or even Pete—about how she envied them.

Pete stepped into the hallway and she could tell from his expression, he wasn't at all surprised to find them listening rather than sharing a shake. "You heard?"

"That Dad still believes he can protect his girlfriend from a killer? Yeah. I heard."

Zoe noticed Pete cringe. He was likely thinking the same thing she was. Harry had saved Zoe from a killer not all that long ago and almost died in the effort.

A chill stirred by the memory made her shiver. She shook it off. "I think it's more than that. He's comfortable here. That's a good thing, right?"

Nadine wrapped her arms around herself. "Not if it gets him killed."

Pete reached out, putting a comforting hand on his sister's shoulder. "Then we'll just have to make sure that doesn't happen."

She looked at Harry's door. "I suppose I could stay here tonight and sleep in one of his chairs."

"Don't be silly, Sis. There's no reason to believe Pop's in any danger."

Zoe caught the glance he shot her way. A silent plea to...what? She wasn't sure.

Pete grasped both of Nadine's shoulders and lowered his face toward her so she couldn't avoid his eyes. "The investigation is focusing on suspects with connections to Kinney. No one else. This wasn't a random murder."

Nadine didn't appear convinced. "Then why were you so gung-ho to pull Dad out of here and take him to your place?"

Pete looked at Zoe, this time a little more insistent. She stuttered. "That's right. We have some new leads in the case. A couple of suspects who have motive to want Kinney dead." Was that what he wanted her to say?

Nadine jutted her jaw. "Who?" she asked Zoe.

Pete jumped in with a response. "We're not at liberty to discuss that right now. Taking Pop home with me would have been a precaution. But he doesn't want to go. Forcing the issue would only upset him more."

Nadine caught her lip between her teeth and scowled. After a moment, she shrugged. "Well, that much is true enough." She stepped out of Pete's grip and aimed a finger at him then at Zoe. Then back at him. "But if anything happens to Dad, I'm holding you both responsible."

Zoe looked to Pete, wishing she could read his mind. Or even his face. But he was in poker mode, and she feared he was running a bluff.

"Nothing's going to happen to Pop," he said to his sister. "You look exhausted. Why don't you go home? Zoe and I will visit with him a while."

Nadine continued to give him a distrustful glare. "All right. But keep me posted. I want to know the minute you make an arrest."

He snapped a half-hearted salute at her.

After Nadine had disappeared into Harry's room to get her purse, Zoe backhanded Pete's arm.

"What was that for?"

"Your sister does not look exhausted," Zoe whispered. "She looks great. And even if she didn't, you never ever say that to a woman."

He snickered. "Point taken."

Zoe eyed a pair of residents chatting in the hall a few doors down. She wanted to ask him what he knew about the case that she didn't, but this was not the place. "We need to talk about suspects."

"Yeah," he said, his voice low. "Later."

Nadine breezed back into the hall, zipping her jacket. "Call me," she said, pointing at Pete, but shooting a look at Zoe. Unlike Pete's incomprehensible attempt at silent communication, Nadine's was clear. *If he doesn't call me, you better.*

They watched her plod down the hall and enter the elevator. Pete waited until the doors closed to turn to Zoe. "I need to ask you a favor. It's about Seth."

Not the topic she'd expected. "What about him?"

"He's resigned from the force."

"What?"

"He hasn't turned in the paperwork yet, and I don't intend to accept it without a battle."

"Good." She knew the young officer would eventually regret his decision. "You want me to talk him into staying."

"If you wouldn't mind."

"I'll head there after we visit with Harry."

Pete stopped her when she turned toward Harry's door. "Why don't you go see Seth now. I'm going to hang around here a while."

This time she understood his meaning. He may have talked Nadine out of spending the night, but he had every intention of standing guard until he had to leave for work.

A half hour later, Zoe stood outside Seth's door. She'd knocked three times with no response. There hadn't been a sound from within, but she could swear she'd noticed a light on when she pulled into the driveway. A light that had quickly been extinguished.

Or maybe she was imagining things.

She was not, however, imagining his car parked in its usual spot.

Zoe retreated to her pickup and pulled up Seth's name from her contact list. Thumbing the keypad, she texted him. *Sorry I missed you.* She wasn't at all sure she had and glanced at the house, expecting to see him peering at her through the closed curtains. *I was hoping to take you out to dinner. Another time. Soon.* She clicked send and started to put the phone down.

Instead, she scrolled back to her contacts, touching the phone icon next to Kimberly Jackson's name. The ringback tone repeated five, six times, and Zoe figured her mother was dodging her too.

But then the call picked up. "Hello." Not a joyful pitch to the voice on the other end.

"Hi, Mom. It's Zoe." She knew full well her mother had caller ID and knew who was on the phone. "How are you?"

"Tom and I are in the middle of dinner. You and I both know you aren't calling to check on my well-being. What is it you want?"

So much for small talk. Or mother-daughter bonding. "You know I lost everything I owned in the fire last summer..."

After a pause, Kimberly said, "Yes."

"I was hoping you might have some old photos of Dad you'd be willing to send me."

Another pause. "Why would you want a bunch of old pictures?"

Zoe closed her eyes. She considered responding with *because some of us are sentimental and still want to remember Gary Chambers,* but she knew Kimberly would poo poo such an idea. Besides, Zoe wanted to know whether her mother was aware of her first husband's indiscretion and suspected Kimberly would never give her a straight answer if she just came out and asked. "Because," Zoe said, "I found out I have a half brother and I want to show him some photos of our father."

Kimberly's sharp intake of breath sucked the air out the phone lines, all the way to Florida. She sputtered and stuttered several false starts. Then, in an angry whisper, she said, "That bitch."

Zoe wasn't sure if her mother was addressing her or Jason's mother.

"I have no idea what you're talking about." Kimberly's voice was a good octave higher than Zoe had ever heard it before. "And there's no way I'm sending you any photos."

The call disconnected, and Zoe had a feeling her mother would have slammed down the receiver had she been using one of those older style phones.

The hang-up didn't matter. Kimberly had provided the answers to both of Zoe's questions. Kimberly did indeed have old pictures of her late husband lying around somewhere.

And Kimberly did indeed know about his affair.

Pete kept watch over Harry until late that night. He alternated between napping in his father's motorized recliner and prowling the hallways, smiling politely at the staff while covertly studying each male he spotted. Could he be a match to the photo caught by the security cam?

The one man he wanted to observe—Daryl Oliverio—wasn't on duty until morning.

At eleven, Pete slipped out of Harry's room and made his way downstairs. While many of the residents had already turned in, a few still had their lights on, watching TV.

He hoped Zoe would be up when he got home, but he found her buried under the covers, only the top of her blonde head visible. Quietly, he retrieved a clean uniform from his closet before changing in the bathroom and heading to the station to relieve Kevin Piacenza by midnight.

The graveyard shift in Vance Township carried a different feel than his usual eight-to-four duties. He hung the "Out-On-Patrol" sign in the front door and spent the night cruising the thirty-five square miles that made up his jurisdiction. In the hours before dawn, he answered a call about a prowler. Searched, but didn't find anything out of the ordinary. He stopped two erratic drivers and wrote them both up for DUI. One had a very sober and very miffed passenger—Pete guessed his wife—who took over the driving. Pete also guessed the woman had wanted to drive all along but Mr. Three-Sheets-To-The-Wind insisted he was fine. The second impaired driver was flying solo, so Pete called in the county police to transport him to a nice cold bed at Monongahela County Jail.

By eight thirty, the sun was up, and he was back at his desk with a fresh cup of coffee and his computer in front of him. Five minutes later, the bells on the front door jingled followed by the buzz of his intercom.

"Officer Abigail Baronick is here to see you," Nancy said.

He double-checked his clock. She was early. "Send her back."

Pete wasn't sure what he expected from Wayne Baronick's little sister—cocky, smart ass, cheesy smile? Instead, the young woman who showed up in his office appeared deadly serious. Attired in her Marsdale uniform, she tucked her hat under one arm and extended the other toward Pete.

"I'm Abigail Baronick. I have a nine o'clock meeting with you. Sorry I'm so early."

Her grip was as firm, if not more so, than many men Pete encountered. "No problem. Have a seat."

She adjusted her duty belt and eased into the chair across from him, her posture ramrod straight. "I pulled midnight shift last night. I was afraid if I ran home to change out of uniform I'd be late, so I came straight here."

Pete chuckled, hoping to put her at ease. "I'm in the middle of a double myself."

"Yes, sir. We do what we must."

Over the next half hour, he asked her about her education and work history even though he already knew what was on her résumé. When he asked why she went into law enforcement, a sparkle lit her eye as she told him about her grandfather and uncle who'd been cops—something Pete somehow didn't know about Wayne Baronick. She did mention her brother, but with less sparkle and more spark. Pete sensed there was more than a little sibling rivalry between the two.

While thinking about the detective, Pete's curiosity prompted him to ask her how she'd heard about the opening. "I haven't advertised that I was looking for a new officer yet."

"My brother told me he'd heard you were shorthanded and planned to hire. He suggested I send in my résumé before word got out."

Her eyes never wavered. She had no idea Baronick had paved the way. Pete leaned forward on the desk, his hands folded. "I want you to be clear on my situation. I have a full-time officer who was in an officer-involved shooting last winter. It was a righteous shoot, but he took a life and has been having problems coming to terms with it."

The young woman listened, her face somber.

"He's a good officer and I hope he comes back. If and when he does, there will be a place for him."

Pete could read the dawning disappointment on her face.

"However, for now, I'm down one full-time officer. For how long? I have no way of knowing. If you want the job, knowing that it may only be temporary, it's yours."

She mulled it over for several long moments. "May I ask a question?"

"Please."

"If your regular officer comes back, would I be completely out of a job?"

"That depends on you. Prove yourself a good cop? I'll make sure you have a spot in my department."

"A part-time spot?"

He answered with a shrug.

For the first time that morning, he spotted a hint of a familiar self-confident smile. "And if I prove myself not only good, but indispensable?"

Finally, the Baronick family resemblance showed through. Pete chuckled. "You never know. Let's take one step at a time. Are you interested in the job?"

She reached across his desk. "Yes, sir, I am."

Their handshake was interrupted by Nancy on the intercom. "Chief, we have a report of an incident out at Professor O'Keefe's."

Pete stifled a growl. He hit the button to reply. "What kind of incident?"

"He didn't specify. He just said he needs the police ASAP and that his life is in danger." Nancy's tone suggested skepticism.

"Got it." Pete climbed to his feet. "Are you available this weekend and for daylight tomorrow?" he asked Officer Baronick.

She popped up out of the chair. "Yes, sir."

"Good. Report here, eight a.m. You'll ride with me day shift tomorrow and afternoon shift this weekend. Then we'll take it from there. Does that work for you, Abigail?"

"Yes, sir." An eager smile lit her face. "But two things. First, I'd like to start today. Right now." She nodded toward the intercom. "This call. If it's all right with you."

Pete hesitated. Meeting O'Keefe might scare the young woman away. On the other hand, he'd like to see how she handled the current resident problem child. "It's all right by me. What's the other thing?"

He finally got a full-blown look at the female version of the Baronick smile. "Call me Abby. Please."

TEN

The clouds overhead showed breaks where the sun might eventually peek through. Zoe stuffed her hands deep in her Carhartt coat's pockets, fingering the apples hidden there, and gazed up at the blue tarp covering a large expanse of her barn roof. According to the weather forecast, the weekend looked rain-free followed by plunging temperatures and the possibility of frozen precipitation on Monday. A brief window of opportunity to get up there and put down the tar paper she had stored inside.

Four horses—her gelding Windstar, Patsy's Arabian mare Jazzel, and her boarders Duchess and Gypsy—stood at the fence behind the barn, nickering impatiently for their breakfast. Duchess, a chunky sorrel and notorious digger, pawed vigorously at the ground as if that might speed up the feeding process.

Zoe waded through the rainy spring slop to the barn door, but as she reached for it, the morning stillness gave way to the hum of an approaching vehicle. With passing traffic a rarity out here, she looked toward the road. The hum grew into a growl. A moment later, a dark sedan rumbled into view. It slowed and turned into her lane. She had a pretty good idea who was behind the wheel, confirmed when the car stopped next to her truck and Wayne stepped out.

"I thought I might find you here."

She crossed her arms. "I'm here every morning and evening to feed the horses. What's up?"

"I'm on my way to Dillard to talk to Pete."

Her pulse kicked up a notch. "Did you learn something?"

Wayne picked his way through the mud toward her. "Not really. I talked to Robert Welsh again. According to him, Daryl Oliverio should be next in line for sainthood and John Kinney was a bastard."

"What about the aide who sent Oliverio out for some air?"

Wayne grunted. "I talked to him too. He said he didn't file a report because Oliverio was a good guy who was just protecting his grandmother. He didn't want to get him in trouble over a one-time incident."

"So, we have nothing?"

"As soon as I get back to Brunswick, I plan to drop by Golden Oaks to have a little chat with Mr. Oliverio. He's supposed to be back on the schedule this morning."

From behind the barn, Duchess the Digger had moved to the door and started pawing at it with a demanding *thud thud thud*. "*Quit!*" Zoe yelled in her deep I-mean-business voice.

Wayne snapped to attention. "Yes, ma'am."

She shot a look at him. "Don't mess with me, Detective. I can kick a thousand-pound horse's ass."

He chuckled. "Believe me. I do not want to be on your bad side. Anyhow, this afternoon, I'm gonna spend some more time viewing the security footage. Wanna join me? I'll bring popcorn."

More mind-numbing hours of watching people walk back and forth through Golden Oaks' hallways? "Uh. Thanks, but no thanks. I have plans."

The detective shook his head in exaggerated disappointment. "Suit yourself." He looked past her at the barn, his gaze lifting toward the roof. "I like what you've done with the place."

Wayne Baronick. Always the smart ass. "Thanks," she said sarcastically. "I thought the tarp added some much-needed color."

"True. Then again, most people would have accomplished the same thing with some paint on the barn itself." He did a slow pivot, taking in the house and the crumbling outbuildings. "Didn't you say your mother gave you this place?"

"Quite the gift, huh?" Especially since deeding the farm to Zoe was Kimberly's idea of making amends. "At least she paid to have the new fence installed." Although Zoe still wasn't sure if the money had been a gift to her or to her cousin Patsy.

"Uh-huh." He sounded unconvinced. "Maybe she should've paid to have a security system installed."

Referring, no doubt, to his previous visits in his professional capacity—a dead body in the barn and, more recently, stolen merchandise stashed in the house. The isolation could be construed as peaceful, but was also unnerving. She had to admit, leaving the horses unattended out here concerned her. "I'll mention it next time I talk to her."

The banging on the far side of the barn started again.

"I should let you feed them before they tear the place down," Wayne said. "The popcorn offer stands if you change your mind."

"Thanks." Although she hoped he didn't plan to wait for her.

He turned toward his car, paused, and turned back. "By the way, how's Franklin Marshall doing?"

"I don't know," she said. But she intended to find out. "Those plans I mentioned? Visiting him at the hospital is one of them."

Pete had seen his share of citizens with their lives in danger. Professor O'Keefe looked nothing like any of them. He'd reclaimed his umbrella from his wife, although it was currently closed, and he gripped it as if afraid Pete might again take it from him. Otherwise, O'Keefe waited in the same spot and wore the same raincoat despite the clearing sky. He also wore the same sour expression.

Pete climbed out of his SUV. "What seems to be the problem, Professor?"

O'Keefe's gaze flitted from Pete to Abby, whom he assessed with a sneer before lifting his chin in Pete's direction. "That homicidal Neanderthal next door has threatened my life."

"How so?" Pete asked.

The professor's gaze was back on Abby. "And who are you?"

"I'm Officer Baronick, Mr. O'Keefe. Pleased to meet you."

He sniffed. "It's *Professor* O'Keefe." His mouth drawn into a smirk, he took in her attire from her boots to her hat. Tipping his head toward Pete, he told her, "You don't match."

Pete wasn't about to explain the departmental differences in uniforms. Or why she wore one from Marsdale. "How did Mr. Anderson threaten your life, Professor?"

He shot a look over his shoulder, as if expecting his machete-wielding neighbor to charge around the corner of the garage. "He's been out in his pasture on his tractor. And he keeps looking over here."

"Has he approached you?"

"Well. No."

"Has he called you? Spoken to you?"

"No, but I can tell he wants to kill me."

Pete glanced at his new officer, glad to see she wasn't laughing. Hell, she hadn't so much as cracked a smile. "Professor, you need to give me more to go on," he said. "If I arrest everyone who looks at you—"

O'Keefe waved the umbrella as if it was a magic wand and could make the situation disappear. "All right, all right. I do believe he'd kill me given his druthers, but he hasn't done anything improper recently."

"Then why did you call us?"

"Because you need to investigate the man. There's most definitely something..." O'Keefe searched for the proper word. "...*criminal* about him."

Pete removed his ball cap and ran a hand through his hair. "I realize he frightens you—"

The professor's chest puffed. "He most certainly does not."

"Let me rephrase. He gives you cause for concern."

O'Keefe apparently didn't recognize the sarcasm in Pete's voice. He gave a satisfied nod. "Yes. He does. *Great* concern."

"But I can't lock him up for running his tractor on his property. I can't even lock him up for giving you dirty looks."

The professor took a step toward Pete, lifting both hands. The one without the umbrella opened, palm up, beseeching. "Please. If you can't arrest him, I implore you to look into his past. He's a dangerous man. I have a sixth sense about this." He looked at Abby and then back to Pete. "And there's something else. The man is besotted with my wife."

"Besotted?"

"Yes. He finds her...alluring. She's totally unaware and doesn't reciprocate the feelings of course."

"Of course," Abby said, her tone serious. Too serious.

Pete looked at her. She glanced back at him and shrugged. For the first time, he spotted a chink in her uber-professional armor. He rubbed his upper lip to hide a grin. Yep. Abby Baronick was going to work out just fine. "You want me to arrest your neighbor because he's attracted to your wife?"

O'Keefe's face darkened. "You find me amusing." His voice lowered to a growl. "I want you to do your job and investigate a dangerous man with an unhealthy interest in my wife. Is that asking too much?"

Pete tugged his hat back on. "No, sir. I don't suppose it is."

Zoe found Franklin shuffling down the hospital corridor toward her, wheeling an IV pole at his side. She stopped and waited. "It's good to see you up and around."

He grunted. "They darned well better let me out of here tomorrow or I'm going to tie bed sheets together and climb out the window."

"Is that what they're telling you? Tomorrow?"

His color was still off, and he definitely wasn't his usual energetic self. "They've been telling me 'tomorrow' for two days now." He stood a little taller, stretching his back. "Tomorrow, and tomorrow, and tomorrow," he said in a Shakespearian stage voice.

"Don't rush it, Macbeth. You don't want to have to come right back here if you leave too soon."

"Bah. I just need a good night's sleep. Which, by the way, is something you cannot get in a hospital." He maneuvered an awkward turn with his IV pole and motioned for Zoe to follow. "Walk with me."

She sneaked a glance at the bag of fluids as she strolled beside him. Half normal saline. Not what she'd expected. "Have they given you any kind of explanation for what's wrong?"

"I don't want to talk about my problems. I want to know about my office. What's going on?"

As they continued toward Franklin's room, Zoe told him about Baseball Cap Man on the security camera and the employee with anger management issues. Franklin stopped at his door. "Good. But this isn't the only case you have to deal with."

She blinked. "What do you mean?"

Gripping the IV pole he faced her. "I put you in charge of my office, not just this one case. Paulette informs me you haven't stopped by to fill out any of the reports. There's paperwork waiting for you, Young Lady."

Reports? Paperwork? She'd been so focused on Kinney's death— and on her brother—she hadn't even thought of the boring stuff.

"Paulette can answer any questions. She's in the office right now. Once you've filled everything out, bring the reports back here, and I'll sign them." Franklin teetered into his room and took a seat on the edge of the bed, struggling to keep from getting tangled in the IV tubing. Once settled, he looked at Zoe. "Well? Get moving."

She studied him for a moment, wondering how long before he could reclaim his duties. "I'll be back in a little while."

As she walked away, his voice trailed after her. "Don't rush. I want the paperwork done *right*."

Paperwork. Terrific.

Suddenly, the stench of autopsy didn't seem so bad.

* * *

A familiar dark sedan sat in front of the Vance Township Police Department when Pete and Abby returned from speaking with Professor O'Keefe. Pete glanced at his new officer's profile. From the set of her jaw, he surmised she recognized her brother's unmarked car.

This should be interesting.

Baronick leaned on the front counter chatting with Nancy and looked up when they entered. "Hey, Chief." He nodded to his sister. "Officer."

Pete removed his hat. "I don't suppose introductions are necessary."

Abby glared at her brother. "What are you doing here?"

Baronick ignored her. "I wanted to update you on the Kinney investigation," he said to Pete.

He noticed Nancy eyeing the three of them, her fingers touching her lips barely covering an amused grin. "Go on back to my office, Detective. I'll be there in a minute."

"Yes, sir."

Sir?

Baronick nodded politely to his sister. For a moment, Pete thought Abby might stick her tongue out at her brother, but she settled on a look Pete had seen on Nadine's face more than a few times.

Once the detective had disappeared down the hall, Pete turned to Nancy. "Get our new officer set up with a badge, uniform, and gear. And don't forget the W-4s and whatever forms need to be filled out."

Nancy stood and winked at Abby. "Glad to have you aboard. We're way past due for some female energy on this force."

Alone in the station's entry vestibule, Pete faced his new officer. "Once Nancy takes care of you, go home."

"But I thought I'd finish the shift here."

"You just came off one shift at Marsdale. I want you rested for tomorrow and the weekend."

"Yes, sir." She gazed down the hallway where her brother had gone, and Pete expected her to ask about him. Instead she said, "That professor. Is he...?"

"An asshole?"

She snickered. "I was going to ask if he's for real, but okay. We'll go with asshole."

"The jury's still out. I'll look into the neighbor's background and then let you know."

"You're really going to do that? Just because the professor thinks the man is attracted to his wife?"

"No. I'm going to do a little digging because the neighbor did attack him with a machete a few days ago."

Abby appeared thoughtful. "I guess it would be irresponsible not to. I mean, if we ignore the professor's complaint and then something did happen..."

"That's right," Pete said. He held out a hand to her. "Eight o'clock tomorrow. Don't be late."

She clasped it, her grip firm. "I won't. Thank you, Chief."

Leaving Abby with Nancy, Pete found Baronick, his feet propped on Pete's desk, his typical grin on his face. Pete shut the door, swiped the detective's size twelves to the floor, and slid into his chair. "Checking up on your sister?"

"No. Actually, I was surprised to see her car parked out front. You didn't waste any time hiring her." He winked. "My recommendation must carry a lot of weight."

"Her résumé was impressive. I hired her in *spite* of her pedigree."

Baronick chuckled then grew serious. "She's a good cop." He shook a finger at Pete. "Don't ever tell her I told you that."

Pete shuffled through a stack of reports in front of him. "What's the update on Kinney's homicide? Have you IDed the guy in the ball cap?"

"Not yet."

"You drove out here to tell me you have nothing."

"I drove out here to tell our acting coroner *and* you that I have nothing."

"Zoe?"

"I stopped out at her farm on my way here. She hasn't gotten much done out there, has she?"

"I replaced some boards on the porch so she wouldn't fall through. Dug up the water pipes to the barn and put in two frost-free hydrants so the horses can get a drink. And we had an electrician run power to the barn so she has lights. But the whole house needs to be rewired." And that was just for starters.

"I hate to say this, but the place is a dump."

Pete couldn't argue. But Zoe insisted she needed a place for her horse. Good ol' Kimberly to the rescue. Some day he and Zoe's mother were going to have a long talk.

ELEVEN

Zoe'd had no idea how much paperwork was involved in the coroner's job. Sure, she'd filled out her own reports and handed them in to Franklin. But the stack of death certificates, coroner's reports, cremation authorizations, and State Police reports left her dumbfounded. Thankfully, Franklin's secretary handled most of the details and helped her with the rest. By the time Zoe completed as much as she could, lugged the pile back to Franklin's hospital room for his signatures, and returned it to Paulette, she'd missed lunch.

She escaped the office before more unfinished forms surfaced and headed to Golden Oaks with one of Harry's much-loved milkshakes on her mind.

Many of the residents at the assisted living home were still gathered in the dining room when Zoe arrived, although a slow-moving exodus of wheelchairs indicated mealtime was over. Going against traffic, she crossed the Bistro and peered into the dining room, searching for Pete's dad. Neither Harry nor Barbara were anywhere to be seen. Zoe skirted the residents filing out and jogged up the stairs to the second floor. At the far end of the hallway, she spotted them. Barbara on her walker, Harry at her side, and a third person, one of the staff members, strolling with them.

Zoe caught up to the trio before they reached Harry's and Barbara's rooms. "Hey there," Zoe said, coming up behind them.

All three turned, which was when she realized the man walking with the old couple was Daryl Oliverio. She stuttered, battling to cover her unease. Could he be the mysterious Baseball Cap Man? Had Wayne been there to question him yet? Did he know he was under suspicion?

"Hello," he said, not sounding like a murderer.

Not that she'd ever been able to detect a killer from his voice. "Hi." She smiled—maybe too big of a smile—at Harry and at Barbara. "Looks like I missed lunch."

Barbara laid a gentle hand on Harry's arm. "Oh, look. It's Pete's friend. Zoe."

"Yes, of course." Harry stepped past Oliverio to give Zoe a hug. "How are you, Sunshine?"

Oliverio backed away. "I'll let you guys visit."

Zoe called "thank you" after his retreating back and tried to picture a ball cap on his head.

"Is Pete with you?"

She turned back to Harry. "Not this time. Sorry."

He waved a hand as if shooing a fly. "No need to apologize. It's good to see you."

Zoe smiled. He recognized her. "I know you've already had lunch, but I wondered if I could interest you both in milkshakes down at the Bistro."

Harry's eyes widened in childlike glee. "I'm always interested in milkshakes. And you know, they're free here."

"Yeah, I know. Cool, huh?"

"Cold, actually."

She pursed her lips against laughing.

He turned to Barbara. "You'll join us, won't you, Sweetheart?"

"I'm sorry." She looked at Zoe. "Would you mind terribly if I take a rain check? I'm tired and really need to lie down."

"I don't mind a bit."

Harry shuffled over to his lady friend and gave her a peck on the cheek. "Have a nice nap."

Zoe's cheeks warmed. Young love wasn't always limited to the young.

After Barbara closed the door to her room, Harry offered an arm to Zoe. "I hope you know where we're going. I don't."

"I do. Just stick with me."

"Like glue."

Pete had run Boyd Anderson through the National Crime Information Center when he'd arrested him for the machete incident. He'd found a couple of traffic violations and a decades-old misdemeanor charge of simple assault that had been dismissed without even a fine. Considering Anderson would have been nothing more than a kid and had been clean ever since, Pete hadn't paid much attention.

Now, though, he pulled up Anderson's name on the NCIC database again for a closer look.

The simple assault arrest had occurred in Pittsburgh. Pete did some math and determined Anderson had been all of nineteen at the time. Details were sketchy and took some digging. Whoever had entered the information into the database hadn't been thorough. Pete imagined some harried officer just trying to get through the task so he could go spend time with his wife and kids. Or meet his buddies at the neighborhood bar. Since the arrest had taken place in Pittsburgh, Pete switched to a different site to search Allegheny County's records for the date in question.

There it was.

Pete scanned the report. The original arrest hadn't been for simple assault. Instead, Boyd Anderson had been arrested for aggravated assault. According to the arresting officer, Anderson and another teen had gotten into an altercation over a girl. Anderson pulled a knife and slashed the other kid. Later records showed the victim gave conflicting versions of the story and the only witness, the girl, claimed Anderson had been defending her honor. Hence the case was pled down. Anderson was sentenced to time served and released.

Pete might have dismissed the incident as nothing more than what it appeared to be. Except for the name of the arresting officer.

John Kinney.

Pete leaned back in his chair. Kinney and Anderson, both in Monongahela County. As a coincidence, Pete could buy it. A great many former Pittsburgh residents now lived in Monongahela County, including himself. But Anderson living next door to Kinney's sister followed by Kinney turning up dead? That was a bit higher on the coincidence scale than Pete was willing to accept without a closer look.

The dining room had emptied out except for a couple of stragglers by the time Zoe and Harry made it downstairs. A quartet of residents claimed one of the tables in the Bistro. Zoe pointed Harry toward one of the others. A young woman in a staff polo stood behind the counter. "Can I get you guys anything?" she asked.

Harry held up two fingers. "Chocolate milkshakes, please."

The woman grinned. "I should've guessed. Two chocolate shakes, coming up."

"What brings you here today?" Harry reached over and squeezed Zoe's hand.

"Can't I just stop in to see my favorite guy?"

He chortled. "Better not call me that in front of Pete."

From the corner of her eye, she spotted someone breeze through the front doors and head for the currently unoccupied receptionist desk. She took a second look. "Wayne," she called to the detective.

He wheeled midstride and headed toward them.

"Harry, have you met Detective Wayne Baronick?" Zoe knew he had but didn't expect him to remember.

"Don't believe I've had the pleasure." Harry struggled to rise.

Wayne grabbed a chair. "Don't get up." He extended a hand, playing along. "You're Pete Adams' father, right?"

"Yes, sir, I am. And proud of it."

"As you should be." Wayne turned to Zoe. "Have you checked on whether Oliverio's here today?"

"Didn't have to. I saw him." She explained how their suspect had been walking Harry and Barbara to their rooms after lunch.

Wayne scowled. "Did you question him?"

"No. I thought you might've been here already and spoken to him."

"What's going on?" Harry asked.

Zoe exchanged a look with the detective. How much should she share with Harry? Wayne didn't offer a response. And Harry would likely forget by the time they finished their milkshakes if not sooner. "Do you remember John Kinney being killed a few days ago?"

"Sure I do." The quick shift of his eyes told her otherwise.

"Detective Baronick and I are investigating his death."

"Oh?" Harry's face lit. "You know I've been saying for years that people have been getting murdered around here."

He'd only lived at Golden Oaks for a few months, but Zoe didn't argue. "I know. And I've looked into every potential homicide and they've all been determined to be death by natural causes."

Harry grunted. "Not this time."

"It doesn't appear so," Wayne said. He looked around. "I don't suppose you know where Oliverio is right now, do you?"

"Not at the moment," Zoe replied.

"Who?" Harry demanded.

"The tall man who was with you and Barbara upstairs. Daryl Oliverio."

Harry's brows dipped in what Zoe had come to recognize as confusion. He wanted so badly to remember.

"It's okay. There are too many people here to expect you to

remember one of them."

"Don't soft pedal it. I know my memory sucks. The number of people around here has nothing to do with it."

The woman from the counter arrived at the table with two tall milkshakes and set them in front of Zoe and Harry. She looked at Wayne. "Can I get your anything?"

"Yeah." He drew his long raincoat aside to reveal the gold shield clipped to his belt. "How can I locate Daryl Oliverio?"

Her eyes widened for a moment at the sight of the badge. "He's working on Two East today." She turned to Zoe. "That's Harry's wing." The woman swallowed. "Is there a problem?"

Zoe wasn't sure it had been necessary for Wayne to flash his badge. Or wise. "We just need to talk to him and make sure he didn't see anything on Monday." She shot a look at Wayne daring him to contradict her.

"Monday? You mean the day John Kinney died?" The woman stuttered over the word "died" clearly unable or unwilling to say he'd been killed.

"That's right," Wayne said.

The woman caught her lip between her teeth and retreated behind the Bistro's counter.

Harry sipped on his straw. "You should've had her make you a milkshake, Sonny. They're really good. And they're free."

"Maybe later." Wayne stood and looked at Zoe. "I'm going to track this guy down and talk to him. You wait here."

"Like hell, we will," Harry said before Zoe had a chance to protest. "I'm not going to sit back like a useless old fool. I can help."

Wayne's patience with Pete's dad appeared to be dwindling. "You can help by staying here and finishing your milkshake. You said it was good."

"It is. And I'm going to help you by telling you to sit the hell down."

"What?" Wayne snapped.

Harry took a slurp, smacked his lips, and aimed a finger toward the receptionist desk. "Your Daryl Oliverio guy is right over there."

Wayne spun, and Zoe followed Harry's gaze. He wasn't kidding. Oliverio, wearing a light jacket zipped over his polo shirt, said something they couldn't hear to the receptionist and then strolled toward the front door.

"Daryl," Harry called, waving at him. "Come on over here. There's someone I want you to meet."

With a relaxed smile, the man ambled toward them. Zoe tried to compare his gait to that of the man in the ball cap. Did Oliverio's jaw match what little could be seen on the security tape? She wished she could hand him a hat and tell him to put it on and lower his head.

"Hey, Harry," Oliverio said. "You guys havin' a nice visit?"

Harry put a hand on Zoe's shoulder. "This here's my future daughter-in-law. Provided my son ever gets off his backside and proposes."

Heat crept into her cheeks. Now wasn't the time to mention Pete already had. "I'm Zoe." She shook Oliverio's hand.

He turned to Wayne. "So, that makes you Harry's son?"

The detective choked. "No, I'm Detective Wayne Baronick, Monongahela County Police."

Oliverio flinched. "Police?"

A moment of uncomfortable silence was punctuated by the gurgle of Harry draining the last of his shake. He gave Oliverio a Cheshire Cat grin. "Pull up a chair, Sonny. Let's chat."

TWELVE

Pete had driven past and admired the Anderson farm for as long as he'd lived in Vance Township. Unlike the newer homes popping up that tried to copy the farmhouse style, Boyd's residence was the real deal. Probably built in the late 1800s, the house was pristine with fresh white paint on wooden clapboard siding. None of that aluminum stuff. More upkeep but the love and effort showed.

As Pete climbed out of his SUV and approached the wrap-around porch, he thought of Zoe's ramshackle handyman special. She had big dreams of creating a cozy and inviting home out of the wreck, probably imagining a place just like this.

Wasn't going to happen on a paramedic's budget. Not even with a police chief's budget thrown in.

The white wooden screen door swung open with a whisper instead of a squeak, and a tall slender woman with short-cropped blond hair stepped onto the porch.

"Mrs. Anderson?" Pete said from the base of the steps.

Worried creases lined her forehead. "Yes. Is everything all right?" She looked toward the field, probably searching for Boyd.

"I'm sorry. I didn't mean to frighten you." Pete introduced himself. "Is your husband around?"

"He's out riding his horse. I expect him back…" She glanced at her wristwatch. "…in about fifteen minutes or so. He's been gone for a couple hours already."

"Do you mind if I wait?"

"Not at all. Would you like to come in? I just made a fresh pot of coffee."

Pete smiled to help put her at ease. "I would love to."

A few minutes later, he sat at an oblong table, which was covered with a blue checked cloth, and took in the quintessential country kitchen. Vintage plates, teapots, and a cow creamer with a sugar-bowl bucket occupied a Hoosier cabinet on one wall. Zoe'd had one like it in her kitchen when she lived in half of Mr. and Mrs. Kroll's farmhouse.

Boyd's wife set a stoneware mug in front of Pete. "Sugar? Cream?"

"Black. Thank you." He made a point of looking around the room. "You have a lovely home, Mrs. Anderson."

She blushed and slid into the chair across from him. "Thank you. And please call me Linda. Mrs. Anderson is my mother-in-law."

Pete sipped the steaming brew. "Have you and your husband lived here long?"

"It'll be twenty years this June. I grew up on a farm near Lancaster. I moved to Pittsburgh to go to Duquesne. That's when I met Boyd."

"At the university?" Pete thought of the assault charge.

"That's right. We were college sweethearts. Boyd was a city boy with a country heart." She smiled at the memory. "That's what I always told him anyway. After we got married, we found this property for sale. It was run down. Neglected. But affordable."

"You mean you and Boyd did all this?"

"Uh-huh. Boyd mostly. Says it keeps him out of trouble." As soon as she said the words, she winced.

"He does good work." Pete wondered if he'd want to help fix up Zoe's place. Provided he had nothing to do with Kinney's death.

"Yes, he does." Linda looked down at her own mug of coffee. "And he loves it here. Loves the horses. I think he was a cowboy in the Wild West in a previous life." Her smile faded, and she met Pete's gaze. "You're here about Professor O'Keefe, aren't you?"

Pete shrugged sympathetically. "The professor is concerned for his own safety."

Linda huffed. "That old bag of wind. Tell me, Chief, why do city people move to the country if they have no interest in learning country ways?"

It wasn't the first time the question had been posed to him, yet he still had no good answer.

Linda didn't wait for one anyhow. "Both Boyd and I have spoken with the O'Keefes about grass clippings. Last summer, we spent over a thousand dollars in vet bills because one of our horses colicked. I'm pretty darned sure it was due to those clippings. And yet he still insists on throwing them over his fence."

Pete fingered the rim of his mug. "Are you well acquainted with Mrs. O'Keefe?"

"Elaine? Oh heavens, yes. We've become good friends. Her husband may be an obnoxious ass, but she's lovely."

Footsteps on the wooden porch interrupted the conversation. The door slammed shut and the footsteps moved down the center hallway.

"We're back here, Boyd," Linda called.

The man appeared in the kitchen doorway. Attired in a denim jacket, dirty jeans, boots, and a western hat, Boyd Anderson did indeed look like he'd walked out of an old western. "Chief? Is there something wrong?"

Pete stood to shake his hand. With a conciliatory grin, he said, "Your neighbor doesn't like the way you look at him from across the field."

"Oh, for cryin' out loud." Boyd removed his hat and hooked it on the back of the chair. "I haven't gone near his fence line." He gestured at his wife. "Linda's going over to visit Elaine next time we hear his lawn mower. Maybe the two women can convince him to mulch his clippings somewhere away from my pasture."

"Sounds like a good idea."

Linda set a cup at the head of the table, and Boyd claimed the chair, thanking her. "Plus," she added, "I'm going to lock the horses in their stalls the moment O'Keefe fires up that mower. We won't let them out until we know it's safe."

"Also a good idea." Pete took a sip and pretended to gaze into the mug, but kept a covert eye on Boyd. "Speaking of Elaine O'Keefe, I suppose you heard about her brother."

"Yes," Linda said. "Tragic."

Boyd's face clouded. Pete noticed the man's grip tighten on his cup.

Dropping the pretense of a casual visit, Pete shifted to face the man. "You knew who her brother was, didn't you?"

From the look on Linda's face, she had no clue what Pete was talking about. But Boyd nodded. "Yeah."

"When did you find out?"

He glanced at his wife. "Linda mentioned it a couple weeks ago."

She looked from Boyd to Pete and back. "What are you talking about?"

"You told me Elaine's maiden name was Kinney," Boyd said. "And you mentioned her brother John."

"So?" Linda scowled at her husband, but her mind must have been processing the name. Her eyes widened in recognition with a touch of fear. "Oh. My God. *That* John Kinney?"

Boyd continued to contemplate his coffee. Pete kept still, watching their reactions.

The woman's eyes shifted. After several long moments, she turned her laser focus on Pete as realization struck. "I read he died under mysterious circumstances and that the police were investigating. You certainly don't think Boyd had anything to do with it."

Pete pushed the coffee away and looked squarely at him. "Did you?"

Boyd appeared startled by the question. "No."

Linda jumped to her feet, bumping the table and tipping her cup. Spilled coffee soaked into the blue checked tablecloth, but she made no move to mop it up. "Don't say another word," she told her husband. To Pete, she said. "I have to ask you to leave, Chief."

He sighed. Stood. "Thank you for the coffee."

She trailed him down the hallway, as if making sure he didn't veer off into any other rooms or stop to snoop through a closet. At the front door, she crossed her arms. "If you wish to talk to my husband again, I'd appreciate a phone call first, so I can make sure our attorney is here."

Pete tugged his ball cap onto his head and wondered what Boyd would look like with one. "Yes, ma'am. I'll do that."

"I already answered the cops' questions the morning John died." Oliverio had refused the offer of a milkshake or a cup of coffee, explaining that he was on his way out for a smoke break, but he agreed to sit with them for a few minutes.

"We know you did," Zoe said. "But—"

Wayne interrupted. "But we thought there might be something else you'd remembered. It's easy to miss details under all that stress."

Zoe eyed the detective. Did he think she was gonna mess up this interview?

As if reading her mind, he winked at her.

No wonder Pete wanted to choke the guy more often than not.

Oliverio looked from Wayne to Zoe to Harry and then back to Zoe. "You're a cop?"

"Acting coroner."

"Oh." Her answer either surprised or impressed him. "And you were here that morning too. I saw you."

"I was visiting Harry." She patted Pete's dad's arm.

"When I saw you, you were with Miss Barbara."

Zoe felt Wayne's gaze on her. "And you were with your grandmother."

"Yeah. It's the best part of working here. Spending time with her."

"You and your grandmother are close?" Wayne asked.

"Very." Nothing defensive in Oliverio's voice. Simply stating a fact.

"I could tell," Zoe said. "John was being..."

Oliverio filled in the blank. "Insensitive. Grandma doesn't like the loud pushy types."

Zoe shot a look at Harry, hoping he didn't pop up with his comment about Gladys crying at the drop of a hat. But he was too busy sucking on the straw of an already empty glass. "I could tell," Zoe said. "It was sweet, how you jumped in to comfort her when she started crying."

Oliverio shrugged. "I'd comfort any of my people who were upset, but Grandma responds better to me than to the others."

Wayne cleared his throat. "How about Robert Welsh?"

Oliverio gazed at the detective, a blank look on his face. "Huh?"

"I heard Robert's quite fond of your grandma."

"Yeah." The grandson still appeared clueless.

"Are they an item? Does your grandmother 'respond' to him too?"

Zoe contemplated kicking Wayne under the table.

"Look, I don't know what you're insinuating, but Grandma and Robert are good friends. Yeah, she likes him, and he helps me make sure she's okay. But you're making their friendship sound dirty. For cryin' out loud...They're *old*."

Harry suddenly came up for air and shook a finger at Oliverio. "Hey. Don't go thinking that just because we're old, we don't have feelings for each other."

Wayne and Oliverio appeared equally stunned by the outburst. Zoe bit her lip to conceal a smile.

Harry sat a little taller and touched his hair. "Just because there's snow on the roof doesn't mean there isn't fire in the furnace."

Zoe choked. Good thing Pete wasn't there.

Wayne squirmed in an effort to regain his composure.

Zoe jumped in to keep this interview on track. "I think the point Detective Baronick is trying to make is that your grandmother is very lucky to have you and Robert watching out for her. You must be grateful for his help too."

Oliverio forced his appalled gaze from Harry to Zoe. "Yeah. Robert's a good guy."

"He probably didn't like John either."

"Huh? What?"

Wayne had recovered and slid his phone across the table to Oliverio. Zoe spotted the still photo of Baseball Cap Man. "Do you recognize this guy?" Wayne asked.

Zoe watched for a reaction.

Oliverio squinted at the photo without touching the phone. "Who is that?"

Wayne rested his forearms on the table. "We don't know. That's why I'm asking. You were here that day. I thought you might have seen him."

Oliverio still didn't pick up the phone but leaned in for a closer look. "It's hard to tell. You can't see his face."

"No, you can't." Wayne leaned back in the chair and crossed his arms. "Tell me, Daryl. Did you know John Kinney was a cop?"

Oliverio shrugged. "Yeah."

"Did that bother you?"

"That he was a cop? No."

"What does bother you? Besides people making your grandma cry, that is."

The clueless look was back. "Huh?"

"Although, I suppose people upsetting your grandmother is enough of a reason to get pissed off."

Harry pushed his empty glass aside. "Cries at the drop of a hat," he said softly.

Oliverio either didn't hear Harry or ignored him. Instead he eyed Wayne, who kept his expression relaxed.

Sounding curious rather than accusatory, the detective asked, "Do you ever get angry at the residents? You know. The ones who upset your grandmother for example."

Oliverio shifted in his chair and shot a glance at the front doors. Planning an escape? Or jonesing for his cigarette? "I might get a little riled."

The detective came forward again. "Riled enough that you wanna shut them up?" He sounded sympathetic. "I couldn't blame you." He made a fist. "Sometimes you just wanna pop some people in the mouth."

As Wayne spoke, Oliverio was nodding, but he said, "No. I mean yeah. I'd like to..." He made a fist too. "But I would never."

"Tell me something, Daryl. Do you own a Pirates baseball cap?"

The change in direction kept him off kilter. "Well, yeah. Everyone does."

Wayne fell silent, but Zoe noticed a hint of a victorious gleam in his eye.

Oliverio scowled at the detective. He shot a questioning look at Zoe. Then his gaze fell to the phone, its screen now dark, still sitting on the table in front of him. "Wait a minute." He touched the phone and the screen woke up to the photo. "You guys think that's me?"

Wayne didn't reply.

"Is it?" Zoe asked.

"No. Oh, hell, no." Oliverio leapt to his feet, his chair scraping and crashing to the floor. The few stragglers in the dining room and the half dozen or so residents in the atrium turned to look.

Oliverio sputtered. "Uh-uh. You guys ain't pinning this on me. No friggin' way." He stumbled over the tipped chair, spun, and bolted out the door.

Wayne sighed dramatically and grinned. "I guess he really needs a smoke."

"You think he's our guy?" Zoe asked.

"Obviously, he is," Harry replied before Wayne had a chance. "That boy's guilty as sin."

THIRTEEN

Tired of seeing all the campaign placards for Dr. Charles Davis and none for Franklin, Zoe swung by the party headquarters after leaving Golden Oaks. By the time she made it back to Dillard, she had a stack of *Re-elect Franklin Marshall for Coroner* signs in the bed of her pickup and a load of groceries on the seat next to her. She had no idea what to do with the signs. The groceries, though, had a purpose.

She pulled into Seth's driveway and parked behind his car, which showed no indication of having budged since yesterday. The curtains in the front window swayed. He was home.

Zoe slid down from the pickup's cab and circled to the passenger side where she dragged the plastic bags out, a bundle of three in each hand. She lugged her load to Seth's door, hoping he'd see her coming and open it.

No such luck.

Setting the bags at her feet, she knocked. Waited. Knocked again.

Still nothing.

The third time, she switched from knuckles to fist and pounded. His upstairs neighbors should have heard her. Hell, the neighbors in the next house should have been aware of her presence.

Still no response. "Seth Metzger, I know you're in there," she shouted. "I've brought you groceries and I'm not leaving. I'll camp here all night if that's what it takes."

Sure enough, the curtains on the next house drew aside, and his neighbor peered out.

But nothing from inside Seth's house. Maybe he really wasn't home.

Zoe beat on the door. "Seth! Open up. The ice cream's melting."

Seconds ticked by into another minute. And another. She looked down at the groceries at her feet. Should she leave them there? Or take them back to Pete's?

Behind the closed door came a thump, a scrape, and a click—the sound of the deadbolt. The door swung open revealing a scruffier version of the formerly clean-cut young man.

She tried to hide her shock at his appearance with a smile. "Hi." She bent down and threaded the plastic handles into her grasp before hoisting them to shoulder height. "I have food."

"Yeah. I heard." Seth held the storm door open, allowing her to enter.

She left the question "Why didn't you answer sooner?" unasked. Instead, she crossed to the kitchen and searched for a spot to set her bounty. The counter was covered with dirty dishes that overflowed the sink. The table was covered with mail, some opened, some not.

Zoe lowered the bags to the floor and started digging through them for the ice cream and other perishables.

From behind her, Seth said, "I guess I need to clean the place up some."

She opened the refrigerator, fearing the worst. Instead of green fuzzy science projects, it contained cans of beer, ketchup, mustard, and little else. "Looks like I showed up just in the nick of time."

"I've been eating a lot of takeout or frozen dinners."

A glance in the freezer confirmed the latter. Half a dozen boxes of assorted microwave meals took up space along with some clear zippered bags of what looked like ice crystals. Whatever was in those had fallen prey to freezer burn, but at least they didn't stink. "When was the last time you had a real meal?"

He grinned sheepishly through his beard. "You mean in the last decade?"

She growled at him. "First things first. I hope you have trash bags, because that's something I didn't bring."

Seth held up a triumphant fist. "Yes, I do."

An hour later, the groceries had been put away, and a pair of trash bags had been filled and deposited outside. Chicken thighs simmered in a black cast iron Dutch oven on the stove while Zoe worked her way through the dirty dishes in a sink full of suds. She'd assigned Seth the task of sorting his mail, tossing the junk and dealing with the bills.

Once he'd finished that chore, he joined her at the sink and grabbed a towel to dry. Having run out of small talk and orders to bark at him, Zoe broached the real reason she'd shown up at his door.

"I hear you tendered your resignation from the department."

Seth kept his head lowered as he wiped a plate. "Yeah."

"That makes me sad, you know."

"It's for the best."

"How do you figure that?"

"I don't have what it takes to be a cop. Not a good one anyway."

Zoe placed both soapy hands on the edge of the sink and turned to look at him. "What exactly do you call a 'good' cop?"

He paused, and she could tell he was mulling it over. "One that does his job without freaking out."

Zoe thought back a few short months ago to a snowy night when she'd been up to her elbows in blood instead of suds, a night when she'd stared down the black maw of a gun being held by a killer. She shivered at the memory. "You saved my life. If you hadn't been there—"

He cut her off. "Someone else would've taken the shot." He sniffed and ran a sleeve across his face. "I wish like hell someone else had taken the shot."

She flung the dishrag into the water and grabbed a towel to dry her hands. "Who? Who else? Pete was trying to de-escalate the situation and had his gun holstered. He couldn't have drawn it in time."

Seth's shoulders hunched around his neck. "Maybe he wouldn't have needed to. Maybe—"

This time Zoe was the one to cut him off. "I would be dead. Bottom line. If you hadn't been there, if you hadn't taken the shot when you did, I would be dead."

For the first time since she'd mentioned that night, Seth met her gaze. "You don't know that."

"Yes, I do."

"I don't. I killed someone that night and I honestly don't believe I had to."

Zoe knew what he meant. The shooting had been a suicide by cop. The killer may or may not have followed through and pulled the trigger but had nothing to lose at that point. "You saved my life, and nothing will convince me differently. You did your job and you did it well."

Seth opened a cabinet door and set the plate inside with the slow, thoughtful precision of a brain surgeon. "But I can't deal with the aftermath. Someone died because of me."

"And *I* didn't. Because of you."

He made a pained face, shaking his head.

Zoe had been trying to avoid laying the biggest sledgehammer guilt trip on him, but nothing else seemed to be getting through. She drew a breath. "The fact that you want to give up your law enforcement career because you saved my life makes me feel like my life doesn't matter to you."

She was glad Seth had already put the plate away. The statement staggered him. "What? No. I mean yes, your life matters to me." His face reddened and for a moment she thought he might burst into tears. He clenched his fists. "You don't understand. This stuff about taking another life—I can't do it again. I can't put myself in that place. Maybe next time I need to pull the trigger, I won't be able to because of this."

Zoe sensed there was more and kept quiet.

After a long moment, he lurched to a chair and half fell into it. "I see other cops—Pete for example—handle this kind of thing and just keep going. They have what it takes to do the job." He met her gaze, pleading. "I don't."

The wafting aroma of the chicken signaled that Zoe needed to pay attention to her cooking. She moved to the stove and added some water to the pot before grabbing a metal spoon to gently loosen the almost scorched meat from the bottom. The simple act of covering the Dutch oven and lowering the heat gave her time to think about Seth's words.

She turned away from the stove to face him. "Pete said he left you a business card for a therapist. Have you called them?"

"No." Seth's lip curled as if the very idea left a bad taste in his mouth. "I don't want to talk to another shrink who has no idea what it's like out there. I've read the books. Taken the psychology classes. It doesn't prepare you for what it's really like."

Zoe nodded slowly. Maybe a shrink or a book wasn't the answer for Seth.

But she had an idea of what might be.

It was after six by the time Pete made it home that evening. He found Zoe in the recliner, one cat stretched out on her legs, the other curled against her shoulder.

She lowered the book she'd been reading. "There's a plate in the microwave for you."

He stretched. "I'm more tired than hungry. Think I'll get a shower and catch a couple hours of sleep first." He bent over to kiss her. The cat at her shoulder meowed its annoyance and vacated its nest.

The feline blanketing her legs didn't budge, and Zoe fingered its ginger-orange fur. "I'll put the plate in the fridge as soon as Jade gives me permission to move."

Pete took a seat on the couch and leaned back. If he closed his eyes, he'd never make it to the shower. Or bed. Or to his midnight shift. Instead, he looked at Zoe. "How well do you know Boyd Anderson?"

"The guy with the corn knife? I don't know him at all."

"What? I figured you horse people all know each other."

"I hate to disappoint you but no. He wasn't in 4H with me and he's never gone trail riding with our group from the Krolls' farm. I've driven past his place and love what he did with it, but I don't 'know' him." She stuck a bookmark between the pages and set the book aside. "Why? Has there been more trouble out there?"

"In a manner of speaking. O'Keefe thinks Anderson is out to kill him in addition to lusting after O'Keefe's wife."

Zoe opened her mouth. Closed it. And raised one gorgeous eyebrow. "Professor K is nuts."

"Professor K?"

"Professor Kristoffer O'Keefe," she said mimicking the man's highbrow speech pattern, "with a K, not a C-H."

Pete snickered. "He is unique. But there's more to it. O'Keefe's wife is...was...John Kinney's sister."

"I know."

"You knew?"

"Wayne mentioned it."

Of course, he did. "Did you know Boyd Anderson had been arrested for assault when he was younger? And Kinney was the arresting officer?"

Zoe blinked. "No."

Pete told her about his visit to the Andersons' place and his chat with the couple.

The lines creasing her brow told him she was giving the revelation considerable thought. But all she said was, "Huh."

He interlaced his fingers behind his head. "How was your day?"

She blinked, as if the question woke her from a trance. "I visited Franklin and learned the coroner does entirely too much paperwork."

Pete chuckled and listened while she grumbled about being ordered to tackle a stack of backlogged reports.

"In spite of all that, I'm still trying to help him get re-elected."

"I noticed the campaign signs out front."

"I hope you don't mind I stuck them in your yard."

He wished like hell she'd think of it as her yard too. "You know I don't mind."

She grinned. "Good." The grin faded. "I don't like the way Franklin looks."

"What do you mean?"

"He thinks they're gonna release him tomorrow, but I have my doubts. He's really pale."

"He's always pale." Pete wondered if the time Marshall spent with dead bodies had anything to do with his chronically pasty complexion.

"No, I mean, he's *really* pale. More than usual." Zoe scowled. "I'm worried about him." She shifted in the recliner. The cat chirped in protest but didn't move. "Then I went over to Golden Oaks to see your dad."

"Is he okay?"

"He's fine. We had a nice chat with one of our suspects."

An image of Zoe and his father interrogating a killer flashed across Pete's brain. "You what?"

"Wayne was there too." She shared how she'd invited Harry for a milkshake and ended up in the middle of an interview with Daryl Oliverio.

Pete mulled over the idea of Oliverio as the killer. "I don't buy into a guy committing murder because an old man made his grandmother cry."

"True. But factor in Oliverio's history with anger management issues. You saw him. He's a hothead." She stroked the lap cat's fur. "Your father's convinced Oliverio's guilty."

"Pop thinks everyone who dies at Golden Oaks has been murdered too. What about you? What are your thoughts on the guy?"

"Up until now, I've thought he was our best bet."

"What's changed your mind?"

"Boyd Anderson." Zoe gazed across the room. "Could he be our Baseball Cap Man?"

"I've wondered the same thing. I wish we had a better view of that guy."

"So do I." The cat in her lap rolled over to reveal its belly. "By the way, I went over to Seth's this afternoon."

"Did you convince him to rescind his resignation?"

"Not exactly. I cleaned up his kitchen and made him supper. And we talked. The shooting has really done a number on him."

"I know. I told him to call that therapist."

"He won't. Says he doesn't want to talk to anyone who doesn't know what it's like."

Pete ran both hands through his hair in frustration. "That therapist is the best in the field. She works with police departments all across the state."

Zoe held up a hand to silence him. "It doesn't matter how good she is if Seth won't talk to her. But I think I know who he will talk to."

"Who?"

She lifted her chin, holding his gaze. "You."

FOURTEEN

The midnight shift had been quiet. One drunk and disorderly outside Rodeo's Bar at closing time—a sad, harmless area resident who had spent many nights sleeping off a bender in the Vance Township Police Department. Pete escorted the man back to the station and set him up in one of the holding cells with the door unlocked.

Pete watched the guy pass out within seconds and decided he looked pretty darned comfortable. With his phone at his side, Pete stretched out on the bunk in the other cell for a power nap. County EOC cut his snooze short with a report of an alarm at a business over in Elm Creek.

It proved to be nothing, but Pete gave up the idea of sleep. He stopped back at the station to refill his coffee and check on his drunken guest who was snoring loud enough to disturb folks within a four-block radius. Then Pete climbed behind the wheel of his SUV and cruised the streets and roads of his jurisdiction.

Around six, he headed back to Dillard. As he neared the station, he noticed the lights blazing at Seth's house. On a whim, Pete turned the vehicle around and pulled into his officer's driveway.

Seth opened the door before Pete had a chance to knock. The kid looked just as bad as he had earlier in the week. Maybe worse.

"Sorry for dropping in at this hour."

Seth gave him a sad smile. "Most of the time my body still thinks I'm working the night shift. But even when I do sleep, I have nightmares. Come on in."

At least the house looked better. Zoe had done wonders.

"Is everything all right?" Seth asked.

"Other than I'm working your shift yet again?"

"Sorry." He didn't sound sorry. "Want a cup of coffee?"

Pete barked a sarcastic laugh.

"Okay. Stupid question." Seth pulled a mug from his cupboard.

Pete took a seat at the table. The piles of papers had been cleared.

And the therapist's business card was noticeably absent too.

Seth must have read his thoughts. "I know you meant well with that doctor stuff, but I really don't want to talk to some stranger." He set the filled mug in front of Pete. "Nancy told you I'm not coming back?"

"I don't accept word-of-mouth resignations. I haven't received written notification."

Seth slumped into the other chair. "I'll get on it."

"Don't. I won't accept that either."

"You have to."

"No, I don't. Not until I'm convinced."

"Of what?"

Pete took a sip. Of what? A good question. Like so much of police work, it was one of those things he'd know when he saw it. "You don't want to pour your soul out to a stranger. I get it. But I'm not a stranger. Talk to me."

Seth blinked. "You?"

"Yeah. You think someone who hasn't been on the front lines won't understand. Well, I've been there, done that. There's nothing you've seen that I haven't. Talk to me."

The younger officer cradled his cup and stared at the brew as if it held the secrets of the universe. Other than the second-by-second ticking of a battery-operated clock on the wall, the house was silent. After a minute or so, he lifted his gaze to meet Pete's. "How many lives have you taken?"

The question wasn't one he'd expected, but he didn't have to think about it. "Two."

Seth nodded thoughtfully. "The first one was that young boy."

A dark street in Pittsburgh more than a decade ago. A report of shots fired. "Fifteen years old. Yeah."

Still holding his cup, Seth came forward and pressed his forearms against the table. "Tell me about it. And about how you got over it."

A clear sky overnight plummeted the temperatures with no blanket of clouds to hold in the spring warmth. By morning, frost whitened the landscape as effectively as a light dusting of snow. Zoe eased her pickup to the edge of the pockmarked road in front of her farm, left the motor running and the heater blasting, and stepped down from the cab. Posting campaign signs out here might not provide a lot of visibility, but she figured not posting them might suggest she wasn't supporting her boss.

The rhythmic *thwank, thwank, thwank* of hammer strokes rang out, cutting through the cold stillness. Zoe looked toward the source of the racket. Her house.

No. Not her house. Her barn. A gray pickup was parked in front of it. The blue tarp on the roof had been swept aside and someone was up there swinging a hammer. *Thwank, thwank, thwank.*

Who the hell...?

Campaign signs forgotten, Zoe climbed back into her truck, shifted into gear, and swung into her driveway.

She'd never before seen the visiting pickup—a shiny Dodge Ram four-door with Illinois state plates. Nor had she hired anyone to repair her leaky roof. She leapt out, slammed her door, and stormed around to the side of the barn to get a look at her uninvited carpenter.

"*Hey,*" she yelled at the man's back.

He turned and grinned around a mouthful of roofing nails.

"Jason?"

He removed the nails he'd clenched in his teeth. "Hi, Zoe. Surprise."

Surprise didn't begin to cover it. "What are you doing here? How'd you even find this place?"

"I tracked *you* down, didn't I? Finding a big ol' farm was a piece of cake." He waved the hammer around indicating the barn, the house, the pasture. "You told me your place needed some work. You weren't kidding. I thought I'd give you a hand."

"But you went back to Philly."

"I did. I told my boss I was collecting on the vacation time I've accumulated, packed my work duds, and took the next flight back to Pittsburgh. Aren't you glad to see me?"

A laugh exploded from her heart. "Yeah. I am." She couldn't believe how badly she'd missed him. "Where'd you get the truck?"

"Rental place at the airport. Nice, huh?"

"Uh, yeah."

"I could get used to this country boy stuff. Big ass trucks. Fresh air—"

One of the horses whinnied and the others followed suit.

"Horses," Jason tacked onto his list.

Zoe noticed though that Windstar, Jazzel, and the others weren't standing at the fence. "Where—?"

"They were raising one unholy racket back there, so I put them in the barn with some hay. I hope you don't mind."

"I don't mind at all."

"I left the grain for you. Feeding hay is about the extent of my horse knowledge."

"That's fine." Zoe realized her cheeks were hurting from smiling. "I'll feed them and then come up and help you out."

"You better not. It's slippery up here with the frost." As if illustrating the point, one foot lost its grip. He yelped.

Zoe's heart slammed into her sternum as she watched her brother scramble to grab something—anything—to steady himself. She reached upward, as if she could catch him. But he managed to regain his balance and his grip.

When he met her gaze, his blue eyes had widened. He grinned but it wasn't the light-hearted one of a moment ago. "Oops."

Images of Jason sprawled, twisted, and broken on the ground at her feet vanished. Zoe closed her eyes for a moment. "Maybe you should come down and wait for the frost to melt."

Still wide-eyed, he nodded. "I think you might be right."

After doling out the grain rations and taking a moment to scratch Windstar's itchy back, Zoe washed her hands at the new water hydrant Pete had installed inside the barn door. She dried off on a thread-bare towel she kept handy. Catching Jason's raised eyebrow, Zoe shrugged. "If you need to wash up around here, this is the only option. Someone stole all the copper plumbing inside the house."

"You have got to be kidding."

She hung the towel over the hydrant and offered to give him a tour of the house. "I can't even call it a nickel tour. I'd owe you at least four cents change."

A few minutes later, he stood in the middle of the kitchen, taking in the same crappy flooring, cabinets, and gaps where appliances should be that continued to vex Zoe. "Your mother gave you this?"

"Yeah. I plan to tackle it a little at a time as my finances allow. The barn took first priority, but once I get the roof out there fixed, I'll start in here." She heard the futility in her own words.

"Start where?" Jason asked, giving voice to her thoughts.

"New wiring. New plumbing. I think the roof on the house here is okay for now." She hoped. She was afraid to venture into the attic for a closer look.

"Uh-huh." He wandered to one of the windows but said nothing.

He didn't need to. Zoe already knew the ancient single panes weren't broken but did little to keep out the cold air. Replacements, though, were way down the list in her budget.

"I guess I'll get a hotel out by the airport instead of asking to bunk in your guest room."

She couldn't very well invite him to stay with her and Pete. "I guess so. Unless you want to stay in the barn. At least there's electricity and water out there." She meant it as a joke, but her voice caught in her throat.

Jason faced her, and she looked into his sympathetic blue eyes. Her father's eyes.

Their father's eyes.

Without a word, Jason closed the distance between them and wrapped his arms around her. Enveloped in his embrace, she buried her face against his shoulder. In that moment, she was eight years old. A skinned knee. Or some boy had been mean to her on the school bus. Finding solace in her daddy's arms. Sobbing little-girl tears.

"Hey, hey, what's this?" Jason drew her away from him, cupping her face in his hands, his voice and his expression concerned. "Why are you crying?" he asked softly.

She choked a laugh and used both gloved hands to wipe her damp face. "I just—it's nothing. Really."

"You sure?"

"I'm sure."

"Because if you're gonna go all weepy on me every time I give you a hug, I'm gonna stop right now." He threw up his hands as if afraid to touch her.

Zoe dug in her coat pocket for a tissue. All these years, she'd steadfastly refused to cry in front of, or because of, men. For the most part, she succeeded. Now here she was, reverting to that ponytailed youngster. Always a Daddy's girl, Kimberly would chide. "I won't. I promise," Zoe said through the Kleenex. "I didn't realize how overwhelmed I've felt over this house." She sniffed. "Pete keeps telling me I should've turned it down. Now that the deed's in my name, he thinks I should sell it."

Jason looked around again.

"You probably agree."

"No."

"No?"

"No." He met her gaze, his eyes narrow and determined. "Yeah, it's a money pit. Yeah, it's more work than you can do yourself. But didn't you say it used to belong to your uncles?"

"My great uncles. On my mother's side."

"Then you have to keep it." He tipped his head down until his forehead touched hers. "Family's important."

"But you just said it's more work than I can handle."

"More work than you can do yourself," he repeated. "Not more work than we can do together."

"But you have a job and a life. In Philadelphia. Clear across the state."

"And I have a little sister on this side of the state. I plan to visit. A lot. I mean, you have horses. You can't just pack up and come spend weeks with me. Although..." He aimed a finger at her chin. "...I do want you to come out east so I can show you my city. In the meantime, I need to get this house fixed up so I have a guest room to crash in when I come to stay with you."

"But—"

"Stop with the buts already. Do you want to make this place your home or not?"

Zoe closed her eyes, picturing her fantasy. A farm she could call her own. A quaint and cozy home where she could have friends and family over for dinner. A place where she and Pete could grow old together.

A place where her older brother could crash in the guest room.

"I thought so," Jason said.

She opened her eyes and realized she was smiling. So was he. "Where do we start?"

"I'd say finishing the barn roof for today."

Zoe pictured him thrashing about on the frosty sloped surface. "After the ice melts."

"Definitely." Jason made an exaggerated pained face and rubbed his neck. "I'd rather not fall and break something vital before we even get started."

Her phone's ringtone interrupted her laugh. The Who. She didn't have to check caller ID to know it was Franklin on the other end. "I have to get this." She stepped toward the kitchen sink and swiped the green button. "Hi, Boss."

He didn't bother with pleasantries. "Get out to the intersection of Routes 15 and 218. There's a vehicular accident with a fatality. These damned doctors won't let me out of here, so you'll have to take it."

"I'll leave right now, but it'll take me about forty-five minutes to get there."

"The victim isn't going anywhere. Call if you have any questions. And keep me posted."

Zoe opened her mouth to reply, but Franklin had clicked off. She pocketed her phone.

"Duty calls?" Jason said.

"Afraid so." She pulled out her keys, located the ones to the house, and began wresting them off the ring.

"What are you doing?

"Giving you the keys to the house."

"Don't do that. Just lock up. I won't need back in."

"I want you to have them. I've got another set at Pete's." When she looked up at Jason, she swore she spotted tears welling in his eyes. "It's not much now. But if you plan to claim the guest room for yourself, you'll need to be able to get in." She pinched the freed keys and held them up to him.

He blinked and sniffed. And accepted them. "Only because I might need to drop off materials and I wouldn't want to leave stuff outside."

Zoe stood on her tiptoes and planted a quick kiss on his cheek. "I gotta go. Be careful on that roof. I don't want to come home and find you splatted on the ground."

FIFTEEN

Pete returned to the station shortly after seven a.m. He hadn't planned on Seth's "therapy" session delving quite so deeply into his own past. His officer had known about Donnie Moreno, the boy he'd gunned down. Hell, everyone in the department knew. Moreno shot Pete's partner, and Pete stopped the threat. But when he learned the threat was nothing more than a kid, Pete had been shaken to his core. His old partner left the force after the incident, taking a job in Hawaii as head of security at some swanky hotel.

The shooting wasn't the sole reason for Pete's move from Pittsburgh to Vance Township, but he'd be kidding himself if he tried to believe it wasn't a factor.

Not exactly the life lesson he'd wanted to share with Seth. How do you "get over it?" *Move to another state or at least to another department.*

Not at all what he wanted Seth to take away from their pre-dawn chat.

Pete was still in his office mulling over the conversation, sipping a cup of coffee, and scanning the overnight reports from surrounding jurisdictions when the bells out front jingled. Snippets of female voices drifted back to him. Nancy and Abby.

Before his secretary could buzz the intercom, he yelled, "Send her back."

Officer Abby Baronick appeared in his doorway a moment later. Her crisp new Vance Township uniform shirt hung off her shoulders and bagged around her waist. The trousers, while cinched tight, clearly were made for a larger person.

She must have known what he was thinking. "This was the smallest size your secretary could dig up. She said she'd order something that fit me better today. I thought she might want to wait until you decide whether or not you wanted to keep me."

Was Abby testing him? Trying to find out how serious he was

about hiring her full-time? "We need another officer." This morning hadn't bolstered his hopes of Seth's immediate return. "Your vest will hide a lot of the bulk, but we still can't have you running around looking..."

"Like a little kid playing grownup?"

Pete was grateful for the hint of a grin on her face. At least she wasn't taking herself too seriously. "I was going to say, 'looking like you'd borrowed someone else's clothes,' but okay. Your description works too." He climbed to his feet. "Let me show you around and find you a desk back in the bullpen."

He pointed out the conference room across the hall before escorting her toward the rear of the building where the hallway intersected at a T. To the right, the evidence room and a garage bay for processing vehicles. To the left, a pair of holding cells and a doorway leading to the large but crammed "bullpen." Six battered metal desks sat at odd angles to one another, separated by rickety partitions. Two of them bore stacks of papers, a few personal photos in small frames, cups of pens. Their partitions served as bulletin boards with assorted case notes and department memos tacked to them. A third cubicle had been cleared of the paperwork, but family photos and a few personal items remained. Seth's.

Pete wasn't ready to turn over his workspace to Abby just yet.

Two other desks contained no personal mementos but had full in-boxes and a few stacks of papers. These cubbies were shared by the part-timer guys.

The final desk was a spare. Stark and neglected, it lurked against a wall as if afraid to join the party.

Pete looked from the lone desk to the others, trying to figure out the best way to fit it in.

"I'm okay with leaving it there," Abby said, sounding less than enthused about the prospect.

"I'm not." Knowing the young Baronick had a rough enough road ahead—new kid, only female, not to mention possibly being seen as a threat to Seth's return—Pete didn't want to physically isolate her in addition to the other invisible walls. "How do you feel about helping me move furniture?"

She flexed biceps hidden by her baggy shirt sleeves. "I'm tougher than I look. I have to be."

He didn't doubt it for a moment.

A half hour later, they'd rearranged the five desks to allow space for the sixth. Pete figured he'd tell his other officers they could make additional changes if they felt too crowded. Provided those changes didn't include nudging out the new member of the department.

He looked at Abby. "Does this work for you?"

"Yes, sir."

"All right then. That's about all there is to see here. Let's go out on patrol, and I'll introduce you to Vance Township."

Nancy was on the phone when they returned to the front of the building but responded to Pete's questioning look with a dismissive wave of her hand.

Out in the parking lot, Abby paused before climbing into the passenger side of Pete's Explorer. "Chief?"

"Yes?"

She squirmed. The first sign of insecurity Pete had witnessed in her. "I wanted to ask about...Detective Baronick's visit yesterday."

Here it was. She wanted to know whether he'd been behind her hiring. "I am aware he's your brother. You can refer to him as such."

Her expression soured. "Yes, sir. My brother mentioned the Kinney homicide when he was here."

Maybe Baronick's connection to her hiring wasn't what was on her mind after all. "He did." Pete slid behind the wheel.

Abby climbed in beside him. "That homicide took place in Brunswick. Is there a link with Vance Township?"

The slight eager note in her voice clued Pete in on the real reason for the question. She wondered if she was going to be involved in a major investigation right out of the gate. And after what he'd uncovered about Boyd Anderson, she might. "Mostly a personal one." He considered telling her about Harry but decided to keep his father's situation out of the equation. "John Kinney was my FTO when I first came out of the academy."

"Oh. I'm sorry."

Pete steered the SUV onto Dillard's Main Street, heading north.

"You said 'mostly.'"

Pete kept his eyes on the road but smiled. Abby Baronick was sharp. "I did, didn't I? Remember Professor O'Keefe?"

"He's a hard one to forget."

"Agreed." Pete told her about delving into Boyd Anderson's past and discovering the tie to Kinney.

Abby fell silent as Pete relayed his meeting with the Andersons and remained pensive once he finished his story. After a mile or so of quiet, she shifted in her seat. "Did you start digging into Anderson because of O'Keefe? Or did you have a hunch there was more to him?"

"To be honest, I looked beyond what I'd found during Anderson's arrest only because the professor was so insistent."

She sighed and punctuated it with, "Huh." After a few more silent miles, she added, "I don't know that I'd have followed up like that. My instincts told me O'Keefe was more of an attention seeker, crying wolf to get the neighbor in trouble without any real justification."

The fact that she'd admitted her mistake impressed Pete. It also reminded him of his own early days on patrol, making wrong judgments with John Kinney behind the wheel. Pete echoed the words he remembered Kinney saying to him. "Your instincts grow sharp with experience. You'll learn."

Armed with photos, sketches, measurements, and notes, Zoe gave the deputy coroner in charge of transportation—a guy named Gene with eyes that reminded her of a Basset Hound—the all-clear to move the body to the morgue. Once Gene had the victim loaded in the coroner's van, Zoe released the scene to the state police and local fire company to clear the debris and get the road re-opened.

During her examination of the deceased, she'd managed to stay detached, but as she headed back to her truck, the weight of the scene hit her. A carload of young women, not more than girls really, on their way to a spring vacation. Probably laughing. Maybe singing along with some tunes. The driver, texting the guys they were supposed to meet at Virginia Beach that evening, drifted into the other lane.

Zoe knew all this because two of the passengers, while bloodied and bruised, had escaped with only minor injuries and had been able to tell the tale. The driver and the other passenger were on their way to Allegheny General in Pittsburgh by way of Life Flight. They'd survive, most likely, but had a long road of reconstructive surgeries and physical therapy ahead of them.

The driver of the car they'd hit head on wasn't so lucky. The paramedics stated the man had been alive when they arrived but had bled out before they could free him from the mangled mess of his minivan. At least the child's car seat in the rear had been vacant. A silent witness to a young father who'd never see his kids grow up.

Zoe climbed into her truck, closed the door, and took some deep ragged breaths, fighting back the tears of her eight-year-old self. A child, learning her dad was never coming back home. Fragmented memories. Riding on his shoulders. His delighted laughter at something she'd said or done. Ghostly echoes she couldn't quite grasp after all these years. Did the man in the minivan have any kids old enough to remember him decades into the future?

She swallowed the lump in her chest and pulled out her phone.

Jason answered on the second ring. "Hey, Sis. You checking up on me?"

She choked out a laugh. "Well, you don't sound like you've fallen off the roof."

"Nope. Not even a mashed thumb. But you, on the other hand, don't sound so great. You okay?"

"Yeah, I'm fine."

"Don't lie to me. What's wrong?"

She closed her eyes and smiled. How was it possible to bond with someone so deeply so fast? Somehow, she must have always known another part of her heart existed out there.

"Zoe?"

"I'm here. I'm just having severe doubts about my new career."

"Do you want to talk? How about I meet you for a late lunch?"

"That would be great. Can you come into Brunswick? I have a stack of reports to fill out and Franklin will pitch a fit if I put it off."

"Franklin?"

"The *real* county coroner. Can you meet me at his office and we'll go from there?"

"Sure. Give me an address."

She recited the street name and number. "It's in his family's funeral home across from the hospital's rear entrance."

There was a moment of silence. "Kind of a one-stop shopping experience? Hospital. Coroner. Funeral home. Bam."

Zoe stifled a laugh. Jason even shared her warped sense of humor. "Yeah. Something like that."

"See you in a half hour. Bye."

He clicked off before she could respond. She set the phone on the seat beside her and reached for the ignition, but the phone rang. Had he changed his mind? Forgotten something? The caller ID, however, named another of the men in her life.

She skimmed the green button. "Hi, Wayne. What's up?"

"I have something you need to see. Where are you?"

"On my way to Franklin's office."

"I'll meet you there." And he hung up.

Zoe stared at the phone. Franklin's office might be an interesting place this afternoon.

Wayne sauntered in a few minutes after Zoe sat down to make sense of her notes. "I gather Franklin's still in the hospital."

"For the moment. He thought he was getting out today, but I think he's gonna be disappointed."

"You look good behind that desk." Wayne made a point of surveying the display of urns, memorial books and cards. "But when you take over, you might consider moving your office someplace a little cheerier."

She glared at him. "I have no desire to take Franklin's job." To be honest, she was having second thoughts about even campaigning for him. "This isn't quite what I expected it to be."

Grinning, Wayne slid into one of the chairs across from her. "Been watching *CSI* reruns?"

"Not recently."

He studied her a moment and his smile faded. "What happened? Anything I should be involved in?"

She shook her head. "Traffic accident. Texting while driving. Carload of college girls headed to a long weekend at the beach crossed the center line. Driver of the car they hit didn't make it."

Wayne winced. "Sorry to hear that." He held her gaze. "But you've been to these calls before. I've never seen you this shaken up by one."

Zoe didn't want to go into how the victim and the senselessness of his loss had struck a nerve. "I guess I prefer to focus on saving the living."

"Then you might need to reconsider the whole coroner gig."

"In the meantime, what is it you wanted me to see?"

Wayne pulled his phone from his coat pocket. "You have no idea how many different security cameras are in Golden Oaks." He swiped and tapped and swiped again. "Or how many hours of absolutely nothing we've been viewing. However..." Instead of completing the sentence, he set his phone in front of her and tapped once more.

The footage playing out before her had no audio. It didn't need any. The camera had captured two men—Daryl Oliverio and John Kinney—engaged in an animated and probably loud exchange. Oliverio waved his arms, punctuating whatever he was saying to the older man.

Kinney stood tall, one hand on the back of a chair, the other fist planted on his hip. He wasn't saying much, but Zoe could tell from his expression, he was pissed. Defiant. Then Oliverio jabbed Kinney in the chest with one finger same as he'd done in the activities room. He jabbed again. The third time, he kept his finger on Kinney. Until Kinney slapped it away. The older man said something that must have put Oliverio in his place. They stood like that for a moment before a third person, also wearing a Golden Oaks polo shirt, entered the frame. At that point, Kinney turned and hobbled away.

"Wow," Zoe said.

Wayne reached for his phone, but a knock at the door interrupted.

Jason stood in the doorway. "I hope you don't mind." He looked from Zoe to Wayne. "The lady out front told me to come on back."

Zoe leapt to her feet and rounded the desk. "I don't mind at all." She hugged him and turned toward the detective, whose eyes and mouth had opened into one big question mark. "Detective Wayne Baronick, I'd like you to meet my brother, Jason Cox."

Wayne staggered out of his seat, stuttering. "Brother?"

Jason stepped toward him, arm extended. "Detective."

The men shook hands, but Wayne's patented toothy smile was gone. He raised both eyebrows at Zoe. "Brother?" he repeated with more emphasis.

Jason looked at her with mock disappointment on his face and in his voice. "Sis. You never told him about me? I'm hurt."

She laughed. Jason maintained his wounded expression. And Wayne's bewilderment deepened.

"I'm sorry," she said to the detective. "I just learned earlier this week that I had a sibling I never knew about." She swept both arms in a Vanna White flourish.

Wayne eyed Jason. "Nice to meet you."

"He's here to take me out to lunch. Provided I can get away." Zoe returned to her seat behind the desk and gestured for Jason to take the vacant chair next to the detective.

"Are you sure? I don't want to interrupt your work."

She glanced at Wayne.

"Please." The detective gave Jason his hungry-predator smile. The one that always reminded her of a python.

Once her brother was seated, Zoe told him, "We're working on the homicide case I mentioned."

"You sure I shouldn't wait out front?" Jason aimed a thumb at the door. "I mean, you know, if this is top secret or classified or something."

"Hardly," Wayne said. "We've been showing photos around to anyone and everyone who might be able to ID our guy."

Jason pointed the image frozen on the phone. "Is that him?"

"Could be." Wayne looked at Zoe. "Did you notice the date on this one?"

"No." She picked up the phone and enlarged the screen, positioning it so the timestamp filled the frame. "This was the day before Kinney was killed?"

Wayne's python smile widened. "Exactly."

She rolled the significance around in her mind. "The animosity between Oliverio and Kinney ran deeper than Kinney making Gladys cry."

A light sparked in the detective's eyes. "And his buddy who didn't report him because it was a 'one-time incident'...was lying."

SIXTEEN

Pete spent the morning introducing Abby to Vance Township. The back roads. The residences that were notorious for frequent visits by law enforcement. The bars where she should always call in backup before entering. And the best places to grab a meal. Once she hit nightshift, the options would diminish, so he pointed out the late-hours convenience store between Dillard and Phillipsburg and suggested she stock up before they closed.

They stopped at the Dog Den for lunch. Footlongs with the works. Despite her trim figure, Abby wolfed her meal like a hotdog-eating champ.

As they climbed back in the Explorer after depositing their trash, she asked, "Now what?"

Pete clicked his seatbelt and shifted into drive. "We're going to swing by the O'Keefes' place."

"Oh? Any particular reason?"

"Several. For starters, John Kinney's visitation hours are this afternoon and evening. His sister will definitely be at the funeral home."

"But not O'Keefe?"

Pete pulled out of the lot. "That's one of the reasons I want to drive by. I'm curious. O'Keefe had some animosity toward his brother-in-law."

"From what I've gathered, he has some animosity toward almost everyone."

Pete chuckled. "You're catching on. I'm interested to know which is stronger. His support of his wife? Or his dislike of her brother? And if he did go to Pittsburgh with her, that means their house is vacant and a prime target for bad guys who read the obits looking for easy pickings."

"Don't they have some kind of home security system?"

Pete grinned at her. "Probably. But it's a good excuse."

She appeared to consider his words. "And you never know. A good thief might know how to circumvent those things." They drove in silence for a mile or so before she turned in her seat to look at him. "You mentioned that Kinney was your FTO. I'm surprised you're here and not at the funeral home yourself."

"I'm short-staffed, otherwise I would be. I'll drive into the city this evening. And I'm attending the funeral tomorrow morning."

Abby shifted to face forward again and fell silent. Watching the road? Learning the lay of the land? Or lost in thought? Pete wasn't sure.

Ten minutes later, they approached the intersection with Silver Maple Drive and the O'Keefes' residence on the corner lot. Pete's question about the man being at his wife's side during this difficult time was quickly answered. The professor was bumping along on his riding mower with its bagger attached.

Pete slowed but cruised past.

"I guess we don't have to worry about burglars taking advantage of their absence today," Abby said.

True. But something else concerned Pete. Boyd Anderson's horses grazed peacefully in the pasture. "Dammit."

Abby shot him a puzzled look.

He pulled into Anderson's driveway. A battered red Honda Civic, which hadn't seen a fresh coat of wax in years, sat in front of the garage. No sign of the pickup. No movement from the house.

"What am I missing?" Abby asked when he shifted into park and opened his door.

"Anderson and his wife agreed they would bring their horses into the barn next time O'Keefe mowed grass in case the good professor hasn't gotten the message yet."

Abby climbed out of the SUV and jogged to catch Pete as he headed toward the porch. "Message?"

He thumped up the steps and knocked on the door. "I'll explain later."

No response. He pounded again. Nothing. He looked across the pasture. The horses had lifted their heads, their attention drawn toward O'Keefe, who had pulled his mower next to the fence.

"Dammit." Pete thudded down the porch steps and jogged toward his vehicle. Behind him, Abby hustled to keep up.

He slid behind the wheel, jerked the shifter into reverse. As soon as Abby leapt in beside him, he mashed the gas pedal to the floorboard.

Tires spewed gravel. A quick check for traffic revealed none, so he didn't brake until he'd backed onto the road. Slammed the shifter down into drive and stomped on the accelerator. He didn't bother with lights for the two-hundred-or-so-yard trip to the next property. The horses were ambling their way toward O'Keefe. The professor had climbed off his mower and was fiddling with the bagger. Pete hit the siren for one short whoop as he passed O'Keefe and wheeled into Silver Maple Drive and then his driveway. Abby clawed at the dashboard and armrest to keep from being flung into the center console.

Pete slammed on the brakes short of careening into the corner of the house, exited the car, and charged around the corner of the house toward O'Keefe.

The professor stood tall. Too tall. Too stiff. A kid caught with his hand in the proverbial cookie jar and determined to play innocent. "Chief Adams. What seems to be the problem?"

"*You're* the problem," Pete said, gesturing at the bagger. "If you're about to do what I think you're doing."

O'Keefe's gaze shifted to beyond Pete to Abby and back. "I have no idea what you're talking about."

"Don't play dumb, Professor. You've been told not to dump your grass clippings over the fence."

O'Keefe wrinkled his nose in disgust. "Oh, please. The Neanderthal has you serving as bodyguard to his ponies now?"

"Part of my duties is to keep the peace. That includes preventing your neighbor from killing you."

The professor perked up. "You finally agree that the man's a menace?"

Pete wasn't about to mention Anderson's possible involvement in Kinney's homicide. "Only if you continue providing him with motive."

"What motive?" O'Keefe waved an arm toward the horses lined up at the fence, ears pricked. "They're livestock. They eat grass." His tone suggested he was explaining the situation to a toddler. "I'm helping the man feed his beasts."

Pete might have thought the same had Zoe not educated him about the delicate equine digestive system, something he knew Anderson had tried to tell O'Keefe numerous times. No wonder the horse owner had shown up with his machete last weekend. Attempting to reason with the professor was a waste of energy. "Let me put it this way. If you dump even one handful of your grass clippings over that fence, I'm going to haul your ass into jail and charge you with criminal trespass, animal cruelty, and anything else I can come up with. You can pay your attorney to sort out which charges stick."

The color drained from O'Keefe's face. Pete wasn't sure whether it was the threat of jail or the idea of having to fork out big bucks to a lawyer that grabbed the professor's attention. "You wouldn't." He stuttered. "I'm not breaking any laws."

Pete moved closer, intentionally invading the man's personal space. "You might want to read up on Pennsylvania statutes. Especially the part about defiant trespass." Pete knew a halfway decent attorney would get any charges tossed, but he was counting on O'Keefe not wanting to sully his good name with even the hint of an arrest record.

The professor's eye twitched. "What do you propose I do with these clippings then?"

"Bag it for the trash. Compost. Mulch. Frankly I don't care. As long as you don't continue to create problems with your neighbor by dumping it on his property." Pete leaned closer yet. "Have I made myself clear?"

O'Keefe did his best to maintain his superior posture while conceding. "Fine." He looked toward the horses at the fence before slapping the bagger's latch closed.

Pete stepped back. The man climbed onto his mower and turned the key. Shooting an angry glance Pete's way, O'Keefe roared off.

"Were you seriously going to arrest him for defiant trespass?" Abby asked.

Pete turned to find her watching him with a look that said she was debating if he was as nuts as the professor. "Probably."

"Even if he never set foot on the neighbor's property?"

Pete shrugged. "That's why I threw in the animal cruelty part. Willfully or maliciously poisoning a domestic animal is a misdemeanor of the second degree in Pennsylvania."

"I don't think he intended to poison anything."

Pete strode past her, heading back to the SUV. "You working for his defense attorney?"

"No." Abby jogged to keep up. "But I'm not sure charging the man would have been the wisest move. He seems like the type to turn around and file a false arrest lawsuit."

"Which he would lose." When they rounded the corner of the house, Pete spotted O'Keefe standing next to his bagged load of clippings at the weeds edging the road. A good spot to start a compost pile. Pete opened his car door and climbed in. When Abby settled into the passenger seat, he turned toward her. "Have you ever dealt with farmers?"

"Not much."

"Have you ever played poker?"

She started to reply, but closed her mouth, a slow smile spreading across her face. "You were bluffing."

Hell, yes, he was bluffing. But he replied, "Maybe."

"What if O'Keefe had called your bluff?"

"He wouldn't. He's a lousy poker player."

"You've played cards with him?"

Pete chuckled. "I don't have to."

Abby's smile turned into a puzzled scowl. "But..."

Pete shifted into reverse. "You want to know if I really would have arrested him."

"Yeah."

"Yes. I would have. Would the charges have stuck? Maybe. Probably not. But Anderson has asked him repeatedly to stop. He threatened the professor with a machete for crying out loud. Maybe the threat of being jailed is what's needed for him to take this seriously."

"You're that concerned about a herd of horses?"

"No." Although Zoe would be. "I'm actually concerned about the professor." Pete gazed across the pasture to Boyd Anderson's farmhouse. The man had been arrested in the past for aggravated assault. He'd used a machete against his neighbor. Could he have taken revenge on the man who arrested him all those years ago? "O'Keefe's not smart enough to realize he's poking a bear. I'm doing all I can to get him to put down the stick."

"My little sister, the detective." Jason scoured through his takeout container of roast pork with Chinese vegetables, pinching a chunk of broccoli with his chopsticks.

"Some detective. I can't figure out how to use these things." Zoe fumbled with her own chopsticks as a piece of General Tso's chicken slipped free from her grasp. In the time she'd struggled to get her first bite, Jason had wolfed down half his meal.

He tossed her a plastic fork. "I don't think it's a job requirement."

Once Wayne had left, Jason offered to bring back lunch, allowing Zoe to work on her reports. She could definitely get used to this family stuff.

"Now what?" he asked.

"What do you mean?"

"Sounds like you and that detective have your man. Do the two of you go out and arrest him now?"

"Not the two of us for sure. My job is dealing with the body and the evidence on and around it. Wayne's humoring me by letting me be this involved on the police end of the investigation." Zoe forked a piece of succulent chicken into her mouth and chewed. The spice sent an inferno through her sinuses and into the top of her head. She grabbed for her bottle of water.

Jason chuckled at her. "So, Wayne'll make the arrest by himself?"

She swallowed and sniffed at her heat-induced tears. "He'll probably do more investigating first. Look for additional physical evidence so they have a solid case before getting an arrest warrant."

"I thought that video stuff looked pretty solid. What's the word? Incriminating?"

Zoe picked up a cellophane-wrapped fortune cookie and winged it at him. "Stick with your computer stuff and leave the dead bodies and homicidal maniacs to me."

Jason missed the cookie and had to bend down to retrieve it from the floor. "You can keep the dead bodies. I'm not crazy about you and homicidal maniacs though. Make you a deal. I'll stay out of your coroner work, and you stay out of the police work."

Pete had made a similar request on more than one occasion. Not that she'd ever listened to him. "You do realize I'm involved with a cop, right?"

Jason squinted into the takeout box and set down the chopsticks. "Speaking of...When do I get to meet the man who's won my sister's heart? How about dinner tonight?"

Before she had a chance to answer, her cell phone rang. The screen identified the incoming caller. Zoe held up a finger to Jason and answered. "Hello, Dr. Abercrombie."

"I'll be at the morgue to do the autopsy at seven. Do not be late."

"Tonight?"

"Tomorrow morning. I have to give a luncheon speech in Erie at noon, so there's no time for dilly-dallying."

"I think Franklin plans to be discharged sometime today—"

"I just spoke to his doctor. He's not going anywhere for a few more days. You're acting coroner. Be there."

The line went dead.

"Problem?" Jason asked.

"Not exactly." She wasn't going to bore her brother with her calculations of what time she needed to get up in order to grab breakfast, run to the farm to feed the horses, and make the half-hour drive to Brunswick for a seven a.m. autopsy.

"I gather something's come up for tonight?"

"Uh. No. I have to be in autopsy, but not until early in the morning." Very early.

"Wow. You have all the fun. What about dinner then? You? Me? Your cop?"

Zoe dragged her mind away from the body across the street in the morgue. "I think we're going to the funeral home in Pittsburgh."

"Oh?" He brought the corner of the box to his mouth and tilted his head back to drain the last of its contents.

"John Kinney, the murder victim? Pete wants to go to his visitation."

"Okay. How about lunch tomorrow?"

"No good. That's the funeral." She did some more calculations. Autopsy in Brunswick at seven. Funeral service in Pittsburgh at eleven.

"You spend entirely too much time with dead people."

"True. How about an early dinner tomorrow? I'll cook. Pete has to be on duty starting at four, but you're welcome to stick around and keep me company."

"Sounds good." Jason ripped the cellophane from the cookie. "In the meantime, I'll keep working out at your place. I'm almost done with the tarpaper. What kind of shingles do you want?"

"Shingles?" The mental image of her brother working up the barn roof all alone set off her guilt alarm. "You don't have to do that."

"I know I don't. I want to. I heard the forecast. They're saying a rain and snow mix for Monday. I started this project. I'm not gonna let it get ruined now."

"But shingles are too much work." Not to mention too much money. "I was just going to put down some of that rolled roofing stuff."

He made a disapproving face at her. "Tell you what. I'll take care of picking the material for the roof."

"But—"

He held up a finger, silencing her. "No buts," he said firmly.

Zoe feigned anger. Or tried to. Stubbornness must run in her family.

Jason cracked open his cookie and pulled out the tiny slip. He read it and nodded his approval. "Even my fortune bears me out." He slid it across the desk to her.

If you refuse to accept anything but the best, you very often get it.

"I'm refusing to accept rolled roofing crap for my little sister's barn." Jason stood and gathered the empty containers, stuffing them into the bag from the restaurant. "Take your time finishing yours. I'm outta here." He came around the desk to plant a kiss on the top of her head. "See you later, Sis."

Zoe watched him head for the door. "Love you," she called after him.

He froze. Turned.

She thought she spotted a gleam in his eyes.

"I love you too," he said, his voice strained. And then he ducked out.

Zoe sat for a moment, basking in the sweet warmth of having someone who shared her blood, her DNA, in her life. She noticed the remaining fortune cookie next to the container of rice and picked it up, shucking the wrap. Breaking the cookie in half, she unfurled the paper inside. And shivered.

Be on the lookout for coming events; they cast their shadows beforehand.

SEVENTEEN

Pete wasn't sure which had been harder to take—last night's visitation at the funeral home or the service this morning. At least last night, Zoe had been at his side. During the memorial service, he'd stood with his fellow brothers-in-blue as the bagpipers played "Amazing Grace" over the flag-draped coffin. Zoe had been somewhere in the rear of the too-small church, crammed in with the other civilian friends and residents from his old neighborhood.

For someone who'd been forced into retirement almost two decades ago, courtesy of the accident, John Kinney's funeral had drawn quite the turnout. Somewhere in the midst of it, a chill crawled upward along Pete's spine, like the breath of the Grim Reaper himself. *This could be me. Tonight. Tomorrow. The next call could be the one. The last.*

He'd quelled the premonition at the time, but now that he was back home, it floated to the surface as he changed from his dress uniform to his everyday work one. He shook his head to chase the demons away. Those were the kinds of self-fulfilling prophecies that made officers second-guess themselves and end up dead.

Instead, he shifted his focus from what could happen to what was about to happen. Jason Cox was coming for dinner.

Zoe said Cox wanted to meet the man with whom his sister was involved. Pete wanted to meet the brother too. For a fleeting moment, Pete had resisted, but then decided where better to meet this guy than on his own turf? Home field advantage.

Pete finished tucking in his shirttails, left two cats sleeping on his bed, and followed the savory aroma of baking meatloaf to the kitchen. Zoe still wore the curve-hugging black dress from the funeral, but she'd traded her heels for a pair of moccasins. While she stood over the stove, her back to him, he admired the view a moment before letting his presence be known. "Smells good."

She turned toward him, a lid in one hand and a grateful smile on her face. "Thanks. I hope it tastes good." She replaced the lid and cracked open the oven door to peek inside. "I wish I'd had time to roast a chicken."

Zoe's specialty. As it was, she'd been up until midnight putting together the meatloaf so she could throw it in the oven the moment they got home from the service. "It'll be fine. You're a great cook."

She gave a self-deprecating laugh just as a knock came at the door. "That's him."

Pete moved to let their guest in.

But Zoe scurried past him. "I'll get it."

Pete folded his arms. She threw open the door with a squeal of delight, sounding like a damn kid welcoming Santa Claus on Christmas Eve.

The guy Pete'd been hearing so much about stepped inside dressed in khakis and a dark brown rain jacket. Definitely the man from Facebook and not either of the two from the police database. So far, so good.

Zoe flung her arms around his neck, and he slipped one around her waist. In his other hand, he held a four-pack of beer. "Something smells incredible."

She released her grip on him. "It's just meatloaf."

"I love meatloaf." He turned toward Pete, a nervous smile on his face.

Zoe clung to her brother's arm. "Jason, this is Pete Adams."

Pete extended a hand.

Jason had to ease free of Zoe's hold to grasp it. The guy had a good grip. Strong, but not one of those testosterone-driven hand crushers.

"I've been looking forward to meeting you." Jason looked him square in the eye and held out the four-pack. "I know it's traditional to bring wine to dinner, but I got the impression you're more of a beer kinda guy."

Pete examined the gift. A dunkel from Pittsburgh's Hofbrauhaus. Not too shabby. "Thanks."

With the initial ice broken, Zoe took Jason's coat, hung it on the hall tree behind the door, and ordered the men to sit at the table and drink the brew while she mashed potatoes and made gravy. Pete noted she didn't send them off to the living room where she wouldn't be able to keep an eye on them.

Jason leaned back in his chair, giving Pete a long appraising look.

"So, you're the man who's won my sister's heart."

"So, you're the man who claims to be her brother."

From the corner of his eye, Pete noticed Zoe wheel toward them, a wooden spoon clenched in her fist.

But Jason laughed an easy, full-throated chuckle. He aimed the long neck of his bottle toward Pete as if to toast him. "True. I appreciate a man who doesn't simply take things at face value." Jason took a slug from the bottle. Swallowed. "Do you want to test my DNA?"

The word "yes" was on Pete's tongue, but he choked it back.

"Seriously." Jason reached to his head as if to pluck a strand of his blond hair. "I'll give you a sample. Not a problem."

Pete didn't need to look at Zoe to see the threat of anger in her eyes. The tension coming off her body radiated from across the room. "That won't be necessary. However, I do have a few questions."

"I have a few for you too, but it's only fair that you go first."

Zoe slowly returned to her cooking.

"Where are you from?" Pete asked.

"I grew up near Philadelphia. A town called Abington." Jason went on to tell Pete what he already knew. How his birth mother had been shipped off to the east where he'd been born and adopted.

Pete listened and studied the man. He appeared relaxed on the surface, but Pete sensed he was covering an underlying nervous edge. Not surprising. Pete would have been more concerned if the guy wasn't even slightly anxious. Appearance-wise, Jason matched his online photos. But did he have any familial resemblance to Zoe? She thought so, but Pete didn't see it. Then again, he and Nadine didn't look anything alike. She resembled their mother. He took after Harry.

"I was finally able to track down my birth mother and found out about our dad." Jason cast a smile toward Zoe.

"What's her name?" Pete asked.

"Huh?" Jason brought his attention back to Pete.

"Your birth mother. What's her name?"

Jason held his gaze without blinking. "Brenda Patterson."

Pete made a mental note to check out Ms. Patterson. "And how'd you find Zoe?"

"My birth mom told me my father's name." Another glance at Zoe. "*Our* father's name. Gary Chambers. It only took a couple minutes to find his obituary on record, including his next of kin. I was disappointed to learn he'd died but thrilled to find out I had a sister."

All of which made perfect sense.

"You don't believe me?"

"I'm just being cautious."

"Fair enough."

"Tell me about your work," Pete said.

Jason took a long draw on his bottle of brew. "No."

Pete blinked. "No?"

"I think it's my turn to ask some questions." Jason set the bottle down and came forward, planting his elbows on the table. "What are your intentions toward my sister?"

A muffled laugh came from the direction of the stove.

Pete searched the man's face for some sign he was joking. This guy had been in Zoe's life for a matter of days and was sitting here at Pete's kitchen table questioning his intentions? But Jason's gaze held steady. His lips didn't twitch into a grin. "I asked her to marry me." Pete looked toward Zoe's back as she drained the potato water into the sink.

"Did she accept?"

"Not exactly."

Which prompted her to turn away from the sink. "Hey. 'She' is standing right here."

Jason flapped a hand at her. "You just go back to what you're doing. The men folk are discussing your future."

She hiccupped a sarcastic laugh. "Really?"

Jason snickered.

Pete forced a grin. This easy rapport between the two of them bugged the hell out of him. He knew it shouldn't. He knew he was being petty.

"Maybe I should be asking you," Jason said to Zoe. "What are your intentions toward the chief here?"

She stood with her mouth gaping for a moment, then scowled and turned back to her potatoes. "None of your business."

Jason chuckled, picked up his beer, and winked at Pete. "You have your hands full, dude."

"Tell me about it."

The conversation remained light while Zoe finished mashing the potatoes and removed the meatloaf from the oven. As they dived into the meal, they settled into a good-natured debate over Pittsburgh's sports teams versus Philadelphia's followed by Philly cheese steaks versus Primanti Brothers. Pete noticed Zoe kept out of the discussion, but merely ate with a contented smile.

Which made him feel even guiltier about his distrust of Jason Cox. Pete hadn't seen her this blissfully happy in ages. If ever.

By the time Zoe brought out the bakery-bought apple pie she'd picked up on their way home from the funeral, they'd run out of cross-state-rivalry small talk.

"How's the barn roof coming along?" Zoe asked.

"Tarpaper and wood stripping's done. I bought steel roofing instead of shingles."

"Whoa," she said. "That stuff's expensive, isn't it?"

"Not in the long run. It'll last way longer than the cheaper stuff. You know what they say—you get what you pay for." Jason caught Pete's eye. "I could use a hand getting the stuff up there."

"I can help you once we're done here," Zoe said.

"Uh-uh. That stuff is awkward and heavy. I don't want to risk having you fall off the ladder."

Was there something more in Jason's expression as he and Pete locked eyes? A challenge? Had he thrown down a gauntlet?

"I'm stronger than I look." Zoe either hadn't noticed the staring contest or was ignoring it.

Jason didn't blink. "I'd rather have Pete help me."

She put down her fork. "Why? I'm perfectly capable. I climb up and down out of the hayloft every day. I sling bales of hay. Every day."

Jason broke the eye contact with Pete and held up a hand at Zoe. "Whoa there. I wasn't implying you aren't capable. I just—"

But she was on a roll. "And it's my farm."

Jason rested his arms on the table, leaning toward her. "Listen. If Pete truly intends to marry you, I just think he ought to be willing to invest a little labor in the place."

"Pete's pulling double shifts at work because he has an officer on leave," Zoe said.

Now Pete was the one who wanted to point out he was still in the room. Before he had a chance, her phone rang.

"Excuse me." She stood and pointed a finger at Pete and then at Jason. "Play nice."

After Zoe had grabbed her phone from the microwave stand and disappeared into the living room, Pete turned to Jason. "Don't you dare let her try to help with those steel sheets."

"I wasn't planning to."

"If you're trying to make me look bad in front of her—"

Jason held up a hand to Pete, same as he'd done a moment ago with Zoe. "I'm not. I'm simply trying to find out how invested you are in my sister's dream."

"Her dream?"

"I've only been around a few days and already I can tell how much she wants to fix up her farm and make a home of it. But I have a feeling you'd be happier if she sold the farm and her horse and just played the happy homemaker here in your house."

Jason's words struck a guilty chord inside Pete's head. Although he'd never suggest she sell her horse, the rest was painfully close to the truth.

Zoe saved him from having to respond to Jason's assessment by breezing back into the room. "That was Wayne. There's been a development on Kinney's homicide and I have to go to Golden Oaks."

The mention of Harry's home tied a knot in Pete's chest.

Zoe must have sensed it. She looked at him. "Your father's fine. Wayne said they found the evidence tying Daryl Oliverio to the crime."

Jason popped what was left of his dessert into his mouth and picked up his plate. "I'll do the dishes."

Pete reached across the table to take the plate. "No, you won't. I've got it."

Jason maintained his grasp on the dinnerware.

What the hell? Were they going to play tug of war now?

Zoe sighed in exasperation. "Will you two alpha males crank down the testosterone level please?"

Jason released the plate.

She walked over to him and kissed him on his cheek. "Thank you. I'll meet you at the farm tomorrow morning to help with the roofing." She circled the table to plant a kiss on Pete's lips that ratcheted the temperature of his blood up to a simmer. Standing on her toes, she brought her mouth and her breath to his ear. "Behave," she whispered.

She exchanged her moccasins for her heels, grabbed her coat, and darted out the door, still wearing that curve-revealing dress. Damn. Baronick was going to have trouble concentrating on the case once she got there.

"I was serious about helping clean up."

Pete crossed his arms. "Zoe's gone. You don't have to try to earn brownie points with her anymore."

Jason mirrored his crossed-arms pose. "I'm not trying to earn anything. Whether you like it or not, she's my sister."

Pete glared at him. Longed for Jason to give him an excuse to slug him. And then remembered another dinner a number of years ago. The dinner when Nadine had brought her future—now ex—husband to meet the family. Pete hadn't acted all that differently toward his younger sister's boyfriend than Jason was acting toward Pete.

Except Pete had been Nadine's older brother for a couple of decades at the time.

"Well, I offered," Jason said. "You don't want my help? Fine. You're on your own doing the dishes." Jason stepped away, retrieved his coat from the hall tree, and reached for the doorknob. "And just so you know, there's no way I'd allow Zoe to handle those sheets of roofing."

"Damn straight," Pete growled. "I'll be the one helping you at the farm tomorrow morning."

Trace evidence of a smile flitted across the man's self-satisfied face. "See you then."

Pete stood alone in the silence of his house and looked down at the plate and fork in his hand. The fork Zoe's brother had licked clean.

The fork that contained a healthy dose of Jason Cox's DNA.

EIGHTEEN

Zoe maneuvered her pickup around three police cruisers parked in front of Golden Oaks. A fourth car, a dark sedan with no fancy trim and no markings, had to be Wayne's.

Inside, an officer stood near the door. A quartet of residents in the Bistro appeared unaware of a police presence. Several others gathered in the sitting area, keeping an eye on the cop or gazing out the window at the vehicles.

Zoe identified herself to the sentry as acting county coroner. He took in her high heels and her dress, making no effort to hide his skepticism. She wished she could give him a whiff of the morning's autopsy aroma that still clung inside her nostrils. "If you don't believe me, call Detective Wayne Baronick."

Apparently, invoking the lead detective's name was enough. The officer directed her to the rear of the building, past the elevator and the stairs. "Down the hallway to the left."

She located Wayne, Connie Smith, and a City of Brunswick officer near a door at the end of the hallway. The detective looked up and whistled when she approached. Her cheeks warmed, and she covered with a snarky retort. "Don't be a sexist pig, Baronick."

He shrugged. "If it walks like a duck and talks like a duck..."

The facility director looked from Zoe to Wayne, uncertainty in her eyes.

"Don't mind us," Zoe said. To Wayne she asked, "What's going on? You said there was a break in the case."

"Ms. Smith reported she'd received an anonymous phone call strongly suggesting she check Daryl Oliverio's locker. I obtained a warrant." He thumbed toward the open door. "They just broke the lock and started searching."

Zoe gazed past Wayne and Connie. Two officers were digging through a locker. Another cop stood next to an anxious Daryl Oliverio.

One of the officers looked their way. "Detective Baronick. You're gonna want to see this."

Zoe followed Wayne inside. The officer who'd beckoned held up a jacket very similar to the one their suspect on the security footage had been wearing. And a Pirates baseball cap.

Oliverio's face flushed. "That's not mine."

Wayne took the jacket and held it up by the shoulders, facing Oliverio. "Looks about the right size to me."

"I'm tellin' you, man. That ain't mine."

Wayne handed it back to the officer, who stuffed both items in a brown paper evidence bag. "Do you mind coming down to the station with us to answer some questions?"

"Yeah, I mind. I'm workin'."

Connie joined them in the locker room. "No, you aren't. Effective immediately, you're on leave."

"But I need this job. And that ain't my stuff. Someone's framing me."

"I hope so, Daryl." She shook her head and walked away.

Wayne nodded to the county officer. "Take him in. I'll question him as soon as we're done here."

Zoe watched them go, the image of Daryl Oliverio's shocked expression when they'd pulled out that jacket and cap stuck in her mind. The other officers continued to dig through the locker, bagging its contents.

Wayne ambled to her side. "I bet you're eager to tell Pete we've arrested Kinney's killer and he can quit worrying about his father."

"You're convinced you have the right man?"

"Aren't you?"

"I don't know."

Wayne crossed his arms. "Why not?"

"He looked more surprised than anyone when you pulled that jacket out of his locker."

"He's a good actor."

"I guess."

"You've seen him get confrontational with the victim. You were with me the day in the Bistro when he blew up and stormed out." Wayne reached over and slapped her on the shoulder. "Even old man Adams pronounced him guilty."

"Yes, and Harry is such a reliable resource." She watched the officers work for another few moments. "You don't need me here, do you?"

"No. I just thought you'd want to be present when we tied up this case."

Zoe shot him a look. "You be sure to call me when you do that." She pivoted on the balls of her high-heeled feet and sauntered away.

"I did," he shouted after her.

Her shoes were beginning to take a toll, so she took the elevator rather than the stairs to the second floor. Halfway down the hall to Harry's room, she found him deep in conversation with a man wearing dark glasses and carrying a slim white cane.

"Hello, Harry," she said as she approached.

He looked toward her. The other man didn't. Harry smiled. "Hello, Sunshine."

She kissed him on his cheek. "I wanted to let you know Pete will be in tomorrow to visit."

Harry's face lit up. "You know my boy?"

"I do. Quite well, actually."

He made a point of checking her out and grinning. "He's a lucky man."

The old flirt.

Harry grew serious. "I'm glad he'll be in tomorrow." He tipped his head toward the blind gentleman. "Arnie has some information Pete needs to hear."

"Ernie," the man said. "And I really don't want to get involved."

"My boy's a good cop. I told you, he's working on this case. You're a witness."

A blind man as a witness? "What kind of information?" Zoe asked.

The man squirmed. "I don't want to get anyone in trouble."

Harry huffed. "Do you want a killer to go free?"

"I prefer to mind my own business. Keeps me out of hot water."

Harry turned to Zoe, his jaw clenched. "Will you tell Pete that Arnie knows who killed that other guy? What was his name?"

"Ernie," the man corrected.

"No, that wasn't it."

"John Kinney?" Zoe asked.

"Yeah." Harry nodded. "Him."

"But I don't know. I told you that. I just overheard John and someone else arguing."

Zoe blinked. "What exactly did you overhear?"

Ernie shook his head adamantly. "I don't want to start rumors. If I must, I'll talk to Harry's son. But nobody else. Now please. Just leave me alone." He extended his cane, whacking Zoe in the shin.

She bit back a yelp and stepped out of the man's way.

Harry reached out to touch her arm. "Are you okay?"

Zoe smiled to reassure him. "Bruised but not broken." She watched the blind witness finger a door before opening it and vanishing inside the room. She should go downstairs and get Wayne. But she'd seen the detective in action. If he steamrolled over the old man, they'd never get any answers. He'd already said he'd speak to Pete.

A young woman in a Golden Oaks polo shirt appeared at the end of the hall and paused at one of the doors. She smiled in their direction. "It's about time for supper, Harry. You'd better start down to the dining room."

He waved at her. "Thank you." Once the woman entered the room, Harry grinned sheepishly. "Do you happen to know how to get to the dining room? I've managed to get myself a little bit lost."

"I do." She reached a hand to him.

He one-upped her with his own arm. She tucked her hand into the crook of his elbow and they strolled toward the elevator. "You will make sure Pete comes tomorrow, won't you?"

"Absolutely."

Harry hugged his arm and her hand closer to his side. "And you'll come with him?"

She wasn't about to miss hearing what this new witness had to say. "Count on it."

Pete managed a couple hours of slumber Saturday night after Nate Williamson, his regular weekend officer, took over the shift at four a.m. Any hopes he'd had of sleeping in were quashed when Zoe shook him awake at eight with talk of a new "witness."

She called Jason from the passenger seat on the drive to Brunswick. "Pete'll be there to help with the barn roof as soon as we're done at Golden Oaks." After she ended the call, she picked up Pete's phone from the console. "I'm adding Jason's number to your contacts in case you need to call him about running late or something." She hiked an eyebrow at Pete. "Do *not* be late."

Pete sighed. "I wouldn't dream of it."

They tracked down Harry in his room, tying his sneakers. He looked up when they entered, and a smile lit his face. "Well, hello.

What a nice surprise." With one last tug on the laces, he stood to accept Zoe's hug and Pete's handshake. "What brings you here?"

Zoe hooked an arm through Harry's. "You told me to bring Pete to talk to Ernie."

"I did?" Harry's eyes shifted, searching his failing memory. He either found what he was looking for or faked it. "Of course, I did."

Pete suspected the latter. "Do you want to take us to see him, Pop?"

That vacant look again. "I'm not sure where he lives."

"I know," Zoe said.

"Wonderful. Lead on, young lady."

Pete handed Harry his cane and fell in behind the two of them.

They'd almost reached the elevator when Zoe stopped at a room. "This is it." She pointed at a small plate next to the closed door. A plate none of the other rooms had. Braille. She rapped lightly.

After a moment, there were some scuffing noises from inside. A click. And the door swung open revealing a man Pete guessed was in his late eighties, who wasn't wearing the tell-tale dark glasses of the vision impaired but was clutching a skinny white cane. "Yes?"

"Hey, Arnie." Harry stepped forward to put a hand on the man's arm. "It's me. Harry Adams. I brought my son the cop to talk to you."

"It's Ernie." The old man had the appearance of someone who's developed a hard shell to survive in a world not designed for him. From the tone of his voice, he'd been tolerating and correcting Harry's misuse of his name for a long time. "And I'd really rather forget the whole thing. I'm sorry you made the trip for nothing."

Pete glanced at Zoe. She'd warned him about the man's hesitance to cause trouble and made an I-told-you-so face.

"Oh, come on," Harry said. "You might have the information they need to crack this case wide open."

"We've already arrested a suspect," Zoe told Ernie.

"Good. You don't need me after all."

"On the contrary. You might be able to confirm what we already think happened, or you might help clear an innocent man of homicide charges." She spoke quietly, a note of pleading in her voice.

Ernie's stony expression softened. Zoe had a way with these old folks. "Well..."

"May we come in?" Pete asked.

The old man considered it a moment longer then stepped aside.

The room was filled with genuine antiques unlike the reproduced items that decorated the rest of the facility. Ernie crossed to a wood-and-leather easy chair with practiced ease. His fingers grazed the wide, flat armrests before he lowered into it. Pete pulled a battered footstool directly in front of the old man and sat on it.

Harry remained with Zoe just inside the door. "Tell Pete what you told me."

Ernie folded his cane and tucked it next to his thigh. "It was probably nothing. I heard John call out to someone. You know. 'Hey. You.' That sort of thing. It sounded like he was coming toward me and I thought he was talking to me. But I heard footsteps and felt someone pass me. That was who John was hollering at. I got the feeling the person didn't want to be bothered because John said it two or three times."

Ernie fell silent. Pete waited and after a minute considered asking, "is that it?"

Harry shuffled toward them. "Don't stop there. Tell him the rest."

The blind man fingered his cane. "John started saying, 'I know you. I know you. How do I know you?' He was hounding the guy, you know?"

"Yeah." Pete could picture the stubborn, gruff retired officer browbeating someone, especially if that someone was being evasive. "Did you hear what the other person replied?"

"Not at first. I think he was pretending he didn't hear John. But John must have caught up to him. When he did speak, I couldn't make out most of what he said."

"Were you too far away?" Pete asked.

"No. Thankfully, I have very good hearing. Compensates for my eyes." He tapped his temple. "I think he was just mumbling. Seemed like he didn't want to talk to John. Or maybe he didn't want to talk to anyone."

"You said you didn't hear him 'at first.' What about later?"

"When John didn't let up, the other man raised his voice and said, 'Back off, old man.' Or something to that effect."

"Did he? Back off, I mean."

"As I recall, John said, 'Now I remember how I know you.' But all I heard after that was footsteps, so I assume the other man left."

"Where did all this happen?"

"Downstairs near the front door. I had been playing the piano and was on my way to the elevator. I believe John was coming from the dining room. Or maybe the Bistro."

A memory whispered in Pete's ear, stirring a chill at the base of his brain. He looked over at Zoe who was chewing her lip. "When was this?" he asked the piano-playing blind man.

"Almost a week ago. Monday morning."

Zoe's baby blues widened.

Pete leaned closer to Ernie. "Did you happen to recognize the other man's voice?"

"No. Never heard it before."

"Are you sure?" Zoe asked.

"Very." He tapped his temple again. "I've learned to compensate for my blindness. As I mentioned, I have excellent hearing. I play the piano by ear. You hum the song, and I can play it. And I'm better at remembering voices than most people are at remembering faces."

"Would you recognize it if you heard it again?"

"Absolutely."

"Excuse me," Zoe said. "Ernie, do you know Daryl Oliverio?"

"Gladys' grandson? Yes."

"Could he have been the man you overheard?"

"No. Definitely not."

Pete thanked him for his time, replaced the footstool where he'd found it, and escorted Harry and Zoe out of the room.

"Did that help you with your case?" Harry asked.

"Yep, it did, Pop."

They walked with Harry downstairs to the dining room where breakfast was being served. After saying their goodbyes, they stepped out into the April sunshine and Pete caught her arm. "Ernie was playing the piano when we were having coffee with Kinney."

"I remember. The confrontation between John Kinney and Ernie's mystery man must've happened right after we left."

"Kinney recognized him. If Ernie never forgets a voice, Kinney's the one who never forgot a face. If he was having trouble putting a name to this one, it was someone he hadn't seen in while."

Zoe's eyes narrowed in thought. "Or someone who disguised their appearance."

"Or that. One thing's for sure. Kinney was like a dog with a bone. If he thought he knew this person, he wouldn't let go until he figured out who the guy was."

Zoe didn't respond. Pete suspected she was thinking the same thing he was. Kinney's dogged determination and photographic memory for faces may have been the motive for his murder.

NINETEEN

Zoe phoned Wayne as she and Pete left Golden Oaks with a request to view more of the videos from the security cams. Then she insisted Pete drop her off and go help her brother with the roof. Pete didn't complain, and she wasn't sure if that was a good thing or a bad one.

At least she and Jason had bonded sufficiently. Pete shouldn't scare him off.

She hoped.

Wayne leaned against the front counter inside Monongahela County Police Headquarters, waiting for her and clutching a venti Starbucks. Instead of his usual suit and tie, he wore a pair of faded jeans and a sweatshirt. He also wore a dark scowl on his face.

Except for the miffed expression, Zoe kind of liked the new look. "You should wear jeans more often."

"I do. On Sundays. When I'm not on duty."

"Sorry. But I may have some information about John Kinney's homicide."

"Have you forgotten? We made an arrest. The world of Golden Oaks is safe from the Baseball Cap Man."

"We may have the wrong guy."

"Why do you keep saying that?"

She'd wanted to see the video and get a few answers for herself before telling Wayne about the new witness. But the detective, his arms crossed, didn't display any willingness to indulge her whims. She told him about the threatening conversation Ernie had overheard and how he was convinced the man Kinney had confronted was *not* Daryl Oliverio.

Wayne eyed her skeptically. "Your new witness is blind?"

"And very convincing."

The detective didn't blink.

"Come on. What can it hurt to view the footage and find out who Kinney was arguing with?"

Wayne glared at her. "I liked you better when you were just a paramedic." He pushed away from the counter and turned toward the desk sergeant. "Give her a pass."

A few minutes later, with her visitor's badge clipped to her Monongahela County EMS t-shirt, she followed Wayne down the hallway to the same room where they'd viewed the security footage last week. She told the tech to pull up the camera at the Bistro and the approximate time they'd been there—around a quarter after nine in the morning.

Wayne leaned back in his chair and slurped his coffee.

Zoe had made a good guess. The camera trained on the Bistro caught the four of them entering around the nine fifteen mark. "Okay. Fast-forward until we get up to leave."

Minutes passed while she watched the sped-up footage. She hadn't noticed how much she used her hands when she spoke until she watched them flapping at high speed. The woman behind the counter zipped in to deliver coffee and zipped back to her post. Finally, they rose.

"Stop it there and play it at normal speed," Zoe told the tech.

Wayne issued a loud and obnoxious yawn.

She glared at him. "Why don't you go make popcorn?"

"I'm fine."

Pete shook hands with Kinney and his father. Zoe hugged both older men. Harry tottered out of the frame, away from the front door. Kinney remained at the edge of the frame, watching Pete and Zoe exit. Then he turned to follow Harry.

Zoe lifted a hand to signal the tech to stop, but another figure entered the frame, moving toward the door, same as she and Pete had.

Wayne saw it too and came forward, suddenly wide awake. "Wait. Freeze that."

The black-and-white image on the screen showed the same unidentifiable mystery man they'd been pursuing for almost a week.

Zoe blew out a breath. "Okay. There he is. Baseball Cap Man." But was he the same guy that Ernie had overheard? "I need the other camera angles on the entryway"

The tech pecked at the keyboard and brought up the camera over the door, placed to capture anyone leaving the facility.

Zoe pointed at the screen. "Now back it up."

After a few tweaks, he played the video.

Pete and Zoe left the building. John Kinney's back was to the camera as he watched them go. He turned, shuffled toward the camera and under it, out of view. At that point, Baseball Cap Man entered the frame from the seating area side, moving toward the exit doors. As always, he kept his face shielded from the camera. He reached for the door and stopped. Kinney stomped back into the picture, clearly addressing their suspect, who kept his back turned.

"That must have been when Ernie heard John calling to the guy. 'I know you.'" Zoe caught her lip between her teeth.

Wayne grunted.

Baseball Cap Man turned. Slowly. His face lowered, the bill of his hat blocking any chance to glimpse his features.

"Son of a bitch," Wayne muttered.

Zoe didn't need sound to know what was being said. The blind man had already provided the dialogue. John Kinney shook a finger at the man. *"I know you. How do I know you?"*

Baseball Cap Man had been motionless once he'd turned. Afraid to make a move and show his face? But then he leaned toward Kinney. Menacingly. *"Back off, old man."* He brushed past Kinney, who pivoted and hobbled after him.

Zoe and Wayne sat in silence a moment. Had the room grown chilly? Or had Zoe's blood turned cold?

When Wayne spoke again to the tech, his voice was low and tense. "Give us the view from the front room sitting area. And start back at the nine fifteen mark."

Zoe looked at him. Nine fifteen? They'd been up to nine forty-five. But she kept her questions to herself. From Wayne's tone, he had something in mind.

And that something quickly became apparent. A minute or so into the footage that showed roughly a dozen residents gathered to listen to Ernie play the piano, Baseball Cap Man strolled in. If she didn't already know the man was a killer, she wouldn't have paid any attention to him.

In fact, she hadn't. He'd been sitting only yards from her that morning. In plain view if she'd only known to look. Every few minutes, he'd turn his head ever so slightly toward the Bistro, but never revealed his face to the camera. "He's keeping an eye on Kinney."

Wayne made a sound like the growl of a bear. "Yeah."

She watched the rest of the video—different angle, but same result—in silence. The killer had been stalking his prey and was about to leave until his victim recognized him.

When they reached the end of the sequence, the tech hit pause. When neither Zoe nor Wayne spoke, he asked, "Do you want me to pull up any other views?"

Zoe expected the detective to go in search of Kinney or Baseball Cap Man or both. Instead, Wayne rubbed his eyes and heaved a sigh. "Not right now. I have something I have to do first. Go grab some lunch."

Lunch? Zoe checked her watch. Almost noon. Crap.

The tech logged out of the computer and left the room, but Wayne didn't budge.

"What do you have to do first?" she asked.

"I have to go over to Golden Oaks and talk to your blind witness. I want to make sure his hearing's as trustworthy as you seem to believe."

"It is." She had no doubt. "And that means Daryl Oliverio isn't our guy. Ernie would've recognized Daryl's voice. And John wouldn't have said 'How do I know you' to one of the regular employees."

Wayne grunted.

Zoe stared at the paused image on the monitor and thought back to something Pete had mentioned. "What about Boyd Anderson?"

The change in direction caught Wayne off guard. "Who?"

"Pete arrested him a week ago for assaulting Kinney's brother-in-law with a corn knife."

"Oh. Him. What about him?"

"Pete told me Kinney had arrested him once."

"When?"

"I don't know. Pete just said when Boyd was younger."

Wayne didn't appear impressed. "Kinney was a cop. He made a lot of enemies over the years. We've been looking at a lot of them. But an old arrest?" He shrugged. "I'll check him out though."

She continued gazing at but not really seeing the image on the monitor. "There's one other thing I can't quite shake."

Wayne looked at her.

"How," she asked, "did the baseball cap and jacket get into Daryl Oliverio's locker?"

After some initial swearing and bickering about the best method to transfer the sheets of green metal from the bed of Jason's truck onto the barn roof, and after a heated debate about installing the material from the front of the barn to the back, left to right—Pete held out for left to right—they'd developed a rhythm to their work.

Pete envied how fluidly the other man moved—kneeling, crawling, squatting—in spite of the steepness of the roof's pitch. Pete's own knees were screaming, and he and Jason were less than halfway done with one side. Pete shrugged off the jacket he no longer needed since the sun had turned the roof into a griddle. He removed his cell phone from its pocket, propped the phone against one of the wooden strips Jason had nailed over the tarpaper, and folded the jacket into a pad for one knee while using the tread of his other boot as a brake.

"So, do you like being a cop?"

Jason's question came out of nowhere and stopped Pete with his finger on the power drill's trigger.

"Yeah, I do." Pete squeezed the trigger and zipped the screw home.

"Why?"

He preferred it when Zoe's brother worked in silence. "What do you mean?"

Jason crouched near the peak, holding the panel firm. "I thought it was a simple question. Why do you like being a cop?"

Pete gave the query some thought. "I've never considered doing anything else. I like being able to help and protect people." He ran another screw into the roof. "I feel I'm making a difference." Another screw. "And there's never a dull moment." He chuckled. "Except for the paperwork."

Jason powered in the rest of the vertical row of fasteners and repositioned for the next one. "Making a difference," he echoed. "Have you ever considered the difference you make might not be for the better?"

Pete looked up at Jason expecting to see a challenge in his eyes. But his gaze was steady. Either the guy had a hell of a poker face or he was simply making conversation. "What exactly are you getting at?"

Jason lined up a trio of the roofing screws between his teeth and spoke from the other side of his mouth. "Have you ever shot someone you later wish you hadn't?"

Pete thought of the two times he'd discharged his weapon and taken a life. The same two he'd talked to Seth about a couple days ago. He might have wished things had gone another way, but both times, he managed to save lives by stopping the threat. "No," he said.

Jason nodded thoughtfully. "Okay. Have you ever sent someone to prison who didn't deserve it?"

Pete bristled. "I don't send people to prison. The courts do that." He took out his aggravation on the next three screws, driving them too far into the metal and mashing the gasket. "Dammit." He forced down his ire and backed the screws out a quarter turn.

Jason eased his way down the slope. "So, you lay the blame on the courts?"

What the hell was this guy's problem? "Do you have personal issues with law enforcement as a whole or just with me?"

"I'm only trying to get a better sense of who you are. My sister thinks you're one of the good guys, but where I grew up, the cops I encountered were megalomaniacal bastards."

Pete had a snarky retort on his lips. But reconsidered. He took a breath. "There are good and bad in every profession. Mine included. And yeah, the idea of carrying a weapon can lure those power-hungry types. I like to think the officers who are sincerely trying to do good work in their communities outnumber the ones you had the misfortune to run into."

Jason gazed into the distance, his jaw working as if chewing on Pete's words. After a few moments he nodded. "Fair enough." He leaned down and zipped in the last screw of that row.

They shifted to the next. Jason crab walked back up to the peak. Pete eased to the right and down, closer to the edge.

The sole of his boot, the one giving him traction, settled on something—a stray screw or two perhaps—that rolled, taking his foot with it. His knee slammed the shiny, slick metal. And slid. A flash of pain knifed through his patella. He scrambled to gain purchase. The power drill sailed from his grasp. Loosed screws skittered down the slope. And he wasn't far behind.

The edge, already close, rushed up at him. Neither his jeans nor the jacket still pinned under one knee slowed his descent. Dragging his fingers, his palms, along the steel didn't help. For one fleeting moment, he saw himself sprawled on the earth beside the barn. Broken. Zoe standing over him. Hysterical.

A hand latched onto his wrist. He looked up. Away from the inevitable drop. Into Jason's wide blue eyes. But instead of stopping the plunge, Jason was belly-sliding too. They were both careening over.

And then they jolted to a stop.

Suspended there, Pete remembered to breathe. His legs hung in midair. The razor-sharp edge of the steel sheets sliced into his thighs. Jason clung to Pete's arm with a vice-like grip. Zoe's brother's face had lost all color. Except for maybe a tinge of green. He spread-eagled above Pete, motionless.

"What stopped us?" Pete asked, his voice sticking in his throat.

Jason swallowed. "My foot."

Pete started to turn his head to see what Jason's foot had snagged. "Don't move," he choked.

Pete froze, but shifted his eyes. In his peripheral vision, he could see the only thing keeping them from skiing off the roof was the toe of Jason's boot caught on the wooden strapping where the next metal sheet should go.

Pete closed his eyes and swore. The honest truth was the only thing keeping *Jason* from skiing off the roof was his boot on the wood strapping. The only thing saving Pete was Jason's hold on his wrist.

And from the agonized grimace on Jason's face, the strain of supporting a combined weight of close to four hundred pounds was rapidly taking a toll on his ankle.

Pete looked around for his cell phone. It remained where he'd set it—which was now above him. He reached for it. Strained.

"Stop. Moving," Jason said.

The phone remained beyond the tips of Pete's fingers. "Can you reach it?"

"My hands are a little full at the moment."

"What about your phone?"

"You mean the one that's on the charger down in my truck?"

Dammit. Pete gritted his teeth. "Let me go."

"No."

"If you don't, we're both going down."

"Shut up."

"If you let me go, you can save yourself and call 911 for me."

"Just shut the hell up already."

"Don't be stupid."

"If you don't shut up, I'm gonna punch you in the face with my free hand."

Either their predicament, his impending demise, or the mental picture of Jason slugging him under their current conditions struck Pete as funny. He chuckled.

"Stop that." Jason's voice took on a higher pitch. "It's hard enough to hold onto you without you shaking. Besides. *It's not funny.*"

He was right. But so was Pete. Jason needed to let go. The fall would be roughly two-stories. He'd land in the muddy slop surrounding the barn courtesy of non-existent gutters. Although, it hadn't rained in a few days and the mud was drying up.

"By the way," Pete said. "You were right."

"About what?"

"If we'd worked right to left, we wouldn't have had to stand on the steel sheets."

"If we live, I'll tell you I told you so."

Pete needed to do something to get them out of this predicament. He bent one knee up. If he could get a grip with his boot somehow...

"Stop. Moving."

"We can't stay here all afternoon." Hell, Jason's toe and ankle probably weren't going to hold them for another five minutes.

Jason shushed him. "Listen."

"What?"

"Just listen."

The faint rumble of a motor mingled with the birdsongs and the breeze-induced rattle of the big maple's branches, still sporting buds instead of leaves. If Pete wasn't mistaken, a Chevy motor. An older Chevy motor that sounded a lot like Zoe's. Except he'd dropped her off in Brunswick at the county police HQ.

It felt like an hour before the approaching truck appeared around the bend although Pete knew it was less than a minute. He'd have to twist to see the vehicle, which wasn't a good idea at the moment.

But Jason lifted his head. "It's Zoe."

Pete could tell the moment she saw and recognized their situation because the throaty rumble turned into a gas-guzzling roar.

The pickup churned into the driveway and skidded to a stop behind the two vehicles already parked there. Pete couldn't see but imagined her diving out. He could hear the muffled pounding of her boots, the little cry bursting from her throat.

"Are you okay?"

"Get the ladder," he grunted.

"I am."

The aluminum extension ladder banged against the edge of the roof not yet covered in shiny new steel. She clanked up the rungs, and in another moment, her beautiful blonde head appeared. "What in the...?"

Jason shot her a panicked smile. "Hey, Sis."

Pete could only imagine what must be going through her mind.

She scrambled the rest of the way up and in a matter of seconds, dragged him by his belt over onto the tarpaper. Jason managed to rescue himself once he'd released Pete's wrist.

The three of them sat on the roof in a row with Pete in the middle, their feet braced firmly on the wooden strips, breathing hard and allowing their heart rates to settle. Zoe still clutched a handful of his t-shirt as if afraid to let go.

Jason broke the silence with a low chuckle.

Pete looked at him. "*Now* you think it's funny?"

Zoe's brother shook his head, either responding in the negative or out of sheer disbelief. Or both. "I have one thing to say to you."

"Only one?"

"For now." Jason held up one finger. "You need to lose some weight, dude."

Zoe squeaked out a short, hysterical laugh. A million emotions and retorts played across her face, but she clamped her mouth shut and shook her head. "I brought lunch." She pushed up to a squat. "Please be careful coming down."

After Zoe had clanked down the ladder, Jason started to rise.

Pete caught his arm. "Hey. Thanks."

"Forget about it."

"Tell me something. Why didn't you let me go?"

Jason fixed him with an acerbic glare. "You wanted to fall off a roof and break your back today?"

Pete ignored the sarcasm. "We didn't know Zoe was on her way. The smart thing to do would have been to save yourself."

Jason looked out across the farm country and appeared to give the question deep consideration before bringing his gaze back to Pete. "Because of Zoe. This is her farm. One day, it'll be her home. I didn't want her living the rest of her life with the memory of you dying here."

TWENTY

Zoe sat on her lowered tailgate flanked by her brother on one side and Pete on the other and looked across the expanse of spring-green grass to the row of *Re-elect Franklin Marshall* signs at the far edge of her yard. She'd brought two bags from her favorite sandwich shop in Brunswick and had imagined a lovely little picnic on a lovely spring day. The first of many, she hoped. Approaching her driveway to see two men sprawled on her barn roof, on the verge of going over the edge wasn't part of the dream. She wasn't sure she'd ever get that picture out of her head.

The incident had ruined her appetite. However, it hadn't put a dent in either Pete's or Jason's. After splashing around at the inside water hydrant in what took the place of washing up, they'd bickered over who got which sandwich. Zoe thought they were going to launch into a game of rock, paper, scissors, but the decision didn't come to that.

"How'd you get home?" Pete asked around a mouthful of smoked ham on rye.

"Wayne gave me a lift back to your house. I got my truck and came here."

Jason swallowed and wiped his mouth. "May I say, Sister Dearest, that your timing is impeccable."

Pete held up his can of root beer. "Amen to that."

Zoe smiled to herself. His opinion of her brother seemed to have improved since Jason saved his life.

Pete took a swig and set the can down next to him. "What did you find out at headquarters?"

She'd completely forgotten the main reason she'd wanted to talk to him. "It looks like Daryl Oliverio isn't our guy." She told Pete about the video footage matching Ernie's story with the Baseball Cap Man. "Since Ernie insisted the voice he overheard wasn't Daryl..." She shrugged.

Pete didn't respond right away. Instead, he gazed toward the road. "What are you thinking?" she asked.

"Kinney knew his killer but hadn't seen him in a while."

"Professor K?"

"Maybe. But I'm thinking the neighbor."

"The Machete Man?"

Jason crumpled the paper that his sandwich had been wrapped in. "Who the hell are Professor K and the Machete Man?" He snorted. "Sounds like a bad '80s rock band."

Zoe had to admit Jason was right. "Professor Kristopher-with-a-K O'Keefe was the victim's brother-in-law who's a jerk. The Machete Man is the professor's neighbor who kinda went after him with a corn knife."

"A corn knife?"

"A machete by any other name is just as deadly," Pete said dryly.

"And this machete guy went after your old dude in the nursing home?"

"No," Zoe said. "He went after Professor K."

Jason leaned an elbow on the side of the pickup's bed. "I'm confused."

It was Pete's turn to snort. "Welcome to my world."

She tried to picture the farmer, who'd been protecting his horses from a citified clod, as a cold-blooded killer of an old man. "I have a hard time believing Boyd Anderson killed John Kinney."

"Why? Kinney arrested him years ago, so it might've taken him a while to place Anderson when he saw him again."

"But why go after him now?"

Pete wiped his mouth and balled the paper, stuffing it back in the empty bag. "Anderson learns their new neighbor was related to Kinney and learns where Kinney's staying. He wants to see what's become of the cop who put him away. Maybe that's all he intended to do. But then Kinney recognizes him and won't let it go. There's an argument. Things escalate, and Anderson ends up killing him." Pete picked up the second bag and peered inside. "Aren't you going to eat yours?"

"I'm not hungry."

He set the bag in her lap anyway. "Look. I know you're sympathetic to Anderson because he's a horseman." Pete reached over and gently caught her chin, turning her head to meet his eyes. He lowered his voice. "But you know better than anyone that not all horsemen are good guys."

She flashed back to a night of terror from more than a decade ago. A night she'd long tried to forget. "Point taken."

"All right then." Pete tapped the bag in her lap. "Eat." He turned away and slapped Jason on the shoulder. "We've wasted enough time. We still have a lot of work to get done. Let's go."

"Aye aye, Captain." Jason snapped off a salute and jumped down from the tailgate. "I mean Chief."

Zoe's cell phone burst out in Franklin's signature song from The Who. She ignored it. "You're *not* going back up there."

Pete eased down a little slower than Jason. "Sure, we are. We can't leave the job half done. It's supposed to rain, maybe even snow, tomorrow. And I'm on duty tonight so daylight's burning." He made a phone-to-ear gesture. "You'd better answer that."

She seriously considered spending the afternoon keeping her eyes on Pete and Jason. She'd been on that roof many times. There was no reason she couldn't help.

Except for the insistent question "Who Are You?" pulsating from her phone.

Pete squeezed her knee affectionately and strode away. "Thanks for lunch," he called over his shoulder.

"Don't worry. We'll be careful." Jason winked at her and followed Pete.

She watched them swagger toward the ladder. "You said that before." It hadn't comforted her then, and it sure didn't comfort her now. She swiped the green button on the screen. "Hello."

"I need your report on yesterday's autopsy." Franklin didn't sound any happier than he'd been the last time she saw him.

"I thought I'd swing by tomorrow—"

"Today. Now."

"Are you out of the hospital?"

"No, I'm not out of the hospital," he snipped. "If I was, I could handle it myself. Paulette is at my office waiting for you."

He hung up before she had a chance to ask him how much longer they planned to keep him. Which was probably just as well considering he'd been convinced they were discharging him two days ago.

Zoe hopped down from the tailgate, tossed the crumpled bag containing her sandwich into the truck's cab, and jogged across the soft—although no longer squishy—ground to the barn. Jason had already climbed the ladder to the roof. Pete had a foot on the bottom rung. "I have to go back to Brunswick to take care of some more paperwork for the coroner's office."

"Weren't you just there?" Jason called down to her.

"Yeah." She glanced at her over-twenty-year-old truck with its mismatched front fender. "If I have to keep running to town to fill in for Franklin, it might be cheaper to rent a room than to keep filling up my gas tank." She knew she shouldn't have said it the moment the mention of gas mileage slipped from her lips.

Pete shook his head. "You really should trade that old tank in on something newer and more fuel efficient."

They'd had this argument more times than she could count, but she couldn't part with the old beast. "Forget I said anything. Just please be careful."

The rest of the roofing job had been uneventful. By three fifteen, Pete had to leave for his afternoon shift although almost half of the second side remained unfinished. He suggested they use the blue tarp to cover it, but Jason insisted on staying to complete the project alone. Zoe's brother proved as stubborn as she was. No amount of arguing about safety swayed his decision.

Pete sped home, grabbed a quick shower, dressed in a clean uniform, and arrived at the station in time for Nate to report on the previous shift. Other than the usual complaints and traffic issues, Sunday in Vance Township had been quiet.

With a few spare minutes before Abby was scheduled to join him on duty, Pete poured a cup of coffee and pulled up Pittsburgh's police database on his computer. He hated to admit it, but Zoe had a valid point. Why would Anderson go after Kinney after all these years?

Once the database's search page loaded, he typed in Boyd Anderson's name and waited for the arrest record to come up. Pete had already seen it but had missed details the first time he searched Anderson's history. Maybe he'd overlooked something else too.

The bells on the front door jingled. "Hello?" Abby's voice floated down the hallway.

"I'm in my office."

She appeared in his doorway and knocked lightly on the jamb. "Reporting for duty, Boss."

Pete glanced at the clock at the bottom of his computer screen. 3:59. He wondered if she was really that punctual or if she'd sat in the parking lot, waiting for the start of the shift.

She must have noticed him checking the time. "I'm not late, am I?"

"Nope." He aimed a thumb at the pot in the corner. "Help yourself."

"Thanks, but I just had a cup on my way here. What's up?"

"I'm taking another look at Boyd Anderson."

Abby cocked her head. "Because of the professor?" She sounded like she already knew the answer.

"Because of John Kinney. The guy your brother arrested? Let's just say the case isn't as solid as it once was."

She nodded at his computer. "Are you having any luck?"

"Not really." Pete looked over the monitor at his newest officer. "How well do you know your way around the social media sites?"

The Baronick grin spread across her lips. On her, it appeared less obnoxious. "Pretty well. Do you want me to see what I can find out about him?"

Pete checked the time again. Four o'clock on a Sunday afternoon. "Later. Right now I think we should work on a more personal approach. Let's go chat up Anderson's neighbors."

"The O'Keefes?"

"No. We already know how they feel about him. Let's get a more diverse taste of the local grapevine."

The problem with the populace in Vance Township was the spacing. In the little mining towns like Elm Grove and Dillard, the early twentieth-century company houses were lined up side-by-side in stair-stepped rows up the rolling Pennsylvania hills. But in the miles and miles of rural areas, the nearest neighbors were often a quarter mile or more away.

Pastures bordered Boyd and Linda Anderson's house on both sides and to the rear. Across the road, woods provided homes to deer, squirrels, and assorted other wildlife, none of which made good witnesses.

Not surprisingly, the O'Keefes' neighbors in the housing development had better things to say about Boyd than they did about the professor. Most of the residents of the newer homes were recent transplants and only knew Boyd as the man who owned the horses. The few who had encountered him said he was helpful, considerate, and pleasant.

The adjectives used to describe the professor leaned more toward antisocial, unfriendly, and pain-in-the-ass.

Giving up on the development dwellers, Pete and Abby headed on down the road. A vegetable farmer, who ran a small roadside market during the summer months, was outside tidying up the place. On a whim, Pete pulled into the gravel lot and stepped out. "Hey, Gino. Are you planning to open early this year?"

The farmer removed his straw hat and pulled a red bandana from his back pocket to mop his bald head. "Nah. Just taking advantage of what's left of the nice weather to get a jump on clearing out the boxes and crap I stored in here over the winter. S'posed to snow tomorrow. Might not get another day this nice until next month."

Abby had climbed out of the passenger side but remained next to the vehicle's front fender.

Pete thumbed at her. "Gino Marcini, meet Vance Township's newest officer, Abby Baronick."

He nodded to her. "You stop by when I open up in a few weeks. I carry the best strawberries in the county."

Pete couldn't argue the fact.

Gino plopped his battered straw hat back on his head and secured it with a tug. "You didn't just stop by to see if I was opening early. What's up?"

"How well do you know Boyd Anderson?"

Gino shrugged. "Pretty well, I guess. He and his wife are regular customers during the summer. Remember that storm on the Fourth of July a couple years ago? Uprooted three big old pines in my yard. One of them came down on my roof. Made a helluva hole. Boyd came right over and helped me cut up the trees and patch the roof."

"Sounds like a good guy."

Gino's head bobbed ever so slightly. "For the most part."

"Care to elaborate?"

Gino scuffed the heel of his boot against the slab of concrete he'd poured in front of his roadside market. "Part of being a good neighbor is minding one's own business."

"Minding your own business is interfering with *police* business, Gino."

That raised an eyebrow. "Boyd in trouble?"

"Maybe. Or maybe I'm looking in the wrong direction. If I am, I'd like to know so I can look somewhere else."

The farmer gazed toward the horizon, mulling over Pete's words.

"Anything I say...would it be...what d'ya call it? Confidential?"

"Absolutely."

Gino crossed his arms. "Boyd has a temper. A bad one."

"Care to be more specific?"

"I once saw him put a hand around a man's throat and pin him against a car."

"Where?"

Gino pointed. "Right over there."

"And you didn't call me?"

"Didn't seem to be a need."

"Boyd Anderson tried to choke a man right in front of you, and you didn't see a need to call the police."

"The man had it coming, if you ask me."

"I *am* asking, Gino."

The farmer wrinkled his nose as if he'd gotten a whiff of sewer. "This man—not a regular customer, mind you—had outta-state plates—was being an ass. He'd been handling all my produce. And I do mean *all* of it. Rough, you know? Squeezing the pears, bruising 'em. Helped himself to a couple of peaches. Ate one. Gave the other to his kid and told him to eat it. Said it would be the only lunch he'd be gettin'. Never paid for any of it. Just bulldozed his way through my inventory and then headed back to his car. Well, Boyd was standing here the whole time watching. When the man and his kid went to leave, Boyd followed him. I could tell he was gonna confront the guy and make him come back and pay for the stuff he'd eaten and damaged. That's the kind of person Boyd is."

Pete had a feeling there was a "but" coming, and he was right.

"But then things got nasty. The man's kid must have said something to him."

"To Boyd?"

"No. To his father. Maybe he didn't think his old man was doing the right thing either. I dunno. Didn't hear what he said. But the man backhanded the kid so hard the boy went down on the gravel. That's when Boyd lost it. He pounced on the man. Caught him by the throat and shoved him up against the car. Hard. I still couldn't hear what Boyd was saying, but from the look on the man's face, Boyd got his point across, if you know what I mean. Pretty soon, the man was digging in his pockets and came up with some cash. Boyd wiggled his fingers, like he wanted more, you know? And the man gave it to him. Then Boyd let him go and went over to the kid, who was trying to dust himself off. Boyd told him to stay right there a minute, loud enough so the father could hear. Boyd came to me with this wad of cash. I told him it was too much for what the guy had damaged and eaten, and Boyd said that was okay. And he picked up a chip basket of pears and another one of tomatoes and took them out to the kid. Since the father wasn't gonna feed him lunch, he said."

Pete covered his smile and glanced at Abby, who had lowered her face. But he could tell she was grinning too. Damn. He hoped he wasn't going to have to arrest Boyd Anderson for murder. He'd rather pin a medal on the guy's chest.

"That's it?" Pete asked the farmer.

"Yep. Didn't see any use in calling you about it."

"No, I guess not."

"But you know what? Even with the extra produce Boyd gave to that kid, the money he gave me from the father was way too much."

"I don't suppose the guy was about to file robbery charges against him."

"No." Gino rubbed his chin. "But I tried to give the extra to Boyd. For his help, you know? And he wouldn't take it."

"Seems like the kind of guy he is."

"Oh, yeah. But considering how deep in debt he is, I'd have thought he'd gladly take a few dollars."

TWENTY-ONE

Zoe found Franklin sitting in a blue vinyl recliner next to his hospital bed, his reading glasses perched on his beak of a nose and a magazine open in his lap. She wondered if he'd been reading it or if the periodical was all for show, because he seemed to be watching the door. The second she appeared, he tossed the magazine aside.

"Took you long enough."

She could have pointed out that she'd dropped everything to drive fifteen miles back into Brunswick, stopped at his office to pick up the needed paperwork, and battled the hospital's sluggish elevators. Instead, she set the reports on his tray table. "I think everything's in order."

Franklin pushed up from his seat and rounded the foot of the bed. He looked better. Or maybe it was the lighting. He picked up the stack and thumbed through the papers, scanning each. "I suppose it'll do." He took a seat on the bed and held out a hand to her. "Pen."

Zoe dug around in her purse until she came up with the requested writing implement.

"I'll be back at work tomorrow afternoon," he said as he scrawled his name.

"Oh?"

"They're discharging me in the morning once the doctor makes his rounds."

She hoped it was true this time since she had to be back on duty at the ambulance garage tomorrow evening and had been wondering how she'd juggle both jobs. "So, you're all right then?"

He went back to the paperwork without responding.

"Franklin?"

"I'm good enough for now. There'll be some surgery in my future, but we'll deal with that when the time comes." He returned the pen and the reports to her. "Take these over to Paulette."

Zoe scooped up the documents and rapped the edges on the table. "What kind of surgery?"

He waved away the question. "Nothing to worry about. Catch me up on what I've missed. I understand an arrest has been made in the Kinney homicide."

"Yeah, but it appears we busted the wrong man."

"I thought the police found the clothing worn during the homicide in the suspect's locker."

"We can't explain the clothing, but it's pretty clear Oliverio's not our guy."

Franklin grew pensive. "You must have missed something back at the beginning."

"What do you mean?"

He shook his head. "Never mind. I'll look into it as soon as I get out of here. Now go. I want everything in order when I get back to my office."

She wandered down the hall pondering Franklin's words. What had she missed?

As Zoe waited for the elevator, the signed paperwork tucked under one arm, her cell phone rang. The doors swished open, and she stepped inside joining two doctors while retrieving the device from her pocket. "Hi, Wayne."

"Where are you?"

"At the hospital on my way to Franklin's office."

"Good. When you're done there, come over to Headquarters."

"Why?"

When Baronick didn't reply, Zoe looked at the screen. He'd ended the call. She pocketed her phone. "I'll be right there," she muttered to dead air.

Wayne had on the same faded jeans and sweatshirt that he'd worn earlier in the day. He waited for Zoe at the same counter. She assumed it wasn't the same coffee clutched in his hands. The exhaustion and the scruff of five-o'clock-shadow darkening his face were definitely new.

"What's up?" she asked.

"I've been to Golden Oaks and chatted with old man Adams' buddy."

"Ernie? So, what do you think?"

"I think for a blind guy, he makes a damned credible eyewitness."

"You could've called and told me that much."

Wayne pushed away from the counter. "You dragged me in here this morning to watch video. I'm returning the favor." He gestured for her to follow before leading the way down a now-familiar hallway.

The tech who'd run the computer that morning was gone, and Wayne flopped into the empty seat. Zoe reclaimed the chair she'd come to think of as hers.

"I'll have you know, you and Ernie ruined my entire day." He pecked a few keys and clicked the mouse, bringing up a segment of footage she hadn't seen before. "Since the two of you pretty much killed my case against Oliverio, I decided to drive the final nail in its coffin." Wayne pointed at the screen. "I decided to spy on Oliverio's locker to learn how Baseball Cap Man's gear ended up there."

The black and white security video showed the employee lounge with people coming and going in fast forward. "Did you find anything?" Zoe asked when he didn't hit pause.

"No."

"So, you brought me back here to see nothing?"

He chuckled a tired laugh. "Not quite. I didn't find anything because we'd picked up all this video right after Kinney's homicide. While I was at Golden Oaks, I requested their more recent films. They were very cooperative." Wayne paused the image. "When I viewed the new stuff, I found this." He advanced the film at normal speed.

A man entered the frame carrying a bag. He looked around at the otherwise empty lounge, approached what Zoe knew to be Oliverio's locker, opened it, and shoved the bag inside. He closed the locker, glanced around again, and left. But unlike Baseball Cap Man, this guy made no attempt to conceal his face.

"Who is he?" she asked.

"I showed the photo to Oliverio who IDed him as Reggie Kershaw. Another Golden Oaks staffer."

Zoe leaned back and ran this new revelation around in her mind. Wayne had paused the footage and zoomed in on the guy's face—soft and round with a slack jaw and nervous eyes. "I don't remember seeing him when I've visited Harry."

"Kershaw works in the kitchen, so you probably wouldn't have."

She met Wayne's tired but intense gaze. "He made no effort to keep his face turned away from the camera."

A trace of a smirk touched Wayne's lips. "You noticed that too? Yeah. He didn't even seem to be aware there *were* cameras."

"He's not our guy."

"I don't think so either."

"You haven't questioned him?"

"Not yet. He's off today and tomorrow. I went to his apartment, but according to his landlady, he went fishing somewhere near Ohiopyle. I tried calling his number, but they have notoriously bad cell coverage along the river out there. The state and local police in Fayette and Somerset Counties have been notified to keep an eye out for him."

Zoe looked back at the face on the screen. "How did he get into Daryl's locker? I didn't notice him breaking the lock."

"That I can answer. Kershaw and Oliverio are buddies and Oliverio had given him the combination."

"They're friends?"

"According to Oliverio."

Zoe huffed. "Some friend. Framing him for murder."

"A fact that wasn't lost on Oliverio." Wayne closed out the video footage and stretched back over his chair, eliciting a muffled pop from his spine. "Okay, I'm done for the day. But I believe we're close to catching our man. Once we find this Kershaw guy, I think we'll get some answers."

"Do you feel ready to go solo?"

Pete and Abby stepped out of the Vance Township station into the chilly midnight air after updating the part-timer who would work the graveyard shift until morning.

Abby only hesitated a moment. "Yeah, I do."

Pete crossed to the Explorer. "Good. Get some rest. You'll take the four-to-midnight shift tomorrow through Friday."

"Today."

He stopped and looked over at her as she beeped open her Subaru Outback. "Excuse me?"

"It's after midnight, so technically, I take the afternoon shift *today* through Friday."

Pete's new officer was detail oriented. Good. "Right."

Instead of opening the car door, she leaned back against it and crossed her arms. "Do you mind if I say something about the Kinney homicide case?"

"Please do."

"All the theories I've heard have been that he was killed because he upset an old lady. Or he was killed because he arrested a guy decades ago. A guy who seems to be doing pretty well for himself by the way." Abby shook her head. "Doesn't it bother you that the motives of the two main suspects are so flimsy?"

Pete weighed his words before replying. "It would if we were taking this case to the DA tonight. We aren't. We need to keep investigating and follow the leads as they come up. We might be looking at the right suspect but for the wrong reason. Or maybe we're completely off base. That's why it's police *work*. No one said it was easy."

She lowered her head, nudging a piece of broken concrete with her boot. "Okay." She lifted her chin and nodded to him. "See you at four."

Pete watched her climb behind the wheel, back out of the space, and head south on Route 15. He stepped into his own vehicle. Home was less than a half-mile away, but the drive took him past Seth's house where every light blazed. Pete steered into the driveway.

Seth opened the door after the first knock. "Hey, Chief."

The kitchen, which had been spotless after Zoe's visit, once more showed signs of a careless bachelor in residence. A pizza box balanced precariously on top of a full trash can. The sink didn't overflow, but dirty dishes had begun to accumulate. A television blared from the other room.

Seth shoved his hands into his jeans pockets. "My internal clock is still set for working the night shift."

"Does that mean you're staying prepared to come back on duty?"

Seth looked away with a wistful smile. "How's the new officer doing?"

"Good. But I'm still not accepting your resignation."

He didn't say anything, but his eyebrows reminded Pete of a sport's stadium crowd doing the wave. Not promising at all. "Can I get you a beer?"

"Sure."

They took their bottles of Iron City into the living room. Seth grabbed his remote and clicked off the retro network's long-cancelled cop show—something Pete had seen commercials for but had never watched.

He thumbed at the now dark screen. "Any good?"

Seth chuckled. "Not really. The main characters shoot a half dozen bad guys every episode. No one goes on desk duty. No one gets investigated by a review board."

"And no one feels any regrets for taking a life," Pete said, filling in the blank he knew was there.

Seth grunted.

Pete claimed one end of the overly soft couch. Seth flopped into the stuffed armchair, and they sipped their beers in silence for a couple of minutes.

"I've been thinking a lot about consequences," Seth said.

Pete crossed an ankle over a knee and thought of the cartoon character with the wooden stand. *The doctor is in.* "What kind of consequences?"

"Of our actions. Especially as cops."

At least he was still thinking of himself as a cop. Pete watched the young officer, waiting for him to continue.

Seth took another sip from his bottle. "I mean, we arrest someone, put them in jail, and their lives are changed forever. They're a convict. After they get out, they're an ex-convict. But the label is always there."

"That's not our doing. We don't arrest people for no reason. The courts don't put them in jail for no reason. You want to talk about consequences of your actions? It's the criminal's actions that have consequences."

"But what about the innocents?"

"You know we do our best to make sure we arrest the right person. And it's not just us. The jury, the judge...they're all working to make sure the person paying for the crime is guilty as charged."

Seth made a pained face. "That's not what I mean. I'm talking about the family left behind after we do our thing. The wives. The parents." He paused before adding, "The kids."

He wasn't talking generalities anymore.

"I maintain, the responsibility lies with the criminal." Pete watched the skepticism and doubt play across Seth's face. "What about the other side of the coin?"

"Huh?"

"The victims. The future victims if we aren't out there doing our jobs. Their lives are forever changed too. Aren't they entitled to see the criminals pay for their actions?"

One of Seth's eyebrows lifted. His expression vacillated.

"You mentioned consequences," Pete said. "Do you remember the oath you took the day you became a cop?"

Seth lowered his gaze. Nodded. "On my honor, I will never betray my badge, my integrity, my character, or the public trust..."

Pete picked up the rest. "I will always have the courage to hold myself and others accountable for our actions."

Seth continued to inspect his knees.

"That oath says we're accountable for our actions and we hold others accountable for theirs. It does not say you're accountable for someone else choosing to pick up a firearm and aim it at another person. That's on them. Steal from the elderly. That's on the thieves."

Seth remained motionless, pensive.

Pete slid to the edge of the seat. Leaned forward, on the verge of reaching across the space between them to grab his officer by the shoulder and shake sense into him. "You may not want to hear this, but by choosing to hide here in your house, that's on you too. You're not only accountable for your actions, you're accountable for your *in*action as well. You're a good cop with good instincts. You took a life, and in the process, saved a life. Now you can't bring yourself to face the consequences of having been the one to do that." Pete took another long slug from the bottle. "I'd hate to see you have to deal with the consequences of not being there when someone needs you. When you could make a difference...and choose not to."

TWENTY-TWO

Zoe lay awake most of the night, wondering what she might have missed in the Kinney homicide case. She must have fallen asleep at some point because she didn't hear Pete come in. Nor did she hear him get up and leave for his morning shift. The phrase "ships passing in the night" floated through her mind.

She dressed in layers—long-sleeved T and a zippered hoodie to start. But the forecast called for falling temperatures, rain and even snow as the day wore on, so she tucked a fleece vest under one arm on her way out. Providing added insurance, she had a battered barn coat behind the seat of her pickup.

Her first stop was the farm to feed the horses. It had been dark by the time she'd done her chores last night. Jason's truck had been absent, so she assumed he hadn't fallen and broken his back. In the daylight, she was awed to see the roof had been completed. And looked incredible, gleaming in the early morning sun. With only the horses to witness her joy, she squealed and danced an awkward but enthusiastic jig of delight.

She fired off a grateful text to her brother, signed it with a *TTYL* and a heart, and stepped inside the barn to feed the insistent equine quartet.

An hour later, she was still pondering the investigation as she reached the traffic light at the edge of Brunswick. She'd intended to go straight to Franklin's office to take a fresh look at the autopsy results, but on a whim, decided to visit Harry.

And Golden Oaks.

She found Pete's dad in his room. A game show blared on his TV, but he seemed to be watching the painting on the wall, a vacant stare on his face. "Good morning, Harry," she called as she breezed in.

He blinked, looked up, and smiled. "Good morning, Sunshine."

"How are you today?"

The smile faded to a baffled scowl. "Oh, fine. I guess. They left me in this room and never came back for me."

She made a point of looking around as if she'd never seen the place before. "It's a nice room."

"I suppose. I'm ready to go home though. Do you know my daughter, Nadine?"

"Yes, I do."

"Have you seen her? I wish she'd come get me."

"How about we go for a walk until Nadine gets here." Zoe glanced at the television. "Unless you'd rather watch your show."

Harry wrinkled his nose. "I'm not watching that. Someone else must've turned it on." He climbed to his feet and offered Zoe his arm. "I would love to take a walk with you. As long as you keep an eye out for Nadine."

Zoe picked up Harry's cane, handed it to him, and tucked her hand into the crook of his elbow.

They stepped into the hallway and came face-to-face with Barbara and her walker. She wore a powder-blue sweater set over matching polyester pants. Outdated, perhaps, but classic. As were the pearls draped around her neck. "Oh." Her eyes widened briefly in surprise. "I didn't realize Harry had company. I was coming to check on him." Her expression saddened. "He seemed a little out of it at breakfast."

Out of sorts or not, Harry was forever the flirt. He hooked his cane over the arm Zoe held and reached his now-free hand to Barbara. "Well, hello, lovely lady. I don't believe we've met."

She raised an eyebrow at Zoe in a silent *I told you so*, then took the offered hand. "I'm Barbara. I live across the hall."

Zoe winked at her. "We were taking a walk until Harry's daughter shows up."

"Yes." Harry released Barbara's hand and resituated his cane. "Join us."

"I hate to interrupt your visit—"

"You aren't." He tipped his head. "Please?"

Barbara looked at Zoe.

Investigating a homicide with Harry tagging along was one thing. Bringing an entourage hadn't been in her plans. But she wasn't about to stand in the way of young love. Or old love for that matter. "Yes, please walk with us, Barbara."

The three of them with one cane and one walker strolled, hobbled, and rolled down the hall toward the staircase and the elevator. No one complained as Zoe led the way past them and down the opposite wing.

She'd expected yellow police tape to remain across the door to what had been John Kinney's room. But the county crime scene techs had completed their search and collected all the evidence they could find. The door stood open. She stopped at the entrance and gazed inside.

The bed had been removed. So had the lamp that had first been thought to be the cause of Kinney's fall. Personal photographs no longer hung from the walls. The only piece of furniture remaining was an institutional-style dresser with chipped veneer. However, three large, dented cardboard boxes sat in the corner. A fourth smaller one perched on the dresser. They'd all been closed by folding and overlapping the top flaps.

"Hello?"

Zoe released Harry's arm and turned to find Connie Smith.

"Oh." Connie rested a hand on her chest. "It's you. That door is supposed to be kept closed and locked, but I just finished a tour and had shown the room to the family as an example of what was available." She moved forward, a key in her hand. "I'll lock it up now."

Zoe moved to block her as inconspicuously as possible. "What's in the boxes?"

"Those are John's personal effects. You know—blankets, throw pillows, the photos from the walls, and such. After the police gave us the all-clear, I had our staff pack up John's things, so the family wouldn't have to."

"I'd have thought his sister would've picked all this up already."

"Different families react differently. Needless to say, I'd prefer she collect his things sooner rather than later, so I can get the room cleaned and painted for a new resident. But I don't have the heart to rush her." Connie smiled sadly.

Zoe thought of the tarp crammed behind the seat in her truck and its empty bed. "As a matter of fact, I could haul it. I have a pickup and live near her."

Connie's eyes lit for a moment before turning downcast. "I can't simply turn over a resident's personal property to someone without authorization. I'm sure you understand."

Zoe also wondered if the crime scene team might have missed something that was now packed in one of those boxes. "Why don't you call John's sister? Tell her I'm Pete Adams' girlfriend."

In her peripheral vision, she noticed Harry turn to look at her.

"I suppose I could do that." Connie rested a finger on her lips.

"Yes. I suppose a verbal authorization would be fine under the circumstances."

"Circumstances" meaning a vacant room lying fallow with paying clients waiting in the wings.

She motioned to the room. "You're more than welcome to wait inside while I place the call. If you like."

Zoe thanked her and watched as the director hurried eagerly down the hall.

"Now, I remember you." Harry's vacant stare had bloomed into a grin. "You're Pete's girl. Zoe, right?"

"Right."

Barbara beamed. "How about me? Do you remember me too?"

"Absolutely."

Zoe brushed her fingers over her lips to hide a grin. Maybe Harry remembered Barbara. Maybe he didn't. The man was a pro at covering his lapses. She tipped her head toward the room and lowered her voice. "Do you two care to help me snoop?"

Barbara looked like she'd have clapped her hands if she'd dared take them both from her walker. "Sounds like fun."

Harry swept an arm toward the door. "After you, ladies."

Zoe moved toward the boxes but paused, trying to recall where things had been that afternoon when Kinney sprawled lifeless on the floor. Divots in the carpet indicated the placement of the bed and nightstand. Unlike on bad TV shows, they didn't do chalk outlines to show where the body had been. But a rust-colored stain on the beige carpeting marked where Kinney's head wound had bled. Zoe's memory filled the gaps. Plaid shirt. Khaki pants. A lamp cord.

Someone had taken the time to wrap the cord loosely around Kinney's ankles to give the illusion of an accidental fall. Where was the lamp now? The crime scene guys most likely confiscated it. There might be fingerprints.

She crossed to the boxes and glanced back over her shoulder. Barbara and Harry stood just inside the room watching Zoe. She gestured to them. "Push the door shut."

Harry did as he was told.

"Barbara, listen for anyone coming and let me know if you hear someone in the hall. Harry, can you come over here and give me a hand?"

Barbara re-positioned her walker and leaned an ear against the door.

Harry shuffled to Zoe's side. "What are we looking for?" His tone was joyfully conspiratorial.

"I wish I knew." If Elaine O'Keefe permitted Zoe to haul the boxes back to Vance Township, she'd have plenty of time to snoop through them. The dresser, however, was another matter. Then again, if Elaine said no, this was the only opportunity Zoe would have. "Go through the drawers and make sure nothing gets left behind," she told Harry while she flipped open the smaller box.

The contents had been tossed inside with no attempt to pack neatly or conserve space. Or protect breakables. With the sound of each drawer scraping open and thunking shut next to her, Zoe skimmed through a stack of framed family photos, some old, some newer. There were a couple of vases, a snow globe, and a carved sandalwood jewelry box. She thumbed open the lid to find Kinney's badge, several masculine gold rings, and a nice dress watch.

Harry moved around her, and she sidestepped out of his way.

On closer look, it was a *very* nice dress watch. She removed it from the box and turned so the light from the window fell on it. Rolex. Knock off. Had to be.

Harry straightened. "All I found was a crumpled-up letter. Shoved way in the back of one drawer. The rest were empty." He squinted. "What do you have there?"

She handed him the watch. "Nice fake, don't you think?"

He held it up, studying the timepiece.

Zoe shoved the jewelry box aside and skimmed through several books by Tony Hillerman and Larry McMurtry. Sandwiched between them was a black and white composition notebook. She slid it out and opened it. At first glance, it appeared to be a handwritten wish list of wines. She'd never been a connoisseur and knew nothing about what she was looking at, but the names seemed impressive. And French. Which she had never studied in school. Chateau something, 2009. Bordeaux something else 2000. Chateau Lafite, 1865.

Chateau Lafite *1865*?

Next to each listing was a price. Some were in the hundreds. A few were priced well into the thousands.

Zoe looked at the top of the page where the words *Wine Inventory* were hand printed in block lettering. It was dated six months ago.

"Someone's coming," Barbara said in a stage whisper.

Not even a second later, the metallic click of the doorknob sent Zoe's heart slamming into her throat, plugging her breath like one of those wine corks. So much for Barbara as an early warning system.

Harry either felt the same panic of being caught as she did or picked up on hers. She glimpsed him stuffing the crumpled paper into his pants pocket.

Barbara thumped back away from the door as it opened a crack. And stopped. Connie's voice filtered in. It sounded like someone had stopped her in the hall with a question.

Zoe shoved the notebook inside her hoodie and yanked the zipper up. She slammed the flaps closed on the box, clumsy hands struggling to tuck the final corner under to secure it.

The door creaked the rest of the way open. Zoe and Harry struck innocent poses, their backs to the dresser. She crossed her arms over her chest—casually, she hoped—to conceal the notebook and keep it from dropping to the floor at her feet. Barbara gazed toward the window and primped her sprayed hairdo.

If Connie noticed they'd closed the door she'd left open, she didn't mention it. "I spoke to Mrs. O'Keefe on the phone. She asked me to thank you for the offer, but she plans to come in today to collect everything and take care of her brother's final bill."

"Oh." Zoe wondered if Connie noticed how out-of-breath she sounded. "Okay. Well, we should get out of your way then."

"Yes. I want to lock up so no one is tempted to help themselves to John's belongings."

Keeping one hand resting on her belly, protecting the notebook, Zoe caught Harry's arm with the other. "Let's go." She winced at her too-cheery chirp.

The trio had made it to the door before Connie's voice stopped them. "Excuse me."

Zoe's heart plugged her throat a little tighter. She turned.

Connie held Harry's cane. "Don't forget this."

He chuckled. "I wouldn't get very far before I missed it."

Connie met him midway across the room to hand it back. "You all have a nice visit."

"We will," he said. "Thanks."

He sounded so relaxed, Zoe wondered if he didn't realize they'd been doing something they shouldn't.

None of them spoke as they strolled, hobbled, and rolled back to Harry's room. Zoe regained her ability to breathe once they were inside.

His face lit with an impish grin. "That was fun."

Barbara risked taking both hands from her walker to clap. "Yes. The most I've had in ages."

Zoe sagged against the door she'd just closed. "That's not what I'd call it."

Harry hooked his cane over one arm and dug in his pockets, coming up with the crumpled paper. "What should I do with this?"

She unzipped her hoodie, retrieved the other ill-gotten gain from their mission, and tossed it on his bed. "Let me see," she said, holding out her hand.

Harry plopped the paper ball in her palm. Barbara shuffled over to sit on the edge of the bed and picked up the notebook.

Zoe smoothed the paper. Not a letter as Harry had thought. A credit card statement. Oh, good. Not only had she swiped an ex-cop's personal wine inventory, now she had a document that could be used for identity theft.

She would just fold it up and stick it back in the notebook when she returned it to the family. How she'd manage that without giving herself away, she had no idea. But before she made the first crease, the long list of transactions on the statement caught her attention.

Apparently, John Kinney was quite the online shopper. And not cheap stuff. Wine seemed to be a favorite item, but not his only big expenditure by any means.

Behind her, Barbara said, "My heavens." Zoe turned to find her reading through the notebook.

"Do you know about wine?" Zoe asked.

"As a matter of fact, I do. My late husband and I loved Paris and Tuscany. We used to pick our vacation spots according the vineyards. We had a wine cellar filled with the best vintages we could afford, but these?" She pointed to the open page. "My husband would be green with envy."

Zoe looked over Barbara's shoulder and followed her finger as she slid it down the list. "I can't imagine John owned all these." There had been no bottles of wine in his room. And he wouldn't have kept stuff of this quality in a box under his bed.

Barbara lifted her eyes to meet Zoe's gaze. "It says 'inventory'."

"It does, doesn't it?" And the credit card statement with a charge from an online wine seller—a rather mind-boggling charge—supported the theory that John Kinney had quite a collection.

What did it mean? Anything? The police investigators had left the notebook behind, so they apparently hadn't thought it was important to the case. Still, a high-priced wine inventory seemed out of place when in the hands of a retired cop.

Zoe took the notebook from Barbara, tucked the credit card statement inside, and closed it. "I'll give this to Detective Baronick. If he doesn't think it has any value to the investigation, he can at least return it to John's family." And Zoe wouldn't have to try to explain to Connie Smith or Elaine O'Keefe how she came to steal it from a box of his possessions. "Thanks for your help."

"My pleasure." Barbara winked at her. "Beats playing pinochle at card club."

Zoe crossed to give Harry a kiss on his cheek. "I should be going."

"Come back again," he said with a grin.

"I will." With the notebook clamped under her arm, she headed for the door.

"Oh. Hey, Sunshine?"

She stopped and turned.

Harry brought his hand out of his pocket and opened his fist. Nestled in his palm was the fake Rolex.

"Crap," she breathed.

"This belong to the same guy who has the wine?"

"Yeah." And it was going to prove a bit more embarrassing to explain how she not only confiscated a two-dollar notebook from a dead man's personal effects, but also a dress watch. Even if it was a knock off.

Harry picked up his glasses from his nightstand and put them on to inspect the Rolex. He blew a low whistle.

Zoe returned to his side and held out a hand.

He ignored it. "I used to collect old watches. Pocket watches mostly. I'd take Pete to flea markets and antique stores when he was small just to look for old timepieces. It was kinda my hobby, I guess you could say. Found some real treasures during those shopping trips." Harry looked up from the Rolex to gaze out the window. "I wonder whatever happened to them."

She knew Pete had one. "Yeah, well, that's only a fake," she said, touching the watch in Harry's hand.

His attention snapped back to her. "A fake? Oh, no, Sunshine. This Rolex is the real deal, all right. And worth a pretty penny too."

TWENTY-THREE

After spending half his morning catching up on paperwork and phone calls, Pete grabbed his coat from the hook by the door and headed out on patrol. The mild weather over the weekend had given way to falling temperatures, wind-chased clouds, and a cold, misty drizzle. As much as he disliked being shamed into yesterday's roofing job, he was glad they'd made a good dent in the task. He wondered if Jason had managed to complete the job or if the blue tarp was flapping in the breeze over the unfinished portion.

Driven by curiosity, Pete turned off Route 15 and cruised up Covered Bridge Road toward Ridge Road and Zoe's farm. By the time he made the left at the top of the hill, the drizzle had grown into steady rain, forcing him to turn the wipers from intermittent to the rhythmic beat of the regular setting.

The gray Dodge Ram sat in front of the barn, but there was no sign of a fluttering blue tarp. Or Zoe's brother. Pete slowed and passed the row of *Re-elect Franklin Marshall County Coroner* signs Zoe had planted at the edge of the road. As Pete turned into the driveway, Jason stepped out of the barn.

"If you've come to help finish the roof, you're too late," Jason, his hair wet and plastered to his head, said as Pete climbed out of the Explorer. "It's done."

"Good." Pete glanced into the bed of the Ram. A tarp, possibly the same old blue one, covered the contents. He flipped back an edge to reveal lumber. "You plan on starting on the house's roof next?"

"I don't think it needs it." Jason looked skyward at the dark clouds and falling rain. "Although I'll check the attic for leaks if it keeps this up." He ambled toward Pete. "That decking's for the porch. I figured I'd finish what you started."

He wasn't sure if Jason intended the words to be a dig at Pete's patch job or if he simply took them that way. "It was January. I planned to finish once the weather broke."

"And it has," Jason said matter-of-factly. "So, I will."

Pete wanted to ask him what the hell he thought he was gaining from all this do-goodery. Zoe was already enthralled with her new brother. He didn't need to earn her affection. Unless he planned on moving in here and mooching off her.

The idea made Pete's jaw ache, but he reminded himself of yesterday afternoon. Hanging off the roof. Jason holding onto him when he could have easily let go. He'd saved Pete from some broken bones. At the very least.

Pete exhaled a breath. "Can I give you a hand unloading this?"

"No, thanks. There's no sense in letting it sit out in the rain. I'll start ripping up the old stuff while I'm waiting on the plumbers."

"What plumbers?"

"The ones I hired to replace all the copper that was stolen. They're bringing a hot water tank too. By the time they're done, Zoe'll have hot and cold running water in the house."

Smug bastard. "Not without electricity to run the water heater, she won't. And she won't have electricity without new wiring. The stuff in those walls right now isn't safe."

"Then I'll have to find a good electrician."

Pete's internal calculator started tallying. Barn roof. Plumbing. New wiring. "I hope you don't expect to stick Zoe with the bill for all this."

Jason's face reddened. "You son of a—" He swallowed the rest of it, and Pete watched him take a deep breath in followed by a slow exhalation. When Jason spoke again, his voice and expression had relaxed. "Look. I have a good job. I'm not a big spender, so I have a pretty nice cash reserve. I've missed a lot of years with my sister. This is my way of making up for lost time."

Pete held Jason's unwavering gaze, wanting to catch a hint of insincerity. A glimmer of something—anything to give credence to Pete's dislike of the man.

There was none.

Was Pete's biggest beef with him the simple fact that Jason was opening the door to Zoe's exit from Pete's home by giving her a place of her own?

A life of her own?

The radio attached to Pete's uniform squawked, interrupting his flash of self-loathing. "Unit Thirty, this is Vance Base. Do you copy?"

He keyed his mic. "Base, this is Thirty."

There was a pause, almost long enough for Pete to think Nancy hadn't heard him. "Unit Thirty, call the station. Urgent. Call the station." Her clipped voice upped the status of the request from "urgent" to full-blown emergency.

He shot a quick "excuse me" at Jason and walked away to place the call. "Nancy, it's me. What's up?"

"You need to get out to the O'Keefes' place. Now." Nancy's tone told Pete this was more than the usual neighbor dispute.

"What's the nature of the emergency?"

"Elaine thinks her husband is dead."

Although Nancy had told Pete EMS was en route, he was first on the scene. Elaine stood in front of the garage door, her hands intertwined and pressed to her mouth.

He jumped from his SUV and tugged his ball cap down on his head. The raindrops, which now had a slushy core to them, soaked her hair and darkened her thigh-length cardigan. "Mrs. O'Keefe?"

She kept her fingers clasped but lowered them to her chin. "He's around back." She made no move to show Pete the way.

Which was fine. He touched her arm. "Go inside and get warmed up."

She nodded but didn't budge.

The shrill wail of an approaching siren rose above the patter of rain-turning-to-sleet. Pete strode around the side of the house to the backyard where he spotted O'Keefe's lawn tractor, its attached bagger, and a mound of wet clothing on the ground next to the machine. Except Pete knew it wasn't merely clothing. He broke into a jog.

The professor sprawled face-up, a look of surprise frozen on his grayish face. His wide-open eyes already had the milky appearance of death. The misty rain-slush mixture hadn't yet washed away the huge volume of blood soaking the middle portion of the body.

Pete squatted next to the body and pressed his fingers into the groove in O'Keefe's neck. Procedure. He didn't need to feel the cold skin or palpate for a pulse that wasn't there to know the man was dead.

The sirens grew louder. The paramedics would have to confirm Pete's assessment, but the only aid they could render would be to the widow. He pulled out his phone and scrolled to Zoe's number. As it rang, he glanced at the rain-soaked mower. The grass around it sparkled with rain droplets and watered-down blood spatter.

But not the grass beneath it.

Zoe answered on the third ring, and her voice warmed him in spite of the sleet transitioning to snow.

"Are you still acting coroner?"

"I guess. I haven't heard from Franklin yet today." A pause followed by a cautious "why?"

"I have a DB."

She groaned when he told her who it was. "I'll be there in twenty minutes."

Zoe parked her Chevy pickup next to Medic Two, the unit she'd be manning this evening, provided she could wrap up her coroner's duties in time.

And not end up in jail herself.

In front of her, the black Monongahela Crime Scene Unit van took up half the driveway. In front of it, Pete's SUV. A marked County Police cruiser and a State Police SUV flanked the driveway.

Fat snowflakes swirled through the air, whitening the grass, but melting on the pavement. April snow. It'd be beautiful if she wasn't so darned ready for spring to set up shop and stay for an extended visit.

Pete's call had reached her while she was on her way to see Wayne. Before she'd had a chance to turn over Kinney's possessions.

She opened her glove box. The door had one broken hinge and nearly fell off. Holding it steady, she stuffed the notebook with the wine inventory list, the credit card statement, and the not-so-fake Rolex into the cubby. She closed the wobbly door, inserted the key into the latch and locked it. Anyone who knew what was in there could pry the thing open if they had half a notion.

The breeze had kicked up, so she retrieved the barn coat from behind the seat along with the duffel bag Franklin had provided. She slipped into the coat, snugged her EMS ball cap down on her head, slung the duffel's strap over her shoulder, and locked the truck. Might as well make it a little harder to break in and steal the evidence that she had also stolen.

She found the gathered representatives from the various police jurisdictions behind the house. They'd cordoned off the bulk of the backyard with yellow police tape, and at the center of the restricted area, the crime tech guys wrestled with setting up a tent to protect the evidence from the elements. A uniformed county officer with a dusting of snow on the brim of her hat stopped Zoe from entering. "You can't go in there, ma'am."

Ma'am?

She realized neither the EMS emblem on her cap nor her barn coat properly identified her official position. "I'm with the Coroner's Office."

The officer made no attempt to hide her doubt. "Can I see some ID, ma'am?"

Before Zoe could start digging for her wallet, she spotted Pete waving to her. With a bundle tucked under his arm, he approached her and the sentry.

"Sign her in, Officer," he said. "Acting Deputy Zoe Chambers."

"Yes, sir." The officer produced a clipboard from under her raingear and held it and a pen out to Zoe.

Once she'd added her name to the security log, Pete handed her the bundle. A disposable biohazard suit. "Can't have you contaminating our crime scene with hay and whatever else is stuck to that coat."

She ripped into the package and started to slip into the one-size-fits-all garment, but her phone vibrated in her pocket, interrupting. "It's a text from Franklin." Tapping the screen, she read the message aloud. "'Just released from hospital. On my way to your location. Go ahead and start processing the scene.'"

"Looks like you've been demoted."

"That's fine by me." She handed her phone to him while she finished wiggling into the biohazard gear. "Better?"

Pete tossed the phone back to her. "Yep." He lifted the fluttering yellow tape, and she ducked under it.

"What happened?" she asked.

"I'm hoping you can tell me. Elaine phoned it in about thirty or thirty-five minutes ago. Said she thought her husband was dead. She was right."

Thirty or thirty-five minutes ago would have been shortly after Connie Smith had phoned her about Zoe's offer to move Kinney's personal possessions out of Golden Oaks.

The techs secured the sides of the white tent to the pyramid-shaped roof. Beneath it, a tarp covered what she knew must be the professor's body. A smaller tarp covered the ground between O'Keefe and the fence. "What's that?"

"A smear of blood." He grumbled. "The rain probably contaminated it, but I did get a few swabs as soon as I was able and tried to cover the rest."

"A smear? Do you think there was a second victim?"

"I didn't find any additional blood. If you ask me, it looks like our killer tried to clean the murder weapon on the grass."

"Were you first on the scene?" she asked.

"Yep. I checked for a pulse even though it was evident he was deceased. The paramedics confirmed it. Other than that, and covering him to protect the crime scene, no one's been near him."

"Photos?"

"Got them."

They stepped into the shelter provided by the tent. "Let's see what we have."

Pete gestured, and two county patrolmen lifted the tarp and moved out of the way.

Zoe studied the supine and blood-soaked body of Professor K, his bluish-gray face frozen in an expression of surprise. She pictured the man in life. Uppity. Self-important. Rude. In death, there was nothing but shock and loneliness. Had he ventured out to do some lawn work before the weather moved in? Whatever his plans, they surely hadn't included dying. She may not have liked the man, but no one deserved this.

Zoe reached into the duffel and withdrew a digital camera, which she handed to Pete. "Care to get a set for the coroner's office?"

"Yes, ma'am."

Ma'am. *Again*. She glared at him. "That's 'miss' to you, buster." While he snapped pictures of the body from various angles, she looked around. "Where's Elaine?"

"In the house with the paramedics. She was pretty shaken up."

"I bet." Zoe wiggled her fingers into a pair of black Nitrile gloves before moving in for a closer look.

She knelt next to O'Keefe and started her physical exam with his head and jaw. "No sign of rigor yet."

A voice, not Pete's, spoke up behind her. "He's not been dead very long."

She looked up at Wayne. "You know there are too many variables to give a TOD at the scene." Or probably even at autopsy.

"What time did it start raining?" Pete asked.

She noticed he was staring at the lawn tractor.

"Why?" Wayne asked.

"Because the grass under the mower is dry."

The detective did some pecking on his phone's screen. "According to the local weather station, the rain started falling here around eight thirty this morning. Do you think he died before that?"

"Maybe." Pete crossed his arms. "All we know for sure is he parked the mower there before it started raining."

"When we move the body, if the grass under him is dry, we'll know he was here too."

Zoe secured brown paper bags over each of the professor's bloody hands, which rested on his abdomen. "You're not moving the body until Franklin gets here."

Wayne narrowed his eyes at her. "I thought *you* were acting coroner."

She glanced at her watch. "Only for another ten minutes or so." After which, she needed to drag the detective aside to tell him about the contraband in her glove box.

Pete elbowed Wayne. "The widow may be able to fill in some blanks on our timeline."

"Has anyone spoken to her yet?"

"Nope."

Zoe gingerly re-positioned O'Keefe's arms at his side, revealing a congealing crimson pond at the base of his breastbone. Pete lifted the camera to capture a series of photos before she started undoing the buttons of the quilted plaid flannel shirt. When she reached the pool, the shirt reluctantly lifted free revealing a jagged slash in the fabric.

Wayne whistled. "Wow."

The professor had a polo shirt on under the quilted flannel. It was equally saturated with his blood and bore a matching wound—a wound that plunged deep into the flesh just below the sternum.

"That was a helluva knife."

Zoe glanced at the detective. Then met Pete's eyes. *Our killer tried to clean the murder weapon on the grass*, he'd said. A mental image played out inside her head. The killer. A bloody knife. He knelt and swiped the blade across the grass. Probably intended to wash it off better once he got home.

Home.

Pete turned away from the body.

Zoe followed his gaze. Across the pasture.

To Boyd "the Machete Man" Anderson's house.

TWENTY-FOUR

Pete and Baronick left Zoe to finish up with the body and headed around to the front of the O'Keefe house.

"You're thinking about the neighbor," the detective said. "Boyd Anderson."

"Maybe."

"He has a past history of violence and already attacked the victim with a machete. Didn't seem too apologetic about it as I recall."

Pete grunted. "Maybe," he repeated. Anderson was the obvious choice, but he had to know that. Why would he show up in the early-morning hours today and kill his neighbor? Annoying as his neighbor might be.

One of the paramedics, who'd been sitting with Elaine, met Pete and the detective at the door.

"She's a wreck," the medic reported. "I really think she needs to see her doctor."

"I'll make sure she calls him before we leave," Pete said before excusing the EMS crew to return to available status.

They found Elaine O'Keefe curled up in a recliner, hugging her knees and clutching a tissue. A cup of tea sat untouched on the end table. Pete dragged an ottoman across the room, placed it in front of her, and sat. "Are you up to answering a few questions?"

Her dark eyes met his for a moment and then lowered. "I think so."

Baronick stayed next to the front door, his phone out. Pete had worked with him enough to know he wasn't texting. He was taking notes.

Pete kept his voice soft. "When was the last time you saw your husband alive?"

The creases in her forehead deepened. "Yesterday. Late afternoon."

The answer surprised him. "Not this morning?"

She swallowed. "No. When I got here this morning...he was dead."

He shot a glance at Baronick, who gave a barely noticeable shrug.

After several long moments, Elaine dabbed at her nose and said, "Kristopher and I haven't been getting along. I guess since burying my brother, my tolerance levels are lower than usual. We—Kristopher and I—had a bit of a disagreement yesterday, and I packed a bag and left."

"Where did you go?"

"I got a room at the Brunswick Inn." She choked a laugh. "It's such a pretty place. I've always wanted to go there, but Kristopher never wanted to spend the money."

"What was your disagreement with your husband about?"

She shifted her weight to her other hip, squirmed to find a comfortable spot, and settled with a sigh. "Honestly? I don't remember. We disagree over just about everything. Even more so lately."

"Try to remember."

She rolled her eyes toward the ceiling. "This house. Money. My brother. His attitude. Pick one."

Pete waited a beat before his next question. "What about your neighbor?"

"The Andersons? Heavens, yes. Boyd and his horses were one of Kristopher's favorite rants."

"Have there been any recent confrontations between them? In the last week, I mean."

She took a moment to think. "No. Not that I'm aware of. Nothing face-to-face anyway."

"Anything *not* face-to-face?"

She leveled her coffee-colored eyes at him with a hint of a smirk. "I once told you he's passive aggressive. Kristopher had a talent for the underhanded."

"That doesn't really answer my question."

"It's the best I can do. Kristopher was always plotting some kind of revenge against those who upset his delicate sensibilities. But he rarely took credit for his actions. And never accepted the blame."

After suggesting Elaine call a friend to come over and sit with her, Pete stepped outside.

Baronick had slipped into another room to talk on his phone but joined Pete on the front porch. "I've confirmed that Mrs. O'Keefe spent the night at the Brunswick Inn. Checked in a little before four."

"Has she checked out?"

"Nope. Still registered as a guest."

So, she hadn't planned to move home this morning. "Anybody notice what time she left?"

"No."

While they'd been inside, the County Coroner had arrived, his van taking the place of the ambulance among the array of vehicles clogging the driveway. Pete looked past it toward the road and the police vehicles from assorted jurisdictions.

And to the weeds at the edge of the yard. The spot he'd thought would make an excellent compost pile for the professor's grass clippings.

"Dammit."

"What?" Baronick asked.

Pete didn't answer. Not yet. He took off at a jog around to the rear of the house and the crime scene. He slowed to a fast walk when the gadgets on his duty belt threatened to bruise his hip.

Franklin Marshall and Zoe were zipping the body bag and looked up when Pete stormed over to the lawn tractor and its attachment. He released the latch and lifted the lid. Instead of being greeted with a whiff of fresh-cut grass, a slightly sour wave of moldering compost smacked him in the face. The stuff on top was dry and brown. He plunged his arm into the filled bin, only slightly surprised at the heat inside, and pulled out a clump of steaming, fermenting grass.

Baronick caught up to him. "What are you looking at?"

"Friday, I caught O'Keefe about to dump a load of clippings over the fence. Anderson wasn't home, so I stopped him by threatening to arrest him."

The detective grunted. "For what?"

"Doesn't matter. I told him to start a compost heap, and when I was leaving, that's what I thought he was about to do." Pete dropped the grass back in the bin and shook off the stuff sticking to his hand. "He was down at the weeds along the road. But just now I noticed there was nothing there."

Zoe joined them, having skimmed off her bloody gloves and biohazard suit. "You mean the professor had this saved since Friday?"

"Looks that way" Pete said.

"It's a wonder he didn't burn down his garage. Or wherever he parks this thing."

Baronick looked puzzled.

Pete thumbed toward the grass. "Stick your arm in there. It's hot."

"Spontaneous combustion," Zoe said. "It's why you never bale hay when it's wet. Farmers have lost their barns that way." She sniffed. "Smells like this could ignite at any minute."

"Might be why O'Keefe was out here so early." Pete eyed the wisp of steam rising from the center of the bin. "Dumping the load before it caught fire."

Zoe raised an eyebrow at him. "If he was smart enough."

O'Keefe's intelligence—or lack thereof—wasn't on Pete's mind at the moment. The motive he'd been seeking for Boyd Anderson showing up with his machete was. Pete caught Baronick's eye. "*Now*, I'm thinking of the neighbor." He turned to Zoe. "What can you tell me about the murder weapon?"

She glanced toward Marshall, who was busy overseeing the transfer of their body-bagged victim onto a stretcher.

Pete touched her hand. "You may not be acting coroner any longer, but you can still answer the question."

"It's not that." She lowered her head for a moment before meeting Pete's gaze. "We can't tell the exact size or type of knife until after the autopsy—if then."

"But?"

"But we can tell you it was a single-edge blade."

"From what I saw, I'd say a big one."

"That's probably a safe assumption."

Pete looked at the detective. "We need a search warrant for Boyd Anderson's property. I want to see that machete of his."

"I'll get to work on it," Baronick said with a predatory grin.

Zoe hated the idea that Boyd Anderson had killed his neighbor. She'd understood—even supported—protecting his horses from a citified moron. Despite that long-ago arrest on his record, she'd never have guessed he was capable of the brutality she'd witnessed this morning. But as she'd told Pete, she didn't really know the man. And as Pete had told her, not all horsemen were good guys.

Perhaps this one had killed more than once.

The burst of fat snowflakes had transitioned to a steady spring rain, dripping from the bill of her ball cap. Pete was engrossed in conversation with Franklin allowing her to slip away unnoticed. She hoped.

Zoe circled the house and found Wayne backed against the garage door, sheltered from the rain, talking on his phone. She sidled in next to him in time to hear him thank whomever he was speaking with.

"Are you okay?" he asked, pocketing his phone.

"I need to talk to you."

"Okay. Talk."

She glanced toward the corner, fearing she'd see Pete coming around it.

"You don't want Pete to find us together? I'm flattered."

She elbowed the detective. "I've sort of done something illegal."

"And you think I'm less likely to arrest you than he is?"

"I sort of involved his father in this illegal activity."

"Oh." Wayne nodded knowingly. "What did you and Harry get into?"

"I sort of stole some of John Kinney's personal items from his room at Golden Oaks."

Wayne opened his mouth to reply, but no words came out. He shut it. Appeared to mull over her admission. After a few moments, he said, "When?"

"This morning."

"Kinney still had personal items at Golden Oaks?"

"Still does. Elaine was supposed to go in and pick up the stuff today, but I doubt that's gonna happen now."

"What exactly did you steal?"

"A Rolex."

"A what?"

She held up her wrist and pointed to her not-Rolex. "And a credit card receipt and a notebook containing an inventory of really expensive wine."

"Why?"

The question puzzled her. "Uh. Because he liked to keep track of his collection?"

"No, I mean why did you steal his watch, credit card receipt, and wine inventory?"

She'd thought Wayne would question the fact that Kinney had this stuff more than her pilfering it. At least, she'd hoped. "I didn't mean to steal any of it. In fact, I have it in my truck and want to give it to you."

"Why not give it to Elaine?"

He wasn't grasping the potential importance of her discovery.

"Because it might be evidence."

"How so? The killer didn't take it. Or leave it, for that matter." Wayne's phone rang. He silenced Zoe with an upheld finger and answered the call. "Baronick...Yes, sir...That was fast...Thank you...Uh-huh...Yes. Thanks." He slipped the phone back into his pocket. "Our warrant's on its way."

Which meant Wayne and Pete would be leaving in a matter of minutes. "Don't you find it odd that a retired cop has a Rolex? And a wine collection worth more than...than..." She looked around frantically. "Than this house. And where is all this wine? I didn't see any of it in his room?"

Wayne shook his head. "Zoe, John Kinney wasn't destitute. He'd won a rather large insurance settlement years ago, invested well, and as a result enjoyed a few of the finer things in life. As for where the wine went, you said you have one of his credit card receipts. Look at it. You'll see a monthly charge for a company called Vintage Locker. They store fine wines for restaurants and collectors."

"Oh." Deflated, she chewed on her lip and on this news. "You knew about all this?"

"I've been working the case since the beginning. That includes looking into the victim's background. Yes, I knew. My investigators left that stuff there because none of it was deemed relevant to the case."

She spotted movement from the corner of her eye. Pete appeared, helping Franklin and Basset Hound-eyed Gene wheel the stretcher holding the body of Professor K to the van.

"The warrant's on its way," Wayne called to Pete. "I'll meet you over at the neighbor's house."

Pete shot a questioning look at her and the detective but kept going. Zoe slumped against the garage door. She did indeed need to turn Kinney's watch and notebook over to Elaine O'Keefe. The grieving sister and distraught widow. She pictured the scene. Elaine hysterical. Crying. Shouting at Zoe for having the nerve to rob from the dead. Calling the cops to arrest her.

Calling Pete. To arrest her.

"Give it to me."

She blinked and looked up at Wayne. "Huh?"

"You said you have the stuff in your truck?"

"Yeah?"

"Give it to me." Wayne rolled his eyes. "I'll make sure it gets back to her with the rest of Kinney's possessions."

She'd have thrown her arms around the detective's neck and kissed him, but thought Pete would have some serious questions if he spotted them. "Thank you."

Wayne shook his head. "Just promise me you'll stick with the bodies from now on and leave the police work to us cops."

Pete and Baronick parked their vehicles across the road from Boyd Anderson's driveway to await the arrival of the warrant and additional county officers to assist in executing it. The detective slid into Pete's passenger seat and flipped back the dripping hood of his raincoat.

"What was that all about?" Pete demanded.

"What?"

Pete glared at Baronick. "With Zoe."

"Nothing." Baronick flashed his veneered smile. "Jealous?"

Pete didn't dignify him with a response. As much as he wanted to press for an answer, he wasn't in the mood for Baronick's BS.

They sat in silence for several minutes watching the Anderson place through the rain-streaked windshield. There was no movement. Even the horses were nowhere to be seen.

"What are your thoughts on Zoe's brother?" Baronick asked.

The fact that, between the detective and Jason, Zoe had been spending a lot of time with other men wasn't lost on Pete. "She told you about him?"

"I met him."

"Oh?"

"He showed up at Franklin's office Friday when I was meeting with Zoe about the Kinney homicide."

"What'd you think of him?"

Baronick chuckled. "He's not *my* future brother-in-law. Besides, I asked first."

What were Pete's thoughts on Jason? He rolled around a few possible answers. Some more diplomatic than others.

When he didn't respond immediately, Baronick chuckled. "That good, huh?"

"He doesn't think much of me, I can tell you that."

"Really?" The detective's voice dripped with faux shock. "You being so soft and cuddly and all."

"Smart ass," Pete muttered. He considered the question. "Jason Cox has been going above and beyond to help fix up Zoe's farm."

"It needs all the help it can get."

Pete huffed a laugh. "No argument there."

"Is he spending Zoe's money?"

"No."

"Is he asking anything in return?"

"Not that I'm aware of."

"So, he's sinking his own cash and his own time into Zoe's dump—I mean farm. You want my advice?"

"Not really."

"Let him."

Pete gave Baronick the sternest glare he could muster.

"I mean it. Let him. I know you'd rather Zoe sell the place. Well, how much do you think she'd get for it the way it is now? All her brother is doing is raising its property value."

The detective had a point. Damn him.

A black sedan came around the bend with its turn signals on. "There's our warrant," Baronick said. He turned to face Pete. "As for Jason, if you have your doubts about whether or not he's legit, check him out."

"I did."

Baronick narrowed his eyes at him. "I don't mean with something as fallible as a law enforcement database. Ask your former secretary." The detective opened the door and stepped out to approach the car that had pulled off next to them.

Pete closed his eyes. Of course. Sylvia Bassi. Why hadn't he thought of his greatest resource earlier?

TWENTY-FIVE

The sight of the now-familiar gray Ram pickup greeted Zoe as she eased past the campaign signs and into her driveway. She caught herself smiling, eager to let her brother comfort her after a trying day and before the night of EMS duty ahead. But a large white box truck with some sort of lettering on the side parked next to the Dodge darkened her mood.

When she rolled closer to the barn, she spotted Jason sitting on her rickety porch. What the hell? He knew those rotted boards weren't safe.

Zoe pulled behind his pickup and looked up at the box truck. *24/7 Plumbing.* She cut the engine, bailed out of her Chevy, and squished across her wet front yard toward her brother seated on the dangerously dilapidated porch.

Except, it wasn't dilapidated anymore. The unstained decking might as well have flashing lights proclaiming "new, new, new." And where in the world had he dug up the pair of lawn chairs?

"What have you done?"

"You like?" Jason spread his arms in a flourish.

She stood at the edge of the porch, not entirely believing her eyes. Pete had repaired a narrow section last winter. But now raw wood marked with muddy boot tracks replaced the old rough and rotted planks, and new six-by-sixes held up the previously sagging porch roof. "You've been busy."

Jason patted the molded plastic chair next to the matching one on which he sat. "Take a load off, Sis. I bought these on sale. They're cheap, but they'll do for now."

She really needed to keep moving. The horses had to be fed. She still had to get back to Pete's and change into her uniform. But a few minutes sitting on her porch with her brother wouldn't hurt. She collapsed into the chair.

Jason aimed a finger skyward. "I climbed into your attic while it was raining. No leaks."

"Good. But..." She glanced at the truck in the driveway.

"They're in there now." Jason pointed the same finger over his shoulder. "By the time they're done, you'll have all new pipes and a water heater."

"Jason, this is too much. You're spending way too much on me."

He dismissed her protest with a wave of his hand. "I have the money. You don't. Helping you out makes me feel...like I'm making up for stuff. Lost time, you know?"

"You don't have to make up for anything. Least of all by dumping money into my house."

"You need hot and cold running water. You can't afford it. I can." His expression soured. "Pete pointed out we still need to have the house re-wired before the heater will work."

"Yeah. We don't have natural gas out here." She paused, the rest of Jason's words sinking in. "Pete knows you're doing this?"

The peevish expression remained. "He stopped by earlier."

"Why do I get the feeling you don't like him much?"

Jason gazed across the yard toward the road, and Zoe studied his profile. His set jaw. His narrowed eyes.

"Jason?"

He looked at her and his face softened. "It's nothing. You look tired. How was your day?"

"Ugh," she groaned and let her head drop back against the window behind her.

"That good, huh?"

"Well, it's not every day that you steal a Rolex watch and notebook containing a dead man's wine inventory list."

Jason choked. "What?"

She poured out the day's events from involving Harry and Barbara in her illegal activities, to having to work a homicide where the main suspect was someone she'd once stood up for, to learning her thieving was all for naught.

Jason scooted his chair over until it bumped hers and slung an arm around her. "I'm sorry, Sis."

She rested her head on his shoulder. Frustrated tears bubbled just beneath the surface. She sniffed them back.

"You're not gonna start crying again, are you?"

"No. Maybe."

He laughed, that beautiful full-throated chuckle that reminded her of their dad. "What'd you do with your stolen loot?"

"I confessed my crimes to Wayne Baronick. The detective you met when you showed up at the coroner's office? I turned it all over to him."

"What about Pete?"

"What about him?"

"You didn't tell him?"

She swallowed a lump of guilt. "No."

"Why not?" There was an edge to Jason's voice.

And it was a question she didn't have a ready answer for. "I will." Eventually. "I guess I feel bad for dragging his father into it."

"No one is going to arrest an old man for burglary. You either for that matter."

"I know. I guess I didn't want to get lectured. Not by Pete."

Jason grew quiet. He pressed his cheek against the top of her head. For several blissful minutes, they sat in comfortable silence watching the clouds part to reveal patches of blue. A tease or a promise?

He exhaled and broke the stillness. "There's something I want to say, but I don't think you're gonna want to hear it."

She sat upright and faced him. "Go ahead."

A muscle in his jaw throbbed. "I don't think Pete Adams is the right man for you."

Boyd Anderson's machete couldn't have cut any deeper than Jason's words.

"I'm sorry. The last thing I want to do is hurt you," Jason said.

She managed to choke out a laugh bordering on hysteria.

"I just don't think the two of you have as good a relationship as you want to believe. He resists all efforts to fix this place up."

Inside her head, she shouted what she knew. Pete loved her. He wanted her to think of his house as hers too. And she didn't want to live out here alone. She wanted Pete with her, but he was a city boy and had his doubts about farm life.

Her unspoken words started to register on a deeper level. Pete wanted her to live in town. She wanted him to live on the farm. Would either of them be happy in the other's world? Truly happy?

"And you," Jason went on, "are keeping things from him. Maybe not important things but stuff you should be able to share with the man you plan to spend the rest of your life with. Instead, you're confiding in that Wayne guy. And in me."

Through the parched desert of her mouth, she managed to

squeak, "Wayne's my friend. And you're my brother."

Jason tipped his face toward her. "And what is Pete?"

Linda Anderson opened the door, her face pale against her wide eyes, which flitted from Pete to Baronick and back. "What's going on?"

"Is your husband home?" Pete asked.

"Yes." It sounded more like a question than an answer.

"Is there anyone else in the house?"

"No." Another question.

"We need you both to step outside."

Her eyes shifted in the direction of the O'Keefe's place, but she forced her gaze back to Pete. "You haven't told me what's going on."

He figured she knew exactly what was going on.

Baronick handed the court document to her. "We have a warrant to search your property."

Her mouth opened but no sound came out. Swallowing, she turned and called over her shoulder. "Boyd? The police are here."

Pete kept his hand on his Glock, his finger on the holster's release. He was taking no chances, even though a menacing-looking pair of county officers in their heavy-duty body armor stood in plain sight behind him and Baronick.

Footsteps thudded across the ceiling and clomped down the stairs. Boyd Anderson came into view wearing dark jeans and a crisp plaid cotton shirt. Not that Pete expected him to show up covered in his neighbor's blood.

"What's this all about?" Anderson asked.

Linda met him short of the door, clutching the warrant, and tucked in under his arm. "They want to search the property."

He took the document and scanned it. "I assume this has something to do with O'Keefe."

"You know about that?" Pete asked.

Anderson aimed a thumb at the ceiling. "I could see a lot of commotion going on over there from my upstairs window." His gaze stopped on one item. "Is he dead?"

"Yes."

Linda let out a sob and covered her mouth with a thin hand.

Anderson aged a decade on the spot. He pulled his wife closer against him for a moment. "Get your cell phone and call the attorney," he said to her. Then he looked at Pete. "What do you need me to do?"

Once the Andersons had gotten their jackets and joined Pete and Baronick on the porch, one team of investigators stepped through the door and set to work. Linda and her cell phone moved to the other end of the porch.

"I notice your horses aren't out in the pasture," Pete said.

Anderson looked toward his barn. "We kept them in today because of the rain and snow."

"I thought maybe you'd put them in because you noticed O'Keefe had his mower out."

"I didn't know he had it out until I got home."

"You went somewhere this morning?"

"Yeah," Anderson said, a growl in his voice. "I took a load of scrap out to Strunk's Iron and Metal."

"Can anyone confirm you were there and when?"

He made a face. "I wish. They changed their schedule and are closed on Mondays now. I should've called first but didn't. It was a wasted trip."

"Did you stop anywhere else? Get gas? Hit a drive-through for coffee?"

"Nope."

"Where's this load of scrap now?"

"Still in the bed of my truck." He pointed toward the garage and its closed door. "In there."

Linda stomped across the porch toward them. "Don't say another word, Boyd. Our attorney's on his way."

He shrugged. "I got nothing to hide." He looked at the warrant in his hand. "I noticed you specifically mention my corn knife in this. Is that what happened? Someone killed O'Keefe with a knife?"

"Something like that."

"Would it help if I just showed you where it is?"

"Boyd," Linda snapped.

He turned on his wife. "I didn't kill anyone, so I don't see where cooperating will hurt."

She blew an exasperated breath.

"Yes," Pete replied to Anderson's question. "Showing us where it is would help a lot."

He gestured for them to follow and stepped off the porch. "It's in the barn."

Anderson led the way with Pete and Baronick trailing behind. Linda stayed on the porch, her arms crossed. Pete wasn't sure if she was about to blow a gasket or burst into tears.

Pete shot a glance at the detective. "You're being uncharacteristically quiet."

"I'm thinking."

"Well, *that* can't be good."

Baronick didn't react, which made Pete all the more curious.

Anderson crossed the gravel separating his house from the barn, weaving around the county police cruisers. At the door set in the barn's stone foundation, he slid the bolt, swung the door open on well-greased hinges, and entered.

The structure showed evidence of having once been a milking barn with the remnants of stanchions in the one corner, but stalls constructed of heavy newer lumber took up the bulk of the space. The horses, which had been the source of all the animosity, nickered.

The smell of horse and hay brought Zoe to Pete's mind. This was the kind of world where she thrived. Where she belonged. Forcing her to spend the rest of her life living in town, even a village as small as Dillard, would be depriving her of her natural element, like a flower, cut from its roots and stuck in a vase with only water. Eventually, she would wilt. And part of her would die.

"Hey." Baronick nudged him. "You coming or what?"

"Right behind you."

They followed Anderson through another door into a room used for storage. Saddles, bridles, large trash bins that probably contained feed. One wall held a peg board on which hung assorted tools. Anderson crossed to it but stopped short and swore. He turned toward them, his face void of all color, his lips a thin tense line.

"It's gone."

Zoe let the intensity of Jason's words burn into her brain. Into her heart. "You're right."

Her brother turned his face away.

"About part of it."

He brought his gaze back to her.

"I've been wrong to keep this from Pete. I need to tell him everything. But you're wrong about him not being the right man for me. Yeah, he drags his feet where this farm is concerned." She looked around. A new porch deck didn't solve all the problems with the house. Even new plumbing only put a dent in the work that needed to be done before the place became even remotely habitable. Never mind comfortable. She sighed. "Maybe Pete's been right about it. Maybe the best thing I could do is sell it."

"No." Jason choked. "I mean, I don't want to see you give up your dreams."

Zoe thought about Pete. Their first kiss in her old kitchen at the Krolls' farm. She'd been keeping secrets from him then too. They'd had highs and lows ever since. Disagreements over cases. Disagreements over her dilapidated pickup. But when it came down to it, she knew he'd walk through hell for her.

And she'd do the same for him.

"My dreams aren't worth holding onto if they don't include Pete."

Jason studied her for a long moment. "You really love him."

"Yeah. I do."

He lowered his eyes and nodded.

From inside, came a thud and some heavy footsteps. The door swung open and two men carrying a pair of toolboxes stepped outside. "We're all finished, Mr. Cox."

Jason leapt to his feet. "Great." He introduced the plumbers to Zoe. Then he told her, "I'll be right back." He pointed toward their truck. "I'm gonna square up with them."

"I've told you. You don't need to foot the bill for the work on my house."

He waved her off again and flashed the smile she'd come to love. "You can repay me by letting me crash in the spare room when I'm in town."

"You darned well better stay here when you come to visit."

She watched him walk away, chatting with the plumbers. Her gaze drifted to the barn roof, new and shining in the snippets of afternoon sunshine. Looking down, she smiled at her new, sturdy porch decking. And plumbing. Did she really have running water now? Jason had his wallet out and was looking over the paperwork, so she ducked inside to the chipped and stained cast-iron kitchen sink and turned the pitted faucet. It sputtered and hissed. And gushed. Water. Running water. For the first time in the house since she'd taken possession.

Zoe stepped back out onto the porch as the plumbing truck's engine roared to life and Jason ambled toward the house.

He held out the papers in his hand. "You should file these somewhere."

Without looking at the totals and only a glance at the word "paid" scrawled across the bottom, she took the receipt and threw her arms around her brother's neck. "Thank you."

He froze for a moment before wrapping his arms around her and holding her close. "You are very welcome, Sis."

TWENTY-SIX

With the disappearance of his machete, Boyd Anderson wisely heeded his wife's advice to shut up until their attorney arrived. Baronick had placed the horseman in the backseat of his unmarked car and stood guard. Teams of officers from county, state, and a few neighboring jurisdictions prowled the barn, house, and outbuildings. One team, armed with a metal detector worked a grid in the pasture between Anderson's farm and the professor's property.

All bases seemed to be covered for the moment, so Pete slid behind the wheel of his Explorer and pulled out his phone.

Sylvia Bassi, his former police secretary and current township supervisor, had been in New Mexico visiting her grandkids and daughter-in-law for the last two weeks. Since he rarely had luck with the Four Corners area's cell service, he didn't expect her to answer.

But she did. "What's wrong?"

"Can't I just call my best girl to say hello?"

"Absolutely, but that ain't me. What's going on?"

He rubbed his forehead. Where to start? "You knew Zoe's father before he married Kimberly, didn't you?"

"You know I did." There was a pause at the other end of the line, and for a moment, Pete thought the call had been dropped. When Sylvia spoke again, her voice was softer. "Why are you asking about Gary?"

"Did you know anything about him having an affair before his marriage?"

Another long silence before she whispered, "My God."

So, it was true. Somewhere deep in Pete's heart, he'd hoped Sylvia was going to completely debunk Jason's story. "Zoe has a brother. And he's here."

A long, soft "Ooohh..."

"Did you know the girl?"

"It was a long time ago. But I'm sure I must have known at the time."

Pete flipped through his notebook. "Name was Brenda Patterson."

"Brenda Patterson?" Pete could hear Sylvia breathing. "I seem to remember a Patterson family. Lived over in Elm Grove. They moved before you came to Vance Township."

He noticed some action with the team searching the pasture. A shout went up, but he couldn't make out what was said from inside his vehicle. Then he spotted Baronick waving at him. "Sylvia, I have to go. If you think of anything about the woman, call me back."

"Wait. Why? Do you have reason to doubt this guy's word?"

"Not really. I just don't care for him much."

"What about Zoe?"

"She's nuts about him. I have to go. Thanks." Pete thumbed the red button and stepped out of his SUV. "What's going on?" he called to Baronick.

"They found the machete."

The county crime scene unit had moved their van and their base of operation from the professor's backyard to the middle of Boyd Anderson's horse pasture. Another crime scene tape barricade had been set up. Pete and Baronick stood at the edge of it, letting the forensics guys do their thing.

"It was half buried in the dirt and grass," the officer who found the machete told them. "There's what looks like blood on the blade. Once the lab matches it to our victim, we'll know for certain this is the knife used in the homicide."

"Odd place to hide a murder weapon," Pete mused.

Baronick pulled up his collar against the breeze. "Maybe he dropped the thing and couldn't find it."

Pete glared at him. "You just stabbed a man to death. A man you've already threatened with this very knife. You're leaving the scene of the murder and drop your weapon. You think you wouldn't take the time to stop and look for it?"

"The grass is high." Even Baronick didn't sound convinced by his own argument.

"Not that high. And it's a damned big knife." Pete looked around. "And another thing. This is Anderson's horse pasture. He wouldn't leave a sharp object out here where his horses might get cut on it."

"But he didn't turn his horses out today, did he?" Baronick said smugly.

Pete had to concede that point to the detective. "Okay. Maybe Anderson intentionally stuck the knife in the ground on his way home from committing murder, and after we left, planned to retrieve and do a better job of disposing of the evidence when he was no longer under scrutiny."

Baronick nodded. "I like it."

"Well, I don't."

"It was your scenario."

"I know, but I still don't like it."

"Why not?"

Pete crossed his arms and pondered the question. Why not? The man had it in him. Of that Pete was certain. But he couldn't help feeling they were missing something important. "Your sister and I talked to Anderson's neighbors yesterday. Everyone likes him."

"Likable guys kill people."

"Sometimes. And if he spotted O'Keefe over there with his bagger full of clippings and thought he was going to feed them to his horses—again—it's possible, even probable, that he would have stormed over there."

"You still don't sound convinced."

"I'm not." Pete turned to look off in the other direction. Toward Gino Marcini's place. "The man who owns the farm market told me about an incident. Anderson was there one day when a customer helped himself to some produce without paying. And before he left, he belted his own son. Anderson snapped. According to Gino, he had the guy by the throat."

Baronick grunted. "I would've too if I'd been there."

"The part that's been bothering me is what happened next." Pete told the detective about Anderson demanding money from the man and then turning it over to the farmer. "Gino said he was surprised Anderson gave it all to him."

"Why? So what if it was way more than the damaged merchandise was worth? I mean, if the guy's being choked, he's not gonna stop and calculate exactly how much he owes. He's gonna throw a wad of cash at his attacker and then get the hell outta there."

"Agreed. Gino even offered Anderson a reward. Which he turned down. In spite of being deep in debt."

Baronick's face darkened. "Anderson's in debt?"

"According to Gino."

The detective's jaw tightened. Clearly, he had something on his mind.

"What?" Pete asked.

"We've been focused on O'Keefe's murder. But you've been looking at Anderson for the Kinney homicide as well, right?"

"And have a damned weak motive there too. A decades-old arrest doesn't seem good enough."

Baronick's lip started to curl into his wolfish sneer. "No. But money does. Money's always a good motive." He swore under his breath. "I should have caught this sooner."

"Am I supposed to know what you're talking about?"

"You'd know if you'd talk to Zoe."

"What the hell does Zoe have to do with any of this?"

"John Kinney had money. Lots of it."

The detective told about settlements and investments, none of which explained what he meant about Zoe. "You're suggesting Boyd Anderson killed Kinney for his money?"

"Like I said, money's always a good motive. And Anderson could easily be our Baseball Cap Man. He's the right size, right build."

"There's only one flaw in your thinking. How does killing Kinney get Anderson any money?"

Baronick deflated. "True. He didn't even take Kinney's Rolex."

"That was real?"

"Yeah. You really need to catch up with Zoe."

Pete wanted to demand answers about Zoe, but Baronick's hypothesis sparked an ember of an idea.

The detective must have read it in Pete's face. "You have a theory of your own."

He looked toward the Andersons' farmhouse and recalled his visit there last week. "Linda Anderson told me Boyd did all the restoration work on the house. Even a do-it-yourself project can't be cheap. She also mentioned some big vet bills thanks to the professor and his grass clippings." Pete paused a moment. "What does Boyd do for a living anyway?"

"He's had a run of bad luck in recent years." Baronick scrolled through his phone for his notes. "He worked for a big firm in Pittsburgh as an environmental engineer."

Pete grunted. "Sounds like good money."

"I imagine it was. Past tense. They phased out his division and offered a transfer to Seattle, but he didn't want to move."

"He and his wife love his farm," Pete mused.

"A few years ago, he got a job with Federated Petroleum Resources at the peak of the Marcellus Shale boom. But when the gas industry flattened out, they cut jobs. His included."

"He's probably one of the landowners who would've made a small fortune had FPR continued with their plans to expand into Monongahela County."

"Exactly. Currently, he's employed at Stoneking's Hardware and Lumber. And he does odd jobs for anyone who needs a handyman."

"Okay." Pete started thinking out loud. "Anderson needs money. Lots of it. He has vet bills. Maybe he stands to lose this farm that he's put his heart and soul into. Kinney has money. Lots of it. The problem is Anderson doesn't stand to inherit."

"I got that much," Baronick said flatly.

"Elaine O'Keefe does."

Baronick's lips thinned. "And coincidentally, her husband has also just turned up dead."

"Yeah," Pete said. "I hate coincidences."

Pete found Elaine O'Keefe wheeling a large suitcase from her front door to her car.

"Going somewhere?" he asked as he climbed from his vehicle.

"Back to the Brunswick Inn." She glanced at her luggage. "Since I already have the room there, I thought I'd pack a few things and stay a while longer." Her smile looked battle-weary. "In all honesty, I don't want to be here right now. Especially knowing that Kristopher died right out back."

"Understandable." The possibility that the widow might be about to make a run for it crossed Pete's mind, but as long as she believed they didn't suspect her, she had no reason to bolt. Not with her brother's money waiting to be inherited. "Let me give you a hand."

"Thank you." She popped the Camry's trunk, and Pete hoisted the suitcase into it.

What did she have in there? Gold bars?

Elaine lowered the trunk lid and tipped her head toward the corner of the house leading to the backyard. "I saw a lot of action out in the pasture. Did you...?" Her voice trailed off, unable or unwilling to say the words.

"We believe we've located the weapon that killed your husband, yes."

Tears edged her dark eyes. "Boyd?"

Pete shrugged. "It looks that way."

She lowered her face. "I can't believe it. I guess you never know what a person is capable of."

"That's a fact."

She traced a finger under each eye and then raised her head, meeting Pete's gaze. "I trust you'll keep me apprised of the situation."

"Yes, ma'am. Can I reach you at the hotel?"

"Oh. Yes." She dug in her purse and came up with a business card and a pen. After jotting something on the back of the card, she handed it to Pete. "That's my cell phone number. It'll save you from trying to track me down if you need me."

He noted the front of the card. Elaine's name and position as a manager at an insurance company in the city. He made a mental note to check on her brother's and her husband's life insurance policies. "Thank you. I appreciate that," Pete said and tucked the card into his pocket. "You already have my number in case you remember anything that might help our case."

"I don't know what that might be, but yes, of course."

He moved around to the driver's door and opened it for her. She thanked him before sliding behind the wheel. "Drive safely."

After watching her make a right turn onto the main road, Pete dug out his phone and keyed in Baronick's number. "She's on her way back to the Brunswick Inn."

"I'll have one of my men make sure she gets there. After all, as distraught as she is, we wouldn't want her wandering off and getting lost."

"You do that." Pete checked his watch. Four fifteen. "I need to get back to the station to check in with my new officer."

"All right. I'm taking Mr. Anderson to County HQ for interrogation."

Pete climbed into his SUV. "I'll meet you there. Don't start without me."

TWENTY-SEVEN

Earl leaned over Zoe's shoulder and scrutinized her phone. "That's him, huh?"

"Yep." She sat at the desk in the ambulance service garage and held the photo of Jason closer, so her partner could get a better look. He swiped through the series. She didn't need to see them to know what Earl was looking at. She'd memorized each one. Jason posed on her porch—one full-length showing his handiwork and one close-up. Jason next to the barn with his arms raised triumphantly toward the new roof. A couple of selfies of the two of them, cheek-to-cheek, goofy grins on their faces.

Earl handed the phone back to her and she smiled at the third and final selfie. Jason had wrapped his arms around her shoulders. She hadn't been quick enough to capture the kiss on the side of her face. But she felt it when she looked at the photo.

She also noticed the gleam in Jason's eyes, emotions boiling up and threatening to spill over.

He almost looked sad.

The phone in her hand started ringing, the image replaced with the notification of an incoming call from Franklin's secretary. "Hi, Paulette. What's up?"

The voice on the phone sounded frantic. "It's Franklin. He's collapsed. They're rushing him back to the hospital."

"What?" Zoe glanced at the scanner. She'd tuned out the staticky chatter of calls being handled by police, fire, and the other EMS outside of their response area.

"He was here at his desk...talking to Doc about scheduling...the autopsy." Paulette hiccuped, and Zoe realized she was sobbing.

"Is he...?" She almost asked if he was dead, but no. Paulette had already said they'd taken him to the hospital. That meant he was alive. Zoe hoped.

Earl leaned down, and Zoe tipped the phone, so he could listen in.

Paulette ignored the fragment of a question. "His color was so bad...almost gray...and I knew he probably hadn't eaten. I went to get him some orange juice...and when I came back..." Her voice broke. "When I came back, he was on the floor. Unresponsive."

"Orange juice?" Zoe's mind raced back through Franklin's symptoms. And the IV bag of half normal saline. "Is he diabetic?"

"He doesn't want anyone to know. But, yes. They say he's going into kidney failure and will probably need a transplant." Paulette's voice spiked and dissolved into sobs.

Zoe braced an elbow on the desk and buried her face in her hand. Kidney failure. She visualized Franklin, fresh out of the hospital, spending the afternoon outside, in the snow and rain and cold.

Paulette sniffed. "I'm sure he took his insulin but forgot to eat."

"Insulin shock," Zoe said. More dangerous than a diabetic coma.

"I called the paramedics immediately." A long pause. "It doesn't look good."

Earl straightened and strode out of the door to the crew lounge.

"Zoe," Paulette said, her voice solemn, "you need to take over again. Indefinitely."

Zoe closed her eyes. "Did Franklin schedule the autopsy with Doc before he..." Before he collapsed.

"Doc told me to call him back after I spoke to you. He's supposed to give a talk to a group of university students in the morning and wanted to do it tonight."

"I'm on duty with the ambulance tonight." Heavy approaching footsteps and the appearance of Earl with their crew chief, Tony Deluca, stopped her. "Wait. Can you hold on a minute, Paulette?"

"Okay."

Zoe muted the call.

"If you need to go, go," Tony said.

"But—"

"I'll get someone to cover for you." He managed a sad smile. "You'll owe whoever agrees to come in. Big time."

She nodded. "Thanks." Unmuted the phone. "Paulette? Call Doc and tell him I'll be at the morgue in a half hour."

Pete found Baronick on the phone at the front desk of the Monongahela County Police Headquarters. From his grim expression, the call wasn't pleasant. After telling the person on the other end to keep him posted, the detective pocketed the device.

"Franklin Marshall's back in the hospital."

"Oh?" Pete was only slightly surprised. The man hadn't looked good at the crime scene.

"Collapsed in his office. Looks like Zoe's handling O'Keefe's autopsy tonight."

"She's on duty."

Baronick shrugged. "Death waits for no one. And neither does Doc Abercrombie apparently." He picked up a file from the counter, tipped his head toward the hallway leading to the interrogation rooms, and started walking. "How's my sister?"

Pete fell in beside the detective. "I left the township in her capable hands."

"How often are you gonna call and check on her?"

"I'm not. Why? Should I?"

Baronick chuckled.

"Dammit. You're the one who referred her. If she screws up, I'm holding you accountable." Pete was only half-kidding.

"She's a good cop. But I've said it before." Baronick aimed a finger at Pete. "If you tell her I said that, I'll have to kill you."

Typical sibling relationship.

They arrived at Interview Room A, but instead of reaching for the doorknob, Baronick faced Pete and flipped open the folder. "Anderson's attorney is in there with him."

"I assumed as much. His wife was pretty insistent."

Baronick handed the folder to Pete. "While I was waiting for you, I did some digging. Anderson is definitely in debt. He's taken out two mortgages on his farm. Behind on both of them. Meanwhile, he's making slightly more than minimum wage at the lumberyard. If he doesn't come up with some money somewhere, he's likely gonna lose his property. Sounds like a pretty good motive to me."

"Now he has legal expenses." Pete shook his head. "It's a shame. That's a nice farm."

"He won't need it. The state'll provide his accommodations if he's convicted."

"I was thinking of his wife." Linda Anderson had seemed so content when she'd welcomed Pete into her home last week. He couldn't help but think about his discussion with Seth. The guilty weren't the only ones who suffered the consequences of their actions.

"Maybe you can buy it for Zoe. It's already in move-in condition.

Unlike her current property."

Pete shot him a look. He didn't want to admit the thought had briefly crossed his mind. "I see the search didn't produce any bloody clothing. No blood anywhere inside Anderson's house."

"Nope."

"If he stabbed a man, he would be covered in blood. What'd he do with his clothes?"

"Maybe he buried them like he tried to do with the knife."

Pete also wondered where he'd cleaned up.

And he thought about that suitcase Elaine O'Keefe had dragged out of her house.

Baronick reclaimed the file. "Let's do this." He pushed open the door.

Boyd Anderson lifted his head when they entered. He sat with his hands folded on top of the table. At his side, his attorney, Anthony Imperatore, had set up shop with an open leather briefcase and a legal pad and pen at the ready in front of him. He made no move to rise, but nodded politely. "Chief Adams. Detective Baronick."

Pete extended a hand, which the lawyer grasped. They'd been on opposite sides of many cases over the years, but Pete respected Imperatore and had gone so far as recommending him a time or two. The man was tough but honest.

The detective shook hands with the lawyer too, but grudgingly. Pete took a seat across from Boyd and caught the look Baronick directed his way. The detective had wanted that spot.

Pete ignored him. "Mr. Anderson, how long have you been married?"

The question brought a look of surprise from their suspect, but Pete wanted to see the man's reactions to the softball questions before lobbing him the tough ones.

"Twenty-one years. It'll be twenty-two this summer." He winced.

Pete imagined Boyd wondering if he'd be a free man for his anniversary. "And how long have you owned the farm?"

"Two years less than that."

"Bought it as newlyweds, huh?" Pete struck a relaxed pose aimed at helping calm their suspect.

"Yeah."

"Where are you employed?"

Boyd shot a glance at Imperatore who remained motionless but wary. "Stoneking's Hardware and Lumber. Plus, I do whatever odd jobs I can scrounge up."

Imperatore rapped on his legal pad with the pen. "I'd much prefer you don't volunteer anything beyond directly answering the question," he told his client before scowling at Pete. "You already know all of this. Why don't you save us some time and get on with it?"

Baronick leaned forward. "You mean get on to the questions you won't let him answer."

The attorney lifted his chin. "We'll see."

"All right." Pete reached for the folder still closed in front of the detective. "Tell me this. How does your wife feel about the possibility of losing the farm on which you've lived most of your married life?"

"Chief Adams," Imperatore said with the inflection of a disapproving parent. Pete half expected him to throw in a *tsk-tsk* for good measure.

But the question hit its mark. Boyd flushed. "She doesn't know. And I'd prefer it stay that way."

"You don't think she'd figure it out when the bank seizes the property and the sheriff serves her with an eviction notice?" Baronick asked.

"I hope it doesn't get that far," Boyd said, a note of panic in his voice.

The attorney clamped a hand on the man's arm. "That's enough, Mr. Anderson."

"Okay, let's try this one." Pete flipped a page in the folder. "Where were you this morning?"

Boyd shot a nervous glance at his attorney. "I already told them. I went to Strunk's Iron and Metal, but they were closed."

Before the lawyer could protest, Pete asked, "And you didn't stop anywhere else?"

"No. I came straight home."

"Anyone see you?"

"My wife."

"Anyone besides your wife?"

"No."

Imperatore made a loop with his pen signaling Pete to move on.

He flipped back a few pages. "How about last Monday morning between ten and noon?"

Boyd's eyes widened, and he looked to Imperatore who'd already raised a hand. "He's not going to answer that, gentlemen. In fact, I'm recommending he not say anything else."

Baronick growled deep in his throat.

Pete made a show of closing the folder before leaning forward to rest his forearms on the table. "Fine. Do you mind if I speculate a moment?"

Imperatore capped his pen. "You're wasting your time, Chief."

Pete shrugged. "It's my time to waste. And you're getting paid by the minute, so I don't see what you have to complain about. Mr. Anderson, on the other hand, is footing your bill. But he's also under arrest."

The attorney held Pete's gaze but didn't speak.

"Here's my theory." Pete looked at Boyd. "I don't think you killed Kristopher O'Keefe." From the corner of Pete's eye, he spotted Baronick's head snap in his direction.

Imperatore also appeared interested, although mildly so. "Do tell, Chief Adams."

"Elaine O'Keefe." Pete said the name and let it hang there a moment.

Boyd's jaw moved, but his lips stayed pressed closed, as if he wanted to speak but feared his attorney would bust his chops for it.

Imperatore, an old pro at the waiting game, didn't even blink.

Pete leaned back and crossed an ankle over his knee. "Elaine O'Keefe's brother had a considerable amount of money stashed away. Money he was squandering on fine wine and other little luxuries. Or at least it was her opinion he was squandering it. Poor Elaine also happened to be married to an asshole."

Baronick choked.

"I think Elaine wanted her inheritance sooner rather than later," Pete said, "but she couldn't bring herself to kill her brother. Or maybe she figured she'd be caught. After all, everyone at Golden Oaks knew her."

Baronick pulled out his phone and started tapping.

"Elaine found out you were in desperate need of money and already had an unpleasant history with her brother, so she made you a deal. You take care of the dirty work, and she'd share her inheritance with you."

Boyd's eyes grew wider with each sentence, but he still kept his mouth closed.

"It was a good deal. Except—" Pete held up one finger. "Poor Elaine is still married to an asshole and now she's only going to get a part of her brother's money."

The realization of where Pete was going with this must have hit Boyd. Lines creased his forehead, and his gaze shifted.

"Elaine managed to slip over to your place—or maybe she just stopped by for a neighborly visit with your wife. I understand they'd become friendly. Either way, she goes into your barn and steals your machete. Then she kills Professor O'Keefe with it and frames you." Pete brushed his hands together as if wiping off dust. "Now the grieving widow is free of her asshole husband *and* she gets to keep her entire inheritance."

Boyd had shifted forward in his seat and appeared ready to pop. However, Imperatore stopped him with a hand on his arm.

"A very interesting supposition, Chief. But there's a problem with it. You're still accusing my client of a murder. One he did not commit." Emphasis on the "not."

Before Pete had a chance to reply, Boyd swiveled toward the attorney and whispered something in his ear. Imperatore's mouth twitched. He blocked the view with his hand and whispered into Boyd's ear. The exchange went on, Boyd clearly excited, for several moments.

"Would you like some time alone with your client?" Pete offered. If they were hammering out a proposition for a deal, he'd gladly give them a little privacy.

Imperatore held up a finger. Wait. He finished what he was telling Boyd, who nodded sharply.

They faced Pete and Baronick across the table once more. "Understand, my client is admitting no guilt in the homicide of Mr. John Kinney, but he does want to give you one bit of information."

Boyd came forward, placing both hands, palms down, on the table. "What you said makes sense—"

Imperatore stopped him. "Just tell them the one part I agreed to."

Boyd nodded again. "Elaine did come over to our place yesterday to see my wife. I'm not sure what they talked about. You'll have to ask Linda. But I can tell you Linda took her out to the barn to see the horses."

Pete shot a glance at Baronick, who spun out of his chair while keying a number into his phone. As the detective slipped out of the room, Pete fixed their suspect with a hard stare. "Is there anything else you'd like to tell me?"

The answer came from the attorney. "No. But I want to be present when you speak to Mrs. Anderson as well."

They'd see about that.

Pete continued to watch Boyd. "If you think of anything else—"

Imperatore slipped his legal pad into his brief case and clipped it shut. "I'll be in touch."

Pete picked up the folder Baronick had left behind and found the detective on his phone in the hallway. "Yes, put out a BOLO on her," he snapped.

"What's going on?" Pete asked as the detective jabbed at the screen.

"The widow's gone, and she's not answering her phone."

"What do you mean, 'gone'?" I thought you had someone watching her."

"I did." Baronick clenched his fist so hard, Pete expected to hear the phone shatter. "They apparently weren't watching closely enough. She checked out of the Brunswick Inn. Elaine O'Keefe is in the wind."

TWENTY-EIGHT

Pete had expected to find the out-on-patrol sign hanging on the front door when he swung it open, setting the bells to jingling. Instead, Abby's squad car sat in the lot, and when he stepped inside, voices greeted him from Nancy's office.

"Hey, Chief." Seth sat in one of the chairs and swiveled toward Pete.

Abby sat in the other, her back turned to the phone and radio base.

Pete couldn't help but notice the smitten grin on Seth's face. "I gather you two have met."

Abby flushed.

"I was out for a walk and saw the car, so I thought I'd drop in and check out my replacement."

"I'm not—" she stuttered.

Seth's easy laugh silenced her.

It was a laugh Pete hadn't heard in months. "No one's replacing anybody," he said for the benefit of both young officers. He looked from Seth—who seemed to be having a hard time prying his eyes from the new member of the department—to Abby and her red cheeks. Pete wondered if he was witnessing the start of a police-station romance. Had Seth stopped in to check out the new kid on the block but stayed for an entirely different reason?

"How'd the interrogation go?" Abby asked, interrupting Pete's musing.

"About the way you'd expect when a suspect lawyers up." He hooked a thumb in his duty belt. "Did you get the BOLO on Elaine O'Keefe?"

"Yep." Abby swiveled in her chair and picked up a sheet of paper on Nancy's desk. "But I don't understand. I didn't think the widow was a suspect."

"The spouse is always a suspect," Seth said. His face clouded.

"Any family member is."

He was right. And Pete should have paid closer attention to her. "She had motive, means, and opportunity. It looks like she hired Anderson to take out her brother. But two things bothered me about Anderson killing O'Keefe."

"It was pretty stupid to use the same knife he'd already used to threaten the victim," Abby said.

"That was one."

"What was the other?" Seth asked.

"Stabbing someone like that is an up-close-and-personal crime. The killer didn't knife O'Keefe in the back. He was standing face-to-face with him."

Abby shifted forward like an eager high school student ready to raise her hand. "And O'Keefe was terrified of Boyd Anderson."

"Right. I can't picture the professor allowing his neighbor to approach his fence, let alone get close enough for Anderson to stab him."

"But his wife could do it," Seth said. "He'd never see it coming."

This was the first time since the shooting last winter that Seth had shown an interest in police work. Whether it was due to an attraction to Abby or simply a result of getting his head together at last, Pete took it as a sign of hope.

Abby pursed her lips and nodded. "I guess I should get back out on patrol. I'm going to swing by the O'Keefes' place just to make sure she didn't return home."

"Don't take any chances. If you spot her, call for backup."

"Will do, Boss." Abby snagged her jacket from the hook next to the door on her way out.

After the bells signaled her departure, Pete turned to Seth. "What do you think?"

"Of my replacement?"

"Of our new officer."

"She's smart."

"She is indeed." At least the kid saw beyond the young woman's appearance. Pete motioned for Seth to follow him and headed down the hall to his office.

Seth stopped at the coffee maker in the corner and poured himself a cup from the pot that had been on since before O'Keefe's homicide. "Zoe working tonight?"

"Yep."

"I figured. Otherwise you'd be in a hurry to get home."

Pete chuckled and slumped into the chair behind his desk. He gestured at the cup in Seth's hand. "You might want to make a fresh pot."

"Nah." He claimed the other chair. "You must be glad to have the man who killed your FTO behind bars."

Another spark of interest. "I'll be happier when we nail down the evidence to convict Anderson."

While Pete booted up his computer, Seth drifted into a thoughtful silence. After a minute or two, he said, "I can't imagine ending up in a place like that." His eyes widened. "I'm so sorry. I forgot your father's in there too."

Pete waved away the apology. "I think the same thing. Not wanting to picture myself in a nursing home. But Harry seems to like it. Hell, he has a girlfriend."

Seth almost choked on his coffee. "Good for him." He swallowed, and the brief grin faded. "I guess I'm thinking more about Kinney though. Being a cop. How do you go from being in total charge of your life and of other officers one day, to having a bunch of nurses telling you what to do the next?"

Pete leaned back in his chair. "It didn't happen quite that fast for Kinney. He's been relying on help for a long time."

"Oh?"

"He was forced into retirement by an accident years ago."

"I didn't realize." Seth took another sip of coffee, winced at the taste, and set the cup on Pete's desk. After he swallowed, he asked, "Was it in the line of duty?"

"Yeah."

"Were you with him?"

"No. I was on duty when it happened, but I wasn't riding with Kinney any longer." Pete let his mind drift back nearly twenty years. "He'd stopped to assist a pair of stranded motorists. Their car had broken down on I-279, north of Pittsburgh. A man and his pregnant wife. Kinney was helping the man push the car off to the side of the road. Another woman, driving under the influence, slammed into the rear of the car they were pushing."

"Shit," Seth whispered.

"Yeah. Shattered Kinney's legs. The other man lost both of his. And that wasn't the worst of it. The pregnant wife saw the car coming. She jumped in to try to push her husband and Kinney out of the way.

She died at the scene."

Seth swallowed hard. "The baby?"

"They couldn't save it." Pete remembered the pall that hung over the Zone One station that night. "Kinney had his wits about him enough to get a description of the vehicle and partial plate number."

"You mean the other driver didn't stop?"

"No. She didn't."

Seth covered his face with one hand.

"She was convicted on multiple charges including two counts of vehicular homicide."

Seth blew out a ragged breath. "Wow. You just never know what day will be your last, do you?"

"No." Pete thought of Kinney, smothered in his room at the nursing home. And of O'Keefe, stabbed in his backyard. "You don't."

A fire-like blaze of orange rimmed the morning horizon as Zoe approached her farm's driveway. Above, a cloudless blue sky promised to melt the frost from the roofs once the sun cleared the tree line. She slowed to make the turn and eyed the row of campaign posters. After the night she'd just had, she seriously considered replacing them with signs promoting the opposition.

The autopsy had been the least of it, revealing nothing unexpected. Professor Kristopher-with-a-K O'Keefe had bled out, the result of a deep stab wound that punctured the small intestine and nicked the abdominal aorta. The type of blade used was consistent with the corn knife belonging to Boyd Anderson.

Before she had a chance to choose between returning to duty with the EMS or going home to Pete's for a long hot shower, she'd been called to the scene of a drug overdose on the far side of the county. The victim was nothing more than a kid. A teen girl with long dirty blonde hair and a life of promise ahead of her, cut short by a needle in her vein. The investigation took until the early hours of the morning and was immediately followed by a traffic fatality in yet another part of the county. Another teen lost his life in a vehicle-versus-tree confrontation. A passenger in the car had been Life Flighted to Pittsburgh, his survival questionable.

It was nearly dawn by the time Zoe climbed behind the wheel of her Chevy and spotted the gas gauge dangerously close to empty. She stopped at the first 24-hour Food 'n' Fuel she encountered and filled her tank. Standing in line inside to pay for her large coffee, she realized not only had she lost an entire night to death scenes, but if Franklin didn't make a miraculous recovery, she'd have a full plate of autopsies ahead of her. The idea left a bitter taste in her mouth, one she couldn't attribute to the convenience-store caffeine.

On the drive home, she'd hoped to find Jason at her house. She needed a brotherly hug. But no gray Dodge Ram sat in front of her barn. The weight of his absence bore down on her tired shoulders. She unplugged her phone from the charger and punched in his number. At least the sound of his voice might tide her over.

"Hey, this is Jason. Leave a message and I'll call you back."

Crap.

She waited for the beep. "It's me. I had a rough night and really wanted to talk to my big brother. Call me when you can. Love you. Bye."

When she hit the button to end the call and her phone returned to its home screen, she noticed the tiny number one next to her message icon. In all the chaos, she'd missed a text. Another tap on the phone and she discovered the message came from Jason.

Something has come up back in Philly and I have to go home. I scheduled an electrician to rewire the house beginning Monday afternoon. My key is on top of the doorframe so he can get in. The bill has been paid in advance.

Please know that I love you with all my heart and always will.

Silly brother, she thought with a smile. Of course, she knew that. Her smile faded. He was gone. Back to Philadelphia. The realization stole her breath away. Why did she feel like he was never coming back?

With a sigh as tired and heavy as her heart, she stepped down from the truck's cab and was greeted by a round of nickering from the horses.

"I'm coming. I'm coming," she told them and headed for the barn door. She shuffled through the process of filling the feeders with grain on autopilot. As usual, Duchess the Digger pawed at the door and ignored her order to quit. They did obey her command to wait while she opened the door. Once she stepped aside, the four horses charged in, dividing into their stalls. She latched each stall except Windstar's, removed her gloves, and took a few minutes to scratch his itches. His warmth lured her to rest her head on his back and close her eyes. He made one slow sidestep, disturbing her potential nap. "Okay, boy. I can take a hint." She patted his neck, slid her gloves back on, and latched his stall before tackling the mindless chore of scattering hay outside. The morning chill kept her moving and awake, but all she could think about was getting back to Pete's and crawling into bed.

Her phone rang. "Please," she whispered to the universe and dug in her pocket, "don't anybody else die today."

"Wayne Baronick" lit up the screen.

She trudged back into the barn. "Good morning," she said without one ounce of enthusiasm.

"Where are you?" He sounded as exhausted as she felt.

"At my farm."

"I need you to come to County Police HQ."

She slumped against one of the stalls. "When?"

"Right now."

"Why?"

"There's something I need you to see. I'll meet you at the front desk."

He ended the call before she could argue.

The horses had cleaned up their grain and were as eager to get back out of their stalls as they had been to get in. One at a time, she opened the doors and let them amble out to the hay. With one last look across the back pasture to the woods beyond, she heaved the big door shut.

She contemplated heading home to Pete's for a shower before returning to the city to meet Wayne, but played the progression of events out in her head. Hot shower. Surrender to the Sirens' call of a warm bed. Wake up at four o'clock this afternoon. As delicious as it sounded, she chose the less appealing option. Yanking off her gloves, she grabbed the bar of soap she kept on an overturned bucket next to the frost-free hydrant. The icy splash of water stung. By the time she washed Windstar's dirt from her hands, shut off the flow, and grabbed the towel, her fingers ached from the cold.

The towel wasn't exactly clean either. Rust-colored smudges didn't look like normal barn dirt. Nor did they look like rust. She sniffed at the towel and winced at its stench.

Zoe looked around. The old bucket she kept under the spigot contained only the water she'd just used. The dirt floor around it showed dark wet spots from the splatter. She knelt and fingered them. A few of the dark spots were dry to the touch.

She shook her head. It had been a long night filled with death and blood. Now she imagined smelling and seeing more of it in her own barn. She looked around for the plastic grocery bag where she stuffed things that needed to be washed. It was gone. She must not have replaced it the last time she took dirty laundry back to Pete's.

Too tired to think about it anymore, she tossed the towel onto a bale of hay, grabbed a fresh one from the cabinet, hung it over the hydrant, and headed to the door.

TWENTY-NINE

"You look awful." Wayne leaned back on the chest-high counter at the County PD Headquarters and held out a large cup from Starbucks to Zoe.

The detective's bloodshot eyes were rimmed with dark shadows, but he'd shaved and was wearing a clean shirt and dress trousers. "Thanks." Zoe took the coffee. "You look pretty bad yourself."

He humphed a humorless laugh. "I'll be glad when I clear this case."

"I thought you had. I heard you arrested Boyd Anderson."

"Yeah. But I have a feeling there's more to it."

"You mean Elaine O'Keefe?"

"Not exactly." Wayne pushed away from the counter and headed toward the hallway, crooking his finger at her.

She followed, her curiosity dampened by the message on her phone. "Wait. I need to make a phone call."

Wayne scowled impatiently but didn't argue. "I'll meet you in there." He tipped his head toward the room where they'd watched the security camera footage.

She had no idea what he could think she needed to see on those videos. They'd viewed hours of them in the last week.

Once Wayne had vanished into the room, Zoe pulled up Jason's number.

"Hey, this is Jason. Leave a message and I'll call you back."

Crap. He was probably already on the road east. "It's me again. Please call me as soon as you get a chance. Love you. Bye." She stuffed the phone in her pocket and entered the AV room.

Wayne sat at the computer.

"Why are we here?" she asked.

Wayne scrolled and clicked the mouse. "There's been something bothering me."

"Besides not seeing Baseball Cap Man's face?"

"Yeah. Besides that." Wayne sped through some video that Zoe hadn't seen before. In fast-forward mode, it looked like day-to-day life in an assisted living facility.

"We figured an employee would know where the cameras were. Do you think Boyd cased Golden Oaks first in order to know where they were located?"

"Huh?" Wayne looked at her and blinked. "Oh. Maybe." He turned back to his video. "But some people are quite adept at avoiding being caught on security cams."

"Adept," she murmured. Boyd Anderson had definitely been adept at keeping his face shielded.

Wayne finally hit pause and swiveled to face her. "Ever since we watched the footage of you and Pete with Kinney and Harry in the Bistro, something's felt wrong."

"When Kinney spotted Anderson and confronted him."

"Yeah. He'd been headed toward the front door before Kinney stopped him. Why?"

Zoe had assumed Anderson had only been getting a look at Kinney, the man who'd arrested him all those years ago, and had only decided to shut him up once Kinney recognized him. But if Elaine O'Keefe had hired him to murder her brother, that scenario no longer made sense. "I...don't know."

Wayne pursed his lips. "Exactly. So, last night I started looking at the videos again. And guess what I noticed." Instead of waiting for her to play his guessing game, he swung back to the keyboard and clicked.

She pulled a chair closer to watch the monitor. The footage showed an angle on Golden Oaks entrance doors swinging open and she and Pete strolling in. "Why are you watching us?"

Wayne shushed her. The video progressed at normal speed for what seemed like ages but was probably a minute or two. The doors opened, and this time, Baseball Cap Man AKA Boyd Anderson entered, his head lowered as always.

Wayne tapped the keys to pull up another snippet from a camera on the second-floor landing. It captured her and Pete reaching the top of the stairs, looking into and then entering the activities room. A couple minutes passed before Anderson also topped the stairs. He paused on the landing and peered into the room.

She nodded at the screen. "There's the footage that positively clears Daryl Oliverio. He was inside the activities room with us."

"Yep. Keep watching."

The camera caught Anderson lurking for a few moments before hurrying down the hall, out of view, when Pete and Harry stepped out of the room.

"I still don't understand why you insisted I come here to see this in person."

"Just wait." Wayne rested his fingers on the keyboard again, only to be interrupted by his phone. "Don't move," he told her and answered it. "Yes?" A moment of silence. "Yes...Yes, I absolutely do...When?" Silence. "Okay. I'll see you then." He ended the call. "That was Connie Smith over at Golden Oaks. Reggie Kershaw just came on duty."

Zoe ran the name around her sleep-deprived brain. "The guy who planted the clothes in Oliverio's locker?"

"We'll head over there to question him once we finish here." He changed the view.

She was about to question what he meant by *we* but the footage distracted her. This time it showed her, Pete, Harry, and Kinney descending the stairs, followed a few moments later by Anderson. Additional clips showed what she already knew. Anderson veered off to the front room where Ernie played the piano while the four of them had milkshakes in the Bistro.

Wayne paused the footage and looked at her, as if expecting applause.

"I don't get it."

The detective groaned. "Look." He ran the clip she'd already seen of her and Pete leaving, Anderson also heading for the door, and Kinney confronting him. "I don't think Boyd Anderson was watching John Kinney. I think he was following you and Pete."

"I'm not buying it." Zoe pointed at the monitor. "We just happened to be with Kinney at the time."

The look Wayne gave her made her feel like a stupid child who couldn't grasp the basics of two plus two. He reversed the footage to a shot of Anderson, his face still concealed by the bill of the ball cap, sitting with the residents who were listening to the blind piano player and hit play. "Now watch."

Anderson's head was turned toward the Bistro, not toward the piano. Zoe had seen that much before. But Wayne slowed the video as Anderson turned to look toward the door, stood, and moved in that direction.

"He doesn't even glance at Kinney, who's headed the other way." Wayne backed up a few frames, froze it, and clicked to zoom in. The image pixilated, but not so much that Zoe couldn't tell the man was clearly looking at the door.

Or more precisely, at her and Pete leaving. Defeated, she leaned back in her chair and sighed. "All right. Maybe he was watching us. But why?"

Wayne closed down the video with a few swift clicks. "I have no idea. Let's go talk to Mr. Reggie Kershaw and see if he can shed some light on the situation."

Pete had touched base with Wayne early Tuesday morning to get an update on the county's investigation into their missing suspect. The detective reported there had been no activity on Elaine O'Keefe's credit cards, and she must have turned off her cell phone. Which left Pete going the old-school route of patrolling his township, speaking with the Widow O'Keefe's acquaintances, and keeping an eye out for her car.

By mid-morning, he'd come up as empty as the county boys had. He made one more pass of the O'Keefes' house, walking around the outside, peering in the windows.

Nothing.

As he strolled back to his SUV, his cell phone rang. Sylvia Bassi.

"When are you coming home?" he demanded. "Vance Township is falling apart without you."

Her snort made him smile. "I'm flying back Friday," she said. "I've had all of this dry desert air I can handle for a while."

Pete reached his vehicle and opened the driver's door. "Glad to hear it."

"Hey, I've been thinking about your call yesterday. You mentioned the girl's name. Brenda Patterson?"

He slid behind the wheel. "Yeah. You remember her?"

"I remember that wasn't her name."

Pete's hand froze on the keys in the ignition. "It wasn't?"

"No. Patterson didn't sound right to me when you first said it, but I couldn't come up with another name to save my soul. Then I woke up at two in the morning and remembered. Melanie Wilson."

Pete's brain stilled. "You're sure?"

"Hell, yes, I'm sure. A girl getting pregnant in high school in a small town was still something of a scandal back then."

"Could there have been another girl along the way?"

"One named Brenda Patterson?"

"Yeah."

"Uh-uh. Those Pattersons over in Elm Grove had all boys. It was almost a joke. For generations, no daughters."

Pete thought of Jason on the barn roof, hanging onto Pete's wrist, risking his own life. "Are you sure?"

Sylvia huffed. "Pete Adams, my memory may not be as sharp as it once was, but I remember Gary Chambers. He was only two years behind me in school and all the girls were in love with him. Junior varsity quarterback. And Melanie was something of a tart. A sixteen-year-old boy can only resist so much, you know."

Pete rubbed his throbbing forehead. Why had Jason lied about his mother?

Then the math started kicking in. Sixteen-year-old boy. Two years younger than Sylvia. "Wait a minute. Gary Chambers went to school with you?"

"Yes. You knew that."

Did he? "How old was he when they had Zoe?"

"Zoe? Oh, I don't know." Sylvia grew silent and Pete pictured her counting. "He was in his mid-twenties when he and Kimberly got married. And they didn't have Zoe right away. Maybe...thirty...ish."

But the high school fling and resulting pregnancy happened at least fourteen years before that. Pete did some counting of his own. "That would make Zoe's brother close to fifty."

"Yes. Why?"

Pete nearly broke his keys off in the ignition and slammed the shifter into reverse. "Because unless he's awfully well preserved, Jason Cox isn't a day over forty."

Zoe accepted Wayne's offer of a ride to Golden Oaks. After the stressful all-nighter, she doubted her safety behind the wheel. Maybe she could crash in Harry's room for a couple hours.

During the short drive from the police station to the assisted living facility, Wayne phoned ahead, requesting Golden Oaks' security detain and isolate Kershaw. Zoe snatched the opportunity to check her messages. Nothing. Surely he'd stop at one of the Pennsylvania Turnpike's service plazas soon. She typed out a quick text. *Please get in touch and let me know you're okay.*

"You checking in with Pete?" Wayne asked.

"No. My brother."

Wayne grunted. "Did Pete ever reach Sylvia?"

Zoe looked at the detective's profile. "Why was he trying to reach Sylvia?"

"To check on your brother. We figured Sylvia is the unofficial township historian, so she would know all the details about what happened back then."

Panic rose like a balloon from her gut through her chest. "Pete's questioning Sylvia about my dad's affair?"

Wayne squirmed. "I think it's more like he's doing a background check from a non-law-enforcement perspective."

Had Pete confronted Jason again? Was that why her brother had left? Zoe glared at Wayne. "Why do you know about this and I don't?"

He squirmed more. "Because it was my idea." His voice lilted upward at the end as if he was asking a question. Or pleading for his life.

Zoe dropped her head back against the headrest and growled. "I can't believe you men. I could imagine my dad acting this way with my boyfriends if he'd lived. But this is my brother."

"We're here." Wayne sounded much too happy—or relieved—to have arrived at Golden Oaks as he made the slow turn into the drive leading to the parking lot.

A concerned Connie Smith waited for them at the receptionist desk. "He's in the employee lounge where the lockers are."

"Perfect," Wayne said and thanked her.

Zoe had to jog to keep up with the detective and caught a glimpse of the blind piano player in a sitting area near the rear of the building, "watching" TV with a few other residents. She'd have to take him aside later and let him know the vital role he'd played in solving Kinney's homicide.

Unlike the day they'd questioned Oliverio, no one stood guard outside the lounge. Inside, three men wearing the standard Golden Oaks polos sat at a table. The one in the middle appeared ready to burst into tears. The other two stood and introduced themselves as part of the security staff. Wayne thanked and dismissed them. "Hello, Mr. Kershaw," the detective said and slid into the chair across from him. Zoe claimed one next to Wayne.

Kershaw's gaze darted from Wayne to Zoe and back. "I didn't do anything wrong. Nothing illegal, I mean."

"We know that." Wayne set his phone on the table between them. "I'm just hoping you can answer a few questions, so I can wrap up John

Kinney's murder case."

Zoe guessed Reggie Kershaw to be in his early twenties. He was baby-fat soft around the edges and wore a hint of scruff on his chin and cheeks, maybe trying—and failing—to look tough. "I'll help any way I can," he said.

Wayne folded his hands and rested them next to his phone. "You put some clothes in Daryl Oliverio's locker."

Kershaw swallowed. "Yeah."

"Why?"

His eyes widened, and Zoe caught the gleam of tears rimming them. "I was told it was a practical joke. I didn't know the clothes belonged to John's killer. Honest, I didn't. I never would have—"

Wayne raised a hand, cutting him off mid-babble. "Who gave them to you?"

"I don't know. I mean, I never saw him before. Or after, for that matter. He seemed nice. And he paid me good money to do it. Like I said, he told me it was a joke."

"And you believed him?"

"Yeah. He seemed like a normal guy. Fun-loving, you know? I figured it was some pal of Daryl's."

Wayne picked up his phone and pulled up a photo of Boyd Anderson. He turned the phone to face Kershaw and set it in front of him. "This the fun-loving guy?"

Kershaw leaned forward, studying the picture and chewing his lip. Finally, he shook his head. "No. It's not."

The answer wasn't the one either Zoe or Wayne expected. "Are you sure?" the detective asked. "Look closer."

Kershaw complied, but again shook his head. "I'm positive." He pushed the phone away just as it rang.

Wayne snatched it, looked at the screen, and grumbled. "It's the office. I have to take it." He glanced at Zoe. "Do me a favor and go fetch us some coffees."

With a quick nod, she slipped out of the lounge and headed toward the Bistro, checking her own phone while she walked. Still no messages or texts. As useless as it felt, she pulled up his number.

"Hello, Sunshine."

Zoe spun to find she'd just passed Harry and his blind friend without noticing. He beamed at her.

She backtracked to them and gave Pete's father a hug. "Hi, Harry. Hello, Ernie."

Harry nudged his buddy. "It's my son's girlfriend."

"Yes," he said. "I recognize her voice."

Which wasn't half as surprising as Harry recognizing her. "Is Pete with you?"

"Not this time, I'm afraid. I'm here on business."

Harry's trademark bewildered look was back. "Oh? What is it you do?"

Zoe glanced around at several other residents within earshot and decided against saying something that might upset any of them. "Right now, I'm official coffee go-fer." When Harry's puzzlement deepened, she smiled. "I'm headed to the Bistro to get coffee for my co-worker. Wanna walk with me?"

"We were already headed that way for lunch," Ernie said. "Lead on."

Zoe tucked in between the two men and their canes. "Ernie, I wanted to talk to you anyway and thank you for your help on that case."

"Oh?"

"What you heard helped us clear one man and has steered us in the right direction."

"Oh. Good. I'm glad I kept an innocent man from being punished for something he didn't do."

She stopped at the Bistro's counter. "Three coffees, please," she told the young woman manning the glorified snack bar.

Ernie touched her arm. "None for us thanks. We'll have coffee with our meal."

"I know. These are for my co-worker and someone we're talking to."

A trio of women on walkers on their way into the dining room stopped to chat with Zoe's two escorts, and the Bistro girl was still pouring coffee. Zoe seized the opportunity to finish what she'd started and called Jason. Again. "Answer, answer, answer," she whispered. The call connected, and she held her breath.

"Hey, this is Jason. Leave a message and I'll call you back."

She exhaled. Crap. "Where are you? I'm worried. Please call or text and just let me know you aren't dead or lying in a ditch somewhere. Love you—" A hand on her arm interrupted her. She turned to see Ernie, a strange look on his face.

"That's him." Ernie tapped her arm. "That's *him*."

She pressed the red button on her phone. "What do you mean?

Who's 'him'?"

"The man I heard that day. The one John said he knew? That was him."

Zoe looked around, expecting to see a man in a ball cap. But all she saw were residents and a few aides, all migrating toward the dining room. "Where?"

"The voice on your phone. That was him."

Did he mean Jason? She laughed. "No. I'm sorry. You're mistaken. That was my brother. I've been trying to reach him and—"

Ernie shook his head insistently and touched his ear. "I can't see, but I have very good hearing. I overheard the message coming over your phone. That was the voice of the man John Kinney confronted."

THIRTY

Pete roared into Zoe's driveway, spewing gravel mingled with the mud. His attempt to call Jason Cox had gone to voicemail.

A white panel van was backed in toward the house. As Pete braked next to it, he read the lettering on its side. *Abbott Electric and Heating.*

But no gray Dodge Ram.

Pete climbed out of his SUV and charged toward the house.

George Winston, owner of the business, met him on the porch. "Hey, Chief. Is there a problem?"

"I don't know. Are you alone?"

Winston thumbed over his shoulder. "My boy, Vince, is in there helping me. Why?"

"What about a Jason Cox?"

"Zoe's brother? No. I haven't seen him today. Talked to him yesterday. He stopped by, dropped off a wad of cash and told me where he'd put the house key."

"A wad of cash?"

"Yeah. I admit I thought it was a little odd. I mean, he insisted on a receipt for it, so I just figured he was one of those guys who didn't like to deal with banks. Usually, it's the older clients who prefer cash, but who am I to argue?"

"I'd like to see some of those bills."

"I don't have them on me. Wait." Winston's eyes widened. "You don't think they're counterfeit, do you?"

It might be one explanation. "I don't know. That's why I want to see them."

Winston ran a hand over his mouth and looked toward the door, probably wondering if he should put a halt to his work until he knew for sure he hadn't accepted funny money.

"What exactly did Cox pay you to do?"

"Rewire the house. Everything. New entrance. Breaker boxes.

Some extra outlets to bring the place up to current code. He said whatever it took to make his sister's house safe and functional."

His sister. The man had a lot of nerve.

Pete held up a hand. "George, don't worry about the money. Do the work. If it turns out he paid you in counterfeit bills, I'll cover the cost."

Winston eyed him. "You sure?"

"The work needs to be done. I understand there's a new water heater in the basement?"

"Yep. He told me to get it wired in too. Should I?"

"You bet. I don't suppose Cox mentioned to you where he'd be today?"

"Nope. Sorry, Chief."

"Okay. Thanks." Pete dug his card from his pocket and handed it to the electrician. "If you hear from him or if he stops by to check on your work, give me a call, will you?"

Winston accepted the card. "Count on it. And I'll tell Sue at the office to hold onto that cash."

"You do that."

There was no way Ernie could hear a voice on a recording, filtered through a cell phone that wasn't even on speaker, and match it with a few sentences spoken at what was probably a low growl over a week ago.

No way.

Zoe tried to shake it off as laughable and made her way back to the employee lounge while balancing three cups of coffee and dodging wheelchairs and walkers headed the opposite direction.

"What took you so long?" Wayne asked.

"There was a line." She set the cups on the table and pulled a handful of sugar packets from her pocket. "I hope you didn't want cream."

Kershaw thanked her and gathered one of the cups and three of the sugars.

Wayne reclaimed his chair and one of the remaining cups. "Elaine O'Keefe is in custody."

"Oh?" Good. Maybe she could provide some of the missing pieces to this puzzle.

"State Police spotted her vehicle heading north and pulled her over. She didn't resist at all. Claims she'd decided to visit family in Clarion, which apparently she does have." The detective turned his gaze on Kershaw. "Now. Where were we? Oh, yeah." Wayne held his phone and the photo of Anderson up to him. "Take another look. Is this the man who paid you to play this practical joke on Oliverio?"

Kershaw looked but shook his head. "I'm telling you. That ain't him."

"Are you sure?"

"I'm positive. A hundred-and-ten percent."

Wayne lowered his phone. "Okay. What'd he look like?"

Kershaw sipped his coffee. Set it down and picked up another sugar packet. "He was about six foot, I guess. Kinda slender, but—and I'm not the type who likes guys, mind you—but he was built good. Athletic, you know? Fair hair. Kinda curly. Blue eyes."

Zoe stared into her cup, her stomach souring as if she'd swallowed battery acid when in fact she hadn't even had a sip of the coffee.

"Would you know him if you saw him again?" Wayne asked.

"Hell yeah, I would."

"All right. I'm going to put together a photo lineup for you to look at. Are you okay with that?"

"Sure."

"Wait." Zoe swallowed a lump the size of her Chevy. She set her phone on the table and pressed the button to bring up the home screen. And the photo of her and Jason mugging on her porch. Sick at heart for even thinking such a thing, she turned the phone toward Kershaw.

He picked it up. Studied the photo for a moment. And nodded. "Yep. That's the guy."

Nancy looked up when Pete slammed through the station's front door. "What in the world?"

He stormed down the hall to his office. "Call Abby and see if she can come in early."

Nancy padded along behind him. "How early?"

"Now." He yanked open the top drawer in his desk and rummaged a moment.

"Do you want to tell me what's going on?"

He found what he was looking for. A brown evidence bag containing a fork. The one he'd actually felt guilty for saving and never sent in for testing. "I have to run something into Brunswick." He didn't mention the other stop he had in mind.

His secretary stood in his doorway, her arms folded and a skeptical scowl on her face. "Anything else?"

He rammed the evidence bag into his coat pocket. "No. Yeah. Have you heard anything from Zoe?"

The look of annoyance softened to one of concern. "No. But she'd call you directly. Wouldn't she?"

Probably. "What about her brother?" The word felt dry in his mouth.

"No. Pete, what's going on?"

"I wish I knew." He scrolled to his phone's contact list and jotted the number Zoe had given him for Cox on a slip of paper. Pete headed for the door and handed the slip to Nancy. "Put out a BOLO on Jason Cox. When Abby gets in, have her ping this number and send me his location."

His secretary eyed the note. "This is the brother's phone?"

"Yeah. Any word at all on him, call me immediately."

"Is Zoe okay?"

"I texted her a while ago. She's working with Baronick today." For which Pete was immensely grateful. He didn't know what was going on with this guy Cox—if that was his real name—but Baronick would keep Zoe safe. Physically. When she learned her so-called brother was a fraud, no one—not even Pete—would be able to make things "okay."

Nancy didn't appear appeased, but she moved aside to let him pass.

Halfway to Brunswick, Pete's cell phone rang. "Yeah?"

"It's Abby. I'm on my way in to the station now. Nancy said you want me to ping Jason Cox's phone?"

"Yep."

There was a pause and Pete thought the call might have dropped. But then she said, "Should I get a subpoena first?"

"No."

Another pause. "Okay. Anything else?"

"Yeah. Dig into this guy, including aliases. Find out anything you can." Pete had already done his own snooping, but maybe his new officer could locate information he'd missed.

"Will do." Pause. "Uh, Chief?"

"Yeah?"

"Is this on the record or off?"

Pete thought about the question. About Zoe and the look of pure adoration on her face when she talked about her *brother*. "You're breaking up," he lied and ended the call. He had too many questions right now. Whether or not this became a matter of public record depended on Cox's answers.

His first stop was County HQ where he scribbled his name on the evidence bag and added Baronick as a contact. He already knew Cox was ten years too young to be Zoe's real illegitimate sibling. But the man's fingerprints hadn't led Pete anywhere.

The desk sergeant accepted the bag and the request and eyed him. "DNA? What case is this?"

"I'm not sure yet."

He raised an eyebrow.

"Look, I'm picking up the tab for it. If it turns out to be nothing, neither Monongahela County nor Vance Township is liable for the expense." And if it did turn out to be something, Pete might have some answers. For Zoe and for himself.

As he climbed back into his SUV, his phone rang again. "Hey, Abby."

"I did what you asked."

"Do you have a location on him?"

Wayne set a plastic glass of water in front of Zoe. She lifted her head from her arms folded on the table to look at it.

"You're not going to be sick, are you?" he asked.

She already was but had no intention of making a spectacle of herself in front of him. They were alone in the employee lounge after the detective had thanked Kershaw and dismissed him to go back to his job in Golden Oaks' kitchen. After that, Zoe collapsed into a chair, unable to breathe, choked by the revelation that her brother was Baseball Cap Man and had very likely murdered John Kinney.

She reached for the water. Took a sip. Forced it down around the barricade in her throat.

Wayne sat next to her and asked gently, "Do you know where he is right now?"

"No." Her voice sounded strange inside her head. Deep. Strangled. She took another sip. "I've been calling and texting him, but he hasn't responded."

From the set of Wayne's jaw, he had some serious concerns on his mind.

So did she. "Why? Why would Jason kill John Kinney?"

"Kinney spotted him. Recognized him from somewhere."

Zoe covered her eyes pressing her fingers in to her forehead to keep her brain from blowing through the front of her skull. *Think. Stop being hysterical and just think.* She lowered her hands. Inhaled. Blew it out. "Jason wasn't following Kinney. He was following me."

Wayne watched her without interrupting.

"Why? Did he want to find out who I was before he contacted me? Make sure I wasn't some nut job?" She laughed even though nothing about this was funny. "Meanwhile he has a history with a retired cop that he's willing to kill to keep quiet. Yet he's checking up on me."

"Maybe."

She looked at the detective and the worried slant to his mouth. "What do you mean 'maybe'?"

"You weren't alone." Wayne drew invisible circles on the table with his finger. "At first we thought he was following Kinney. Now you're assuming he was following you. Isn't it more likely that he was following Pete?"

"What? Why would he follow Pete?"

She must have sounded hysterical, because Wayne rested a soothing hand on her arm. "Kinney was a cop. Pete's a cop. They worked together. Kinney recognized your brother from...somewhere. If he had a past with Kinney, maybe he also had a past with Pete."

"But Pete has spent time with him and didn't recognize him. Besides, Pete's done background checks on him. Jason works in IT at a big bank in Philadelphia."

Wayne gazed across the room, his eyes narrowed in thought. "The fact that Pete hasn't recognized him does punch a hole in my theory."

"And Jason saved Pete's life." She pictured them on her barn roof, her brother clinging to Pete while barely holding on himself.

Wayne acknowledged her with a grunt. "Okay. We need to find your brother. Now."

"I told you. He's not returning my calls."

"Try again."

She sighed. Pulled out her phone and placed yet another call to Jason's number. As before, his voicemail picked up. "Do you want me to leave another message?"

Wayne waved her off, and she hung up. He placed a call of his own. "What's his number?" he asked her.

Zoe opened the screen to Jason's contact page and turned it to face the detective.

"Yes. Baronick here. I need you to ping a number for me."

Pete hadn't been to the Sleep EZ Motel in Brunswick since last summer. Not his jurisdiction. But city, county, and state police frequently visited the place. It had earned considerable notoriety for drug dealings, prostitution, and just about any other illicit activity. The familiar face at the front desk surprised him. "Hello, Gerald." He'd thought the scrawny, pasty kid would have been behind bars or at least moved on by now.

Gerald squinted. He didn't ask, "Do I know you?" Probably didn't care.

"What room's Jason Cox in?"

"He's not here."

Pete put on his best poker face. "I can get a warrant. But if I have to go that route, I'm probably going to have to search a bunch more of your rooms. I don't think your clientele would appreciate that."

Last summer, Gerald had been a nervous wreck. Apparently, he'd gained some experience with law enforcement in recent months. Now, he only looked bored. "You don't need to get a warrant. He's not here. He checked out about an hour ago."

"Don't lie to me, Gerald. I know he was here less than ten minutes ago."

The kid shrugged. "That may be, but the dude checked out and turned in his key. If he's here, he's visiting somebody else."

"Like who?"

Gerald grinned, showing a mouthful of yellow teeth. "For that you need a warrant."

Dammit. Pete turned away from the desk and crossed to the front windows. The parking lot was mostly empty. A few older sedans with faded paint jobs. A dented minivan. An ancient pickup in worse shape than Zoe's. But no gray Dodge Ram.

A dark-haired woman in a stained white uniform shuffled down the sidewalk toward the office and pushed through the glass doors. She tottered over to the desk and thumped something down in front of Gerald. "I find this in trash in 138," she said in a thick accent. "I keep it?"

"No, you can't keep it." Gerald said loudly, no doubt for Pete's benefit. In his peripheral vision, he could tell the desk clerk was looking at him.

The maid spit out some unsavory words in Spanish, turned and retraced her steps out the door.

"Hey. You. Cop," Gerald called to Pete. "It's your lucky day."

"Oh?"

The skinny kid held up a cell phone. "That dude you're looking for? He left this behind."

Pete claimed it. Rolled it over in his hand. "Did he mention where he was headed?"

"Nope. Paid his bill. In cash. And split."

Pete thanked him and returned to his SUV. Once inside, he pressed the home button on Jason's phone. A quick swipe brought up a photo of Jason and Zoe. A cheek-to-cheek selfie. Zoe looked happier than he'd ever seen her. Even Jason's dopey grin seemed genuine. For a moment, Pete questioned his conviction. Could Zoe's father have had another child from another fling? Could Jason really be Zoe's brother? Pete studied the photo. Was there a resemblance? Zoe's hair was a shade lighter, but he knew better than to trust a woman's hair color. They were both blue-eyed. Both slender and athletic. Definitely not the same smile or chin.

As Pete debated, the screen went black. He woke it back up and opened the voicemail. Three. All from Zoe sounding more frantic to find him with each additional message. What was going on with her?

And if something was wrong, why hadn't she reached out to him instead of her brother?

Jason's text messages revealed one, also from Zoe.

She was the only listing in his contacts. His call log hadn't been deleted and contained seven numbers Pete didn't recognize.

He switched to his own phone and called the station. Abby picked up. "I need you to do something," he told her. "I have a list of phone numbers. Run them through the reverse directory and get back to me." He read the list from Jason's outgoing call log.

"Got it. And I was just about to call you."

"Oh?"

"You told me to dig deeper into Jason Cox."

"Yeah."

"Everything about him online seemed legit."

"Seemed?"

"Yeah. But I took a chance and decided to call his boss at the bank in Philly."

The tone in her voice raised the hairs on the back of Pete's neck. "And?"

"And he's never heard of a Jason Cox."

THIRTY-ONE

Pete debated whether to call Zoe. What could he tell her? Honey, your brother may not be your brother. Or if he is, your dad got more than one girl knocked up before he married your mom. Either way, Jason doesn't really work for a bank in Philadelphia. Plus, he seems to have skipped town.

Or had he? All Pete really knew was he'd checked out of a dump hotel.

And tossed his phone in the trash.

Abby called back a few minutes after he'd put her on the number search. "What'd you find out?" he asked.

"Three of the numbers were for local plumbers. Two more were for electricians."

"Abbott Electric?"

"As a matter of fact, yes. That was one of the last numbers called."

"What else?"

"The very last number he called was to Econo Drive, the car rental place on Franklin Boulevard in Brunswick."

The gray Dodge Ram. Pete had assumed Jason had rented it at the airport when he'd flown in from Philly. But if he wasn't really from the City of Brotherly Love...

"You found out he didn't work at the bank he claimed to. Did you happen to find out where he *is* from?"

An exasperated sigh made its way through the cell signal. "He has a huge online presence, but it's all a front. He must have hacked into all those websites to create fake profiles. And his social media pages are all new too. Jason Cox exists only on the internet. Beyond that, he's a ghost."

"Keep digging. I'm headed over to Econo Drive."

Despite the company's name, Econo Drive boasted some rather nice vehicles on their lot. Including a big gray Dodge Ram parked front and center.

Pete pulled up behind it, blocking any chance of escape. He climbed out of his SUV and strode into the office.

A young blonde behind the counter greeted him with a perky smile. "May I help you, Officer?"

"I'm looking for the man who's been driving that pickup." He aimed a thumb toward the window.

Her smile faded. "Is there something wrong? Was it used for illegal activity?"

"I'm not sure. That's why I'm looking for the driver."

She blinked. Glanced down at some paperwork in front of her. Jason's, Pete presumed. "I'm afraid he's already gone."

Dammit. "How long ago?"

"Not more than five minutes."

"Did you see where he went? Did he rent another vehicle? Did someone pick him up?"

"Um." She looked down at the paperwork. More than a glance this time. "He'd left his own vehicle in our lot out back while he'd rented the Ram."

"What lot?"

"Behind the building." She pointed over her shoulder. "You might be able to catch him."

Pete headed for the door. "What kind of car?"

"Red Chevy Cobalt."

He broke into a jog across the front of the structure. He should have snatched that paperwork from the woman, but he didn't want to miss the chance to snatch Cox first. Pete rounded the corner. Saw a high chain-link fence at the rear corner, the gate open. He picked up the pace, his heart pounding. If a red Chevy Cobalt came roaring out of that enclosure, he was set to pull his Glock. Not that he'd fire. Bad enough he was going to have to tell Zoe her brother was a fraud. The last thing he wanted to do was have to explain to her that he'd shot the guy.

Pete reached the gate and stopped to grip the pipe post and catch his breath. Inside, roughly fifty vehicles were parked in four rows. Most looked like rentals, a few appeared worse for wear. But a handful seemed too old or in poor condition. A trio of men engaged in conversation gathered at the far end of the building near a massive garage door. Pete scanned the lot for the Cobalt.

A lone man, oblivious to Pete's presence, strolled down the farthest row. Pete could only see his head above the cars' roofs.

His dark-blond head.

Pete's breath slowed but his pulse continued to throb in his ears. He advanced toward the rear of the lot, keeping his eyes on the man, fearing he'd vanish like that ghost Abby had mentioned.

Jason was younger than Pete. Not weighed down with a heavy, loaded duty belt. And if this man was indeed Jason, he had a hell of head start if he chose to bolt. Pete cut across the next-to-last row and lengthened his stride, paralleling the man he stalked. Half jogged. But didn't want his pounding footsteps or crunching gravel to give him away.

The man was in no hurry, his gait an easy, rolling stride. As if he had all the time in the world. Pete gained ground. Drew alongside, only one row over. He caught a glimpse of the man's profile.

Jason Cox.

But Pete had blown his opportunity to get ahead of Cox, who angled toward the red Cobalt. Pete darted between cars and abandoned his attempt at a stealthy approach.

"Jason!" Pete called in his deepest, most authoritarian voice. He saw the man's back muscles tighten. Saw the slight hiccup in his stride.

But he didn't turn, didn't speak, didn't even speed up. Did he think if he ignored Pete, he'd go away?

"*Jason.*" Pete closed the distance between them. He had to reach the man before he was able to get into the Cobalt.

Still no reaction. Cox kept walking away. Almost to the car.

Pete broke into a run, closing the gap. "Jason." He grabbed the man's arm and forced him around.

In his almost two decades in law enforcement, Pete had looked into the faces of traumatized victims, grief-stricken survivors, conmen, killers, the dead, and the dying. He'd witnessed heartbreak and hatred. Usually, he was able to read the difference in an individual's eyes. But in that flash of a moment, Cox's expression vacillated through the entire roster of emotions while struggling to maintain a jovial façade. "Hey, Pete."

Pete kept a vice-like grip on Cox's arm. "We need to talk."

"How about a rain check? I have somewhere I need to go." He attempted to free his arm with a light tug.

But Pete held on. "The only place you're going is to jail unless you give me a damned good explanation for why you're pretending to be

Zoe's brother."

Cox's eye twitched. "Let go of me, Pete."

"Who the hell are you? Really. And what did you hope to gain by posing as Zoe's brother?"

Cox lowered his gaze. "You need to listen to me." His voice grew deeper, quieter. "Just let me go. And walk away."

Walk away? Was he serious? "Not an option. I already know you never worked at that bank in Philadelphia. I know Gary Chambers never had an affair with a Brenda Patterson, which means you aren't Zoe's half-brother. What I don't know is who you really are and what you hoped to gain by ingratiating yourself into Zoe's life."

Cox's eyes came up. Pete had seen that look before. On the roof. As Cox clung to Pete's wrist, debating the merits of letting go. Back then, he'd held on.

Pete had a feeling he was regretting that decision.

"Please. Let me get in my car and drive away. You'll never hear from me again." Cox swallowed. "Neither will Zoe. You have my word."

Tempting. Just let the guy vanish out of her life. She would always wonder, but Pete wouldn't be the bad guy in the scenario. Cox's word, however, meant little at this point. "Sorry. Not good enough. If you don't want to talk here, you can talk at the station."

Cox tipped his head closer, his eyes imploring, his voice pleading. "Don't do this."

Pete took pride in his ability to read people. Despite the anguish in Jason's eyes and voice, Pete sensed something darker, bordering on sinister buried under the surface. "You don't get a say in the matter."

Jason lowered his gaze and sighed. "That's where you're wrong."

Something steel-hard pressed into Pete's gut just below his Kevlar vest. He knew without looking—but did anyway—at the revolver clutched in Cox's hand.

"Get in the car."

As Wayne parked the unmarked sedan in front of the Sleep EZ Motel, Zoe's queasiness hit a new high. She'd been inside one of these rooms once before and she'd had to take a long shower afterwards. What was Jason doing here?

"Stay in the car," Wayne ordered and climbed out.

Why had Jason lied about staying out by the airport? Was he ashamed of having to take a cheap room at a dump like this? Hell, even with no heat or electricity, her house would have been a huge improvement. Maybe that's why he was working so hard to fix it up.

She shook her head. Where he stayed wasn't the issue. Her brother was a killer. As impossible as it seemed, she needed to accept it.

Wayne wasted little time speaking with the desk clerk. When he climbed back behind the wheel, he said, "Well, Pete's onto him too."

"Oh, no."

"Yep. He beat us here."

"Pete arrested Jason?"

"Nope." Wayne explained that Pete had been looking for her brother, but he'd checked out already and tossed his phone in the trash. "The clerk gave it to Pete. I need to update HQ. You call Pete, find out where he is and tell him we're on our way. Tell him do not attempt to apprehend Cox alone."

At least Wayne didn't tack on "because he's armed and dangerous." This couldn't be happening. And yet, it was.

While the detective placed his call, Zoe keyed up Pete's number and listened to the ringback tones. Part of her didn't want to hear Pete point out that he'd told her so. But a bigger part wondered about Wayne's earlier theory. Had Jason been following Pete instead of her? And if so, why?

The call connected. "This is Vance Township Police Chief Pete Adams. If this is an emergency, call 911. Otherwise leave your name, number, and reason for calling and I'll get back to you as soon as possible."

Why wasn't he answering his phone? A flood of horrible scenarios played across her imagination. Pete with his gun drawn and aimed at her brother. Pete lying crumpled and dead on the floor. Or Jason bleeding out at Pete's feet.

At the beep, she forced her voice to stay level. "It's me. Call me as soon as you get this. It's important." She'd almost said it was a matter of life or death. She prayed it wasn't.

Wayne was still talking to County HQ, so Zoe keyed in the number for the Vance Township PD. A female voice answered and identified herself as Officer Abby Baronick. Zoe shot a quick glance at Wayne. "This is Zoe Chambers. I'm trying to reach Chief Adams."

A pause. "He's not responding?"

"His phone rang and went to voicemail."

Another pause. "Hold on a minute." There was a scuffling sound and then Zoe heard Abby's distant voice saying, "Unit Thirty, this is Vance Base. Unit Thirty, this is Vance Base, please respond." Silence. Followed by Abby repeating the transmission.

"What's going on?" Wayne had finished his call.

Zoe held up a silencing finger as Abby came back to the phone.

"I'm getting no radio response either," she said.

"Do you know his last location?" Zoe asked.

After a moment's hesitation, Abby replied, "Econo Drive Car Rentals, Franklin Boulevard." Another brief pause. "He was following Jason Cox."

Zoe looked at Wayne. "Econo Drive Rentals."

Wayne nodded.

"Your brother and I are on our way," Zoe said and ended the call.

THIRTY-TWO

Relief at the sight of Pete's SUV parked in front of Econo Drive mingled with dread at the realization it was blocking Jason's pickup. Zoe braced one hand against the dashboard as Wayne stomped the brakes, screeching into the empty space next to the pickup's driver's door. The relief evaporated when she saw both vehicles were empty.

"Stay here," Wayne barked.

Zoe watched him storm into the business. Her imagination ran amok with a barrage of what-ifs. Maybe Pete and Jason were inside. They must be. Their vehicles were here. Too revved on adrenaline to sit still one more second, Zoe got out of the car and stepped onto the Dodge's running boards to peer inside. Nothing. No papers, no empty coffee cups, no nothing. She stepped down, and on a whim, tried the door. It opened, and she climbed into the driver's seat. Leaning across the gearshift, she popped open the glove compartment and dug through the contents—the truck's instruction manual and some paperwork showing Econo Drive as the owner of record. The center console contained nothing. Her desperation growing, she flipped down the visor. A slip of paper floated down, skimmed the steering column, and settled on the floor. She bent down to retrieve it.

"Zoe?"

She bolted upright.

Wayne stood in front of the pickup, clutching several sheets of paper, which he used to flag her toward him. No Pete. No Jason. Just Wayne, and his expression hadn't relaxed at all.

She slid down from the truck, snagged the scrap—a receipt—from the floor, and slammed the door. "Where are they?"

He approached her, holding out the papers. "Get back in the car and stay there."

She didn't like his tone at all. "Where are they?" she repeated, taking what she could now see were rental forms from him.

"The girl at the front counter said Cox left his personal vehicle in the back lot when he rented the truck. That's what she told Pete too. Now, get in the car and stay there." Wayne aimed an authoritarian finger at her and strode away.

There was no friggin' way. Zoe tossed the papers and the receipt onto the sedan's passenger seat, slammed the door, and jogged after the detective. She caught up as he turned the corner.

He stopped. "I told you—"

She continued past him toward the rear of the building and the chain-link fence.

Wayne drew alongside and grabbed her arm. "Go back to the car."

"No." She tried to tug free, but he had a firm grip.

"Zoe—"

"That's my brother and my—Pete back there. I am not waiting in the car."

Wayne's jaw clenched so hard, Zoe expected him to chip a tooth. "Fine. Stay behind me."

Together, they approached the fence. Ten feet away, Zoe surged ahead of the detective to the gate.

Cars, pickups, SUVs and minivans filled the lot. She searched for heads above the hoods and roofs. Nothing. They must be behind one of those larger vehicles. She started forward, but Wayne's hand clamped onto her arm again.

"You don't listen very well, do you?"

She wanted to race through the lot, screaming Pete's and Jason's names. All things considered, she thought she was behaving quite well.

"The only way I'm allowing you to come with me is if you stay behind me."

"We'd cover more ground if you go one way and I go the other."

"You're not armed."

"It's Pete and my brother. They aren't gonna shoot me." Nor could she shoot either of them. Even if Jason had killed John Kinney.

Wayne scanned the lot. "I don't have time to argue with you."

Finally, something they agreed upon.

He pointed straight down the first row, which they could plainly see. "You go that way." He pointed toward the back of the lot. "I'll go this way. Circle the perimeter. Call out if you spot anyone. We'll meet back there." He indicated the opposite corner.

"Okay." She took off down the row. Yes, he'd sent her where he felt she'd be safe. But she fully intended to skip between vehicles, especially the big ones where someone could hide.

She fought the urge to run. Instead she prowled, listening for voices, however soft. Listening for footsteps crunching the gravel.

The voice she heard came from the back corner and belonged to the detective. "Jason Cox. This is the Monongahela County Police Department. Step out and show yourself."

Zoe knew from his tone he hadn't located them but was shouting to the wind, hoping to get a response. If there was one, she didn't hear it.

She craned her neck around every SUV, every van, every pickup. Ducked to look under for legs.

Or bodies.

Nothing.

Eventually, she reached the far corner and met Wayne as planned. Frustration and worry creased his face. "They aren't here," he said.

"Now what?"

He looked around, as if a new plan might be hidden somewhere in the lot. Then he pulled out his phone. "You call your brother's phone. I'll call Pete's. Maybe someone will answer. If they don't, I'll have them pinged."

She scrolled to the number she had for Jason and hit send. Listened while it rang in her ear. Somewhere nearby, she heard something else too. Ringtones.

Wayne heard them as well and spun, trying to locate the source.

Not one ringtone. A duet.

Zoe homed in on the general location at the same moment as Wayne. Side by side, they advanced across the row of parked cars along the back fence-line. The tones grew louder. One of them stopped. Zoe pressed her phone to her ear. Jason's voicemail. She hit redial as the second ringtone also fell silent.

They stopped at an empty spot. No car. No phones.

As the re-dialed call connected, the ringing started again. Close. Very close. With Wayne on her heels, Zoe approached the next car—a small, blue compact model—and dropped to her knees. And hands. Dropped to her belly to look under the car.

Wayne flattened next to her but closer to the compact. He reached one long arm under the vehicle and scooped out two cell phones.

"What the hell do you think you're doing?" Pete strained against his own handcuffs in the crammed backseat of the Cobalt, a backseat clearly not designed for a man of his size. He wasn't sure which pissed him off more—having let Jason pull a gun on him, having let Jason disarm him and take the cell phones, or having let Jason overpower him and clamp his own damned handcuffs on him.

Jason drove on in silence. Around them, daylight faded into dusk with shades of orange, red, and violet blazing on the western horizon. It was the type of sunset Pete would have loved to be sharing at Zoe's side.

Not packed into this rolling sardine can with a nut job at the wheel.

From what Pete could see of Jason's profile, the man appeared stoic. Focused. They were headed north on Route 15, back toward Vance Township.

"Can you at least tell me where we're going?" Knowing the intended destination might help Pete come up with a plan.

"Shut up."

"He speaks." Pete twisted. Strained. But the steel held firm. And tight. Cold metal sliced into his wrists. "You're not a stupid man, but you're doing some stupid shit right now. You've been pulling some kind of con on my girl. I don't know why. But whatever you're up to doesn't merit the kind of prison term you'll get for kidnapping a police officer."

Jason's Adam's apple did a slow rise and fall. He lifted his chin. But kept his eyes on the road ahead. "You really don't know what this is about, do you?"

From Jason's tone, Pete suddenly had the feeling he didn't want to know. He caught a glimpse of Jason's blue eyes—not at all the same shade as Zoe's—in the rearview mirror before they shifted forward again. "No, I really don't," Pete said.

"It's about you. This has all been about you." The voice held contempt. But something else as well. Jason sounded...drained.

"Me? Why?"

"You don't remember me, do you?"

"Should I?"

"Probably not." Now he definitely sounded tired. "It was a long time ago. I was just a kid."

Pete studied Jason's profile. Tried to picture him as "a kid." Tried to remember a long-ago encounter. And drew a blank.

"It's funny. You're the one who arrested me, but it was Kinney who recognized me."

Kinney? John Kinney recognized Jason. The realization sent a chill as icy as the touch of the Grim Reaper across Pete's aching shoulders. "*You* killed him?"

"Yeah. I did. I hadn't planned on it. But he spotted me when I was following you, and the old man would not let it go."

That morning at Golden Oaks. The man on the security cam in the ball cap. "Why," Pete asked, "were you following me?"

"Reconnaissance. I was trying to figure out the best way, the best time, to kill you."

Zoe perched on the edge of the Dodge Ram's driver's seat, facing the open door. She stared at Jason's signature on the rental form.

Within one week, she'd found a brother—family—fell in love with him, and now she discovered she didn't know him at all. He'd killed a man. The address on the rental paperwork wasn't in Philadelphia. It was in Pittsburgh. And he'd taken Pete.

Dear lord, where had he taken Pete?

Sirens wailed through the darkening sky as Wayne punched through Econo Drive's front door and headed toward her. "Cox paid with cash. I've put a BOLO out on his Cobalt. County's sending the Crime Scene Team here."

She kept her gaze on the papers in her lap.

Wayne fell silent for a moment. Then rested a hand on her shoulder. "Hey." His voice was soft. "Pete'll be okay. He knows how to take care of himself."

Not if he'd let someone take him hostage. Not just "someone." Jason.

"There was no sign of blood, so we have to believe Pete's not been harmed."

"Closed head injury," she said.

"What?"

She looked at the detective. "I'm a paramedic. I know lots of ways people can be 'harmed' without leaving blood."

Wayne held her gaze. She could tell the idea had crossed his mind too. "He'll be all right."

Zoe wanted more than anything to believe him, but the words felt as hollow as the inside of her chest at the moment. "Did you talk to your sister back in Vance Township?"

"Yeah. She's pulling in extra personnel in case Cox takes Pete back there."

Would Jason take Pete back there? Where? Where would Jason go?

Her farm.

She looked down to hide the revelation from Wayne. If every cop in the county roared into her place, Jason might panic like he had with Kinney. But if she went alone, he wouldn't hurt her. And he wouldn't hurt Pete in front of her. She swallowed, plastered on her best poker face and met Wayne's gaze. "Look. There isn't a darned thing I can do here. It's getting late. My horses are gonna be tearing down the barn if I don't get home and feed them."

Wayne nodded. He looked toward the parade of flashing emergency lights and wailing sirens topping the hill and coming their way. "I'll have one of my men drive you home."

"That's not necessary. You need all hands on deck here." Not a lie. "Just have one of them take me over to Golden Oaks so I can get my truck."

"Are you okay to drive?"

"Yeah. I actually need some alone time to clear my head." Also, not a lie.

"All right." Wayne held out a hand for the forms she'd been holding. Pointed. "What's that?"

The receipt. "Oh. I looked through Jason's truck when we first got here, and this was tucked in the visor. It's from the Gas 'n' Go."

Wayne looked at it. "Dated five days ago. Cash. He seems to pay for everything with cash. Twenty-five gallons of gas." He glanced at the gray Ram. "It probably wasn't even enough to fill this beast up."

Jason had said it with the same emotionless detachment as if he was discussing plans to buy groceries.

Dozens of questions raced through Pete's head, but he settled on one. "Why do you want to kill me?"

For several long moments, Jason remained silent. Pete had just about concluded he wasn't going to answer when he heaved a sigh. "You ruined my life. When I look back to where everything went off the rails, I can pin it down to that night when you arrested me."

"I'm really sorry, but I don't remember you. Do you mind telling me what I arrested you for?"

"Possession with intent to sell."

"Drugs." Pete's annoyance bled through into his voice. He'd seen the consequences of heroin on the streets of Pittsburgh. To a lesser degree, meth. But drugs of any variety had long been his pet peeve.

"Marijuana," Jason said as if that excused him.

"It was illegal."

"It wasn't mine."

Pete had heard that song and dance more times than he could count.

"It was my mother's. My mom had...problems. Okay? She did the best she could, but she was weak. I'd taken the weed from her and planned to ditch it."

"You mean sell it."

"I mean throw it in the freakin' river. But you pulled me over and busted me."

Pete grunted. "Right."

Jason sighed again. "You didn't believe me back then either, but it's the truth."

"So, a drug bust when you were—what? Eighteen? Ruined your life? And now you plan to kill me because of it?"

"I was twenty. I called my mom from lockup. She might have had issues with alcohol and weed and maybe some other drugs, but she was my mom and she loved me. She knew it was her stuff I was busted with, so she got in her car and was racing to come bail me out when she was in a wreck. It was pretty awful. One guy lost his legs. A pregnant woman was killed."

The hair rose on the back of Pete's neck, and he spotted Jason's eyes watching him from the mirror. "John Kinney."

"Yeah. He was there too. Mom was devastated about it. Devastated because she'd killed that girl and devastated because she couldn't help me."

Pete thought back to early in his career. "Your name wasn't Jason Cox back then."

"No. It was William Crawford. William *Jason* Crawford. I served my time. Learned a lot in Crime School. That's what we call it, you know. Prison. Lots of great teachers in there. It turned out I had a real affinity for computer work. Hacking was second nature to me, I learned from the best. When I was released, I took my middle name and my mom's maiden name. Cox. I have no problem hacking into computer systems and databases whenever I need to cover my ass."

"Your bank job in Philly."

"That bank has some serious cyber-security issues. And hey, I said

I worked with computers, so it wasn't a total lie."

Pete thought about all the online digging he'd done. "Your fingerprints weren't in the system." He suspected he already knew the reason.

Jason confirmed it. "They were. But now they're not. And by paying cash for everything, I'm able to fly under the radar. For the most part."

Pete wanted to ask about the cash—where it had come from. But a bigger question demanded answers first. "I still don't see how I ruined your life. You paid your debt to society. You even learned a skill of sorts. I mean, if you can hack, you could have gotten a legitimate job in the field of computers if you'd wanted to. Why track me down after all these years and decide to kill me for an arrest almost twenty years ago?"

"You don't see how prison ruined my life?" Jason choked a harsh laugh. "Okay. How about the job I lost? The honest one that paid our rent and put food on our table. Naturally, that didn't matter all that much because my mom also was being fed and housed by the Corrections Department. Because she was in an accident while trying to get to me. Because you were a hard ass who insisted on arresting me for possession rather than believing I was trying to help my mom." The anger intensified with each sentence. Pete opened his mouth to argue personal responsibility and personal choices, but Jason raised a hand. "Or how about the fact that I couldn't do anything to help my mom either because I was locked up? Or how about the not one, not two, but three times I was assaulted in prison? And you don't think prison ruined my life?"

A discussion Pete'd had recently with Seth whispered in the back of his mind.

"But it wasn't just me. I'm tough. I could handle it. My mom though, she never got over that night. Knowing she'd taken the life of that woman and her baby destroyed her. She served her time for vehicular homicide. And then got arrested for drugs again. And then got arrested for shoplifting. Need I go on? She spent more time in a jail cell than in her own bed. Until two months ago when she found a gun while going through a dumpster." Jason held up the revolver he'd jammed in Pete's ribs back in the Econo Drive lot. "This gun." His voice trembled and then grew soft. "She's not suffering any longer." He lowered the gun. "And after tonight, you won't be either."

THIRTY-THREE

Zoe made a slow approach to her farm. Ditching Wayne and the rest of the police force had seemed like a good idea at the time. Now, she wondered what the hell she'd been thinking. What would she find? What was going on with Jason? What was the connection between him and Pete? All the potential answers made her ill. She wanted to wake up from this nightmare and find herself in Pete's arms.

Her high beams reflecting off the campaign signs were the only illumination. Most nights, she loved the lack of light pollution out here. Right now? Not so much. She rolled into the empty driveway. No Cobalt. But that didn't mean it wasn't there. Not so long ago, she'd found an entire panel van stashed inside her barn.

She parked with her headlights aimed at the barn and left the engine running as she stepped down from the pickup's cab. The horses nickered impatiently, and the *bam, bam, bam* of Duchess the Digger striking the back wall rang out over the distant trilling of spring peepers. So much for a covert entrance.

Zoe's boots squished across the rain-softened ground. Her fingers trembled, releasing the latch. With a heave, she swung the barn door open.

Her truck's headlights flooded the interior and revealed nothing out of the ordinary. Stacks of hay. The water hydrant. Feed bins. Empty stalls.

She blew out the breath she'd been holding and slumped against the door frame. But her relief was short-lived.

Where were Pete and Jason?

The horses didn't care. Windstar whinnied. Duchess pawed the back wall. One thing Zoe hadn't lied about to Wayne. She did need to feed the beasts.

She hit the switch next to the barn door and went back to her truck to turn off its lights and motor. As she headed toward the barrels of feed, she noticed the dirty towel she'd tossed on the bale of hay and veered from her path to pick it up. Those rusty smudges she'd thought looked like blood looked even more like it now.

But whose blood?

One of the horses outside the closed back doors whinnied. Another snorted.

Zoe balled up the towel and tossed it back where she'd found it. Later. She'd deal with it later.

Most evenings, the routine chores—doling out the feed rations and bringing the hungry beasts in for their dinner—soothed her mind and quieted her thoughts. Not tonight. The last week played over and over in her head, the memories a jumble.

Dinner with Jason at Pete's. Jason saving Pete on this very roof. The security footage from Golden Oaks showing a man in a ball cap. The Pittsburgh address on the car rental forms.

Jason had lied to her. He'd been at Golden Oaks following her. No. Following Pete. Kinney had recognized him. And he'd killed Kinney.

Before he'd contacted her about being her brother.

While the horses ate their grain rations, Zoe sank down on a hay bale and covered her face. But her brain kept spinning.

Jason framed Oliverio. Paid Reggie Kershaw to plant his clothes, his baseball cap, in Oliverio's locker. How did he know...?

She dropped her hands from her eyes. That day in Franklin's office. Jason had shown up while she and Wayne were talking about the case. "Oh, my God," she whispered to herself. Wayne had shown Jason the video of Oliverio arguing with Kinney. They'd provided Jason with the perfect scapegoat. All he had to do was plant the evidence.

Boyd Anderson. When the case against Oliverio fell apart, they'd shifted their focus to Boyd Anderson. Sunday, after Jason had saved Pete from falling off her roof, they'd sat on her tailgate and had lunch. And she and Pete had talked about Professor K and the Machete Man.

Sounds like a bad '80s rock band, Jason had said.

Zoe looked over at the dirty, bloody towel balled on the hay bale. Pictured her brother covered in blood after knifing the professor. Pictured him washing up here. In her barn. Using her towel to dry off.

Jason had killed Professor K—in cold blood—to frame Boyd and keep the police looking in the wrong direction.

She doubled over, choking on hot tears and the cold hard truth.

"It's my fault." Zoe fought to draw a breath. "I gave Jason all the information he needed." He'd gleaned information from every conversation they'd had.

Every conversation.

Zoe leapt to her feet, her head throbbing but clearer than it had been in days. She knew exactly where he'd taken Pete.

Pete stepped through the man-door into the dark, cavernous, quiet barn. Until recently, Marvin and Bernice Krolls' farm had been home to a riding stable, which Zoe managed. Tonight, as Pete walked into the vacated barn, prodded by the barrel of a revolver against his back, he missed the aromas of horses and hay, replaced by the musty smell of abandonment—and the tang of gasoline.

Pete had the advantage of knowing this barn well. Even in the darkness, he pictured the massive indoor arena in which he now stood. The tack room to his left, roughly thirty feet away. Box stalls running the length of the arena on both sides. Plenty of places to seek shelter if he had the chance to break free.

"Stop," Jason ordered.

The pressure against Pete's spine released for a moment, and he heard the shuffle of Jason's footsteps moving away. Muscles tensed. This might be Pete's opportunity to regain the upper hand.

But the overhead lights flickered on, hesitant at first, then bathing the arena in illumination, stripping Pete of his advantage.

He took a quick survey. The last time he'd been here was the day Zoe helped load the last of her boarders' horses into a trailer and said goodbye to all that was left of her former home. At that point, the barn had been almost completely empty. The good hay had been sold. The tack room emptied. Marvin Kroll's tractor, quad, and manure spreader were headed for auction. The only thing left had been a stack of old hay bales, too moldy for feed.

Now those same bales had been split open and scattered in front of him. Five five-gallon gas cans were lined up next to the hay. This did not look promising.

However, if Jason planned on Pete politely submitting to being barbecued, he was in for a rude awakening.

"You're planning to send me out in a blaze of glory, huh?"

Jason shrugged. "If you want to look at it that way."

"How do you look at it?"

He kept the gun aimed at Pete and glanced around. "I knew this place was vacant. No one else would get hurt—"

"As if that matters to you."

"Believe it or not, it does." Jason seemed on the verge of elaborating, but pressed his lips tight for a moment. "The gas-fed fire should destroy any evidence."

Pete had no intention of letting this guy treat him like a victim in one of those bad B-movies where the natives tie the hero to a pole and light a pyre at his feet. He pivoted the rest of the way to face the man holding the gun. "Tell me one thing."

Jason held his gaze, unblinking.

"Why go to all this effort? Why didn't you just let me fall that day on the roof?"

"For starters," Jason quipped, "you'd have just broken your legs, and I didn't have my gun with me to put you out of your misery." His expression grew stoic again. "What I told you then was the truth. I didn't want Zoe to have to live with the memory of you dying on her property."

Pete barked a laugh. "You expect me to believe you care at all for Zoe? She's not your real sister."

Jason winced as if Pete had stabbed him with a knife. "I do care for her. You have no idea."

"Tell me." Keep him talking.

"When I first saw her with you at that nursing home, I thought she might be a good way to get close to you. It wasn't hard to find out about her father dying when she was a kid, and it was pretty handy that she and I were both fair-haired and blue-eyed. So, I concocted the whole story about him having an affair and me being her sibling." A predatory grin crossed his face. "She fell for it too. Hard. Bought every word I said." The grin faded. He lowered his gaze, his eyes growing rueful. "She missed her dad so much. And I miss my mom. I guess I started wanting a sister as much as she wanted a brother." Jason's voice grew raspy.

"But all you really wanted was to kill the man she's in love with."

His gaze came back up to meet Pete's. "I wanted to convince her that you're no good for her. Something I believe, by the way. I thought if I could make her see what a manipulative bastard you are, losing you would be easier to take."

Gun or no gun, Pete wanted to wrap his hands around Jason Cox's neck. Even though Pete knew the hard steel wouldn't give, he strained against the handcuffs.

"The problem is Zoe really is in love with you. I finally came to realize how devastated she'd be to lose you."

Pete stopped straining.

"Which is why I changed my mind. As much as I hate you for all you've done to me and my mother, I decided I couldn't do that to Zoe." Jason heaved a resigned sigh. "So, I was leaving town."

His words hung in the air between them. Pete tried to process the man's meaning.

"Except—" Jason's demeanor changed. He tipped his head and shook the revolver at Pete the way a mother might shake an accusatory finger at a disobedient child. "You wouldn't let it go. I pleaded with you back in that parking lot to let me walk away. You'd have never seen me again. But just like that old cop in the nursing home, you wouldn't listen. You just...kept...pushing."

Any appearance of contrition had vanished. Pete had no doubt Jason would squeeze the trigger without an ounce of concern for Zoe's feelings. But Pete wasn't going down without a fight, handcuffed behind his back or not. "You knew full well I couldn't let you walk away."

"No, because you're always right, aren't you?" Jason sneered.

He might have been planning to say more, but Pete didn't give him the chance.

It had been a lot of years since Pete had played college football. And even then, as quarterback, he'd not spent a lot of time practicing the kind of tackles at which the defensive linemen were so proficient. But those guys' lives didn't depend on the play.

He lunged. Lowered his head and drove his shoulder where he'd rather have aimed his firearm. The body blow forced an *oomph* from an off-guard Jason, and he staggered back. The world slanted, balance and equilibrium lost. Pete, his arms bound behind him, had no control over his landing. He hoped his weight hurling down on top of Jason would knock the wind out of the bastard. Send the revolver flying. Break a few ribs.

But Jason twisted when they slammed into sandy dirt that did nothing to cushion the blow. Pete plunged face-first into the arena floor. Ignoring the grit in his eyes, he used the momentum of Jason lurching out from under him to roll onto his back. Pete's shoulders screamed, but he blocked the pain and blindly kicked out. Made contact. Jason crashed sideways. Pete scrambled to beat Jason to his feet, knowing his opponent had the advantage of two free arms. Pete made it to one knee. Heaved to his feet, blinking away the blinding grit. His vision cleared in time to see the revolver's muzzle aimed at him. And Jason's leer.

"Not the easiest way to get you where I wanted you, but it'll do."

Pete looked down and realized, during the scuffle, he'd ended up at edge of the loose, musty hay. He brought his gaze back up to the gun just in time to see Jason's finger tighten on the trigger.

THIRTY-FOUR

Zoe had parked a hundred or so yards short of the Krolls' barn from which lights blazed. The last thing she wanted was the crunch of her tires on the red-dog gravel lane to freak Jason out and force his hand. If she could ease inside—talk to him—she knew she could convince him to stop whatever he was doing.

She'd closed about half the distance when the shot rang out.

She froze for one horrible moment, paralyzed except for her brain. Who had shot? Who had *been* shot? Neither possibility offered a favorable outcome.

Zoe blinked. And launched toward the barn. Fifty yards felt like a million miles. And in spite of her pounding strides, the structure stubbornly seemed to grow no closer. The thud of her boots and the bass drum of her heart overwhelmed all other sounds of the night.

By the time she reached the barn and red Cobalt parked outside, exertion and panic sapped her ability to draw an effective breath. But there was no time to stop and catch it.

She slammed through the door—and cried out at the sight in front of her.

Pete lay on his side in a bed of hay, his back to her. And blood. Pete's blood. Everywhere. The unmistakable tang of gasoline further sapped her breath.

Jason spun toward her, a gun shoved in the waist of his jeans, a gas can in each hand. "Zoe?"

Pete groaned. And moved.

He wasn't dead.

She started toward him, but Jason, still holding the gas cans, took two long strides to cut her off. "Don't," he said.

Pete struggled to roll toward her but floundered. Zoe inhaled to clear her mind and her vision only to choke on the fumes.

He was handcuffed, his arms behind him. Blood streamed from one thigh. That leg appeared useless, the femur likely shattered from the bullet.

With her gaze locked on Pete, Zoe started forward, intent on passing her brother. But he once again stepped in front of her.

"No," he said. "Zoe, just leave. Now."

She pried her gaze from Pete to meet Jason's eyes. Eyes that she'd come to love and trust. Eyes that now pleaded with her.

"Zoe. Go. Forget you were ever here." He swallowed. "Please."

Pete moaned. "Do what he says."

"No." She tried to step around Jason.

As if locked in some horrible dance, he moved with her, blocking her from reaching Pete. Only now, Jason was so close she could feel his breath. He maintained his grasp on the gas cans but bumped her with one shoulder. Lowered his face to touch foreheads with her. The overhead light caught the gleam of tears welled in his blue eyes—the eyes that always reminded her of their father.

She wanted to ask him why. She wanted to beg him to stop this. The gun in his waistband. The gas cans. The stench sickened her. Took her back to last summer when she'd been trapped in the basement of a burning farmhouse.

But all that really mattered in that moment was saving Pete.

Jason must have realized he wasn't changing her mind. This time he didn't get in her way when she sidestepped around him.

Zoe circled Pete and dropped to her knees in front of him. His jaw clenched in pain, his skin pale. Sweat beaded on his forehead. "I'm here," she said.

"You shouldn't be." His teeth chattered.

She studied him. Saw the dread in his face. In addition to the pain, he was afraid for her. But the only thing she feared was losing him.

From the corner of her eye she saw Jason set the gas cans down.

She moved to Pete's thigh and the hole that spewed more blood with every heartbeat. The bullet had struck the femoral artery.

Zoe stripped off her jacket and draped it over him. With no first aid gear, she unbuckled her belt. Yanked it from the loops on her jeans. Her hands trembled as she slipped the makeshift tourniquet around Pete's thigh above the wound, threaded the end of the belt through the buckle, pulled it snug. Muscled it tighter. Tighter. She watched the wound as the volume of blood abated. Straining, she cranked down on the belt even more. The blood flow lessened. Dwindled.

And stopped.

She blew out a breath. But quelling the flow was only the start. She kept her firm grip on the belt and looked at Pete's eyes, glazed in pain, and his arms, bound behind his back. "Jason, take these cuffs off," she ordered. She looked at her brother, hoping her stern expression would bolster her demand.

Instead of reaching into his pocket for keys, he reached into his waistband and pulled the gun. He raised it toward her, his hand shaking. She looked beyond the muzzle to his eyes glistening with tears.

"Don't make me do this," he said, his voice soft, ragged.

Her own eyes burned as she held his gaze rather than looking down the muzzle of the gun. "You'll have to. It's the only way I'll let you kill Pete."

Jason tipped his head slightly and choked a sob. "I am so sorry."

The gunshot rang through the barn, echoing from the rafters.

Zoe's breath caught in her throat. She'd expected pain. Getting shot should hurt. There was none.

Jason's eyes widened. His expression changed from regret to surprise. Without a sound, he crumpled like a marionette whose strings had been cut. Zoe wasn't sure if she screamed out loud or if the anguish stayed locked inside her chest.

Movement at the barn door drew her attention to two police officers who flanked it.

Seth. Still scruffy, but in uniform. And a woman. Wayne's sister?

Zoe's ears rang from the echoes of the gunshot—or was it two?—leaving her deaf, unable to hear what Seth said to the young female officer. He gestured toward Jason. The woman kept her sidearm aimed at Zoe's fallen brother and approached him. Seth holstered his weapon and broke into a jog toward Zoe. He reached into his pockets, coming up with a tactical tourniquet, which he tossed to her, and a handcuff key.

Once Seth had released Pete's bound arms, Zoe ordered the young officer to hold her belt while she applied and secured the tactical tourniquet. The muscle memory of the much-practiced technique steadied her hands. Focusing on the task of treating the wound diverted her brain away from the reality she didn't want to face. "Okay, let it go," she told Seth.

He released the belt, and Zoe breathed a sigh of relief when the bleeding didn't start again.

"We need an ambulance."

Seth nodded. "Already on its way. We tracked your phone and when I saw where you were, we figured out what was going on and called for backup and EMS."

"Do you have a blanket in your vehicle?"

He looked toward the other officer. "Abby, get a blanket from the trunk."

She waved and took off at a jog.

Zoe looked at Seth. "So, that's Abby Baronick?"

"You've never met?"

"We spoke on the phone earlier." Zoe refused to steal a glance in Jason's direction. Although she'd been vaguely aware of Abby securing the gun used on Pete, there had been no sound or movement, no attempts at first aid.

Together, Seth and Zoe eased Pete onto his back. She noticed him watching when she caught his wrist to check his pulse. "I'm so sorry my brother did this to you." She hiccupped back a sob. "You're going to be okay."

Pete didn't look convinced. "I'm cold," he said through bluish lips and chattering teeth.

Seth adjusted Zoe's jacket to better cover Pete's shoulders and then slipped out of his coat and added it on top of hers. "You got this?" he asked her.

"Yeah."

Seth rose and moved to Jason's side.

Pete's heart rate beneath her fingers was rapid, but stronger than she expected considering the amount of blood soaking his pants and the hay around them. Despite her best efforts to resist, she looked over at Seth, who rested his fingers on Jason's neck. Seth spotted Zoe watching and shook his head.

Reality slammed her. In the space of a week, she'd found a brother she never knew she had, and now she'd lost him. And after what she'd learned and experienced this day, she realized she'd never actually known him at all. She took a couple deep breaths, forcing down the agony and the tears.

The distant wail of sirens signaled help was on its way.

Pete reached over with his free hand to grasp hers. Zoe brought her gaze back to him. "I'm okay," she lied.

She could see in his eyes that he didn't believe her.

"Zoe—"

She shushed him. "Save your strength. We can talk once I get you to the hospital."

Pete shook his head. "You need to know this. Jason...isn't..." He took a labored breath. "...wasn't...your brother."

THIRTY-FIVE

A black sedan claimed Zoe's usual spot in Pete's driveway, so she parked at the curb and slid down from the driver's seat, dragging a plastic bag of groceries with her. In spite of the May sunshine and birdsongs filling the air, she still couldn't quite shake the cold or the heaviness that had enveloped her heart since that night over a month ago.

Pete's kitchen door swung open before she had a chance to reach for the knob revealing a smiling Wayne Baronick.

He took the bag from her as she entered. Peering into it, he asked, "Buy me anything good?"

Zoe snatched it back. "I didn't buy *you* anything at all."

He pressed a hand to his heart. "I'm hurt."

Pete hobbled into the kitchen on his crutches. "Get over it, Baronick."

The detective chuckled.

"What are you doing here?" Zoe set the bag on the counter and started unloading the groceries. "You better not be trying to coerce Pete into going back to work early."

Wayne held up both hands in surrender. "I wouldn't dream of it. Besides, it seems Seth is getting pretty damn comfortable in Pete's office."

Zoe caught the smile on Pete's face. If anything good had come out of his brush with death and shattered femur, it was Seth's restored confidence and renewed passion for his job.

Or, as it turned out, for Pete's job.

And, although no one really talked about it, Wayne's sister. The budding intradepartmental romance was the worse-kept secret in the county.

Wayne crossed to the table and set a finger on the newspaper lying there. "You must be happy with the election results. Franklin won."

"Yeah," Zoe said, "but he still has to go against the pathologist guy in the general election this fall." Franklin may have won his own party, but Dr. Charles Davis had run on both tickets and had been unopposed on the other. The campaigning would continue until November.

Provided Franklin's health permitted.

She glared at the detective. "You didn't come here to read the election results."

Wayne shot a look at Pete and didn't reply.

She planted a hand on her hip. "What?"

"We got DNA results back on the blood you found around the water faucet in your barn." Wayne met her gaze. "It matched Kristopher O'Keefe."

So, her theory had been right. Jason had stolen Boyd Anderson's corn knife and had killed the professor with it. Since Professor K didn't know Jason, it was probably an easy task for him to walk up to the man, flash that charismatic smile, and ram the blade home. And then go back to her barn to clean up.

"Show her the rest," Pete said.

"There's more?"

Wayne gave Pete a questioning look but shrugged, picked up an envelope she hadn't noticed on the kitchen table, and handed it to her.

"What's this?"

Neither man answered so she opened it.

The only thing she could make out from the bar graphs and percentages was the heading. "More DNA results?"

"Jason's," Pete said.

Wayne folded his arms. "It confirms that Jason Cox was *not* your biological brother."

"Oh." The weight on her heart continued to bear down. Pete had said as much that night in the barn. He'd elaborated later, in his hospital room after the surgery to repair the damage done by Jason's bullet. Still, she'd had a hard time believing it.

She'd so easily and completely bought into the story of a long-lost brother. She'd convinced herself he looked and sounded like their father.

Her father.

Pete tried to be gentle, explaining she'd longed so badly for family that she'd seen what she wanted to see. And Jason played into that.

All to get close enough to take his revenge on Pete.

Even so, she'd still clung to a thread of hope that Jason had been her blood kin. It seemed like an outlandish hope even to her. But to let it go meant admitting she'd been a gullible fool.

As she continued to stare at the paperwork proving she was, indeed, just that, Wayne whispered something to Pete and slipped out the door

Pete hobbled over to her, tucked both crutches under one arm, and wrapped the other around her shoulders. "I'm sorry," he said into her hair.

"You? I'm the one who's sorry. Because of my stupidity, you almost died." Her voice broke, the crush of guilt becoming too much. She slipped her arms around him and hid from reality, burying her face against his chest.

He held her while she cried it out, soaking his shirt with tears of regret and—heaven help her—of grief for Jason.

And tears of self-loathing. How dare she grieve for Jason? A lying killer who wasn't really her brother. Who had tried to take away the only man who'd ever been completely straight with her.

When the sobbing ebbed, she stayed there, afraid to let go.

"There's something else about Jason I didn't tell you before," Pete said.

She waited, not sure she wanted to learn more.

"It's true he concocted the brother story in order to get to me through you. But as much as you believed it because you wanted him to be family, he started to buy into it too. He admitted he'd come to love you like a sister. More than that, he came to love you *more* than he hated me."

She drew back and looked up at Pete. "But he shot you. He planned to dump gasoline on you and burn the barn down to cover it up."

"Only because I'd figured out who he was and what he'd done." Pete lifted a hand to cup her cheek. "He'd decided to leave town and abandon his plan to pay me back. If I hadn't tracked him down at the rental car lot, he may very well have disappeared forever."

"And Elaine O'Keefe and Boyd Anderson may have gone to prison for murders they had nothing to do with."

Pete shrugged. "I have enough faith in the judicial system to believe they'd have been cleared either way."

Zoe mulled over the path not taken. Jason would be alive, out there somewhere. Pete wouldn't have nearly lost his life. And she'd forever wonder what had happened to "her brother."

"My point," Pete said, "is that you have nothing to be sorry for. None of this was your fault. The responsibility lies solely with Jason. He had a lot of classic sociopathic characteristics. He was adept at lying and manipulating. And he could pour on the charm whenever it suited him."

She wasn't appeased. "Aren't sociopaths incapable of emotion? He sure fooled me on that one." The tears bubbled up through her chest again. "I thought—" She choked, unable to say the words.

Pete shook his head. "That's what I'm trying to tell you. I don't believe you were blinded by a man *pretending* to care for you. He *did* care for you. He loved you—in his own way—as much, or more, than a real brother."

Zoe stared at the damp spot on Pete's shirt and let his words sink in. Jason had loved her *in his own way*. And yet, she'd looked down the barrel of his gun knowing full well he'd have killed her if Seth and Abby hadn't shown up when they did.

Pete thumbed the tears on her face. "Look how much money he spent on your house. I expected to learn he'd stolen or embezzled funds to pay for it. But there's been no evidence of theft linked to him. Maybe spending his own cash was his attempt at retribution."

She suspected Pete and Wayne were still investigating the money trail. But she was pretty sure she'd rather not know.

Her cell phone rang. She ignored it.

"Anyway," Pete said, releasing her and repositioning the crutches, "I've managed to forgive the man. You should too." He tipped his head. "You better answer that."

Zoe watched him swing across the kitchen to the counter and the groceries before pulling her phone from her pocket. The familiar Floridian phone number on caller ID forced a groan.

"Hello, Mother."

"I've reconsidered your request," Kimberly said.

"Excuse me?"

"The photos you wanted. Of your father."

Zoe had completely forgotten. She'd made the request five weeks ago.

"Do you still want them? To show that brother of yours."

Zoe opened her mouth. Closed it.

"Well?"

She drew a deep breath. "Yes, I'd love to have the photos. But it turns out I don't have a brother."

"Of course, you do."

"No, I—what?"

Kimberly's exasperated sigh carried over the miles from Florida to Pennsylvania. "I've known all along that your father had a child before we were married. I didn't know whether it was a boy or a girl. I didn't want to know. I'd quite happily have lived the rest of my life and let that bastard child remain a secret. But since he's crawled out from under some rock, you might as well have these pictures of your father. I certainly don't need them."

Zoe stood in stunned silence after her mother ended the call.

"What's wrong?" Pete leaned on the kitchen counter munching a cookie from the package she'd bought.

She pocketed her phone. "Nothing." She crossed to him and slipped back into his arms. "Absolutely nothing is wrong."

ANNETTE DASHOFY

USA Today bestselling author Annette Dashofy has spent her entire life in rural Pennsylvania surrounded by cattle and horses. When she wasn't roaming the family's farm or playing in the barn, she could be found reading or writing. After high school, she spent five years as an EMT on the local ambulance service, dealing with everything from drunks passing out on the sidewalk to mangled bodies in car accidents. These days, she, her husband, and their spoiled cat, Kensi, live on property that was once part of her grandfather's dairy.

**Books in the Zoe Chambers Mystery Series
by Annette Dashofy**

Henery Press Mystery Books

And finally, before you go...
Here are a few other mysteries
you might enjoy:

PROTOCOL

Kathleen Valenti

A Maggie O'Malley (#1)

Freshly minted college graduate Maggie O'Malley embarks on a career fueled by professional ambition and a desire to escape the past. As a pharmaceutical researcher, she's determined to save lives from the shelter of her lab. But on her very first day she's pulled into a world of uncertainty. Reminders appear on her phone for meetings she's never scheduled with people she's never met. People who end up dead.

With help from her best friend, Maggie discovers the victims on her phone are connected to each other and her new employer. She soon unearths a treacherous plot that threatens her mission—and her life. Maggie must unlock deadly secrets to stop horrific abuses of power before death comes calling for her.

Available at booksellers nationwide and online

Visit www.henerypress.com for details

SHADOW OF DOUBT

Nancy Cole Silverman

A Carol Childs Mystery (#1)

When a top Hollywood Agent is found poisoned in her home, suspicion quickly turns to one of her two nieces. But Carol Childs, a reporter for a local talk radio station doesn't believe it. The suspect is her neighbor and friend, and also her primary source for insider industry news. When a media frenzy pits one niece against the other—and the body count starts to rise—Carol knows she must save her friend from being tried in courts of public opinion.

But even the most seasoned reporter can be surprised, and when a Hollywood psychic shows warns Carol there will be more deaths, things take an unexpected turn. Suddenly nobody is above suspicion. Carol must challenge both her friendship and the facts, and the only thing she knows for certain is the killer is still out there and the closer she gets to the truth, the more danger she's in.

Available at booksellers nationwide and online

Visit www.henerypress.com for details

IN IT FOR THE MONEY

David Burnsworth

A Blu Carraway Mystery (#1)

Lowcountry Private Investigator Blu Carraway needs a new client. He's broke and the tax man is coming for his little slice of paradise. But not everyone appreciates his skills. Some call him a loose cannon. Others say he's a liability. All the ex-Desert Storm Ranger knows is his phone hasn't rung in quite a while. Of course, that could be because it was cut off due to delinquent payments.

Lucky for him, a client does show up at his doorstep—a distraught mother with a wayward son. She's rich and her boy's in danger. Sounds like just the case for Blu. Except nothing about the case is as it seems. The jigsaw pieces—a ransom note, a beat-up minivan, dead strippers, and a missing briefcase filled with money and cocaine—do not make a complete puzzle. The first real case for Blu Carraway Investigations in three years goes off the rails. And that's the way he prefers it to be.

Available at booksellers nationwide and online

Visit www.henerypress.com for details

THE SEMESTER OF OUR DISCONTENT

Cynthia Kuhn

A Lila Maclean Academic Mystery (#1)

English professor Lila Maclean is thrilled about her new job at prestigious Stonedale University, until she finds one of her colleagues dead. She soon learns that everyone, from the chancellor to the detective working the case, believes Lila—or someone she is protecting—may be responsible for the horrific event, so she assigns herself the task of identifying the killer.

Putting her scholarly skills to the test, Lila gathers evidence, but her search is complicated by an unexpected nemesis, a suspicious investigator, and an ominous secret society. Rather than earning an "A" for effort, she receives a threat featuring the mysterious emblem and must act quickly to avoid failing her assignment...and becoming the next victim.

Available at booksellers nationwide and online

Visit www.henerypress.com for details

88697973R00155

Made in the USA
San Bernardino, CA
14 September 2018